Red Velvet

jp roth

RED VELVET
Copyright © 2020 by JP Roth

ISBN: 978-1-68046-979-0

Published by Satin Romance
An Imprint of Melange Books, LLC
White Bear Lake, MN 55110
www.satinromance.com

Published in the United States of America.

Cover Design by Ashley Redbird Designs

Dawn McTeigue, I am dedicating this book to you. Thanks for listening to each sentence at least three times and still feigning interest, thanks for helping me through my endless confusions. Parts of you show up in all the best friends that play in my stories—thanks for being mine.

Special thanks to Stephanie Hansen, my amazing agent, for listening to my worries, and offering constant support. There would be none of this without you.

Special thanks to Lisa Petrocelli, the wonderful author/editor who worked on making this book perfect. You can't know what your words of encouragement meant to me.

A very special thanks to Nancy Schumacher and all the wonderful people at Melange & Satin Romance—thanks for taking a chance on one of my fantastical tales.

PROLOGUE

The Concierge
October 16, 1792

I was a queen and you took my crown; a wife and you killed my husband; a mother and you have deprived me of my children. My blood alone remains—take it, but do not make me suffer long—Marie Antoinette.

Freezing wind tipped in ice buffeted the cold stones of the Concierge. Overhead crows screamed, their wings battling the bruised sky. Marie Antoinette looked up at the foreboding structure that would be her last home. Her arms ached for her children; she could still hear Marie Thérèse's pitiful screams when the soldiers ripped her daughter away, and Louis, her beautiful boy dead and buried for all she knew. Marie imagined his little body lying limp, forever alone, dirt filling his mouth, his precious eyes eaten away by hungry worms. Marie placed her gloved hands over her face. Horror was coming—she knew it, but she would have submitted her neck to *Madame la Guillotine* for just one word of her children. *Were they crying for her? Precious Louis, so sensitive, he couldn't go to sleep without nighttime kisses.* Tears rolled down her cheeks, fell on her lips, she tasted the salty misery and knew she could not stop them; they flowed from her torn, weeping heart.

A metal gauntlet closed around her upper arm in a torturous vise. Marie bit her lip to keep from crying out. She lifted her pale face toward the full moon, a crimson ring circled the orb. It looked blood-soaked. Beneath the pale red light, the *Concierge* hunched like a sleeping dragon. The black gates were its mouth, spiked towers the wicked spine. Clouds of swirling mists covered the wet ground and circled the base of the dungeons. *Dragon breath,* Marie thought. She crossed her heart. In a terrifying way, it was a beautiful structure, one of the finest she could remember. *I will die here,* she thought. *I never desired to be a princess, now I am murdered as a queen.* The thought made a scream rise in her throat. She choked it back, the image of her head falling in that bloody basket hung before her, gruesome pictures painted by the moon-gilded night. Marie turned to her captor, looked deep in his dull, unfeeling eyes; she knew he did not see a queen in her anymore, only a whore who must die. He did not see her at all. Not her—not who she really was.

"May I have a moment?" she asked in a voice that had enchanted kings and peasants alike.

"You may have nothing," he said. The gauntlet latched to her arm hauled her unceremoniously forward. Starving, beaten, and broken, Marie struggled to keep her footing. Loose rocks stabbed her heels, and her hot blood speckled the ground.

In the stillness, the crunch and release of the drawbridge were deafening. Marie fell to her knees. Before the rocks could cut her soft skin, the gauntlet hauled her back up. Marie thought she might faint from the pain.

After what seemed like an eternity the gauntlet released her. Marie fell. The sharp stones did their worst. She looked up through the tattered clusters of her hair. "The *salle de la toilette,*" she whispered. Marie's heart sank; this was it. They really meant to kill her. Tears fell unbidden from her eyes and tumbled onto her lips.

Softly she recited the Hail Mary. Women loitered in the courtyard, backs hunched by toil and age, weaving baskets, telling their stories in mournful songs.

Blood all over the carnation petals;
To the ground, they flutter and fall,
King or duke, princess or maiden fair,
La Revolution takes them all…

Marie stopped trying, she let herself cry—here at the mouth of hell; she let her soul break down. The sobs were for her children, for scandals and lies. She wept for the dead, for the decapitation of innocence, so many lost souls…she cried because she did not wish to die.

"We all die, child, best to remember the moments when we lived."

Marie looked up. The woman who spoke to her was unlike the others as day is from night. Locks of hair so black they held an indigo sheen, swirled around her face. The thick, healthy hair was nothing like the limp grey tatters Marie had grown accustomed to. It framed a pair of chestnut eyes, which were wide and alert, a gaze undiluted by liquor or illness. Time had cut no groves in the flawless, dark skin. Her face held the story of beauty in youth and strength in age. Filth and excrement coated the hem of the woman's skirts, but the rest of the cloth was soft and clean. The basket she weaved was full of a white powder which Marie suspected was flour, though she had little experience of the stuff. She knew only that it made her favorite cakes—sweet, flakey confections she would never taste again. *Let them eat cake!* Gah! Marie had never thought such a thing much less said it. Just another lie, one of the many nails in her coffin. The woman handed Marie a mug that looked too clean to live here. Marie took it with a teary smile. Instantly, the gauntlet knocked the cup from her hands; it clattered against the stones; the earth gulped up the liquid.

"I have my orders," growled the soldier. "No one touches

milady. No one speaks to her. She is a common prisoner of the Republic."

The woman took a step forward, confidence and poise in every line of her slender limbs. The soldier took a step back. "You will let me give Marie a drink of water, or Madame Richard will know the reason. Can you afford to lose this job, Sir? What would the wife say? New child on the way…another mouth to feed…?" She broke off, let the threat of her words hang between them.

"Water only," he croaked and gave them their space.

"Thank you," Marie whispered. "Random kindness is a foreign thing of late."

The woman did not utter a sound, only lifted her basket and threw the contents in Marie's face. Marie coughed and spat out a mouthful of dry, clinging particles. "What are you…?"

"Silence. We have no time, the spell I cast will not hold them long at bay. My magic struggles to exist amidst so much pain and death."

Marie stood up, passed her hand in front of her captor's face. He stared at the unseen distance, stoic and still. "How are you doing this?" Marie asked.

"That is not important now." The woman took a deep, bracing breath. Marie held hers. "I have two of your children," the woman said. "They are alive for the moment, safe."

Marie swayed on her feet, the woman caught and held her steady. "Louis?" Marie begged.

"Yes, I have the Dauphin, and Marie Thérèse."

"How?" Marie thought each beat of her heart may be its last.

"France gave my brother a sack of gold to take their lives; he couldn't do it. He knows I owe you a blood debt, so he brought them to me. Frightened, missing their mother, but alive."

Marie kissed the woman's hand and brought it to her heart. "Why are you doing this?"

"You did me a great service once. The Romani people must settle every debt before death, we do not forget. Ten years ago my starving daughter stole a loaf of bread, and our King demanded her life in payment for the crime. She was eight years old. You went to him, whispered in his ear, and saved my child. You gave us two baskets of bread and a purse of gold. I will use that gold to save your children."

"I'm sorry," Marie whispered. "I don't remember."

"So…" The woman smiled, and the light in her eyes infused her face with beauty and youth. "All this means is you have performed many such acts of kindness. In your mind they blur together like a stream of smiles." The woman leaned in, placed a kiss on Marie's brow, then wiped at the droplets of tears that gathered on her chin. "You are worthy of my help."

"Can you take me to them? My babies…please."

"If it was in my power, I would. I must get them out of France, take them away, to England perchance."

"But, Marie Thérèse? She's only ten and so very brave…the tower guards love her. She reads to them from her diary every night. Someone will miss her. It can't work."

The woman shook her head, and sadness drenched her eyes. "I will leave another girl in her place."

"No, you must not—" Marie began, but the woman held up her hand.

"It honors her to give her life for the princess, though it will not come to that. They will not kill Marie Thérèse, and a pretty peasant girl will become royalty. It is not a bad exchange. All we need is a diversion."

Marie nodded then rubbed her eyes to ease her spinning mind. "A rumor? My people love those." Marie dried her tears and lifted her head; a beam of sunlight touched the broken courtyard, she felt it like a glimmer of hope. "The rescue of a queen perchance?" she whispered.

"You have a keen mind and a golden soul. I know it will never be the same—I will love and care for your children like they were my own."

"My keen mind and my soul—whatever its state—have never been my value," Marie said in a humorless tone. Dropping in a low curtsy, she took the woman's hands in both of her own, pressed her lips to the sun-kissed fingers. "Truly I thank you, they are so easy to love. Marie Thérèse is prone to dark thoughts, but she is pure and strong. Louis is very gentle; he loves people for no reason at all

—" Marie broke off and closed her eyes. "He would have made a glorious king."

The woman lifted Marie to her feet. "I will leave a cryptic note and a single carnation on the floor of your cell, then you will know it has begun. Fate has decreed you die…I wish I could give you more."

Marie pressed a kiss in the center of the woman's palm. Tears gushed from her eyes, but they were tears of pure joy. "You have given me everything," Marie said. "Everything."

On the morning of October 16, 1793, Madame la Guillotine claimed the life of a queen. When the executioner held up her severed head, they say there was pure serenity in the smile forever frozen on her beautiful lips.

～

Letter from Marie Antoinette to her sister-in-law penned the evening of October 15, 1793:

> *"I write to you, my sister, for the last time. I have been condemned, not to an ignominious death—that only awaits criminals—but to go and rejoin your brother. Innocent as he, I hope to show the same firmness as he did in his last moments. I grieve bitterly at leaving my poor children; you know that I existed but for them and you, you who have by your friendship sacrificed all to be with us."*

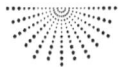

BOOK ONE

Paris, France
October 16, 1792

I have seen all; I have heard all; I have forgotten all. There is nothing new except what has been forgotten. Courage! I have shown it for years; think you I shall lose it at the moment when my sufferings are to end?—Marie Antoinette

Queenie sat on the dusty floor of an abandoned hut situated less than a mile off the Champs-Élysées. The dilapidated house was pressed against a group of soaking pines, hidden well in rainy shadow. In her lap she cradled a dagger, a weapon which had been in her family longer than speech. It was called Seam-Ripper and only had one use. Queenie slid the dagger from its scabbard; she set it down in front of the weak fire she had made using wet wood and sodden leaves. Water leaked from the many holes in the hut's thatched roof, the cold droplets splashed against the blade and her trembling hands.

She meant to perform the most dangerous of all spells this

night, distantly she wondered if the magic was even in her power. She prayed to her goddess that it was. "Am I fool?" she wondered aloud. "Am I tempting fate? Taking more than I mean to give back?" The grey silence offered her no answer. Queenie stood up, passing a hand over her eyes, surprised to find her palm wet from perspiration. *I'm afraid,* she thought. *I go against the natural order. I should be afraid.* "So, what if I am?" she said out loud. "I will turn it to strength. I will not let those children die. I will not!" If her debt to their mother was not paid in full, she would carry it in the afterlife where it would haunt and punish her forever.

The rickety door of the shack flew open. Sheets of rain ghosted through the room, haloing the giant man filling the frame. Her brother Antonio ducked his head and stepped inside; shadow touched all of him save a slice of his bleeding face. In each of his hands he held a crying child.

"Come in and shut the door this instant!" barked Queenie, rushing to the children and pulling them in her arms. "Now, now," she crooned. "You're both safe. Stop your crying and try to take some breaths. Deep ones, they help."

Marie Thérèse lifted her head, golden curls spilling over her small shoulders, her red eyes bubbling misery. "I want to see my mother, please? The cruel man," she said and pointed a slender finger at Antonio's hulking figure. "He said they will cut off her head today!" The little girl clutched at her heart, her voice dropped, and she choked on a sob. "She is so sweet, we need her...Louis needs her."

"I do!" howled Louis. "Mommy, Mommy, Mommy? Where are you? Please, madam. I will be good always. I will never look down on others who have less than me. I will only help them, I promise. Please?" His voice broke. "Please take me to my mommy. Please save her."

The old heart in her chest, the one Queenie believed had turned to stone a long time ago, shattered into tiny pieces. "Oh, darlings," she whispered. "I can't save your mother, but I can save you. Your mother loves you. She wanted you to know that. Both of you. She loves you so much." The word *love* felt strange on

Queenie's tongue; absently she wondered when she had last tasted it.

Antonio offered his sister a harsh look. "Queenie, we don't have time for this. The *gendarmerie* will be on us in moments." He glanced out the hut's single, broken window and searched the empty street.

"They won't come this way; the Republic fears the true *miserables*."

"They will come," he promised.

"You don't know that," argued Queenie.

"I do."

"How?"

"*Parce que*, it's what I would do."

Queenie turned away from her brother's angry face. Closing her eyes, she reached out both hands, and her fingers found the complicated clasp that tenaciously held her heavy necklace in place. Quick, deft movements unlatched it, and she drew a small bag from between her breasts. Without a word she poured the contents of the bag in her cupped palm. Jewels clanged and clashed; the touch of the firelight pulled rainbows from their perfect centers. Tiny motes of light danced over the walls and floors. Marie Thérèse stopped her sniffing and glanced up. Louis looked at his sister, his miserable wails faded slowly while a little bubble popped between his wet lips. Marie Thérèse crawled to her brother and pulled him onto her lap. In perfect trust, he laid his flushed, pudgy cheek against her shoulder and stuck a thumb in his mouth.

Absently, Marie Thérèse's left hand patted her brother's head, and she lifted the right one toward the rainbows. The lights spun over her, illuminating the milk in her skin. "Is this magic?" whispered the princess. "It's so pretty, like dancing angels." The child met Queenie's eyes. "Are the angels here because we will die? Mother says that when you get sick angels come and take you to Heaven."

"I hate angels!" moaned Louis. "They will take Mother."

Queenie said nothing. She chose a chunky amethyst and put the rest of the stones back in the bag. It would not do any good to explain what she meant to do. She heard the joints in her knees

9

creak when she knelt down before the fire, her hand shook as she lifted the knife. Firelight danced over the wicked blade, Louis saw the spark and started crying again. Marie Thérèse hushed him, visibly holding back her own tears.

"Don't worry, the blade is for me. All I want to do is save you." Queenie knelt down beside the children and handed Marie Thérèse the sparkling amethyst. "Will you trust me?" asked Queenie.

Marie Thérèse held out her hand. Queenie placed the charged stone in her palm and the girl's fingers closed quickly around it. "I don't know you," Marie Thérèse said.

"I know," replied Queenie, hearing an unusual softness in her voice. "You just have to look in my eyes. Right here, yes, like that. Look deep in my eyes, can you see my soul?"

Marie Thérèse took a pause to chew on her lower lip. "I think so," she finally said. "I see you."

"Yes. That's right."

"It's quite dark," Marie Thérèse breathed. "Not just the color of your eyes, I mean, that's an exquisite brown. Dark in a way, but also light, *âme fusionnée*. That's what my grandmother called it, she said my father had one, a fused soul."

"You are a smart little girl," said Queenie, smiling despite herself.

Marie Thérèse looked down at the gem in her hand. "It's so warm," she muttered.

"Yes, that is its nature," said Queenie. "It's an ancient, powerful stone. The heat is all the memories it carries in its heart."

"What does it do?"

"It changes things."

"How?" Marie Thérèse asked.

"You will have to wait and see, I am going to perform some magic, say some ancient words. When the spell is finished, and the words have done their changing work, you will be something else. Your memories will fade, and you will learn a new way of life. It will be difficult, yet you will live."

"Will it be painful?" Marie Thérèse wanted to know.

"Only for a moment. It will be over quickly." Queenie said the words and prayed desperately they were true. "Trust me."

"I don't mind the pain," Marie Thérèse said, trying desperately to be brave. "I'm just worried about Louis. He's the heir to the throne. Mother says it's him who must be King. He is the good we have been waiting for. I promised her I would take care of him. I promised her." A rush of fresh tears poured from Marie Thérèse's eyes, salty rivers that sloped over her flushed cheeks. "It was the last thing I said to her before they came to take me away. I promised. It was my last promise to her. I don't want to forget my promise. I don't want to fail her."

Queenie caught the tear that dripped from the girl's trembling chin. "I don't want to fail her either," she said in pure honesty. "I made a vow to her. I will keep it. There is an old magic in my family, so powerful it's forbidden. For centuries no one has dared to use it." Queenie sighed, slowly sitting back on her heels. "I don't fear the price." She rubbed her hands over her tired eyes, it felt so good. "I don't fear death. I may never receive absolution for what I have done." Queenie's hands fell to her lap. "Protecting you and your brother will go a long way toward saving me."

"Alright," Marie Thérèse said, after a tense moment of silence which none of them could afford. "I trust you."

"Thank you," said Queenie. She felt like falling into her best curtsy, the child was her mother's daughter through and through. "Is the stone getting hotter?" asked Queenie.

"Yes," Marie Thérèse gasped. "It's starting to burn."

"*Oui*, that's good. Give it to your brother." Queenie touched the boy's cheek, this time he did not pull away. "When it's too hot to hold," she told him, "give it back to me."

"Yes, madam." Louis sniffed and held out his hand for the jewel.

"Queenie," warned Antonio.

"I know," she said, not sparing him a glance. "I can't rush this. Either the powers that be are on our side, or they are not. We live and die at their will tonight."

"It's hot now…" gasped Louis.

Queenie closed her eyes on an inhale and took the gem. It was time. She held the amethyst in her right hand and the blade in her left, a quick stroke from Seam-Ripper cut her right palm, deep enough to sever tendon. Blood gushed over the purple gem; it dripped through her fingers and trickled down her wrist. Her body started to tremble as she raised her clenched, bloody hand over the children's golden heads.

"*Accipite Spiritum intus contingant animae lumen inferre,*" chanted Queenie, watching the first drop of blood fall. A silent splash landed in on Marie Thérèse's forehead, the second drop fell in Louis's eye.

"It burns," gasped Louis instantly. His little hands came up to wipe it away, and when the blood touched the soft tips of his fingers, he started to scream.

"*Accipite Spiritum intus contingant animae lumen inferre,*" said Queenie once more, hearing the uncertainty in her voice. *No other way,* she thought. *There is no other way.* Two more drops splashed the tip of Marie Thérèse's nose, and shivering, the princess began crying.

"*Accipite Spiritum intus contingant animae lumen inferre,*" gasped Queenie. Her hand began to smoke, it felt like she held the center of a flame. "*Accipite Spiritum intus contingant animae lumen inferre. Accipite Spiritum intus contingant animae lumen inferre!*"

"What does it mean?" Marie Thérèse cried. "What are those horrible words?"

"Take the spirit inside, touch the soul, bring it to light," said Queenie, her voice tear-soaked and wavering.

"That's…" Marie Thérèse gasped. "That's *très jolie.*" Marie Thérèse opened her lips to say something else but found no more breath for words. Her back arched, something there snapped. Antonio cried out, Queenie heard the echo of her own shocked scream, then there were only the sounds the children made while their bones broke, and their small bodies changed. A horrid smell filled the cabin; it was the smell of charred flesh and hot fire. Every instinct in Queenie told her to look away, to stop saying the words, shout denial and smash the stone in a million pieces—she could not, would not. *I will be with them in this,* she thought. *I will be present in their pain, share it in the only way I can.*

Marie Thérèse flipped and rolled onto her stomach, her body quivered, her head turned on her shoulders twisting in an unnatural angle. She screamed terribly, her arms shot out, her fingers curled into claws. The little princess uttered another scream that Queenie would later hear in her dreams, the white skin covering Marie Thérèse's small shoulder blades split apart, blood gushed, and the bones of her ribs reformed. A few more crunching snaps, a warming *whoosh,* and a pair of pearl white wings unfurled. The feathers—tipped in red—were so soft they looked like living velvet. The owl wings flapped once, then folded down the princess's arched, bleeding spine. Antlers sprouted from the young Dauphin's head, his hands and feet transformed into hooves, and he looked at her out of liquid, cerulean eyes as a golden light filled the room. Queenie gasped, it was beautiful and terrible. It was everything they had told her and so much more than she imagined. Heartbreaking brutality, desperate reality.

Then, finally, blessedly, it was done. The following silence was sharp, piercing, almost worse than the screams. White feathers capped in red velvet floated through the air. The night was rank with the burning, bloody scent of what transpired.

"What have you done?" said Antonio, his voice low and shaken. His arms covered his face, his trembling legs rooted to the spot.

What I must, Queenie thought. *Always what I must.*

Antonio lowered his arms and unsheathed his sword. "What...?" He spun full circle, his jaw hanging askew, his eyes darting around the room as if he tracked the flight path of a fly. "Where are they? Saints! What have you done! You have cursed our bloodline by performing this forbidden spell! I told you! Sweet Madonna, I warned you!"

The fear in his voice captured Queenie's attention. "What do you mean? They're sitting right here! Right in front of me! It worked! It actually worked, you hear the stories, legends, never do you believe such a thing is possible, think such a thing will work! They're here." Queenie stretched out her finger whisking the red tip of a single feather. "Right here. Perfect. A golden fawn, and the most beautiful white owl I've ever seen. Just perfect."

Antonio shook his head. "You've lost your damn mind."

"They are right here!" cried Queenie.

"They vanished," swore Antonio.

"You see nothing?" asked Queenie.

Antonio shook his head. "I saw things in the smoke, unimaginable things, wings, a shimmer of horns, then...nothing. They just disappeared."

His words made no sense to Queenie. She turned away from his dumbstruck expression and stroked Marie Thérèse's silky head. "They are breathtaking, both of them. So perfect. I have kept my promise. I may walk in the afterlife unfettered."

"You really see them?" asked Antonio, squinting his eyes and tossing his gaze haphazardly around the room.

"Yes, brother. I really see them," said Queenie. She leaned down and placed her lips against Marie Thérèse's silky brow. "Beautiful princess," she said. "I will call you Velvet."

1

VELVET: FATEFUL ENCOUNTERS

London, Cheapside
October 14, 1800

*A*mbient yellow light poured down from the broken streetlamp standing quiet on the filthy road. The light fell onto the cobblestones and thick puddles between them. The last of the evening raindrops caught the flickering light and turned it to golden diamonds; they were all that sparkled in this dank, cold world. The light touched the shabby faces of the shacks that lined the street, then fell away—its absence pitched the world in darkness. A little mouse skittered to a stop under the lamp and used his cold hands to wipe the water off his twitching nose. His beady eyes looked up at the Ladies of the Night who stood in colorful clusters, calling out their wares to any poor soul who happened along this dreary way. Carriage wheels clattered in the distance; somewhere men shouted, foggy noises punctuated by soft thuds of fists meeting flesh. A booted foot landed in a puddle beside the loitering mouse, and mud sprayed his whiskers. He skittered away before the boot struck again. Only it was not a boot that fell, it was the body of a woman. She fell against the cold stones thumping unceremoniously.

Hot blood trickled from a gaping wound across her ribs, more of it pooled under her waist. There were no screams of outrage or horror; this was the Chepe, and many creatures like Velvet were abandoned or left for dead every day on these storied streets.

Not dead though, Velvet thought. *Not dead yet.* Her eyelids lifted, and when sight returned, she saw the world lying on its side in a wreath of dark clouds. It spun like a fortune wheel. She was the little ball falling from space to space, waiting to see where fate would land her—black or white—life or death.

"Excuse me, are you breathing?" asked a pretty voice. To Velvet, the voice was soft and far away. It spun beside her on fortune's wheel. She opened her mouth to speak—no words came, only the rank taste of blood filling it.

"You look terrible, if you were wondering," said the voice. "Are you…?"

"Alright," Velvet whispered. "I'm alright." Velvet closed her eyes. She had to stop the spinning.

"If you're alright, I'm legitimate," the voice told her. "Gah! Your hair is like sunshine, just who would mess up a girl like you, I'd like to know—it's rude!"

Velvet realized the voice came with a soft pair of hands. They touched her face and shoulders. "Come on now. Sit up, girl. It's a little knife wound, nothing to cry about. My name is Nora, well, actually it's Nora Hartington, people call me Lady N, but for some reason, I don't see you being one of those people." Nora adjusted her hand slightly and chattered on. "Put your arm over my shoulder, yes, that's right."

Velvet gasped. Pain, hot and acid, bit her side. Nora hushed her by a sharp wave of her slim hand. "Nonsense. Make it a few steps with me, you live. Stay here, you die. Your choice, but if you die, I'm stealing your hair."

Nora made this threat with such culture and prim elegance, Velvet laughed. The pain in her ribs almost made her scream, but she laughed anyway. "You would not," Velvet gasped. "*That* would be rude."

"Yes, well, it's a dog-eat-dog world, and yours is far prettier than mine."

Velvet said nothing, it was too difficult. Her only stability was the girl at her side holding her fast. Velvet looked at her face. Nora's sky-blue eyes bridged a slender nose dusted by a sweep of adorable freckles. The hair—piled high atop her head—ended in a luxurious mass of twisted curls, framing gently arched brows that boasted a rare autumn hue, set off beautifully by her gown of midnight blue. The fine bone corset was black, with an indigo etching that framed the décolletage in delicate, embroidered swirls, then fell into yards of flounced skirts made of a material that looked fluffy as a springtime cloud. Nora's skirt swayed, and Velvet felt her body sway with it. It still felt so wrong walking on these spindly legs of hers.

"Hey, stay with me," pleaded Nora. "I can't carry you. To my great misfortune, I am quite a tiny person. Tell me your name, can you do that?"

"Velvet."

"Velvet?" queried Nora. "That's it? That's your name? I introduced myself by three separate titles and all you have for me is Velvet? Well, who are your people, Velvet? Do they all have two-syllable names?"

"Most," Velvet said, distracted, her small uncoordinated feet on the verge of a breakdown. This was no time to comb through the shambles of her family tree. "My family is Romani."

"That's absolute nonsense. You have the bluest eyes I've ever seen, and your hair looks like actual gold. It's upsetting, really."

Velvet's knees were seconds from giving way. In her mind, blood trailed her like a scarlet banner, and fortune's wheel slowed, nearing its final spin. It twirled her back to childhood days where red and gold lights from the caravans pulsed, and flickering evening fires lit up the night. Tambourines shook out their enchanting song, and jeweled dancers flashed bare limbs before the throbbing orange light. Velvet heard her grandmother's voice singing a sad song, while her fingers plucked at the strings of her guitar. She could smell the sweet tang of roasting onions and cabbage boiling in cast-iron pots over open flames, heard the hoot of an owl, saw her brother's face in a world of mist and cannon smoke. Her current reality ever fading by the second, Velvet suspected she might be dying.

"You can make it," said Nora, hoisting Velvet higher against her shoulder and locking her hands around Velvet's bloody waist. "Not much further now. My carriage is just around the corner." Velvet's vision darkened at the edges. Her feet stumbled, and small sparks of pain attacked her toes. "No, no, none of that now!" admonished Nora. "A couple more steps. Don't you fail me after I carried you all this way! This is without a doubt the most physical labor I have ever done in my life without first receiving payment."

"Isn't this a pretty sight?" said a deep, foreign voice that grated on Velvet's nerves. The wheel stopped spinning so fast it exploded and blew apart in a thousand pieces that lit up the sky in her mind like a host of exploding fireworks.

"You get out of my way now, you big brute," said Nora. She struggled to pull the edge of her cloak over Velvet's bowed head and link her arm even tighter around her waist. "My man is around the corner, and I swear I will scream so loud it'll bust your ears."

The man laughed, a rich, dangerous sound that rose the soft hairs on the back of Velvet's neck. She listened to the steady patter of her heart as it slowed to an easy rhythm—perhaps its last? No. Not yet. Velvet adamantly refused the thought. She would not die, not now, not here. She had spent too many years flying in the sky to die in the gutter.

The man took a single step closer. "It seems something squirms beneath your cloak?" he noted. "She's a pretty thing. Come on now, give us a look, sweetheart, there's a good lass."

"Beautiful." Another voice, deeper—like gravel being dragged over glass—came at her from the left.

"We don't mean no trouble," the shattered voice said.

"Nope, no trouble at all," the other confirmed. "We're looking for a girl about so high." He thrust a hand in the air. "She has hair like…" He paused, Velvet assumed it was for effect. "Well, like that one there." He pointed one long, grubby finger at Velvet. "You know, the coward, crouching behind your skirts."

"Get—out—of—my—way," said Nora, spacing each word.

"Sir. You are—" Nora's words broke off as the man's hand closed over her throat.

"Give us the girl!" he hissed. "And we will be on *our* way." His tongue darted out to pass over his bottom lip in a serpentine lick. Velvet heard Nora gasp at the sparse air, and let her body go limp —momentarily giving in to her hollering joints. Nora screamed, swaying when Velvet went to her knees. Nora might have fallen herself, but the man's grip on her neck held her fast.

Growling a stream of foul curses, the man hoisted Nora until her toes hovered inches from the earth. Nora's face bulged. Her attacker leaned in until their noses touched. Nora gagged audibly, her eyelids tumbled closed, her hands grappling desperately with the ones at her throat. Fiercely, she clawed at the leathery skin of his wrists, polished nails leaving bloody grooves.

Velvet tried to stand. Fresh, sizzling pain jolted through her, but she did not utter a sound. She reached for the knife in her boot; it hissed when it cleared the sheath. She was outside the pain, there was only focus, movement, and survival—survival most of all. Every sense spiking, Velvet listened to how her mind amplified the surrounding sounds. Screams from the bawdy houses, the pattering feet of beggar boys running for their loot, or their life— and the men. Velvet could hear the men best of all, accelerated heartbeats pounding over short, excited breaths. Nora's screeching sounds were all that mattered. Her face was turning a mottled shade of purple and there was no time to wait for the ideal moment, time had become a thing they were fast running out of.

Velvet sprang up and buried her knife in the taut neck of Nora's attacker. The man shrieked, as blood filled his mouth, and the scream turned to a slurry, garbled wail. Nora crumpled to the ground, clawing at her throat, gasping for air. Velvet spun around, instinctively dodging the fist aimed at her face. Her arm moved, and this time her knife sunk in the second man's stomach. She stabbed again and again, short quick jabs that were over almost before he registered them. The man stumbled back—smacked a meaty hand to his bleeding gut—and fell on his backside, then lost consciousness with a groan. Velvet heard a sick crack when his skull hit the stone. In front of them, the first man was on his knees, the gash in his neck spewing obscene amounts of blood. Both the hands he pressed to the wound did nothing to staunch the flow.

"I've never seen so much blood in my life," gasped Nora, dragging herself to her knees. "Now I will faint, and who could blame me?" Shaking hands encircling her battered throat, she coughed until tears ran down her cheeks. More hot blood pooled around the man's knees so the cracks between the stones could not contain it. Crimson liquid bubbled up, rushing toward the lacy hem of Nora's dress.

"Run!" Velvet panted. "Get out of here!" Hand shaking, she lifted the bloody knife, her eyes searching for danger—she found only shadows.

"I will do no such thing! *Spencer!*" wailed Nora. "*Spencer!*"

Velvet fell. Regardless of how much she wished it was otherwise, darkness had won the battle for her sight—the world faded to black.

2

ALL OF THEM

*We have a secret, just we three, the robin, me and the big cherry tree—
and nobody knows it but just we three…*

Henry: In Pursuit of Loyalty

enry Thomas Augustus, Earl of Clare and Duke of Newcastle, rested his elbows on the mahogany table before him and pressed the thumb and forefinger of his right hand against the bridge of his nose. He was developing what he assumed would be a migraine of soul-shattering proportions. Dragging in a deep breath, he stared down at his clenched fists, his palms wet and cold; his tense fingers possessed a tremble. Sickness twisted his gut like poison, and he swallowed the sudden urge to retch. Dark curls of hair fell in his eyes, but he did nothing to brush them away.

Henry knew what he was, understood the travesties he had committed in the name of King and country—however, those were par for the course as he had never disobeyed a direct order. He dropped his hand, his eyes returning miserably to the letter laid out on the table. Taking another breath—that broke at the finish—and hoping he had misunderstood, Henry read the missive for the tenth time deciphering it with practiced ease.

Thank you for your invitation we attend you in Newcastle, we find your hospitality perfect as expected. The French candlesticks were exceedingly beautiful. Lady M will get excellent use from them. Many royal heirs from all over Europe will attend the Grandville ball tomorrow night. Most of the festivities will take place in the rose garden, Lady M fervently hopes all the dancing will not kill them.
Sincerely, Lord Grandville.

Earlier that morning, Henry received another missive which read:

Lord Newcastle, please find your carriage waiting for you at twelve minutes past six, the last two packages have arrived.
Sincerely Lord Barton

Henry's eyes returned to the second missive penned in Charles Granville's strong hand. His sharp gaze roved over the twelfth word, then the sixth, finally the last two. *Find French heirs, kill them.*

There was no mistaking it. The command was clear. The missive from the King included a small oil miniature of Princess Marie Thérèse of France. Masterfully painted eight years ago, it showed a beautiful child crowned in blonde ringlets that brushed chubby cheeks, the color of sunlit rubies. Her blue eyes stared out at him from the painting, young and terribly innocent. Hauntingly beautiful—he did not need it; he would remember that face for the rest of his life. As a boy of twelve his father had sent him to French court, told him to learn the way of women and come back a man. He had done both those things—plus trained and studied as a palace guard—that was where he had been the last day he saw her, in the courtyard of the Temple Tower.

He had seen her often as a child, a cheery-eyed doll with a kind word for everyone. Not on that last day. On the last day she had been in the arms of a man wearing the uniform of a palace guard which fit badly in all the wrong places. Mud smeared her perfect face, straw tangled in her long hair, and her bottom lip was badly swollen. In her hands she carried a carnation, all covered in tears—then she had fallen, and the sight of her cheek hitting the mud broke his young boy's heart. He had dropped down beside her, held out his hand, and helped to regain her feet.

"Thank you, sir…for your kindness," she whispered, and her soft words made him feel more man than boy. Then, she had kissed his cheek, and he had remembered her for always. Now—oh God now—the King wanted him to kill her, kill that beautiful girl who had given him his first, free kiss.

Henry pushed back from the table, the old wing chair—which had been in his family longer than his immediate ancestors—creaked in all its joints. A foggy darkness had filled the library while he sat in brooding contemplation; now the fireplace held only dying flames and scattered ashes. A gargoyle sat on the mantelpiece, its mouth hanging askew, its wide, unseeing eyes staring at nothing and seeing it all. Henry had always felt those beady eyes following him around the room—which is why he avoided this place like the Devil. Point of fact: he would have gladly faced all levels of Dante's hell than spend one moment longer than necessary in his father's haunted library, and tonight was no different. Why his father had ever thought the thing held some decorative value would forever be beyond him. Perhaps the old monster had seen bits of himself in the crumbling statue.

Kill children. The old Duke would have jumped to serve his King in such a fashion—Henry feared he could not, yet knew whatever he failed to do, would only become the job of another. A choice he would not wish on an enemy had fallen on him—to disobey his King or take a child's life. Moisture gathered on the back of his neck; he wiped it away and reached for his gun. When his fingers closed around the cold steel of the breach he saw a tremor in his hand. Duty differed greatly from desire, he had no choice of the family to which he had been born, no choice in life bequeathed to him and its accompanying destiny. He was a talented killer yet hated it with all his soul.

The gun securely holstered, he reached for the missive on the desk, crumpled and fed it to the weak fire. It blazed to life for a beautiful second, and Henry watched it turn to vapor and ash. He wondered how the princess would look now, tried not to imagine which of his men would find her first, and how long it would take her to die.

Those morbid thoughts rattling around in his pounding head, he pulled a mask over his face—leaving only his eyes visible—grabbed his hat, walked past his army of servants and out the front door.

"Henry, wait!"

Henry spun toward the rapid beat of footfalls and urgent, wheezing voice. Devon, Viscount of Eden, pitched forward at the waist, hands resting on quaking knees, gulped in great pants of air. "Gone," he gasped. "Both gone."

"Good God, man!" said Henry nonplussed, his voice muffled by the mask. "Did you run all the way from Bath?"

"Not Bath, here in London near Hampstead Heath," said Devon, coughing hard. "You were not moving fast enough to suit the King, and he sent out another contingent of men not an hour past."

"What?" shouted Henry, starting toward Devon, fists clenched. A wave of crashing relief that he would not be the one to carry out the sentence, stopped his feet. Dread quickly washed it away.

"The prince and princess...fled." Devon stood, straightening the crooked collar of his red coat with an impatient jerk. "It was ghastly. A bloody show if ever there was. Every man dead, women and children too. Burnt to crisps." Devon looked sick. "Never seen such carnage, not even during those two years we spent in the Americas."

"Those were not the orders," Henry said.

"They were not," confirmed Devon.

Henry ran his hands through his hair and straightened the mask beneath his eyes. A familiar voice sounded at his back and he spun toward it. "Your horse, sir."

Henry muttered his thanks to his manservant and took the outstretched reins. "I will be out for most of the night, Carthers. Please have the household retire."

"Respectfully, sir," said Carthers, "Miss Penny will disobey that order no matter what."

"Of course she will," acknowledged Henry, smiling reluctantly. "Stay here until I return, Devon. Carthers, please see that Miss Penny has a guest room made up for Sir Devon."

"Nonsense, Carthers," said Devon briskly. "Fetch me a mount." Body stiff, expression unchanged, Carthers bowed and left.

"Henry, wait…" Devon coughed, still battling to clear excess smoke from his lungs. "If it were up to me I would let them go, wish them fortune enough to disappear."

"Alas, it is not up to you," was Henry's curt reply.

"No," agreed Devon. "It is not. So, where to, old chap?"

"To obey the King. Find the French heirs and kill them."

∾

Lady N: Bastard and a Princess

Nora was beside herself; the horror of this evening had officially gone too far. It began with her rather forced, yet grand exit from the opera—a nightmare which she refused to relive—to this? Nora viewed it a suitable punishment for wanting a potion that would remove the child growing inside her. Nora did not know her babe, but his father was pure evil and that did not bode well for his poor little soul. Her hands went to her stomach while something wrenched at her heart. Before she could stop herself from doing so, she hoped nothing had harmed it. That hope told her she would not have done it. It told her another thing. *I will have a child,* she thought. *A baby, a bastard, like me.* It was horrible and wonderful.

"*My Lady Nora!*"

"What?" She snapped back to a reality full of Spencer's horror-struck face.

"I apologize for yelling, my lady. I called your name, you didn't move. Are you alright, ma'am?"

"I am not! I am surrounded by dead bodies!"

Spencer bent down and touched Velvet's wrist. "I think this one is still alive."

"Well, pick her up! We must get her home, then call for Dr. Harper immediately."

Spencer bowed his head. "Yes, ma'am."

"Don't look at me like that," scolded Nora, moving briskly toward the waiting carriage.

"Yes, ma'am," repeated Spencer as he fell in step behind her. "Of course, ma'am."

In a flurry of lace, silk, and petticoats, Nora settled Velvet inside the carriage, arranging her ruined dress against the plush velvet of her seat. Muttering to herself, Nora stuffed a feather-down lap cushion under Velvet's head. "I should have left you where I found you." Her sharp words were a stark contrast to the hands that gently brushed golden curls away from Velvet's closed eyes. The girl was a beauty, Nora acknowledged, sighing, disgusted by the world and all its cruelty. Buried beneath the layers of silk and lace, she found her petticoat and ripped off a strip of clean cloth, then another. Careful not to jostle the girl, Nora reached around Velvet's slender waist and shuffled the makeshift bandage in place.

"We will have to wait on patching up that shoulder," said Nora to herself. "Nothing I can do about it now. The bleeding has stopped, it's just…I'm not sure if that is a good thing or a terrible one." Nora realized it was her nerves talking and distantly wondered if she was going into shock.

Suddenly, the carriage jolted. Nora fell on the seat forcefully enough to make her teeth clack together. She leaned her head back letting out a broken breath, then another, watching the night rush past the open window; she saw crumbling buildings, little more than shifting shadows and people with no faces. Soon they left the worst of the city behind. Now, London was long streets lined by cultured trees. Carriages wearing shiny new wheels drawn by high-priced stallions sped past. No screams in the air now, only soft classical notes flowing out of the fashionable houses.

They neared the Strand and Spencer slowed. Nora saw outlines of townhomes, their gilded moldings glowing under the many streetlamps. The gas flames caused the shadows to dance until it seemed like the world was a kaleidoscope constructed in prisms of marble and gold. Then, she saw it—something that should not have been there—something she would later tell herself she had not seen at all. A golden stag stood in the middle of the empty street, the mists of evening swirling around his glittering hooves. His antlers speared the night, and white clouds of his breath fogged up the space between them, shrouding the moment in mystery. Nora blinked her eyes. When they refocused, the apparition had vanished.

It's all become too much for me and I have gone insane, thought Nora. Her eyes continued to search the torch-lit streets. Just when she believed sleep would take her, Velvet bolted upright and screamed. Nora, hand to her heart, screamed with her.

≈

Velvet: In Desperation

"*Morate! Morate!*" Velvet wailed. Nora screamed again.

Where am I? He's searching for me! Saints, the pain! Velvet's head fell back against the seat and her eyes rolled in their sockets.

"Will you stop that caterwauling?" squealed Nora, her voice three octaves higher than normal. "You have already terrified me to my soul. Besides, if you keep thrashing you'll bleed again, and if I'm being honest with you—and let's face it, myself—having to deal with more blood would likely bring on the faint I have assiduously avoided thus far."

"I see," Velvet said, though in truth she did not. What was faint? "Where are we?"

"We are on the way to my townhome. I didn't know what else to do. I couldn't just leave you lying in the middle of the Chepe, a death sentence to be sure."

"*Nooo,*" Velvet moaned. "Let me out! You're in danger, every moment you spend with me your life is further forfeit."

"Further forfeit?" screeched Nora. "What does that mean, *further forfeit?* One of the most foreboding things I have ever heard, don't you know? I refuse to hear another word about it. I have no time for doom and gloom." Velvet leaned in and took Nora's hands. Nora jumped, though she did not pull away.

"You are in danger!" Velvet said. Her words came out through short bursts of breath. "You helped me. I owe you. Now stop this carriage. Let me out or you will die."

"Really, Velvet," scoffed Nora, turning up her small nose. "Theatrics are tedious. Your face is ghostly pale, your eyes are hectic and delirious. I mean, you look like a lost princess made of dreams and fairy tales, but those wounds are godawful."

"Please," Velvet said. "Please."

Nora opened her mouth—most likely to keep arguing—but three things happened simultaneously to forestall such an event. The screams of a horse in agony shattered the silent night. A gunshot released a deafening boom and the world tilted. Inertia lifted Velvet out of her seat and threw her into the window. Glass shattered falling on them like sharp rain. Nora's back hit the plush ceiling of the carriage, then her body limply slid to the whirling floor. Beams and metal splintered as the carriage rolled and lifted both women in the air. Another roll, an ear-splitting crash, and Nora's fashionable carriage landed on its side, the delicate upholstery breaking on the wet cobblestones. Velvet felt her breath exit her lungs in a hot *whoosh* that took her senses.

Consciousness returned bringing tiny pins and needles that pricked her skin. She could hear the rain lashing the streets and wiped it off her face. Disoriented, Velvet scrambled to a sitting position, wildly shaking the fog from her head. Nora lay sprawled over the shattered remains of her carriage, sooty lashes brushing pale, freckled cheeks. *No!* She wanted to shout. *No more pain! No more death!* What was it about her that attracted such tragedy, she wondered, crawling to the girl who had saved her?

"Nora," Velvet called. "Nora. Wake up." She reached out to touch her hand, praying the dark curse which followed her did not take this particular, precious life. Through breaks in the morning fog, Spencer lay a few feet away, his right leg twisted at an awkward angle, his chest moving steadily up and down. Velvet almost sobbed in relief—too many had died tonight. She tried to stand, stumbled a couple times before finding her balance, then straightened her shoulders and turned to face the danger she knew lurked behind her, the danger raising the hairs

28

on the back of her neck. What Velvet saw had the power to stop her heart.

Dark shapes materialized out of the shadows; everywhere she looked there was another one. Masks covered all but their hateful eyes, naked swords and daggers glinting in the firelight. Velvet fumbled for her dagger. Gone. Lost on yet another street where she had nearly died. Velvet reached for the amulet around her neck; it was a small, violet crystal—the last protection she had left. Energy hummed in its core, reverberated through the ground beneath her tingling feet. Velvet brought the stone to her lips and closed her eyes. Sending a quick prayer to her goddess she threw it to the ground and crushed it beneath the heel of her boot. The enchanted stone instantly disintegrated into a soft powder and released its magic. A crimson cloud enveloped them. It was an old Romani trick used to frighten *Gadje* customers, it would only give them a few moments to escape. Velvet thought—hoped—it would be enough.

"Wha...what? My carriage!"

"Shush." Velvet placed her hand over Nora's mouth. "Come," she whispered, then put a single finger to her lips. "Quiet. Follow me."

"No, you follow *me*," said Nora, her whispers more like falsetto shouts. "I know these streets and you can hardly walk."

"I have to walk so I will," Velvet said and took Nora's outstretched hand.

"Come now," demanded Nora. "Don't argue, and I promise not to talk about this red mist, which I believe you are responsible for."

Velvet gripped her side, clenching her teeth in determined agony.

"*Now!*" demanded Nora. Velvet nodded her lips pressed tight. Her heart pounded as together they ran down the street and the crimson cloud followed them.

"Why are they chasing you?" gasped Nora when they rounded a sharp curve that dropped off in a steep flight of stairs. "Well, both of us now—why are they chasing both of us?"

Velvet shook her head. "I don't know. Men came to our camp

at sunset. Tall, violent, white men. They killed my family and burned all the caravans—but I was truly the thing they searched for—and my brother, of course. Neither of us have stopped running since. They killed my grandmother, cut off her head with a saber, after…after they burned her body." Velvet flinched, regretting the words the instant she said them. Such things were too painful to think about. Now she had to find safety, then she would think about it, then she would cry.

"I feel so helpless," Velvet admitted over a mouthful of tears. "You are being terribly kind to me, I have no way to pay you for it. It's not done. My people always repay a kindness."

"I hate to contradict you, but *I am* your people," muttered Nora.

Velvet went on as if Nora had not spoken. "If I had any of my things, I would give you a good luck charm at least. If I live, I'll find you, I swear it! Please go now, to a safe place, and stay there. I'll lead them away."

Nora paused for a second, her spine straightened, her jaw tensed—then she shook her head, making bouncing curls swish. "Oh! I don't think I could, I feel something would fall out of the sky and bop me on the head if I even considered it."

"Bop?" Velvet asked.

"Yes, bop," affirmed Nora. "Can we go to the constable? Maybe they could help?"

Velvet shook her hand free of Nora's hold, a fresh gush of real fear startling her badly. "No!" she cried. "They will arrest us, lock us away in a metal cage. Throw away the evil key!" It was the worst thing yet, the worst thing of all. She did not know why, but Velvet knew she could not ever be caged again. No, never again, she knew that for certain, yet she wondered what devious actions had designed her fear.

Nora imperiously lifted her auburn brows. "You're a strange thing. Who told you that?"

Velvet bit her bottom lip, only letting up when she tasted blood. "No one told me. I just know."

Yes, she knew, knew better than anyone in the world what it felt like to be locked away, if only she could remember *how* she knew. Her only memories started in the sky, though she always knew in her heart she had not been born to fly. The thought terrified her, as always. Her fear made her lash out, the explosion of angry heat in her chest felt childish and unavoidable. "Leave," she blurted, flinging a hand at Nora's midsection and completing her sentence sans thought. "You're pregnant, if you have no care for your own life, think about the baby!"

Velvet clapped her hands over her mouth, instantly wishing to take back the careless words. Yet what is spoken into being can never be recalled. She took a deep, centering breath. "Forgive me—I..."

Nora looked shattered. Heat flooded her cheeks as her mouth fell in a wide O. "How do you know?"

Velvet dropped her eyes and studied a scuff mark beneath her shoe. "I just do. I've always known things, even when—" Velvet broke off. When? What had she been about to say? Something so close...on the tip of her tongue. She sighed at its loss. Waving her hand through the space between them, Velvet pushed the remnants of it away. "Many of my people are seers," she said.

"*Again*," stressed Nora, rolling her eyes. "*I* am *your people!*" Nora put up both hands when Velvet started to speak. "No one in the world knows about this baby. Having barely acknowledged it myself, I certainly don't know what I intend to do with it."

Velvet took Nora's hand. "Listen. Please. If you decide not to keep it and I am still alive, I'll help you. My grandmother used to make a draft that was painless and..." Velvet flinched again, she tasted ash and saw flames. The thought of her grandmother screaming and burning hurt worse than the knife wound in her side. She locked her lips and tugged at Nora's hand. They ran in silence for a time, and Velvet wished for her lost wings.

"Here!" gasped Nora, stopping so abruptly Velvet nearly ran her down. "This is Mister McIntyre's shop. He always leaves the back door unlocked for me in case I need anything during the night. Bless you, Jacob," she whispered, eyes tilted Heavenward. Nora tugged on the brass knocker and flung the door open, then hauled Velvet inside the shop and closed it firmly behind them.

The cool interior smelt like honey, wheat, and strawberries. The mouthwatering combination of scents made Velvet realize she was starving—distantly she tried to remember her last meal and found she could not. Nora clattered around for a moment before Velvet heard the hiss of a wick igniting. A soft glow expanded through the room.

Unable to stay upright a moment longer, Velvet sat down, leaned her dizzy head against a large burlap sack that smelled of sunshine, and closed her eyes. Shadows moved across the little window at the east of the room; they marked the passage of the rising dawn, and for a while neither of them spoke. Velvet drifted between dreams and reality, wishing always to return to her nightmare, finding it better than the truth.

Nora stirred, and blinking her eyes she yawned hugely, stretching her arms above her head. Beyond the small window, bells rang in the street, quiet at first, then louder. Men shouted, a child cried, and some woman screamed a word Velvet did not understand.

"Spencer," gasped Nora, using her whispered shout. "He must have gone for help. Dear soul! Do you think they saw my face? The men chasing you? I would hate to think they did as it would make me feel quite vulnerable, you know?"

Velvet said nothing. She had no words, and she wished many things tonight.

"I often talk when I'm nervous," explained Nora, taking an apple from a bushel of them and handing it to Velvet.

Velvet took it, smiling her thanks. "I bite my nails."

"You do not!" Nora seemed scandalized. "Ugh! Here I was thinking the urge to retch had passed."

Velvet took a bite of the apple, her teeth pierced through the crisp green skin, and flavor exploded in her mouth. She made a small sound of pleasure and chewed quickly, desperately greedy to taste it again.

Nora cast Velvet a strange glance, but the fruit was sour and sweet, it made her mouth tingle and she hardly cared. She had never tasted anything so wonderful.

"So," Nora tapped her chin. "Let me see if I have this straight, you're British, but you grew up with gypsies?"

"I am French," Velvet said. Yes, she was, that was true. The knowledge was linked to a foggy memory and she struggled to hold onto it, yet like wet-wood smoke, it crackled furiously and flitted away. "My first human memories are of campfires at sunset," she said. "Music after dark, dancing, always dancing. Now they are dancing in the sky. Everyone I knew is dead and my brother is missing." Velvet swallowed the lump in her throat, afraid it might finally leak out of her eyes. "Wherever he is, I hope my dog is with him."

"*Human* memories?" queried Nora. "What on earth are you...?"

Voices on the street rose in alarm. "She's in there," someone called. "Blonde as an angel, there's no missing her," another one yelled.

Nora took a deep bracing breath, "I have decided to help you," she declared. "Even though you are a complete stranger, I feel I must."

"The Romani believe a stranger is just a soul your own is fated to meet," Velvet said.

Nora smiled. She would have said more, but the door banged against the wall so hard the top hinges creaked miserably, then gave way. A huge, dark form filled the entrance dominating all the space. The light from the streetlamps bounced off the silver knob on the hood of his tricorne and turned it to a glowing coal that illuminated his eyes, the only things visible on his masked face. In one hand he held a sword, in the other, the metal of a cocked pistol glinted like polished starlight. He took a step toward them, and Velvet jumped to her feet pushing Nora behind her.

"Why?" Velvet asked him, not retreating when a single stride of his long legs brought him closer. "Why are you doing this? Leave me alone. I've done nothing to you or your kind."

"You can't live," the dark figure said. "One life to save thousands...we must have peace."

"If that were true I would willingly bare my neck for your knife," Velvet said.

"It is the truth," the dark voice replied.

"So you say," Velvet said. "I mean nothing to anyone, so I cannot see how my life or death matters."

The masked man lunged for her so fast, Velvet had no time to react, his hard fingers closed around her arm. He squeezed her knife wound, and pain jolted through her frazzled nerves. Velvet lashed out, blindly enraged. Her nails caught the stubbled skin above his collar and scored long, bloody groves down his neck. He grabbed her arm, twisted it up behind her back. It was like someone had pinioned her wings—gods of earth and sky—she missed her wings!

Screeching her alarm Velvet freed her right arm, and her hand whipped across his face, half-blinding him by her cutting nails.

His sharp green eyes widened in shock at her attack. The man stumbled back. Behind the cloth mask she saw his lips start to move as if he would speak. Velvet was not listening. She arched her body, tensed her foot, and drove the heel into his shin. The kick sent him staggering, he slung his massive arms around her waist—she felt caught between a boulder and a bar of iron. Every second of agony, fear, and loss rose inside her like a dark cloud, the color of her anger obscured vision, and rational thought fled.

She heard herself make a disorienting snarling noise and kicked him again. He cursed loudly, stumbled and fell. Velvet felt her balance give way as his arms tugged dragging her down atop him, and she screamed in panic as they crashed to the floor.

His body felt like an open blaze through the thin silk of her dress, his fingers stunning brands on her hips and waist. Velvet could hear his harsh, panting breaths in her ear as she kicked and writhed. There was an echoing *thunk* when the back of her skull connected to his hard head. Stars obliterated her vision. His hold around her waist slackened, Velvet bucked again, won her freedom, and rolled off his big body with a garbled shriek. She scrambled to her feet and made fists of her hands, ready.

"*Goddamn it!*" the man raged. His shout shook the floorboards. The pad of his hand was pressed to his forehead, and a small trickle of blood marred his vision, it poured from a split in his left brow. He eyed her as if he had discovered some strange species of rabid fairy. Velvet snarled in response, showing him her straight row of front teeth.

"Oh, my God!!" cried Nora, her voice muted, full of disbelief. "Bastards on a biscuit! Good heavens and blessed hell. Henry Thomas Augustus, is that you? *Mon Dieu*, it is!" She clapped a hand to her heart. "Jesus, Henry! Take off that ridiculous mask, you look like a hired killer."

The man, Henry, faltered, then took a clumsy step back as if Nora was a bloodthirsty hound rather than a tiny slip of a girl. Velvet saw something painful flood his eyes before he could mask it, and…something else. Regret, shame? She could not be sure, but whatever it was vanished as quickly as it appeared. "Nora?" he nearly roared. "What the Devil are you doing here? Where the hell is Charles?"

"Hell and the Devil to you too, Henry! And I don't know where your feckless brother is. I left him at the opera with Miss Amanda Clearance hanging on his arm. God knows I want to find something beautiful in every woman, we must stick together after all, but that little slu—"

"Nora!" demanded Henry, cutting her off.

"What?" she squealed.

"Are you quite finished?" His voice was deep and rasping, muffled beneath the thick material of the mask.

"Since you had to interrupt me, it's clear that I was not!" retorted Nora. "No, Velvet, dear. Sit back down, he won't hurt you."

"I will not," she told Nora, and rounded on her attacker. His eyes moved between her and Nora, his hand opened and closed on the pommel of his sword. Velvet eyed his tall, broad-shouldered frame. She wanted to hurt him, make him bleed. The impulse terrified and saddened her. Everything in her life was violence now. *Born in blood*, she thought and shuddered. Her mouth voiced the only question running through her mind.

"Why did you kill my family?" she demanded, trying to keep fresh tears out of her eyes and voice. "They did nothing! They kept to themselves—they were kind, good in soul and heart—" A sob broke through, Velvet gulped it back. "You have innocent blood on your hands—there were children, babies!" she finished, dropping her eyes to the ground as the burnt bodies of her friends flashed before them.

"You must sit down," pleaded Nora.

"Murder," Velvet whispered, though she yielded to the persistent hands that bore her to the ground. Her head fell back against the fragrant gunnysack; unwilling, she closed her eyes. "Cursed," she breathed. "All cursed." His shadow loomed across her. Velvet felt it clear as if he laid his bloody hands on her bare skin. She blinked, seeing him. His eyes were a dark storm encased in an emerald sphere, his skin the color of sunlit honey. The gypsies wrote songs about men like this: iron in their bones and death in their gaze.

"Did you set those flames?" she asked, not breaking their shared stare. It felt like the words took all the air from her lungs, stilled the unsteady beats from her heart. "My brother is innocent, how could you?" Exhaustion unraveled the seams of her sanity. The taste of ashes was in her mouth again, and she heard the haunting screams. Screams she would never forget. Fresh horror washed over her, and Velvet felt her face crumple when she could no longer keep the dark thoughts at bay. It was too terrible, unimaginable, and the grief burning on her tongue was a bitter thing to swallow. "How could you?" Hot tears finally poured out of her eyes, rushed down her cheeks, and she did not bother to wipe them away. The understanding of what had been done this night was heavy. She closed her eyes wishing whatever took her memories so long ago would return and steal them again. "Babies..." she whispered. "Babies...how could you?" Consciousness drifted through her grasping fingers. "We were just babies," she told him, and her mind was filled with a cold dungeon and the familiar sound of crying. The blaze of the rising sun lit the flecks of crimson in his eyes, and when the darkness came to claim her, the stranger sent to take her life visited her dreams.

~

Henry: Guilty and Innocent

The tears of the princess twisted Henry's heart until he felt like the worst villain alive. She was perfect, perfect as she had been all those years ago. "I wasn't there," he said and realized she had fainted. He looked at the fine bones shaping her delicate features and wondered at his motives. He never explained or defended himself —never. Yet, this broken girl—face smeared in bloody tears and body tensed for fight, even in sleep—made him want to fall to his knees and beg absolution. It was pure insanity. How did one apologize for merely fulfilling their purpose?

Could he have killed her? No! Never! Had his own life depended on it, he knew he could not. Henry tugged on the cloth wrapped around his face; he let the mask drop and used his hand to wipe at the sweat on the back of his neck.

He did not—could not—take his eyes off her as he directed his words to Nora, the last person in the world he expected to meet midst the throes of his dark errand. It was fate alone—who seemed ever against him—which had brought her here. A pale warrior, standing between him and his kill. "Why are you not with my brother, Nora? How are you embroiled in this—"

"This travesty?" finished Nora, and he knew it was rage that made her voice tremble. "Honestly, Henry! What on earth is going on?"

Henry shook his head. He felt sick and confused. "Nora," he said again, his voice low and dangerous. "Why are you here?"

Nora let out a long, loud sigh. "Charles found out a secret of mine. The cad said some rather choice things in front of our friends, things I prefer not to remember much less repeat."

Nora knelt down beside Velvet and stroked a blonde lock away from her sleeping visage. "On my way home I nearly tripped over this ethereal creature. Look at her, Henry, have you ever seen such a face?"

"No," he admitted. He had not.

"You weren't honestly going to kill this girl, were you?"

Henry said nothing, only watched the sleeping girl who looked exactly as a princess should, or an angel—perchance a strange combination of both? He had only seen her mother once, on a dark, bloody day, still viewed through the eyes of the boy he had been, walking the stairs that would take her to Madame la Guillotine and the final act of her life. Marie remained Queen till the end, a glowing vision in his mind, yet her daughter seemed to have grown far more otherworldly in her perfection. He was born to protect creatures exactly like the one lying in front of him, he had sworn an oath to do so…how could he obey his King and break it now? Kill the girl with the beautiful smile and kind words? The girl who had kissed his cheek and left a smear of dirt on his nose. It was madness. He could not.

Henry re-holstered his gun and sheathed his sword, standing slowly, feeling painfully older than his twenty-five years. Outside the window, he could see the last of dawn's grey melting under the onslaught of sunrise, and he was glad the night was done. His soul felt heavy, as if he did in fact need absolution. He rubbed his hands over his face and through his hair, messing it mercilessly. "I was following orders," he said finally, finding each word he spoke more difficult than the last, as if anything in speech could excuse what had been done. "We cannot stay here discussing it. Half the King's guard searches for her, and many others."

"You are commander of the King's guard. Command them to stop," said Nora.

"It's not that simple." Henry closed his eyes, but it did not block out the way the morning light cast the princess's features in gold.

"Pick her up then, and oh! She's bleeding again." Gently Nora touched Velvet's bandaged arm. "You wouldn't think someone this frail could be so strong. She's lost so much blood! God! This is awful. Do you suppose she'll be alright? I mean, you've seen wounds like this, I imagine…inflicted them even."

Henry faced Nora's furious figure. The scratches the princess's nails had left on his neck smarted and something in his knee ached. Nora was right in one thing—the girl was very strong—strangely so. "Much as I enjoy your passive aggression, Nora, now is really not the time."

"Pah! Truth can hardly be mistaken for aggression! Don't worry, it's your guilt bringing on that pesky confusion, it will pass when you make amends." Nora lifted her hand when he opened his mouth. "I can see my wit has staggered you, please, just stay silent and obey me, for once, Henry."

There was no other choice, not for him. Henry bent down and lifted the girl he meant to kill in his arms.

~

Velvet: Only Death Awaits

Hands on her waist and thighs left tingles in her blood. Velvet opened her eyes, gasping at what she saw. She was positive that death had finally come for her, and Satan himself was here to carry her to hell.

"What fire?" she heard Nora demand, and Velvet realized in dismay that she was quite alive. Her proof the pounding in her head, and scorching heat slashing her rib.

"What was she talking about?" raged Nora. "What did you do, Henry?" Nora stood under the small doorframe blocking the exit, hands on hips, a defiant cast to her delicate features.

Velvet looked away from them both, her eyes turned to search the grey fog lying over London like a filthy blanket. She wanted it all to be a dream yet knew in her heart it was not. Louis was out there somewhere—Louis and Cerberus; the rest were dead. Everyone she loved—each beautiful soul who had raised her, protected her, left out food for her, cared for her and Louis through the lonely years—was dead. She hissed in a breath, Henry's eyes flew to her face and burned where they touched.

"*Bâtard*," she hissed. "*Meurtrier*— murderer! Put me down!" she demanded. Her round of struggles was terribly ineffective. She was well and truly caught, and Henry's arms were the steel cage she feared. "Please," she begged. Velvet thought she sounded very weak, and hated it, but it could not be helped. She was so exhausted, it was hard to control her roiling emotions, to maintain proper decorum when all she wanted to do was drift into the fever dreams she knew were coming for her. How much blood can a human lose before their heart just stopped beating? Was that why the strange organ stuttered in her chest when she met his hot stare?

"I have to find my brother and my dog, Louis, Cerberus, they need me. Please, just let me go."

"I can't," said Henry. His eyes shifted focus, they looked over her shoulder and narrowed. "Your life is priced high, love. Only death waits for you out there." Velvet tore her eyes away from his face, too hard and angular to be perfect—too perfect to be real.

Nora stepped from the shop and scanned the Strand, stomping her foot to a rhythm only she could hear. "Oh, Velvet…" she worried. "Much as I hate to admit it, Henry has a solid point! *Gad!*" Nora's hands balled into fists. "You know what?"

"What?" Henry almost roared.

"Velvet is right! You are a bastard! And I don't throw that word lightly. Did you leave *any* guards at the palace? We are quite surrounded—" Nora's torrent of words was squelched in a scream. "*Oh my God!* Lord Eden! Devon! Sweet Madonna!" she gasped, clutching at her heart and swallowing dramatically. "You gave me a start! Heavens! What are you doing lurking in the shadows like a highwayman? Pray don't tell me you are party to this nonsense!"

Devon uncrossed his legs, shoved off from the wall, and dropped in an elegant bow, then straightened to take her hand. He inspected the soft skin wrapping her wrist before he pressed his lips to the air hovering above her knuckles. "Nora, I want to say it surprises me to see you here; sadly, it does not."

"Yes, well, it's a good thing I am. You men, running around wild, hunting this poor girl—I never!"

Devon threw up his hands in surrender. "I hunt no one. I am only here to make sure our Duke of Newcastle ends the evening with his stubborn head attached to his obstinate shoulders."

Henry barked out a laugh, cold and humorless. "My head is not the only one in danger, we are all traitors tonight."

"We have to get off the Strand," said Nora, lifting the hem of her skirt while retreating through the door.

Henry had not shifted his gaze. Velvet felt her lips pull into a tight line of defiance. "Put—me—down," she said again, spacing each word, trying to add sufficient venom to her tone. Henry ignored her completely.

"She's too pale!" he barked, loud enough to make Velvet flinch. "How much blood *has* she lost?"

"A lot! I told you!" was Nora's tart reply. "She would be in Doctor Harper's care if your men hadn't shot at me and destroyed my carriage…we arrived at McIntyre's shop hotfoot. I don't mind telling you, tonight has been one of the worst of my life, so unpleasant in fact that if you had anything at all to do with any of this—like she says—I will make it my business to personally to see *your* worst."

"Ah," murmured Devon. "You two at each other's throats—I bask in the soothing sounds of home. Since I've managed to make you both take a breath, perhaps we could see to the situation at hand. I hobbled the horses around the corner, if we can make it…"

"I'll make it," Velvet said, too weak to struggle anymore. There was no real weight in her tone. "I can walk."

Nora made a tsking sound. "Just hush and let him carry you. Henry's a giant brute, make no mistake," she avowed. "He won't hurt you, though, I won't allow it!"

Velvet looked at Henry, seeing the subtle tick in his jaw. "Is that true?"

"Hurt you?" His dark brows narrowed, and he sounded shaken. "I am ordered by the King on pain of death to kill you."

"Ludicrous," scoffed Nora. "You will do no such thing. My father is a dear heart, God save him; sadly my idiot brothers are right, he is unfit to rule, if he meant to kill you. He will thank us later. No one—not even King George—wants the death of an angel on his conscience."

Nora's voice faded away. Death, always so much death. The word singing through Velvet's head brought more chills to wrack a shivering frame. She felt too weak to do anything about them; the world was spinning again, and she held onto the image of her brother's face.

"She's fainted," said Henry, sounding altered, as if this statement pained him. Velvet could voice no words to tell him it was not so. She lay silent, counting each of his breaths by the rhythmic bursts of heat that prickled the chilled skin of her cheek. He had done it. He was the one. The hated red coat beneath the dark cloak that hung down his back like pinioned dragon wings. Velvet let her drifting mind wander and thought of the revenge she would exact when she felt well again—if—if she felt well again.

"Nora…" Henry's voice shook. "*Did you hear me?*"

"I heard you, control your tenor! If she has fainted, it's no bloody wonder! Child had the fright of her life. The knife wound across her ribs is ghastly. Two of your men attacked us earlier, I think, though I can't be sure. Their coats were black instead of red, their movements seemed standard regiment; they both reminded me of your father in a way."

Henry growled, a low sound in the back of his throat. Nora ignored him. "Velvet, and the deadly knife she whipped from her boot, saved my life. She's fast, Henry." A flush rose on her freckle-dusted cheeks, and something serious sparked in her deep eyes. "Did you really murder her whole family?"

Velvet felt Henry's shoulder tense beneath her cheek. "I didn't set the fire myself," he said gruffly. "I didn't even know the King had sent others, but yes—it was on my watch, and yes, I'm afraid it happened. Just know that I mean to find out who and why."

"Yet, you were sent by my father on the same errand? Were these not your orders as well?"

"No. The slaughter of a gypsy community was not required. Only two lives," he said, after a beat of silence that rang like a bell. To Velvet it seemed he choked on every word.

"Did you know you were going to kill *this* girl?" asked Nora haltingly, fear of his answer shadowing her eyes.

"Yes," said Henry, his voice barely audible. "Yes, I knew."

Velvet saw Nora's disparaging look shoot vivid holes through what remained of Henry's composure. "I have known you most my life," she said. "So I am not going to hit you. Just know that I want to. Most ardently!"

"Our orders were to find her and her brother, not slaughter innocents."

Nora's teeth worried at her lower lip. "Why does my father want her dead?"

"I can't tell you, Nora. Trust that the reason is sound."

Nora's face turned the color of a ripe tomato, and under the cap of her vivid hair it looked as if she had just burst into flames. "Sound?" she wailed. "Sound? Are you mad? There is never a good reason to take an innocent life. Never! To that, I doubt I will ever trust you again. This is on *your* head, Henry, you must save her. Is her brother alive?"

"The last I heard, yes."

Nora said nothing, the silence stretched until again it rang in Velvet's ears. *Say more! Say more!* her heart begged. *Please tell me what happened to him. Where is he?* No one answered the silent voices in her mind.

"Devon," Henry called out, sounding deeply relieved. "Thank God."

Velvet felt the steel arms tighten around her. She opened her eyes to see Devon returning leading two sweaty stallions across the street, clinging to the scattered shadows. Velvet's eyes roved over his red coat, and unwanted memories of burning children made her close them again.

"They know you have her," rasped Devon, keeping his voice low and passing a set of reins to Henry. "Damn savage lot out there. Assassins, soldiers, and sell-swords."

Henry took the reins and shifted Velvet in his arms. From beneath her lashes she saw his eyes rove over the slim white column of her throat.

"The neck of an Antoinette," she heard him whisper, or maybe he thought it and she only read the desperate words in his eyes. Either way, a cold chill rushed down her spine.

"Nora," barked Henry as he mounted, hoisting Velvet higher, pulling her tighter to his chest.

"What, Henry?" Nora's voice was made choppy by her own struggle to mount and find a comfortable position in Devon's lap.

"No, don't move like that, darling," cautioned Devon, wincing. "You'll cause a reaction and unseat us both."

Nora ignored Devon and faced Henry. "You were saying?"

Henry cleared his throat. His fingertips brushed Velvet's temple; her eyes were closed, and she feigned sleep. Still she knew his gaze never wavered from her face when he said, "I would not— could not—have killed this girl."

"Obviously," snorted Nora. "This whole thing is absurd!"

"Never thought it, old man, not for a moment," chortled Devon.

"Still…" Nora sighed. "We seem to find ourselves in quite the pinch. Not to mention, like villains, we saved our own necks after the carriage crash and left Spencer lying in the street. His leg looked broken. Who knows where my horses are?" Velvet thought she could hear tears in Nora's voice when she said tremulously, "We have to go back for all of them!"

"Not yet," grated Henry. "They'll be fine. Spencer is an old military man. If anyone can take care of himself, it's that one."

"Now, Lady N," said Devon. "If you don't mind ducking your head and bracing your shoulders, I think we mean to make a run for it."

Velvet's eyes trembled open, shadows of men wavered in the thick fog; some drew their swords, others looked unsure, while still others rushed at them, flowing from the belly of darkness like an army of black locusts.

"Yah! Yah!" Henry snapped the stallion's reins wrapping his right hand, his left cradled her head against his chest. Velvet saw locks of her gold hair swirling in the wind that whipped his cloak out behind them. She imagined how they looked, his mask back in place to obscure all but his eyes, and she realized her previous fantasies of death had almost been true. In her mind it seemed the very Devil himself had kidnapped an angel.

3

BUT NOTHING

Just When You Thought You'd Seen It All

Velvet opened her eyes and saw only Henry's face. "Demons are always beguiling," her grandmother had often warned. "Beautiful faces, words like the sweetest honey, only poison in their souls." Her gaze roved over the rough stubble shadowing his jaw and the downward turn to his mouth. *Poison in their souls, murder in their hearts,* her mind confirmed.

The four of them as one crested the base of sloping dip in the winding street. Velvet locked her teeth to keep herself from crying out, as each clip of the horse's galloping hooves rattled her bones and aching cuts.

"I find it enjoyable being a fugitive," said Devon happily. "Exhilarating, really. Gives me a newfound respect for life."

Beneath Velvet's cheek her captor's chest rumbled when he spoke. "You've been a fugitive for ten minutes—"

"Quite right, Devon," Nora cut in. "Hardly enough time to make an informed decision."

"I'm living in the moment," Devon avowed. "We are all dead men walking, save you, of course, my dear. I doubt you will die for this, though in your father's state anything is possible."

"Don't make predictions of doom and gloom under your breath," admonished Nora, straightening her seat in the saddle, making Devon squirm. "It only adds dread to the ominous, my lord."

"It's the truth, Nora," said Henry.

Velvet never heard Nora's response—though she felt sure it had been tart—because an arrow whizzed by Henry's cheek, so close she felt its tail of wind.

"Yah!" cried Nora. Bent low over the stallion's back, she wrapped her arms around his neck, pressing her face against his sweaty coat. Another arrow blasted past them, then another. Velvet felt Henry's cradling hand draw her even closer to his chest; he pulled up on the reins, when the horse reared. Arrows shot from the wall of fog surrounding them, so close she could see the color of their feathers.

"Are your own men firing at you?" Nora's voice quaked. "Good God, Henry! I never—"

"Of course not!" barked Devon. "Your father has hired himself some sell-swords. Far worse, don't you know? We left the palace guard in the dust, holding their swords and wondering what to do. Not one of them would fire a shot at the Duke; most of them owe him their life."

"If they owe him their lives, they should ride after us and save it!" parried Nora. An arrow struck the pommel of her saddle. It pierced the leather an inch from her hand with a sickening twang. Nora's eyes squeezed tight. "That tears it," she said, calmly removing her hand from immediate danger. "That arrow just pierced my last nerve!" She shuddered and looked up her hand closed over Devon's forearm. "Here, stop!"

Henry tugged on the reins, and the horse's hooves clattered to a halt. Velvet felt him dismount, impossibly graceful as she was still cradled in his arms. Distant shouts echoed through the empty street. Running feet pattered the ground. Henry caught the edge of his cloak and drew it over them both. Velvet gasped, feeling the heat of his body seep under her skin and rush through her icy veins. *She should hate him! Shouldn't she?* Hatred was nowhere in the warm circle of his hold. Velvet wondered how she could feel this safe in his arms—a stranger, a savior, a killer.

"Link your fingers behind my neck," breathed Henry. Velvet obeyed, having already decided she had no choice. She was determined to take his help for now, save her strength, and bide her time—revenge would come, she swore it would! The wound on her ribs screamed in protest but her fingers curled around his neck and touched the tie that held back his hair. Velvet realized they were running. His long legs ate insane distances. So lithe, so strong, she thought—the rare Gadje warrior from her grandmother's songs.

"Here!" said Nora abruptly. "No, Devon, not that way, make a right, we can go in through the gardens." Nora reached out to unhitch a small silver latch, and the delicate garden gate swung open. "There, go to the conservatory. I trust most of my household, but the less of them involved in this the better. I'm sure at least one of them reports to my father."

Nora lifted her skirts and ran ahead of the men, through a dewy garden full of roses and yellow hummingbirds. She opened the glass door of the conservatory and stood back to let Henry brush past. "There, lie her on the daybed under the gardenias. No, not like that, gentle! You'll hurt her neck."

"I'm capable of lying a woman down, thank you, Nora," said Henry.

Nora snorted. "This is not the time to boast of your infamous promiscuity, Henry. Devon, will you go to the house and fetch clean cloths and a bowl of warm water…oh! Wake Katie. Only Katie, mind. I need Katie."

"Yes, my lady." Devon gave his heels a jaunty click, then hurried off.

"Water," Velvet begged. "I'm so thirsty."

"It's the blood loss," growled Henry. "I've seen men die of less."

"Well," said Nora. She knelt down on a floor cushion near Velvet's head then lit a match. A circle of fuzzy light enveloped them. "She is not going to die."

Velvet listened to a stream of liquid falling in a glass, then Nora's hand was behind her head lifting her up. Velvet gulped the cool water, not caring that it bubbled past her cracked lips and ran down her chin.

"Gently," cautioned Nora. "When was the last time you drank something? Or ate for that matter?"

Velvet did not know, so ignored the solicitous questions and took Nora's hand. "Thank you," she whispered over her next gulp, sighing in bliss when the cool liquid soothed her parched throat. "I would have died without you tonight."

"Nonsense." Nora brushed Velvet's worry away, a sweet smile on her tense lips. "Is there no one we can call, Henry? No doctor who would keep our secret?"

Henry shook out a negative that tossed his dark curls around his head. Velvet noticed some of his hair had fallen free of its club and now ran wild. He could have been a gypsy with his broad shoulders and swarthy skin, one of the men who painted their chest and did knife tricks. The sudden smell of campfires made her think of Louis, and every thought further broke her heart.

Henry took a step toward her; he saw her open eyes watching him, then stopped himself. After a moment of indecision he started to pace, giving Velvet visions of a prowling dragon. "When she's bandaged properly we will ride to the Sisters of Saint Catherine, beg them for sanctuary."

"No!" Velvet squeezed Nora's hand. "If I don't live, please find my brother, he is perfect and innocent, please…I know you owe me nothing but…"

Nora's eyes were wide in distress. "You will be fine, I promise. Hush now, rest while you can."

Nora tried to gently disentangle her hands from Velvet's desperate grasp. Velvet made a small sound in her throat and held on tighter. "Please. Nora," she begged, not caring that tears ran unchecked down her face. "Please."

"I do promise to try," whispered Nora, shaken. "Though I have no idea how I would—"

"I'll find him," said Henry.

Velvet felt her eyes fly to her attacker. "You!" she gasped. "Find him, and kill him you mean?"

Nora unlaced the front of Velvet's gown, and Velvet listened to her own short breaths deepen. She had put the gown on yesterday morning—or was it the day before? She found she could not recall, since it was all just a blend of blood and fire. The dress was a rose-white, it had long skirts streaming from a corset weaved in a golden thread that matched the embroidered hem—she had felt like a princess, reveled in being human, twirled under the sunny sky until pure happiness made her dizzy. Her grandmother made the dress for her three days ago, the day she exchanged a pair of wings for human legs. Her grandmother said the dress was stitched by threads of love and starlight, told Velvet that the gown was fit for the princess she was. Now, her blood soaked it, dark red as an eclipsed moon and all the golden trim had turned crimson.

"Henry, help me," said Nora in a sharp tone. "I don't want to jostle her, I have to get this corset off…it's wrapped under her… Oh, Devon, thank God!"

Devon smiled. "People have been saying that to me all day. It's nearly made it to my head."

"Do not let it," commanded Nora, the glare in her eyes softening when she looked at him. "Too stuffed already, the added weight would strain your shoulders. No, don't put that there. Leave the water here and hand me the cloth. You are a saint, Devon, truly."

"I know," he admitted. Nora moved her skirts so he could kneel beside her. Velvet stared at the three of them, a halo of protection surrounding her. Their auras flowed together making all the colors of a burning rainbow. Feelings of joy, gratefulness, and rage battled in her chest.

"On three, Nora," rasped Henry. Velvet felt his hands span her waist. "Don't move, angel. Now Nora, one, two…three."

Velvet bit back a scream until she tasted blood. Small fibers of her chemise twisted in the knife wound slashing her lower ribs—ripped free, taking tissue and skin with them. Consciousness was an ocean, and Velvet struggled to keep her head above the waves.

"Oh, it's not as bad as I first imagined!" said Nora in relief. "A few stitches and some rest will have you feeling right as rain."

Henry's hands went to the tie at Velvet's neck, the one holding the bloody edges of her chemise in place. His fingertips touched the strings and he paused, then his hands fell to his sides in clenched fists. "I will not add the debauchery of a child to the list of my villainous crimes tonight," he said.

"I lost my childhood when the cannons boomed and the children burned," Velvet muttered, glad to be rid of him, wondering why she suddenly felt cold. Regret drenched his eyes when he stepped back; she felt the illogical need to soothe it and cast it away—quickly before the irrational feeling could take hold.

They stared at each other while the sounds in the room muted, stared until Devon stood and clapped Henry on the back. "Well, spotted old chap, debauchery is all quite bourgeois—come stand guard beside me, it's a pastime filled with intrigue."

"Devon, are you ever serious?" asked Nora kindly, not looking up from her swabs and bloody bandages.

"Never, Madam, humor is my lifelong companion who will walk me to the end. Together we will do our best to make the hangman laugh before he slings the noose. Ah! Someone is coming, far too much fog to make them out though—see? There's the intrigue I spoke of—simply scintillating."

Nora rolled her eyes, deftly wringing out a bloody cloth. "Did you wake Katie?"

"She was already out of bed and getting dressed, much to my chagrin," admitted Devon, looking sour at the memory. "I got a pillow in the face for my troubles and received firm directions to hell."

On the heels of his statement, a girl rushed in their sheltered alcove; ashes smudged her white apron and her hair tumbled free of her nightcap, which hung limply around her shoulders. In one hand she carried more bandages, in the other, a cocked pistol.

"My lady," said Katie, her voice calm and controlled as her movements. "If I may have a moment of your time."

"I am rather busy, Katie, perhaps you could tell me why you're carrying a gun?"

"Because, my lady, five men outside are doing the same. I have gold in my pocket and another pistol; I also brought a bit of yarrow and willow bark, Lord Eden said you have a wounded girl. This will help any bleeding."

"You're an angel!" gasped Nora and reached for the items.

"Spencer is waiting by the cellar door. We will use the tunnels to escape, as I feel your home is no longer safe, my lady. We have been invaded."

"Invaded! Really, Katie, the drama!" said Nora dryly, then paused. "Spencer? I thought he broke his leg in the crash. He's here?"

"Yes, my lady, woke the household about ten minutes past. I asked him about the leg, he said it was nothing. He wrapped it himself and fashioned a cane with a broom."

"Good Lord," said Devon. "Quite the household you have, Lady N."

"Yes, well, being the bastard daughter of a king comes with some benefits. There." Nora applied the yarrow to Velvet's shoulder and the deep cut on her ribs. When she had wrapped the bandages in place to the best of her limited medical ability, Nora dried her hands on her skirt and retied Velvet's chemise. "I've done what I can. We will have to dispense with the corset for now. Katie, please fetch me one of my cloaks, a dark color if possible."

"My lady," urged Katie, her eyes a pair of full moons in her flushed face. "I don't think you're grasping the peril."

"Fine." Nora sighed. "Velvet, you may use mine. Now, do you think you can sit up?"

Velvet sat up, trying to swallow. It was useless, her tongue felt dry as sand. "I must go now, thank you for everything you have done."

"You cannot go!" wailed Nora. "You can hardly stand."

"I do not have another moment. My brother could be in pain —he could be dying. I must return to..." *To where?* Her blank mind gave no answer. "I must return to the place where brother and I were separated. When the redcoats caught me, they said they wanted to play a little before they did the deed— I forced him to flee before he was seen. I assume they meant to brutalize me in some fashion or another before taking my life, and I did not want him to witness it—he has already tasted too many flavors of horror. I fought to distract them, they cut me. It was all so..." Velvet put a hand to her spinning head, she did not know how to finish that last sentence.

Nora threw her cloak around Velvet's trembling shoulders. The weight was warm, and she sighed into it. "Is that when I found you?" asked Nora.

"Yes," said Velvet. "I think they believed I was dead." Velvet sighed. "Everyone always wants me to die…it feels very strange," she whispered. She tried to tie the ribbon at her neck, but her numb fingers were clumsy, and the silky strings fought back. Nora brushed Velvet's hands away and retied the ribbon in a bow. Velvet caught the girl's busy hands between both of her own and looked in the face that regarded her with such concern. "I have to go to my brother," she said, needing somehow to explain. "Please, I have to. He's all I have left."

"No," Henry cut in. "It's a death sentence. We will go to the Sisters of Saint Catherine."

Velvet lifted the hood of the cloak to hide her golden curls. When the silk settled in place, she met Henry's eyes. "Restrain me or kill me, sir, that is the only way you will stop me." It was difficult, but she stood up, inordinately proud of herself for not swaying on her unsteady feet. "Please, just show me the way, I will —" A gunshot boomed, leaving her thought unfinished.

Nora flinched and rolled her eyes. "In my house? This is monstrous!"

"Indeed," said Devon. "King George must be in a rare mood."

"Please, my lady," begged Katie, casting furtive glances over her slim shoulder. "It is my job to protect you. I know you have a kind heart, and I love you for it—we all do, my lady—yet if you take a bullet to the head you won't be able to use it! We must go now!"

"Though a tad overdone, I believe young Katie is right, Henry," said Devon. He moved to stand at Katie's side. "We can hold them off while the ladies make a break for it. In the unlikely event we come out on top, we can all meet in the Temple Gardens." He winked at Nora. "By the maze near the *une gousse d'amour,* you know the spot, Lady N."

Nora threw him a sharp look. "Not well as you, my lord, I'm sure."

Velvet took one step toward the glass doors, then another.

"Steady now," said Henry. His strong hands caught her when she stumbled. Velvet wanted to throw his hands from her, grab the candle from Nora, and use its tiny flame to set *him* ablaze. This was his fault, even if he had not lit the fires himself. Instead, she closed her eyes and let the hand at the base of her spine warm her from shaking fingertips to curled toes.

Henry touched her chin, lifting her face. "I give you my word, I will help you find your brother. If it is in my power, I will bring him to you."

"First you vow to kill us, now you swear salvation?"

Henry stepped closer, and the space between them seemed suddenly electrified, each breath hot sparks in her throat. Velvet understood none of it. "Why?" she needed to know.

"Evil was done in the name of justice, I meant to set it right."

"Justice?" Velvet scoffed. "You know nothing of that word!" She shook her head to clear it of the pervading fog drying up her common sense, like desert water dissipating beneath a hot sun. "You could just walk away," she whispered. "Forget me."

Henry's finger traced the line of her jaw. She felt the skin there glow under his touch. "Not if I lived to be a thousand," he avowed.

Another gunshot—dramatically louder than the first— shattered the door of the conservatory, spraying glass through the room and showering them all in painful rain. Devon bore Nora and Katie to the ground, persevering through their squeaks and protests. Henry pulled Velvet against his chest and turned them so his broad back faced the danger.

Three more shots fired off in rapid succession. Nora shrieked. Katie crawled to the other side of the room knocking over a potted plant and smashing a vase. "It's useless!" called Katie. "It is as I feared, the path to the house is overrun. We can use the side entrance, through the rose gardens, enough trees line the way to provide cover."

"Do you still have that second gun, Katie?"

"Yes, my lady. Should I return fire?"

"I say!" protested Devon.

"Do it, Katie," said Henry. His hand fell away from Velvet's face. "Go with Nora, Angel, I'll find you."

"Don't trouble yourself, it is my fervent prayer to never see you again!" Velvet spat, but he was already gone. She wrapped her arms around herself, holding onto a little of his warmth.

"Velvet!" said Nora from the other side of the room, using her whispered shout and wildly waving her hand, beckoning. "This way! Oh, stars! Get down!"

Velvet saw the sharp alarm in Nora's wide eyes. She threw up her arms and ducked her head—it was too late—a shadow brushed past her line of vision; she blinked, and it crashed into her, forceful as a racing stallion.

Her head hit the ground and a burst of stars obscured her sight. A man fell on top of her; the crushing weight of him took her breath as did the elbow digging in her wound. Velvet cried out and shoved at her attacker, using her nails to claw at his eyes. The man, stunned at the violent assault, took a defensive stance, falling back, hands flying up to protect his face, while he used his legs to wrestle her thrashing ones in submission. When Velvet realized her knee was only inches from his groin, she grabbed his shoulders for leverage, then, using all the force in her small frame, Velvet brought her knee up between his legs. Her attacker howled in shocked misery, his body instantly limp. He rolled over onto his back, then curled slowly in the fetal position, both hands holding his injured parts. Velvet scrambled to her feet and ran toward the girls who stood huddled together, pistols drawn, delicate fingers caressing primed triggers.

"I wanted to shoot," said Nora, releasing the hammer and stowing the pistol in the front pocket of her gown. "But it's so dark, I feared the bullet would hit you." Nora turned and gave the wounded man a withering glance. "You don't appear to have needed much help."

"Should *I* shoot him, my lady?" asked Katie.

"If you don't," the man moaned, "I will kill you."

"Very ominous, sir," said Nora in a sugary tone. "However, we hold the guns, you merely grovel at our feet."

"I'll gut you, bit—"

Katie fired her gun, effectively ending the man's sentence in a bloodcurdling scream as his kneecap blew apart. The recoil threw Katie back, but she recovered her footing easily and reloaded.

Nora closed her eyes, pressing a finger to her ears, she shook her head. "For heaven's sake, Katie! That was abominably loud."

"I'm sorry, my lady," said Katie. "I thought it best to shoot him in the leg."

"Right you were," said Nora, then kicked a shard of glass at the man. "That's what you deserve for making nasty threats, you bastard." She kicked another shard, and this one ended its flight buried in the man's thigh. He mewled miserably.

"My lady, we really must hurry, we can leave through the gardens. Spencer is seeing to the rest of the household, I know he is. Your safety is all that must concern us now."

"Let's away then." Nora sighed long and loudly. "I hope Lord Eden and Lord Newcastle are doing something useful; you, dear Katie, have offered more protection than either of them, the hooligans." Nora linked her arm through Velvet's and helped her out the small door.

Early morning light touched the upturned daisy faces and changed their petals to flames, leaving flowery shadows on the grass.

Katie wiped away a drop of sweat that trickled from beneath her cap and looked around. "Quickly, please!" she persisted, holding out her hand. Nora took it. Thus linked, they dashed through the rose bushes, ripping their gowns free when the thorns bit the material, hissing when they gouged skin. A white fence consisting of twirled bars and arrowhead spikes wrapped Nora's property. Through it, Velvet saw the waking world. A bird's song interlaced by the rattle of carriage wheels and the clattering hooves of the shod horses filled the air.

"*Get down!*"

Velvet recognized Henry's husky roar and obeyed without thinking, taking Nora with her. Katie let go of Nora's hand to remain standing. Little over five feet, wispy as a reed, and dwarfed by the weapon in her hands, Katie braced her feet apart and aimed at the shadow which morphed to a man. A sliver of light glanced off the mouth of the barrel. Velvet covered her ears.

"I hate it too," whispered Nora, reading Velvet's mind. Her hands went up to cover her own ears. Katie squeezed the trigger. The shot rang out, but the man kept coming. Velvet's hands dropped to her lap; she clenched her fists wishing for her knife. From the south of the gardens, in a place the sun had yet to touch, she saw Henry and Devon running toward them. Twice the distance to cover, Velvet knew the shadow would reach them first. When she met Henry's eyes, she saw he had come to the same conclusion. The way he held his pistol told her it was useless—there was no time to reload. Velvet got to her knees and positioning herself in front of Nora she curled her body in a low crouch. Katie reloaded.

"What are you planning?" hissed Nora. "Don't you dare charge him! He'll kill you!"

"I'm hard to kill," Velvet said, praying it was true. She tensed her weight on the balls of her feet and prepared to spring. Only a few yards away now, the man drew a long blade from the sheath belted to his waist. The tricorne he wore was a replica of Henry's, it too cast his face in shadow, above the mask his dark eyes shone an evil light.

Katie carefully measured black powder out of a glass jar which she returned to one of the many pockets in her dove-grey uniform. She set a small ball, slick and greasy, atop the powder then capped the pistol. Movements briskly efficient, she drew back the hammer —her shot never came.

The man's fist lashed out and struck Katie's jaw, her head snapped back. She kept her footing—just barely—and fired the gun. The bullet sailed over the assailant's head. Katie shoved her elbow in the man's stomach, and his breath left his lungs in a wordless *ooof*. Growling, his knife slashed dangerously near Katie's stomach. Velvet slammed her body against his legs, wrapped her arms around his knees, and tugged hard, using every ounce of her currently dubious strength. The man flung his arms out for balance; the knife fell from his grasp and his full weight landed on her. Before Velvet had time to gasp back her escaping breath, gloved hands flexed around her throat.

Movements wild and lurching, Velvet felt the ground searching for a weapon—a rock, anything to wound or dislodge him—but her hand grabbed only empty tufts of grass. Spit splashed her cheeks as the man leaned in and laughed, throttling her so forcefully Velvet thought he meant to break her neck.

"Get off!" screamed Nora, pounding the man's back with her fists. "Katie! Shoot him!"

Katie said nothing. Through silted eyes, Velvet watched Katie's light brown locks of hair whipping her face while she carefully reloaded. Velvet's vision rippled and she knew her air had run out. The sound of running footfalls was not far off, someone called her name. The inane noises echoed in her fuzzy brain, and she felt her body go limp.

Just before her world disappeared to a storm of white dots, a black blur streaked through her fading vision accompanied by a low growl. Instantly the hands at her neck fell away.

Velvet gasped, rolled onto her stomach, and coughed until tears ran down her cheeks. Hands massaging her wounded throat, she searched the garden for her savior.

The moment she saw him, Velvet forgot about the ache in her throat and forgot her desperate need for air. She crawled on her stomach, digging her hands in the wet earth and using the grip to haul herself forward. "Cerberus?" she sobbed. "Oh, Cerberus!"

"Holy Saints!" yelped Katie, the sight of Cerberus rustling her nerves in a way the assassins had not. "That's the largest dog I've ever seen."

"I really don't think it's a dog?" said Nora.

Velvet hardly heard their chatter. Cerberus stood over their latest attacker growling menacingly. The contents of the man's throat dangled from his jaw and streaks of darker black marred his scruff. When he saw his mistress the beast forgot his kill and bounded over to nuzzle her cheek. Velvet flung her arms around the monster's neck, sighing in profound gratefulness and thanks then buried her face deep in his thick fur.

"Oh, Cerberus," Velvet whispered, hoisting herself up so she could press her warm nose against his cold one. Tears ran unchecked down her cheeks; she landed kisses on his big face liberally smeared by slobber and blood.

"Good God, is that a bear?" panted Devon, as his harrowing run came to a grinding halt beside Nora. He seemed to consider sheathing his sword, then rejected the notion.

"It appears so," said Nora. "I would stop where you are, Henry, that hairy monster just killed a man."

Henry came to an abrupt halt, a low noise whistling through his teeth.

"I think young Katie here deserves a raise," said Devon to no one in particular.

"I am not that young, my lord," replied Katie in a haughty tone. "I am sufficiently compensated for my services."

"Katie takes whatever she desires." Nora sighed. "I've been in her debt since childhood."

"Are there more men?" asked Katie, already reloading.

"I don't think so," Devon told her, seeing to his own ammunition.

"...two behind the house," Velvet heard Henry tell Nora. "They attacked, they died."

Velvet listened to their words but did not have time to give them her attention. Her whole soul focused on the fact that Cerberus lived, and his life meant a chance for Louis still existed. "Where did you come from?" she purred. "Can you take me to Louis?" Cerberus wagged his tail and licked her cheek.

Still keeping a strong grip on his neck, Velvet swung her legs over Cerberus's back, settled her body along the ridges of his spine, and rested her tired head against his neck. "Good boy," she breathed, "take me to Louis. Take me—take me to him." She was so tired, so unbelievably tired, if she could just rest for a few short moments, just rest, then she could keep going. Then she could fight. She tried to hold them open, yet her stubborn eyelids tumbled closed. Velvet dreamed.

4

RIGHT BEFORE YOUR EYES

Nora, Nora, where are you?
Are you the young lady who lives in a shoe?

*T*he dog Velvet called Cerberus, was a creature of fantasy. Roughly the size of a pony, with a shaggy black mane and lion-sized paws. The beast existed in a child's picture book, not on a misty Thursday morning, and *certainly not* in her gardens. Nora watched Velvet hoist herself onto her dog's back, the girl's golden hair spilling from the hood of her cloak like a veil of starlight.

"Didn't know people could ride dogs," said Nora. Her hands were terribly cold, and she felt shocked to her core, as if this unforgettable dawn had power to change her world.

"I don't think it's the usual, my lady," said Katie. "Are we going to let them traipse off into the sunrise?" Nora let Katie's sentence hang. She had no answer—neither it seemed did anyone else—no way to say why she felt beholden to this girl. Perhaps the fact it was her father who ordered the murder, or just the golden quality of Velvet which made Nora feel she must protect such a thing at all costs—whatever the pull, she would let no harm come to the girl, that she vowed.

Cerberus looked at the three of them pensively, Nora saw their reflection in his huge chestnut eyes. None of them moved an inch, they all—like her—simply stared in wonder as he walked toward them with great loping strides that emphasized his size by the ground they covered.

A stream of light touched Velvet's face spangling her skin with rainbows. Nora walked forward, holding out her hand. She did not think she possessed any great bravery, yet felt no fear when Cerberus drew back his lips and growled. Blood smeared his teeth, Nora saw—noted it for what it was—still she felt no fear. "You're a good boy, aren't you?" she cooed. Cerberus took another step closing the distance between them. He stuck out a massive tongue and licked her hand, then happily sniffed the air, as if yes, he believed he *was* in fact a good boy.

"My lady!" gasped Katie.

"I wouldn't," cautioned Devon.

Nora ignored them. Cerberus tilted his head, a quizzical sound rumbling in his throat; Nora scratched his ear and he sneezed in pure happiness. "Are we safe, Henry?" Nora asked, careful not to change the cadence of her voice.

"I think so, yes. For now," grunted Henry, his mild tone a sharp contrast to his expression. Running a frustrated hand through his hair, Henry looked at the man sprawled on her lawn. Nora followed his eyes, her gaze coming to rest on the missing jugular.

Now, Nora was sure she had gone into shock because the sight of the gore did not bother her the way it should. Why were people dying tonight? She wondered who was this girl they died for? Nora needed answers more than anything else at the moment, including a warm bath. Just the thought of that warm, cleansing liquid running over her skin, washing away the blood, dirt, and sweaty smell of fear was enough to make her grit her teeth in longing. Nora put the needy thoughts out of her mind and tilted her face to Henry.

"Who is she, Henry? Why were you sent to kill her? After all this, I believe I have a right to know who I risked my life for." Cerberus licked her hand again. Nora reached up to scratch his cheek absently, as if her and the big beast had known each other forever. "Henry?" she persisted. "Tonight I have found myself insulted, shot at, and tumbled by a shattering carriage! A gentle monster dog just made a meal of an assassin's throat before my eyes, in my day garden no less... If you chose this moment to give me your famous silent treatment, well then, I would just slap you silly."

Henry gave her an imploring look; Nora returned a frosty glare.

Resignation finally slouched his broad shoulders. He let out a breath and pinched the bridge of his nose between thumb and forefinger. "Her name is Marie Thérèse, she is the daughter of Louis the Sixteenth and Marie Antoinette. If her brother is dead, she is heir to the French throne."

Nora sucked in a sharp breath. "Bastards on a biscuit!" she wailed and drew back a fist to strike his chest. "If this is one of your jests, I swear to Christ, Henry! Just tell me the truth!"

Henry caught her attacking hand. "It's the truth. I swear it. Does this seem like something I would jest about?"

"I never know with you! My God!" Nora took a deep breath that trembled as it went down. "It is strange, though."

"What is?" asked Henry.

"Well, there is already a Marie Thérèse. She resides in Mitau, living large in the home of her last surviving uncle, the Comte de Provence, who is currently a guest of Tsar Paul the First. Also, a complete lecher I'm told." Nora's strokes on Cerberus's nose continued as she gave a mock shudder. The big animal snuggled in her hand, licking at the freckles on her cheeks with a tongue the size of a large trout. Nora scooped a glob of saliva off her chin and felt a smile lift her lips. "The gossips say the old uncle has eyes for his niece. The other Marie Thérèse, that is." Nora tapped her chin pensively, her brain rushing through a dozen scenarios.

"She is a peasant girl," said Henry. "Exchanged by the gypsies a few days before Marie Antoinette's death."

Nora's eyes fell on Velvet. "I knew there was something special about her," she declared. "I mean, of course I couldn't exactly *know* it, but I felt it. Does that make sense?"

"I think so, yes," said Henry, truthfully.

"She lived with the gypsies all this time?"

"I have no idea, I only learned of her life last night."

Cerberus tensed at a street noise, his teeth clashed together, and his lips drew back in a snarl.

"Easy," Nora soothed, softly scratching behind a loping ear. Cerberus submitted to Nora's caresses but watched Henry through wary eyes. Nora stared at the distant trees boarding her property. She looked past the swaying leaves to the shadows now peopled with demons. A feathery thing fluttered in her stomach, and her hand flew to the flutter.

"I'm pregnant," blurted Nora, wanting instantly to recall the words. *What in heaven had made her say such a thing?* Biting her lip and stealing her nerve, she tilted her head to meet Henry's eyes, silently daring him to make a disparaging comment, or worse—a joke.

Henry locked his hands behind his back and rocked on his heels. The arrested expression on his face told Nora she need not have bothered throwing him the look, her ill-timed statement had rendered him speechless.

"It's your nephew of course," continued Nora warily, her voice shrill in the screaming silence. When no one spoke, Nora's playful scratches behind Cerberus's ears turned fidgety, and she twirled strands of his coarse hair through her fingers. "Stop looking at me like I just dropped my gown, Henry! You will catch a host of flies with that gaping jaw! You knew I was sleeping with Charles, saints, all of London knew." She threw up her hands. "Such things do happen, you know? Regardless what the gossips say, I was innocent when I went to your brother's evil bed, thus had no idea how to prevent such a thing."

Henry unclasped his hands, removed his tricorne, and ran one through his dark hair; his lips moved, but no words came. His expression reminded Nora of a time when he had fallen from his horse many years ago. He had been a lad of five or six, the horse a giant gelding of eighteen hands. The fall knocked the wind from his lungs and the look on his young face—one of astounded confusion, which mirrored the one he wore now.

"I say, it isn't yours," Devon cut in. He clapped Henry firmly on the back. "Take a breath, old chap. It's always been the four of us, though Charles has cut in and out over the years. Now there will be five. We shall be uncles, my lad." Devon administered another hearty slap on his friend's back, jolting Henry and causing Cerberus to paw at the ground while he tore up great chunks of earth and howled in a fury of renewed growls.

"I'm going to murder my brother," stated Henry, his voice incredibly calm, almost cheerful.

"Classic," quipped Nora, raising her eyes Heavenward. "Not the reaction I hoped for, yet, sadly, what I expected."

"Now, now, old chap," admonished Devon. "If you kill him, you can't very well force him to marry our girl."

Nora laughed, a deeply unhappy sound. "I wouldn't marry Charles if he were the last man living." Nora kissed the wet tip of Cerberus's nose and buried her fingers in his fur, staring into his liquid eyes until she could see her own flushed face in their reflection. "And I am truly sorry, but we can't go to the Sisters of Saint Catherine just yet, Velvet won't rest properly until she knows her brother is safe, honestly, I understand. If something happened to you I would never stop looking. So…" Nora took a deep breath and gathered her resolve. "Cerberus," she commanded, "take me to Louis."

The dog's ears perked up, and his big nose twitched as he sniffed at the wet air. Nora pressed a hand to the side of her fallen coiffure and tried to pat down the springy, red curls. The gown of blue muslin—which wrapped her in silken moonlight last night—was now a wreck of muddy leaves and dried blood. A deep tear marred the quilted skirts and the beautiful lace bustle was filthy beyond repair.

Cerberus walked past her, and Velvet moaned in her sleep. Nora followed them, placing her foot in a paw print which dwarfed it. She heard Henry and the others fall in step behind her.

"Does Charles know?" asked Henry in a deeply strained voice.

"He does. It seems he has no time for the leavings of a whore or her spawn."

"Nora!" roared Henry. Fury radiated from him to Nora, and it seemed his energy scorched the air.

Nora rolled her eyes. "Those are his words, not mine…needless to say, his charm overwhelmed me."

Henry took her elbow and spun her to face him. Exhaustion stamped a set of half-moons beneath his dark eyes, his full lips were a tight, pale line in his swarthy face. "You will marry me," he declared, startling Nora enough to make her jump. "I will give you my name." Henry dropped his eyes to the still slender lines of her waist. "Protect you both."

Nora felt a sudden rush of tears prickle her eyes. She went up on her tiptoes. Sighing, she placed a kiss on his cheek. "Oh, Henry, much as the look of fear and abject depression on your face carries the promise of many happy years to come…I'm afraid I must decline your gallant offer. Just another wonderful thing about being the King's bastard, I may marry for love—or not at all."

The barest hint of a smile sparkled in Henry's eyes, though her previous assessment of his expression remained. "Nora, I think I could make you very happy. I believe you find me tolerable?"

Nora fanned her face with coquettish flips of her free hand, then threw him a look from beneath her auburn lashes. "Are you fishing for compliments, Henry? You know you're the most desirable man in England and perhaps the continents?"

Henry's shoulders sagged, and he used his hand on Nora's elbow to halt their progress. "Be serious, Nora. I must marry you, to save you ruin."

Nora burst in a choked giggle. "Me?" She had to struggle to keep the laugh from turning hysterical. "Lady N? The most scandalous daughter of England? That's the laugh of the eighteenth century. My reputation was ruined at birth, done in by its circumstances."

"Precisely." Henry ran a hand through his hair and the small tie that held it back fell against the ground. His hair, thus freed, rushed around his shoulders, the dark curls brushing his clenched jaw when he shook her. "I don't want the same thing for your child. It is not gallant. I've loved you since we were children, Nora, from the very day you showed up on our doorstep, a bedraggled little princess wearing the most freckles I'd ever seen."

"I love you too, Henry. Love you for taking pity on a

misbegotten child. I love you for standing up for me when I was too weak to fight." Nora stood back and patted his cheek, then wrested her elbow from his grip. Picking up her sodden skirts she continued after Cerberus. A low-hanging branch reached out to link its bony fingers through her hair, and she batted it away. "But we are not in love and never could be. You are more than my blood, you are family—so our union would be an epic fail." She spoke from over her shoulder; stepping lightly, forcing him to follow at a brisk pace if he wanted to hear her words. Behind him, Devon and Katie strolled side by side speaking in low tones.

"It would be silly," Nora continued. "We are too passionate, you and I, to do things in half measures. That is what our marriage would be, half of what we could have with someone else. Do you believe in soul mates, Henry?"

"Of course not. Do you?"

"I don't know. I would like to think I do, that there is someone special for each person, a soul you knew and loved in another life, so on the off chance that it's true, I would prefer to wait for him."

"We are friends at least, many strong matches in our time are constructed on less."

"True," admitted Nora, looking at him in fond regard. Streams of weak light brushed his Grecian profile, straight nose, and high cheekbones, highlighting his firm chin and a pair of lips that would make Adonis weep in envy.

Nora used her elbow to nick his ribs and tried to give him a reassuring smile. "You honor me with the offer. My answer, however, is still a resounding no. You have not loved a woman since the angels came to take your mother and sister."

"That is not true. I loved you."

Nora snorted. "You tolerated me."

"I did more than that. I got down on my knees, begged God for your life."

Nora's expression turned sad, and she felt an unwelcome moisture gathering in her eyes. "I remember that. In my delirium I heard your prayers, I wanted to tell you that there was no god who would take Lady Rosilia and Charlotte yet let a bastard live. When the scarlet fever burned away leaving only me, I came to realize that Lady Rosilia was too good for this world, Charlotte too perfect. I am sure Heaven suits them far better, your father truly was the very worst sort, they went to a world without him. I imagined it suited them both just fine. I'm sure she missed you though, perhaps Charles less so." Nora reached for Henry's hand and linked her arm through his, borrowing his strength for support —it was a comforting thing in a world suddenly gone insane.

They walked in silence for a time, until Velvet stirred and cried out a stream of words in a language Nora had never heard. Cerberus made a mewling sound; Nora hushed them both, wondering at all the ways of fate and thinking it far too early in the morning to mentally pontificate so.

Heavy rain clouds gathered over their heads and drenched the street beyond in shadow. Faceless people milled about, dark cloaks drawn up against the cold, heads bowed to the wind.

"Devon, be a saint and hail a hackney for us, will you?"

Devon mumbled through a huge yawn, nodding out a lazy affirmative. The aftershocks of adrenaline drained the normal animation from his cherubic features and his steps had lost their usual bounce. He finished the yawn, his final sound a desperate growl, then stretched his arms over his head. He moaned, deeply, ending the stretch with obvious reluctance. "Of course. I can't wait to stuff these aching joints in a rickety conveyance and rattle down the Strand."

Nora huffed. "Well, there's no help for it. Look at me! What if someone sees?"

"Nothing I can't fix, my lady," said Katie, coming to fuss over Nora's explosion of curls and retie the lace at her neck.

Katie gasped. Her scowling features collected in the center of her small face and made Nora bristle beneath the heat of her displeasure. "You lost one of your diamond earrings, my lady!"

Nora shrugged a slender shoulder. "It's of no consequence. I think I lost it somewhere in Cheapside. I hope the someone who finds it needs it more than I."

"If they need it, chances are they don't deserve it," stated Katie.

"Nonsense," Nora replied. "You are too young to be so jaded. Everyone, no matter their station in life, deserves a chance."

"A charming sentiment, my lady," said Katie. Nora could hear her striving for a polite tone.

"There is no charm equal to tenderness of heart," said Henry

"Oh, Henry," Nora purred. "It's so scintillating when you quote Austen to me."

He threw her a lazy wink. "You forced me to love the chit."

"And you are forever grateful to me," Nora finished. She paused a moment scanning their bedraggled group with a quizzical eye. "You know," she continued. "I've always wondered—"

Velvet screamed her wide, sightless eyes fixed on a distant mirage. Every muscle in her small body tensed and quivered. Henry growled, his scabbard cleared its sheath—hissing quietly.

"No, it's alright, Henry," Nora soothed. "Waking up this way is *de rigueur* for her."

Henry re-sheathed his sword; his eyes—wandering between the princess and Nora—blinked meditatively at this performance.

Devon returned a moment later, a pronounced limp in his gait. A few particles of dirt clung to his upper lip, and his blonde hair jutted out in all directions from his head. Several bleeding scratches decorated his palms, a silver button below his chin was missing, and the right knee of his dark trousers held a shaggy tear. Nora felt her mouth fall open. Devon, despite his injuries, dropped into a low, courtly bow.

"Devon?" Nora asked, giving him a quizzical once-over. "You look to have taken a fall."

Devon snorted—in a most ungentlemanly fashion—and brushed his hands over the front of his coat. Slender twines of golden rope hanging from the tasseled cap on his shoulder swung across his chest when he stood and pulled on his lapel, resetting the garment over his lithe frame.

Through clenched teeth, he said, "We were wrong, there are others on the street. A blaggard jumped me moments after I hailed the thing. The driver panicked. Lily livered rabbit! An unfortunate struggle, of which I ended up on the losing end, ensued. During said struggle, my leg became entangled in the flapping reins. I lost my footing and found myself dragged behind a spirited team of horses for near a street block.

I persevered, however," continued Devon. "In the end, I succeeded in my quest like a champion." He dropped in another bow giving Nora a sidelong smile. A small flourish of his hand, that fluffed the lace at his wrist, gestured to the rickety conveyance parked just beyond Nora's front gate. "Your carriage awaits, my lady."

Nora could feel the vibration of a laugh tickle her battered throat. "The carriage" to which he referred was little more than a wooden crate pulled by two flea-bitten horses of questionable heath. Their tails batted at the flies gathering around their backsides, crawling in black clusters over the mountain of manure, steaming in fresh piles on the street

"I would not exactly call that *thing* a success," said Katie. "You shouldn't ride in it, my lady, not in your condition. Let me take you to your father, and safety! Henry will help the girl find her brother."

"To find sanctuary among the Sisters of Saint Catherine," corrected Henry.

"Whatever," said Katie!

"Stuff and poppycock!" Nora declared, casting a furtive glance over her bare shoulder. "I refuse to look at my father right now, the monster! Ugh!" She ran her hands up and down her arms to wipe away the sudden chill that seized her.

"Katie is right," said Henry. "I forbid you to ride in..."—he sputtered for a moment at a loss for the appropriate word—"that thing," he said finally, echoing Katie.

"Forbid?" Nora repeated, and her voice climbed a few octaves. "Forbid? Really, Henry!" Nora rolled her eyes and brushed past him. "We are wasting valuable time chatting about this foolishness. I am not leaving her side until I know she is alright, and that is that!" Rising on her toes, she linked her arms around Velvet's waist, careful not to brush the girl's wounds, and helped her dismount. Henry started, and Nora felt his arms encircle them both. Her weak knees thanked him.

"Devon?" she asked. "The man who attacked you? Were there others with him?"

"None that I could see. But the bounty on Velvet's head is very dear; more will come soon."

"What a mess!" she said. "I want a moment to catch my breath, I may not see these gardens for a while…" She hesitated. "I loved them so."

"This is not your battle, Nora," said Henry.

"So you say, yet it is one that practically fell in my lap. I mean to fight it," she said, and it was true. The shock of the night seemed to be fading, replaced by a heady sort of relief in this brief idyllic reprieve.

"We may be safe for the moment," said Henry echoing her thoughts. "But I fear it will not last long."

"I know," Nora whispered. Realizing she was taking this all a step past common courtesy, she could not shake the feeling of right. Destiny guiding her feet, each of her choices were taking her where she was always meant to go.

Velvet shifted in discomfort, her lips parted; gingerly she touched the wound at her side, then flinched at the pain. Her pearly white teeth worried at her bottom lip. She lifted her head and stared up at Henry's face in astonishment.

"Where am I? Where's Louis?" Her hand clamped over her mouth. "What…where—" Her words broke off. Nora watched memories of the last few hours flood the girl's blue eyes. Behind her golden head, tepid rain fell from the swollen sky in fat steady droplets. Across the street a dirty raven perched on the lip of the gutter, splashing in a puddle and letting the water roll off his oily beak, then he spread his feathers and shivered off a host of raindrops that momentarily haloed the bird in a watery orb. Black wings spread wide showed the wisps of dark purple and sapphire blue hiding in the feathers. The bird cocked his head to the side and gave himself another shake. More water flew adding to the bulk of his watery halo. Nora let her eyes follow the path of the droplets.

Katie asked her a question she did not hear. The drops of water rolled down the sparsely populated street catching the weak shine of a lamp not yet extinguished. A fly buzzed near her lips, and Nora batted it away.

Henry repeated Katie's question, but those words also drifted past her without a sound. There was a heat emanating from the center of the street, warm as a banked flame. It called to her.

A carriage flashed past her disoriented vision, its silver-rimmed wheels ran through a puddle, showering the idling bird in a stream of mud and releasing a noxious brown cloud in the air.

When the cloud cleared she saw it again, a thing she could no longer tell herself she had not seen. Air whistled through the small gap between Nora's front teeth as she inhaled. The exhale never came; rather the breath knotted in her throat and swelled her lungs.

A golden stag stood in the street's center, his shadow falling on the outraged bird, his image shimmering—a dream inside a fairy tale. Soft, glowing light gushed down from the ivory antlers, illuminating large sections of the descending rain. An earth-shaking rattle announced the passage of another carriage. The galloping horses kicked up more brown, muddy clouds. When those too disappeared under the downpour, the silent street held only mist. The trapped air in her lungs hurtled out in a dizzying rush, and against her better judgement, Nora promptly fainted.

5

ALREADY DEAD

Three Wise Men of Gotham went to sea in a bowl; if the bowl had been stronger, my song would have been longer.

Velvet went to her knees beside her fallen friend and brushed the clinging autumn strands of hair off her sweat-dappled face. "She's fainted," Velvet breathed. The corner of her lip lifted in something that was almost a smile. "Not to worry," she mimicked Nora's earlier comment. "This is *de rigueur* for her."

Henry barked out a surprised laugh. He tried to cover it in a cough and failed. His shoulders rocked. Shaking—in what Velvet thought was a very strange fashion—he bent down and lifted the unconscious Nora in his arms. Corded muscles bulged beneath the cloth of his red coat. Velvet thought if she had a guitar in her hands, she could have written a ballad on the allure of his person. She smiled to herself, but the smile turned wistful, of course the Devil would be compelling, beauty was part of the curse—she knew that better than anyone.

"You can let go of her now, Angel," said Henry. Velvet complied reluctantly. Henry handed his frilly bundle over to Devon, who despite his pained grimace, accepted.

"Jesus," groaned Devon, stumbling slightly under Nora's

weight. "How women walk in all this frillery will forever befuddle me."

"Take her to her father. I will take Velvet to sanctuary," said Henry, in his usual tone of command before he turned and reached out a hand to help Velvet to her feet. The morning light played on the golden quality of his skin, rendering his features in brushstrokes of dove grey and platinum. Velvet wondered why her impulse was to take the hand he offered, when everything in her told her she must hate its owner. She thought about it for a tense moment before acknowledging that she had no idea how to hate, no idea how to love, no idea how to live. It had been so much easier living life as a snowy owl. She understood many things and over the years learned the strength of her soul; as a human, there was so much she did not know. Velvet felt the rain plastering her hair to her cheeks, and a beat later she wiped it away.

"I mean you no harm, Velvet," he breathed, meeting her wide gaze with his own blazing stare.

"Oh?" Velvet exclaimed, fighting to keep her voice under control. "I thought you said my death would save thousands. How do I know you are not just waiting for the opportune time to kill me?"

"If I wanted you dead, you would be," said Henry.

"Foreboding," Velvet whispered. "What if you change your mind?"

He looked at her for a long moment, and she watched glittering drops of water run off his face. "I give you my word," he vowed in his low, sincere voice.

"A thing of great worth, I'm sure, but of not much value to me. Having little experience of such a thing, I put no stock in a man's word." Velvet took his hand, her fingers linked through his. "You are very warm for a cold-hearted killer," she whispered.

"You are very blunt for an angel," was Henry's stoic reply as he helped her to stand. Devon came up to them shuffling Nora in his arms.

"Duce heavy!" grunted Devon. He hoisted Nora higher. "To the carriage then, we are foolish to stay here long as we have."

Henry turned toward the street of living shadows, taking

Velvet's elbow in a firm grip and giving her body a small shove forward. Velvet let herself be led. Her mind swirled for a plan, but the truth was she was a lost girl in a foreign world and going at it alone was far too great a risk.

Nora chose that moment to wake with a spluttering gasp. Her arms flew out and her flailing fist glanced Devon's jaw. His head snapped back, he yelped, more in frustration, Velvet surmised, than in pain.

"Good God, woman!" Devon's howl was tormented. "That is the third time someone has hit me in that exact spot tonight! Do control yourself."

Nora's hands clenched into tiny fists. "I will do you far more harm if you do not set me down at once!"

The unruly mop of blonde curls that framed Devon's face rippled over his cheeks, now flushed a peachy pink. Large dots of perspiration glistened atop his lip. "The duke instructed me to carry you to your father. I am merely obeying orders, it's him you must release your ire upon. You are a squirmer, my dear, has anyone ever told you that?"

"No one—" huffed Nora, "has had…had occasion to!" Nora took her small fists and beat on his chest, her voice rising alongside the power of her blows. "I refuse to be taken to my father! He is a monster! Do you hear me? I refuse! Put me down!"

Abruptly, Devon obeyed. Nora landed with a hard thump on the wet ground in a heap of lacy skirts. She shrieked and sat up, her hands flying to her ruined coiffure, her eyes locking on Devon— astonishment slowly morphing into outrage. A single second is what it took for her to recover from the shock of the fall. Hissing a word no lady should know, her silk-stocking leg shot out. Her foot connected sharply to the back of Devon's knee, and she kicked his own foot out from under him with a solid *thwack*! He yelped again and fell flat on his back, his limp body making a soggy noise as it bounced. Uttering a heartfelt groan, he fell utterly still, save his right arm which he threw dramatically across his eyes.

"Damnation, woman! The Devil take you then!" he said, his voice muffled by his arm.

"I've done nothing that was not first done to me," said Nora, giving Devon the full heat of her evil eye, then her lips quivered, and she burst into a peal of tinkling laughter. Lying prone on the ground, his forearm still straddling his face, Devon's body shook. Beside Velvet, Henry was gripped by a similar affliction. A snorting gulp, and he dropped her hand, clutched his stomach then laughed out loud until tears streamed down his cheeks. The sound of his laugh made Velvet feel like she had swallowed sunlight.

Nora placed her fingertips against the lids of her eyes, laughing in long musical peals, kicking her feet, spraying mud in the air. A stream of it struck Devon's face. He seemed not to care, only got up on his knees and howled at the rising sun.

"Oh God!" exclaimed Nora, over another helpless giggle. "I've gone hysterical! We are going to be murdered in my gardens because I've gone hysterical. I so of-often get accused of it…nice…nice…" her words disappeared into another shrill laugh. "Nice to finally know what it feels like."

Velvet did not understand why they were laughing or why she felt the incredible need to do so herself. By all rights she should be a bucket of tears, yet when Henry pitched forward, jolts of laughter rocking his big frame, Velvet felt her lips lift in the smallest smile.

Cerberus sniffed at the air and howled impatiently. Velvet reached up and stroked his neck. "I know, boy," she whispered. Velvet spared a final glance for the convulsing people and felt a pang, an invisible vise twisting her heart. Only a few moments had passed, but they were already too many gone. It was so hard to leave. To Velvet, the scene before her was perfectly idyllic—one her imaginative mind had always treasured—a private family portrait glimmering in a frame of rain, and she, the uninvited voyeur, stealing a few moments from the happiness of strangers.

Velvet moved silently backward. Cerberus understood his mistress's intent; his paw pads made no sound when they met the wet ground. Silent movements took her beneath the front gate, barely a creak from the hinges when the edge of her toe nicked the door. She was having a difficult time making one foot fall in front of the other—there were conflicts inside of herself that she could not settle—she dreamed of finding a huge tree where she could curl up in its wide branches and let her mind trail away in the wind.

The hem of her gown brushed over a rosebush, and a spiked thorn caught hold. Velvet grabbed her skirts, crushing handfuls of red velvet in her palm. She tugged on the material once. Nothing moved, the thorn's curved tooth pierced the cloth straight through, and would not release it. Velvet grit her teeth and tugged again—the cloth gave way with a screeching tear." The roses rustled, loudly—she froze, praying she had not been heard.

A movement in the corner of her eye made her spin around to see Henry closing the distance between them in a miraculous amount of time. Velvet could only stare at her aghast. Cerberus moved in front of her, growls rumbled in his throat, his bare teeth wet from the blood of his last kill. Henry came to an abrupt halt a few feet away.

"Don't force me to fight this monster," he said.

Velvet could see a steady pulse pounding at the edge of his jaw, pulsing in his white lips, all traces of laughter wiped clean—she felt defiance flash in her eyes.

Henry only stared at her as if she was dim-witted, or visibly growing a third eye. "You are a princess," he finally said, as if he explained the structure of the universe to a small child. "Did you know that?"

"I know what has been said, I am unsure of the truth."

"Does it matter? I cannot kill you, so my life is forfeit. Until the Reaper comes to harvest my soul, I've sworn to protect you, I have also sworn to find your brother. Damn it! Do you need my promise inscribed in blood before you will let me?"

"No, I don't need that," Velvet said. Cerberus's growls increased in volume. He snapped at the empty air between him and his target who stood a mere three feet away, holding out his hand to her—yet again. Velvet dropped her eyes to her mud-soaked boots. "It doesn't matter who my parents were, I hardly remember their faces. It only matters who I am now."

Henry raised a dark brow. "And who is that, my lady?"

"No one," Velvet said and hoisted herself onto Cerberus's broad back. "Just a lost owl."

"That is a cryptic sentence, love, one we don't have time to decipher." A smile rekindled in the green flecks of his eyes. The smile changed him from austerely handsome to devastating, and he started to take another step. Cerberus barked in his face. Henry stunned Velvet by barking back with enough ferocity to make Cerberus splutter and go silent. Henry eyed the animal for a few moments more in some austerity, and Cerberus whined in submission. Velvet was so shocked by the exchange between man and dog that she said nothing when Henry completed the step he meant to take.

"Nora is family," he said. "She insists on helping you. That means you're not lost anymore. Come, Velvet, get down. Don't make me carry you again, I fiercely recall your dislike of it."

"Don't joke," she said, trying to be stern. "I will never forget what you have done. The spirits will curse you for your actions."

"I do not believe in curses," he told her.

"The power of a curse does not require your belief," she shot back.

"I would never have allowed it to happen," said Henry. "The proof is your life. I am truly sorry I was not there to stop them." Henry locked his hands behind his back, Velvet thought it was to stop himself from running them through his wild locks of unbound hair. "I was born to obey my King," he said simply.

Velvet did not want to understand, but she did. Not hate, maybe not even love, but every creature that roamed this earth understood loyalty. Velvet felt a set of eyes burning holes in her back; she turned to see Nora on her feet, intently watching the exchange between herself and Henry. Devon hopped beside her on one foot, shaking chunks of dirt out of his boot. He rested his elbow on Nora's shoulder, and muttering a word she batted him away. Devon swayed precariously, and the world went suddenly still.

Henry felt it too; she saw his shoulders tense, his body still as stone, his eyes scanning for danger. No singing birds or clattering carriage wheels filled the morning, just the sound of rain hitting various objects and the unsteady clamoring of her heart. She took a deep breath and let it out slowly—*they were fine*—*no one was coming—it was just her frazzled nerves*—when she took her next one, the entire world exploded.

A huge bubble of fire rose in the sky atop a pillar of swirling black smoke and baked the air with the heat of the desert sun. A thunderous *boom* exploded, and Nora's fashionable townhome blew apart, a thousand burning shards rained down on the wet ground. An invisible force struck Velvet in the chest—a pillowy hand made of hot air intent on snapping her spine. She flew into the street, then landed against the curb with a bone-jarring thud. Acrid smoke filled her lungs, she lifted her arms to cover her face, coughing, trying to see out of her streaming eyes. Shards of splintered wood pelted her, bit at her bare skin, and hissed in bursting pockets of steam when they hit the ground. Trying to make out her caterwauling thoughts, Velvet gasped as a crushing weight settled on her back. Her panic at the new terror was short-lived—Cerberus howled in her ear then licked her neck in a long, sloppy stroke.

"Good boy, Cerberus," Velvet grunted. A moan rose to her lips as she struggled to sit up. She pushed her fingers into her ears and opened her mouth, her eardrums crackled and popped, the sharp pain made her sneeze.

"Christ!" spat Henry. He knelt down beside her. "I thought the beast crushed you."

"Nora, Devon, and Katie?" Velvet gasped, lifting her head to look in wonder at the disaster before them. The remaining pillars of Nora's home smoldered hotly in the distance. Through the gilded white gate she could see only empty darkness edged by an ominous orange glow. "What about Spencer and the rest of her household? Oh, goddess! Are they all dead? Because of me?"

"I don't know," said Henry. "Certainly not because of you. Can you stand on your own?"

"I don't think so. My ears are ringing something awful and…"

"Velvet, you're bleeding," he said, and his voice was wretched.

He touched her. She looked at her blood on his fingertips and sighed. "Not surprising," she said. "It's also possible I might be sick."

Velvet felt his body tense. "If you do so, please have the courtesy to aim against the wind," said Henry.

A jolt of sound escaped her lips before Velvet could smother it with her hand. *Was that...mirth?* It seemed improbable since she could not remember a single moment of laughter in her life.

Henry misunderstood her twisted expression. He touched her again, his fingers rested lightly on her wrists—one, two beats—then he brushed scattered bits of gravel from her skin. "This is not your doing," he said. "There are many bloody hands in this tale—none of them are yours. Nora is right, the edict demanding your life is a grave injustice. We haven't known each other long, but I've seen no proof of the devil in you. I've seen only bravery, loyalty, and selflessness."

They were drawing a crowd of wide-eyed onlookers. A few seemed to know Henry, one even called him by name, using a similar title to the one Nora gave him on their first meeting.

"Are you hurt, milord?" a faceless one asked.

"The constable will be here presently," another said in a cultured tone.

"Is that His Grace, the Duke of Newcastle?" This feminine whisper was closer than the others, Henry barked a response. Velvet squinted her eyes to see through the endless swirling sheets of rain and watched the crowd grow in density as it parted to let another well-wisher through. Standing statue-still, Velvet saw the outline of a man, his face and chest in shadow—the glowing whites of his eyes simmered death. In his hand was a knife, held out in the open for everyone to see, hiding in plain sight.

"Henry," Velvet started.

"I see him," said Henry. "When I say so, I want you to run, unhitch one of Devon's woebegone horses, and don't stop riding until you reach the Sisters of Saint Catherine. Kneel at the altar. Demand sanctuary!"

Velvet reared back. "Certainly not! I will do none of those things. I will not be an anchor to you! I can fight," she finished, struggling to contain her emotions and return her voice to a whisper. She was also trying to remember just what on earth an *anchor* was.

Henry smiled despite it all. "Don't I know it," he muttered.

"Give me a knife," Velvet demanded. "I mean it. I am tired of being unarmed. I...don't look at me like that."

"Like what?" asked Henry innocently. Velvet knew him well enough by now to know that muffled quality to his voice meant he was trying not to laugh. It enraged her.

"As if I was a confused sheep! I know how to use it."

Henry pinched the bridge of his nose and sighed. "Confused sheep..." His shoulders rocked. "Christ, if that isn't exactly what you look like."

Velvet threw her eyes Heavenward in pure frustration. Overhead the smog thickened, the heavy rain did nothing to quench the fire eating ravenously at the remains of Nora's home. The entire world looked burnt around the edges and ocher ashes rode the visible streams of pale wind that thrashed the darkening morning.

"Get ready," commanded Henry.

"I'll distract him," Velvet said.

Henry gazed at her, an indiscernible look in his eyes. "You are a strange, magical thing, aren't you?"

Velvet lifted her chin and tried to look down her nose at him— a method of communication used by English ladies to control men, or so her grandmother said—but his height made it impossible for her to achieve the desired effect, and a little rain went up her nose. She sneezed and coughed simultaneously, so forcefully, Henry nearly lost his hold on her. Velvet rolled her eyes, finishing her cough in a hiccup.

"Maybe," she said, when she could. "Now, give me your dagger, let me fight."

"Fine. I'll give you my dagger if you promise not to use it on me, and only use it on others when forced."

"Hum, I promise not to use it unless forced."

"Clever too," breathed Henry. "A dangerous combination."

"He is less than three feet behind you," Velvet said in a conversational tone, suited more to a picnic than a knife fight, and held out her hand. "Give me your dagger, now."

Two more explosions went off in front of them and the pillars which had so beautifully framed Nora's house only moments ago, crumpled in a smoldering heap. Screams and gasps from the body of onlookers surged in the crackling night.

Henry let Velvet go. Heart on fire and blood pounding, her feet hit the ground; he spun around, and drew his sword. Velvet heard the swish of sharp steel cut through wind and rain. Back to back, Velvet and Henry spun full circle. Knife cutting through the swaths of rain, the man charged. Henry's arm struck out. Velvet heard a chilling scream, then hot fountains of blood lashed her face, and a limp body crashed to the ground, knife still clutched in his death grip. The puddles at her feet ran red.

Chaos exploded in the street. Screaming people were pushing and rushing to get away from the violence.

"Velvet! Get down!" shouted Henry. To Velvet, his every movement was a dark blur.

Too late. Another figure hovered over her, his masked face inches from her own. He held a knife raised above his head. Henry's sword sang a deadly song as it pierced the man's forehead before he could swing his own blade and end Velvet's life. The man's face caved inward, pain and shock wiped the smirk out of his eyes as the sharp tip of Henry's sword busted through the back of his head. Shards of cranium and brain splattered all over the ground. More shadows in the crowd screamed and a pale-haired woman fainted at Velvet's feet. Still more came wielding short daggers and loaded guns.

Henry pivoted and brought his sword up in a blinding, bloody slash. Another body fell. Henry placed a large, booted foot atop the chest of the fallen man and Velvet saw him lock his lips when he ripped his sword free. Grabbing her elbow in his sword-wielding hand, he locked the other behind her knees and lifted her like she weighed no more than a feather in a storm. His sword arm came across her waist forming a tilted crucifix with her body, presenting a formidable defense against the shifting throng.

"Get back!" shouted Henry at the growing crowd. The blood of dead men dripped down his face; his lips drew back in a snarl showing a strong row of white teeth. Cerberus stood to the right, his own teeth bared in a similar fashion, his huge paw resting on a severed head. Henry's first attack had cut through the neck of the bravest fool, dislodging the mask which now lay discarded in a rippling puddle. The head belonged to a man who seemed too old for such tiring work; his leathery face was sun-worn, rolls of skin wrinkled the corners of his open eyes, thick scar tissue gouged out a portion of his rotund nose, and a colorless tongue lolled out of the slack, dead mouth.

Velvet closed her eyes quickly. It was no good, the image would be forever seared in her mind. *All the good memories are gone,* Velvet thought sadly, *so many bad ones to take their place.*

Two men broke free of the crowd, then two more, and it continued that way until the killers outnumbered them three to one. Cerberus prowled back and forth, standing guard just before them, and growling deep in his throat. Whether it was Cerberus's menacing stride, Henry's flashing sword, or the two dead bodies lying at their feet, the killers held back. They ghosted along the edge of the panicking crowd. The storm light touched them, secretly revealing the weapons they concealed.

Then, she heard the rough clatter of hooves, and a soft voice calling her name—relief surged through Velvet. Out of the burning smoke, two horses maintaining a punishing speed galloped toward them, followed by a host of buzzing flies who struggled desperately to keep pace. The wooden cart they pulled clattered over the wet cobblestones. Above the splintered beam of the cart's shabby side, Velvet could see a shock of orange hair hovering like a wispy cloud painted by a sunset. Cerberus let loose an outpour of terrifying howls causing one horse to bray loudly and rear up on its hind quarters. His hooves kicked at the dark rain, and his eyes rolled back in their huge sockets so just the white showed. The horse landed jolting the carriage. When he reared once more, his soaking mane whipped Devon's face showering his coat in mud and random street debris. Devon cursed and juggled the flailing reins in one hand, using the other to wipe the watery muck from his eyes. Velvet watched as he struggled to control the frightened beasts and maintain his seat atop the teetering bench which looked held together by splinters and a sinner's prayer.

"Get in!" screamed Nora. Wide eyes snapping in her flushed face, she held out her hands.

Devon swayed in his seat yanking at the reins; the terrified horses screeched to a halt, nearly causing the rickety cart to jackknife. Nora yelled her command again as the carriage teetered to the left. In the next breathless second the whole weight of it balanced on the two side wheels. Thumping tremendously, the carriage righted itself. Velvet heard a twin pair of groans before it swerved in front of them, less than five feet away.

Henry swung from the waist and threw Velvet in the zigzagging cart. She landed fully on the entwined limbs of Nora and Katie, consequently winding them all. Velvet raised the head threatening to spin off her shoulders, realizing with a pang that she was lying directly on top of Katie.

"Oh, sorry!" she muttered, rolling off quickly as her wounds and exhaustion would allow.

"Don't apologize," groaned Katie, reclaiming her bruised limbs. "It's Lord Newcastle who should do that. No fault of yours where you landed. After being thrown, that is." Katie pursed her lips and scowled at Henry who had leapt onto the moving conveyance and was even now sitting beside Devon, deftly taking the reins from him. The cart pitched forward into the black dawn.

Velvet heard her teeth clack together; Katie flew back, and her head smacked against Nora's freckled nose. Nora yelped in agony. Katie scrambled to a sitting position. Both her hands flew to either side of Nora's face and she crooned out her own sonnet of apologies. "Oh, my lady!" cried Katie, seeming to care nothing for her own pain and smarting eyes.

"It's not broken at least," said Nora in a tight voice. Reaching past Katie's hands she touched her bright red nose. "Does it look crooked?"

Katie smiled, a real smile that flushed her cheeks, casting her plain features in a rosy hue that reached her brown eyes and turned them to gold. "No, my lady. It seems straight. Perfect as ever. Spencer says if the nose is broken you bleed like a stuck pig."

"There's no blood, right?" said Nora. "Oh, God! Spencer!" Her smile shattered. "Spencer! Miss Croy? Laura? Philip?" Tears filled Nora's eyes. "I'll never forgive myself if they're dead. Just never!"

"You're alive," Velvet said. "You both are." She took Katie's hand. "That matters."

"Yes," whispered Nora, wiping at a stray tear. "That matters."

"They might be safe, my lady," soothed Katie. "They knew of the peril, and Spencer will take care of them. I know he will."

"I am so sorry," Velvet said, knowing there was no justice to be had in the words.

"Don't worry, my dear, the world always falls apart when the King wants you dead," said Nora, still gingerly touching the contours of her bruised nose.

"But you didn't have to be a part of this curse with me," Velvet said. She found it difficult to meet Nora's gaze, so she stared over her shoulder and watched the shadows of murderous men shrink to oblivion.

"I think I did," said Nora after a moment. "Only the Devil knows why—you are what matters—you are a princess with a claim to what's left of the French throne. We're already a merry band of traitors. I think on our own each of us would be dead; together, we might stand a chance." Nora squared her shoulders and looked up at the dark sky. "All this talk of curses," she whispered after a time. "Perhaps there is one floating in the air, it has turned morning to night."

There was a faint rumble in the distance as if to add fact to her supposition. Nora shrugged out of her jacket, the rain plastered the silky material to her bare arms, causing it to hold onto her freckled skin in a determined show of vengeance. In the end, removing the garment was a two-person job. Finally, it was done; Katie fell back, winded and flushed. Velvet stared at the slim column of Nora's throat; besides her own she had never seen such pure, white skin.

"Do you never go out in the sun?" Velvet asked, watching the small muscles in Nora's arm bunch as she wrung out the waterlogged material of her coat.

Nora shrugged. "I am a creature of the night mostly, though I love picnics and morning rides in the park...why would you ask such a silly thing?"

"Because your skin is so soft and white," Velvet said.

"No more than yours," said Nora. "You grew up in France, surely you must have seen many a white-skinned lady at the French court."

"I remember little of that," Velvet admitted. "The spell my grandmother cast on me took most of my memories."

Curiosity flooded Nora's eyes, though she said nothing. Only drew a deep breath, shook out her coat then held it up for inspection. It hung in the space between them limp as a used rag. "Ruined beyond repair," said Nora. "The toll tonight was a heavy one, and…what do you mean, the spell? What spell?"

Velvet said nothing, instead she busied herself wrapping her borrowed cloak tightly around her shivering frame, flipping her hair over her shoulder, and trying to wring the water from the curly mess. The silence stretched to the uncomfortable realm, and she listed to Cerberus's howls. From her vantage she could see each stride of his long legs as he ran after the cart, his steady, loping gait easily keeping pace.

Velvet cleared her throat of its nerves and opted for the truth. "My grandmother cast a spell on my brother and I, a few days before they beheaded my mother. Or maybe the day of? I really can't be sure."

"I see," replied Nora after a time, through her tone said she did anything but. "Why would she do a thing like that?"

"To keep us safe I assume. French soldiers were looking for two blonde children, I suppose she did it so no one would recognize us. When it was done, she boarded a ship and spirited us to England."

"How interesting," said Nora, biting her lower lip. "Your grandmother, she was a witch?"

Velvet shook her head. "She was a gypsy," she said, as if the final word explained it all.

"What was the spell?" asked Nora.

"She…she," Velvet stuttered, unsure how much to say. "It was a disguise."

Nora's eyes widened. "I've heard the gypsies can do such things, though I never really believed it. I read a novel once about a frog who changed to a prince when kissed. There was another one too, about a princess who fell under the spell of a dark magician. By day she was a princess, but at night she was transformed into a swan."

"You read too many books," said Katie.

Nora waved away Katie's observation. "Am I right, Velvet? Was it something like that? It was, wasn't it. How scintillating! Were you very different?"

"You could say that, yes," Velvet replied and studied her pinky nail which had apparently shattered sometime in the last twelve hours.

"What did you look like?" persisted Nora. "How long did it last?"

Velvet wrapped her arms around her legs, drew up her knees beneath the cloak and rested her chin on them. "It's a fantastic story and unbelievable."

Nora scooted forward and brushed a fresh sheet of rain off her forehead. Her eyes were alight with curiosity, water droplets sparkling like diamonds in her thick lashes. Despite the terror of the night and the streak of soot that decorated her freckle-dusted cheeks, she looked beautiful, her slightly crooked smile reaching her eyes, making both bubble in effervescent life. "I like to unbelieve the believable," said Nora, scrambling the words in her haste to get them out.

Katie snorted, then followed the glorious noise with a choked hiccup. "That sounded better in your head, didn't it, my lady?" asked Katie, ending the sentence in another giggling snort.

"Vastly," said Nora. She rounded on her maid. "Honestly, Katie, that is really the most disturbing noise."

The horses took a sharp turn, the carriage swerved in a wide arch, making worn rims of the wooden wheels cut the muddy ground and send sprays of gravel to strike Cerberus's face. The beast howled at the injustice, never breaking his stride. Katie's body rattled as it struck the side of the cart, and Velvet's head clapped the base beam of the driver's bench.

"Good Lord, Henry!" cried Nora. "Have a care before you kill us all."

Henry glanced over his shoulder at their prone, bedraggled forms. "In case you ladies haven't noticed we are in the middle of running for our lives. I apologize if the ride is not up to snuff!" He paused to stare at Velvet. "So?" he asked, and Velvet felt her willful gaze locked on his lips. "Regale us with the unbelievable," he said.

Velvet shook her head, averting her eyes from the confusing pull she felt every time he spoke—like it was he alone who she truly searched for. *Wild nonsense!* she thought; out loud she said, "Some other time, perhaps."

"Eavesdropper," muttered Nora. Henry swiveled in his seat and returned his attention to the road. The cadence of the clattering hooves changed, and the surrounding scenery morphed from glittering townhomes to towering smokestacks belching out thick, white steam that rose above a panoramic view of the city. To the east, the Tower of London speared the bellies of the low-hanging storm clouds. Tiny lights glowed in the stone-framed windows, and Velvet thought for a terrible moment she could hear the howls of the dying. She looked away from the structure's foreboding face, watched a cluster of little homes and the remnants of a shipyard fly past, then rose to her knees. "Where are we?" she asked, grabbing hold of the splintered beam for support.

"This is the London Bridge, dear," said Nora patiently.

"I mean, why are we going this way? My brother is behind us." Velvet whirled on Henry. "You promised you would help me find him," she accused.

"I did," he said firmly. "I never break a promise. But we are in a sorry state, you are wounded—even though you fail to properly acknowledge it—we need a place to rest and regroup. Running mad through London at ten in the morning is inadvisable." Henry cast his eyes to the sky and a spray of windy rain washed his upturned face. "Even though it might as well be bloody midnight out here," he muttered.

Devon made a garbled sound of agreement, shuddering visibly. Velvet thought the great Lord Eden looked like a little boy lost in his father's clothes. The image was so endearing it made Velvet say the first thing that popped in her head. "How old are you, Lord Eden?"

Devon looped his arm over the rough plank questionably serving as the driver's backrest. He leaned toward her as far as comfort would allow. A smoky silver infused his blue eyes, then he smiled sinfully and wriggled his brows. "Why ever do you ask, my lady? Do you see something that interests you?" He brought his hand up to his face and let it flow airily down his profile, his fingertips lightly skating the muscles in his arms and chest.

"Oh my God, Devon," Nora said and violently rolled her eyes. "You are an utter cad and a fool."

Devon abandoned the pose and gripped his chest with both hands. "Such words of endearment will steal my heart." He swung back to Velvet, a rakish smile decorating his full lips. "I am nearly twenty and one, my lady. Since I am uncertain whether I shall see another day, I will say it loud and proud as I believe Henry is right, we seem to have found ourselves in the throes of the Apocalypse."

"There, Velvet, you see?" said Nora, clearly trying to keep her voice light, the quiver in it set the tone. "All your talk of spells and curses has us spooked." A peal of deafening thunder punctuated her words, and less than a second later a bright flash of light briefly illuminated the dark sky. Over the side of the swaying bridge, Velvet watched the bolt reflect in the dirty, roiling surface of the River Thames, stared until the crackling light fizzled out, then dissolved in its dark body.

6

GOOD-BYE MY DEAR

And the day went dark...dark indeed. Because of a withering curse and a dastardly deed.

A sweet smell wafted around Velvet when she opened her eyes. Honeysuckle and pine, she thought over a long inhale. The softly scented air did much to dispel the noxious odor of the Themes, clinging to her hair and clothes, stinking like the plague. The front wheels of the cart hit a nasty bump. Velvet sat up, reaching out her arms to steady herself, while the poor cart tried to do the same. Having spent too many years of her life as a nocturnal creature, Velvet had yet to feel her best in the morning. However, she felt sure *this* morning was worse than any that had come before it. Phantom axes cleaved her skull, her eyes dull and throbbing felt like they burned from the inside. Despite the raging fever, her stomach rumbled out a set of ravenous grumbles which to her, rivaled the din of the thunder. Velvet blushed hotly and pressed her hand against the unhappy place.

Henry gave her a sidelong look, a twinkle illuminating the corner of his eye. "Do excuse yourself," he said in an affronted tone.

"I'm hungry," she said defensively while the heat in her cheeks turned feverish. Velvet swallowed, hoping she could keep her voice normal. "Starving, actually."

"Not to fear," soothed Henry. "We'll be there soon."

"When exactly is *soon*?" asked Nora, her voice thick and fuzzy from sleep.

"Not much longer now," he said wickedly. The exaggerated patience in his tone told Velvet it was not the first time Nora had voiced this particular question. "We are on the borders of Newcastle lands now."

Nora groaned and stretched her arms above her head. "You said that a half hour ago. I have never been so uncomfortable in all my life, and that includes when Sister Ingrid made us kneel on rock piles."

"Ah, yes! The old trick of purging sin through pain. Good times," said Henry, rolling his eyes.

"Are you bringing Velvet home?" asked Nora, Velvet knew his home was *their* home—the knowledge made her feel like an outsider again.

Yet she too wanted to know the answer. *Where was he taking her? How long would it take her to escape?* The expression on his face gave nothing away. He did not answer, only clicked the reins, silently asking their tired companions for more speed. The horses ignored the request and clomped along at the same unhurried pace.

Velvet rubbed her aching eyes then looked out at the hazy world. The storm sapped every ounce of light from the day and she could only see three feet in front of her. Even the fog was black and dense as tar, touching fields and sky, streams, mist veils, and crystal waterfalls. The broad trunks of ancient pine trees surrounded them, tall and foreboding. Velvet shuddered under their powerful glare.

A thick blanket of browning pine needles covered the soggy earth. Strings of daisies, their petals liberally splattered in tiny droplets, lined the road like a flowery trim on a lady's day gown. Velvet thought the beauty of the flowers was incredibly out of place in this forest, which loomed angrily around them, haunted as a nightmare.

When she looked up it was to find Henry still watching her, that odd light igniting the crimson flecks in his hazel gaze. His spirit animal was a hawk, Velvet decided, thinking she could see traces of the creature's soul swirling in the velvety-green depths of his eyes, and knew she was delirious.

"Are you staring at me, my lady?" asked Henry, in a voice for her ears alone.

Velvet quickly cast her eyes down to inspect the cart's stained, chipped floor, feeling the flames of the fever ravage her lungs. "No, my lord, it is the top button of your coat which holds my interest." She gasped.

There was a moment of stunned silence. Then, Henry gave a surprised bark of laughter. Conscious of her increasing blush, Velvet crossed her hands over her mouth and exhaled a draft of air that warmed the icy tip of her nose. She was a block of ice and raging inferno simultaneously—she wondered again at the insanity of humanity yet kept her thoughts to herself. "How long was I sleeping?" she asked, and coughed, a long wracking hack that burned from nasal to navel.

"About an hour," Nora cut in. "And I am peeved at you for it, having left us all on the edges of our proverbial seats."

"An hour?" Velvet croaked.

"Don't worry, I saw Cerberus a few minutes ago, he's not far behind." Nora plaited the clump of hair she held. Velvet suspected she needed something to do with her fluttering hands. "Did the spell turn you into a gypsy?" asked Nora. Her fingers flew and a choppy braid materialized.

"Maybe at heart," Velvet said.

Nora let out a frustrated huff. "What kind of answer is that?" she moaned.

"There's a small tavern about a mile up the road," said Henry. "We will find food and proper bandages, if we are lucky, some medicines to bring down Velvet's fever." His eyes scanned their small, sad party, his mouth turning down in distaste at their predicament. "We need reinforcements."

Velvet meant to ask him what exactly he meant by *reinforcements,* but the cart jolted over a fallen log. An old, rusty nail in the back spoke of the left wheel snapped with a popping twang. The stripped hinges creaked loudly, and the misshapen wheel promptly cracked in half. Velvet dimly heard Henry shout a stream of unknown obscenities, then her world was a giant swirl of dark greens, pastel yellows, blue, and gold as the cart flipped in the air. Mentally sighing, Velvet lifted her arms to shield her face and relaxed her body to take yet another fall. It was over quickly, not bad—all things considered—based on their current luck it could have been much worse. The cart rolled once, then tumbled on its side and deposited all of them face-first in the mud before coming to rest in a lopsided pose. The three remaining wheels were spinning uselessly, batting at a fresh surge of rain, spraying droplets in all directions like broken windmills.

Nora growled in frustrated rage, rolled to her side, and slammed her hands on the ground. Her complexion flared until it matched the color of her hair as she pounded her small fists in the mud. Velvet turned over and felt a clump of mud smoosh against her scalp. She looked up at the canopy of trees, watched a flock of migrating birds flutter through the gaps in the high branches, and quietly shivered, internally missing and wishing for her wings.

Henry struggled to his knees, picking up his stream of curses which had been abruptly cut off by the violent tumble. He brushed a few pine needles off the lapels of his coat and pulled a leaf out of his hair. Katie sat up and used both hands to scoop mud off her face. She gave her once-pristine uniform a forlorn glare.

Devon lay on his stomach, a few feet from the cart, half his face submerged in a dark puddle. Without lifting his head he kicked his legs in what Velvet thought was a strange display of childish denial. It took her a moment to realize he was trying to kick the cart and thus inform it of his wrath. After a few more kicks that went nowhere, his booted toe finally made contact in a muted thump that ended in a hollow metal *twang*. Devon cried out in agony as his leather-clad toes struck the uneven metal hinge locking the cart's splintered planks together. Bubbles rose to the surface of the puddle and Devon punched the ground.

Torn between humor and distress, Velvet crossed her arms over her chest and let her tired eyes fall closed. "What now?" she whispered, asking the sky, speaking to the universe.

"Now we walk," Henry told them. A flicker of confusion and

pity crossed his face when he looked at Devon. "Well, those of us who can. Devon, take one of the horses and lead Nora and Katie to the Blind Pig. I will take Velvet and ride ahead."

"The Blind Pig?" cried Nora. Her small nose wrinkled in distaste. Mud dripped from the crown of her fiery hair covering her face and neck. She used the back of her hands to wipe her lips then spat out a few pieces of gravel. "I have fallen more times in the past few hours than I have in my entire life!"

"Hardly," said Henry. "Don't forget my father's early morning jogs."

Nora threw up her hands. "How can I? When you insist on reminding me."

Henry stood up, and Velvet watched his stiff movements as he removed his coat. Mud smeared the red fibers and the gold embroidery looked burnt, touched by storm light. Henry walked to Velvet and tossed his coat over her shoulders, deftly buttoning the garment under her chin.

"Thank you," Velvet breathed. "But the cold is in my bones, I don't think the coat will help much, so you can keep it." She tore her eyes away from him and looked up at the furious sky.

"I'll strip you of it if I have need," said Henry, affecting a Scottish brogue. To Velvet, it seemed he had fallen out of some ancient manuscript, a story of a dark and powerful warrior prince. He illuminated her vision, his features blocking out the rest of their stormy, haunted world. And what was "Scottish" anyway— *yes,* she thought—she was definitely delirious.

"Why aren't you the King?" she blurted before there was time to think better of it.

Henry smiled. "Do you always say the first thing that pops in your head?"

Velvet bit her lower lip. "It appears so, yes. Just one of the many things in my personality which I will investigate when I stop running." Now she did roll her eyes. "If I ever stop running."

"You will," he promised.

"How do you know? I've been running since I could walk."

"Nothing in life stays the same forever," Henry told her. "And I am not the King because my mother married the wrong man. Alas, the poor chit had no choice," he added with some bitterness. "Her own father marched her down the aisle and handed her off to a monster four times her age. She was fifteen when she had me, only seventeen when she gave birth to Charles." He stood up and helped her to her feet.

When she was standing on her own, he let go of her hand and walked to one of the horses. A tall boy wearing a moon-grey speckled coat, glossy beneath a shaggy, dark mane. Henry stroked the tendons standing out in the horse's slender neck and went about checking the hooves for rocks or debris that could catch between the arched metal shoe, potentially causing real damage. He removed the bit, and the horse brayed happily using his cold nose to nudge Henry's face. Velvet watched the ease in which Henry performed these ministrations. The few moments which passed between man and horse told her more about the man than anything else could.

Velvet felt a dazed smile almost reach her yawning mouth and huddled deeper in his coat; his scent was all over it. She would never, could never forget his smell, whiskey and man, leather and wind. The silly sliver of a smile stayed on her lips while Henry locked a strong hand in the coarse wild mane and vaulted on the horse's bareback. The beast snorted, chafing slightly under the new, unaccustomed weight. Henry made a small clicking noise in his mouth and leaned in to stroke the horse's nose, crooning a lyrical phrase in the same beautiful language he often slipped into when unaware. Now that his enchanting words were not being used to temporarily relieve her of sanity, Velvet recognized the language as Gaelic. Her grandmother had taught her many languages over the years, and Velvet was glad to realize she had some memory after all.

"*Ann, ann,*" crooned Henry. The horse stomped his hooves as if he meant to demonstrate his willpower against the spell Henry weaved through soft touch and gentle words. She pitied the beast, having herself fallen victim to the same intoxicating enchantment.

"*Balach math,*" he mumbled. She understood the words "good boy" before Henry's accent smoothed out to proper English. "That's right, you're safe, ya mangy runt. Do you have a name, sir?" he asked the horse in a polite yet respectful tone.

The horse brayed a response, stomping his feet and tossing his head.

"Ah!" said Henry, continuing the same small series of strokes up and down the horse's nose. "Peter, you say? Well, that's a fine name, lad." Henry patted Peter's drenched nose and the animal submitted. To show he was doing so of his own free will, he walked in a little circle, lifting his knees and snorting. Velvet saw that a few more pats and praises from Henry had Peter preening like a prized stallion by the time they returned to her. Henry held out his free hand, and Velvet took it without hesitation. He lifted her onto Peter's back and gathered her close. Signing, she settled easily into the crook of his arm. His linen shirt was wet and clung to him like skin.

"Where is your cloak?" she asked, comfortably aware that she snuggled in his coat. "I'm sure you had one."

"I believe it is currently a pile of ashes on the much-abused floor of Nora's drawing room," said Henry in mock sorrow, then crossed himself. "May it rest in peace."

"Velvet?" called Nora.

Velvet turned her head too fast, a jolt of pain blasted up her neck, and red spots burst in her vision. "*Merde,*" she muttered, rubbing the aching spot.

Nora stood up, shook out the crumpled folds of her skirt, then stomped her foot and threw Henry a withering glare, wagging her finger at him. "If anything happens to her, I'll kill you."

Henry touched his hand to the imaginary rim of his missing hat (resting in peace no doubt beside the cloak) and he winked at Nora. "You may put your trust in me, my lady." Henry's vow made Nora's blistering look intensify. Her lips, trembling and purple from cold, cut a straight line across her slender face. She let out a *humph* and put her palms on her hips.

Devon, who had collected his wayward limbs, was bent forward at the waist rustling both hands through his hair; a shower of leaves, a few pine needles, and a piece of a cone fell loose. He gave the expelled pile of forest debris a pained expression of disdain, then craned his head from side to side, put a hand to the top of his skull and tried to touch his forehead to his shoulder. The joint in his neck released its tension in an audible pop. "My soul for a bath," he muttered, slogging off to unhitch the remaining horse. Velvet returned her eyes to Nora. Dark bags stood out under her wide gaze, shocking against skin gone translucent in the shifting darkness.

Henry readjusted his seat on Peter's slick back and increased his choke hold on the reins. "I will expect you at the inn shortly. This forest can be perilous after dark."

"After dark?" asked Nora, sparing a single glance at the day turned night. "What time is it now?"

Henry looked at the sunless sky and shook his head. "Impossible to say for sure. An hour or two after noon would be my best guess."

It *was* impossible to say. Black clouds bubbled over the surface of the sky; they pulsed and writhed from persistent claps of thunder as if each swirling mass held its own heartbeat. The only light that dared to touch the blustery day came from the brief flashes of lightning occasionally cutting through the stormy murk.

"It is all rather biblical, isn't it?" said Nora. She rubbed a hand over her face, letting out a long, tired sigh. "Fine. Go. We'll be right behind you. Won't we, Devon?"

Devon grunted in agreement and helped Katie to her feet. "You ladies mount up," he said. "I will bravely walk before you and personally lead you to safety."

Nora rolled her eyes at Devon, but Velvet was sincere when she said, "Thank you, Lord Eden." Her voice barely crested the delicate boundaries of a whisper. Absently, her eyes traveled over each of them, and she felt that same sense of wonder that any of them would do any of this for her.

Devon bowed, a spark of his indomitable buoyancy returned. "You are very welcome, my lady. I think by now it is imperative that you call me Devon."

"Alright," Velvet whispered. "Devon it is." She blew them a kiss. Nora gave it back with an airy flare. Katie, clasping Devon's arm and propping her slight weight against him, lifted her free, mud-soaked hand in a small wave.

A thumping crash prevented any other pleasantries. Cerberus

blasted through Velvet's line of sight and came to a stumbling halt in front of her. Peter, caring nothing for the shaggy quality of Cerberus, nor his big, wagging tail that whipped at the rain and threw it in all directions, backed up skittishly. Cerberus ignored Peter's fear, his own excitement far too great. He squared his bulky shoulders, bent his head, and opened his huge, shaggy mouth to lay his treasure in the puddle bracketing Peter's restless feet. It was a small silver chain twinning around itself like a snake. It boasted a teardrop emerald pendant, blissfully floating atop the chunky puddle. The large jewel winked, flashing curiously at Velvet from the glittering center of the chains.

Katie rushed to pick up the necklace. She barely spared it a glance, only handed it to Velvet nodding politely. Velvet's hand folded around the gem. Her eyes fell closed. She drew in a deep, bracing breath.

"Velvet, what is it? What's wrong?" Henry's voice brushed the shell of her ear, deep and wary. His eyes dropped to her hand. "That really is quite the dog you have there? Is that yours?"

Velvet nodded wildly. Her hair flew in her eyes, whipped in her open mouth. It did not matter, in stunned wonder she brought the pendant to her racing heart. "He's alive," she whispered. "Sweet saints! Louis's alive." She blinked rapidly, unable to believe her eyes. The dusky light seared her retinas making them water profusely. Velvet wiped the moisture away, wishing she could do the same for the torrent of emotions surging through her. Relief, exhaustion, fear, and security. Velvet felt her shoulders slump; humans truly were the strangest of creatures.

"Go to him, Cerberus," she said weakly. Cerberus pawed the ground and whined in denial.

"Yes. Go, boy. Take care of him. I'll find you. Keep him safe. Go."

Henry clicked his tongue against the roof of his mouth and pressed his heels to either side of Peter's stomach. Peter obeyed the set of unspoken commands and shot off in a surprisingly competent gallop. Henry clutched Velvet closer to his chest, running his hands up and down her arms trying to quell her shivering. Velvet's tremors stood fast against the onslaught of warmth, her teeth stubbornly chattering in a timed series of sharp snaps.

They rode for a time in this jarring fashion until Henry tilted his face down to hers. Velvet lost track of her breath. "May I ask about this great treasure that brought you proof of life?"

"Y…yes. I mean…of course you can ask." She cleared her throat violently. "Seconds before the soldiers grabbed me I put this chain around Louis's neck. It belonged to our grandmother. Velvet raised her clenched fist to her lips and kissed the pendant. "If Louis gave it to Cerberus, it means he is alive and safe. He wouldn't give up the emerald unless he knew I would need it more than him. It's what I would want, what I would have made him do—he's a good boy." Velvet's words drifted out unchecked, she hardly cared. The sorrow was still there huddled into itself, whimpering somewhere in the back of her mind. It was deep and piercing, but the glowing knowledge of Louis's life backlit all her thoughts in shades of rosy-gold and overshadowed the darkness.

"Good enough for me," said Henry. His black lashes, lowered in defense against the storm, made sooty lines on his high cheekbones, dramatically enhancing the deep slant of his eyes. A small line formed between his brows and it deepened when he spoke. "First we will take care of you, then we will find him. I promise."

"I believe you." Velvet breathed and wondered if it was the delirium bolstering her hope. Her shivers slowed to gentle quakes that gave her brief moments of reprieve. "Tell me more about your family," she said, dreamily lost in the distracted moment.

"I would rather not," he grunted. "It is a deeply unpleasant subject."

"Your mother? Was she unpleasant?"

Henry's full lips softened around the edges. He drew in a breath and released it in a visible cloud. "No. She was an angel."

"Was she fair?" Velvet asked. For some reason she pictured a golden-haired lady in a field of flowers. She voiced her thoughts and Henry smiled down at her.

"No," he said gently. "Dark-haired, green-eyed, like me. She was slender and tall and always wore a gentle, caring smile—the same for lord or peasant. I remember her soft hands, the sound of her voice when she sang to me at night."

Sparks of lightning raced across the sky and split the heavy clouds above their heads. The affronted clouds belched out giant burps of thunder that rocked the soaking ground.

"What else do you remember?" Velvet asked, her voice slightly muffled by his shirt.

"Everything," he said frowning. "I have an unhappy curse of remembering everything. Many times I have drunk to forget."

"Did you?" Velvet asked. "Forget, I mean."

"No," he said distinctly. "I did not."

"I don't remember my mother at all," Velvet said, trying like she always did to recall Marie Antoinette's face. Nothing greeted her mental search, save shadows and billowing mists. Velvet took a shallow breath. Talking about it was more difficult than she would have thought—then again, what in this life was not difficult? "The day before she died, my grandmother showed me a miniature portrait of my mother. She looked so sad, I don't believe the artist did her justice. They say she was a great beauty, all I could see was a girl who experienced a tragic childhood and would later die an unjust death."

Henry nodded his head. "She was…a great beauty…I mean, you look just like her. I saw her the day she died, so innocent and strong. I watched her climb the scaffold." His face grew pale from recalled images.

Velvet's eyes flew wide, for a moment she forgot the fever attacking her head and bones. "Tell me," she said. "Please, I want to know. It's morbid, I understand—I've imagined it so often. I want—" Velvet shook her head. "*Need* to know how it really happened."

Henry dashed a hand through his hair showering her in a blanket of freezing droplets. Velvet said nothing but shivered in silence…waiting.

"It stormed the day before her execution," Henry finally said, his low voice tentative, as if unwilling to go on. Velvet made a noise of encouragement in her throat and tugged the short collar of his white shirt.

"The sun shone on her golden hair when she walked through the crowd," continued Henry, eyeing her in concern. Velvet kept the small smile on her face, though her hands balled into fists. "No one threw anything or yelled an awful obscenity; in fact, as she walked up the one-way stairs of the guillotine, not a single person said a word. Nothing shifted in the air save a few tendrils of floating mist, the entire world seemed stunted in silence. I was very young, but I imagined I could hear her brave, beating heart."

Henry stopped talking and closed his eyes. Velvet knew he was seeing it all again in that strange, distorted clarity, which often chaperoned childhood memories of tragedy. "Your mother climbed the rickety scaffold without incident, and when she reached the dais of death, she stopped to stare at the way the sun sparkled against the blade waiting to kill her. Some kind soul had cleaned it for her execution, a courtesy given to a queen. In the crowd an old voice called her name, and she stumbled slightly, then accidently stepped on the foot of the executioner. '*Pardon, monsieur, Je ne l'ai pas fait exprès,*' were the last words the French queen ever spoke. She apologized to the executioner—sorry she caused his slight pain —when it was him who would pull the lever and end her life. Then she knelt, folded her hands in prayer, lay her neck down at the base of the *lunette,* and waited for the blade to fall. They held up her head to the crowd when it was done." Henry, jaw clenched, swallowed hard, and Velvet saw him cringe. "She was smiling," he said. "I will never forget that smile."

Scalding water—Velvet could not attribute to the boisterous rain—trickled down her cheeks, and swollen droplets dripped from her trembling lips tracing silver trails over her chin. "Why do people destroy beauty?" Velvet asked, knowing as she said the words there was no acceptable answer. "Why do they hate it? Why? Why hate when there is so much to love?"

Henry wiped water from his nose. "Because they can't find beauty or love in themselves, so they envy it in others." He shrugged and liquid coasted down his shoulder like a muddy waterfall. "Envy breeds hate."

"Hate," Velvet whispered. "Such a strange emotion."

"Yes, one I am far too familiar with," said Henry. He readjusted the reins, and a frustrated flick of his free hand pushed his wet hair out of his eyes. "If Lord Norton hadn't done the world a favor and put a bullet in my father's black heart, I would have obliged it myself."

Velvet looked up at his profile, her eyes tearing from the fever, the windy rain…his words. "I'm so sorry you lost your mother, too. I think we will always miss the ones we have lost."

Henry nodded. "Occasionally, I visit her grave," he said. A clap of thunder muffled his thick voice. "My father laid her to rest in our family's crypt. It's a quiet place, always covered in some mist or fog. My mother used to tell me fog was the cloak of the great goddess who stood guard over the ancient ground. She was a fanciful, Scottish lass, my mother was. Many accused her of witchcraft in her short lifetime and much trouble came of it. Her father was the late Lord Brandon, Duke of Hamilton, Laird of the Douglas clan. My mother grew up wild, her head ever stuffed with magic stories, recipes, and tales. She often said her great grandmother was a powerful seer, swore strange talents ran in the blood of Douglas women. Sometimes, when I stand before her headstone, I imagine I hear her voice in the wind; it coasts like a galloping stallion across the empty moors and calls my name."

"Perhaps you do…it does," Velvet said.

He shrugged again, glancing down at her from the corner of his eye. "Perhaps."

"And your sister? How old was she?"

"When she died?"

Velvet nodded, picturing a pretty, female version of Henry, high cheekbones and slanting eyes. She would have bouncing black curls—exotic as an Egyptian princess.

"We celebrated her fourth birthday ten days before she died. I was terribly bitter at first, then I realized her death was probably a blessing since my father would have most likely turned his attention on her. He raped and beat my mother rather frequently." Henry inhaled, and Velvet felt his shoulders shake and knew the next words were difficult for him. "Her heart was that of a warrior, her body rather frail and weak. She tired easily, the brutal way he used her would have broken anyone. She would not have lasted long even if the scarlet fever had never come." Velvet gently touched his arm. Henry shuddered. "I used to sit outside her door until she stopped screaming. After, I would hide in my room, wait for my father to leave her. I would go back and do my best to tend to her wounds. I was only a child, I hadn't the slightest notion of how to save her. Then, one cold winter she died alongside my sister, leaving Father with only my humble self to torment, and Nora of course, though she well knew how to stay out of his way. He beat me often until I grew too old to take the beatings. Ten years later an angry husband, Lord Norton, Duke of Canterbury, killed the bastard in a duel. I became a Duke."

"How old were you?" Velvet asked, empathy infused her voice. The thought of this big, strong warrior, young and afraid, crying in front of his mother's door and listening to her screams, hurt in indefinable ways.

"Eight and ten," he said, and bitterness laced his words. "A young man on the brink of life, ready to embrace freedom, the modern age." He smiled, a wry, self-deprecating smile that did not touch his eyes. The shadows of the overhanging branches danced across his face, darkening his golden skin. His eyes drew together and the gravity in his gaze added a profound depth to the tenor of his voice. "I did not take well to responsibility, initially, that is." Henry laughed. Velvet heard no humor in the discordant tones. "I quickly learned—the hard way I might add—that I am a quick learner."

"So am I," Velvet muttered.

They were both silent for a moment, lost together, visiting the specters of their past. Velvet understood he had just given her a precious part of himself, and she wondered why he had done it— was it a calculated move to make her trust him? Was it pity? If the latter, she was far too tired to ask or really care; it had felt nice. Time passed, clocked only by the steady clip of Peter's hooves.

"I met you once, you know?" he said suddenly, startling her from near sleep.

"You did?" She gasped.

"Yes, you fell, and I helped you to stand—then you kissed my cheek."

Velvet felt herself blush. "I cannot imagine I did such a thing!" she said, trying desperately to remember such a monumental occurrence.

"I swear to you, my lady, you did…and it was a lovely kiss." He winked at her and she averted her eyes.

"Well," she said when she could, "thank you, sir…thank you for your kindness."

Under her hand she felt his heart shudder. "Ah, Velvet…" He breathed, a raspy quality to his voice. "That's exactly what you said to me all those years ago."

They rode on and she felt the beats of his heart steady, her stiff shoulders relaxed as she drifted between hazy veils of awareness. Through slitted eyelids she could see the dark shapes of the towering pines receding in the distance. In front of them the horizon opened in a panorama of rolling hills patched by fragrant expanses of heather-drenched fields. Ebony shades tinted by streaks of purple and scarlet painted the ground.

Henry's gaze stayed focused on the well-washed path where hints of the eerie storm light reflected in the puddles. Not daring to look at him again, Velvet felt intensely aware of his every movement. Each breath he took resonated with her own, and of course she could not be sure, not really…but it seemed that somewhere in the past hour her heartbeats had synced with his.

7

DON'T WORRY, DARLING, IT'S JUST A DREAM

$\mathcal{V}$elvet knew it was a dream. She knew it because she was flying. It had only been a few days since last she spread her wings and soared over some clear blue lake, only a few days since her grandmother sat beneath a blood-red moon, built a fire, and took a soft, snowy owl in her hands. The night was clear, the sky untouched by clouds. Velvet looked at the seam between earth and sky to the place holding the last of the sun's light and first tendrils of encroaching shadow—a break in the fabric of the world where she knew the pagan gods hovered. They listened to her grandmother's chanting prayers and waited to see what she would offer as currency for her request. Velvet remembered the way the spell had crackled, and Seam-Ripper—the knife her grandmother had used to slice her own skin. The red blood and violet smoke that hissed as it ran over her feathers. Then came the changing, the pain when her feathers popped out, her small bones stretched, broke, elongated. Stretched, and stretched again.

Velvet tried to shy away from that particular memory, but it was a dream and she had no control if it as it entered the realm of nightmares. In the dream Velvet swooped down toward the glassy surface of the water; she saw her big black eyes, round as a couple of fat cherries, blink rapidly over her tiny, pointed nose. On the edge of the glimmering lake a dozen caravans dozed in the ocher light. They formed a harmonious semicircle, their colorful roofs, wheels, and walls illuminated by the late afternoon sun. The shadows cast by the low-hanging tents of the fortune-tellers and spell weavers were alive with woke spirits. Horses grazed near the water, happily lapping it up. She watched Louis play in the frothy ripples, casting a golden glow wherever he went.

Suddenly, the dream moved, stretched, and changed. She was a slip of a human girl, standing on unsteady feet. She wore a new red dress, its velvet hem tossed by a light breeze. A cannon boomed, and a giant burst of flame engulfed a bright yellow caravan with purple wheels. The flames ran over the wheels and up the door, eating at the jeweled tassels hanging in front of it, melting the happy yellow paint. Velvet looked up at the tearing sky and screamed her brother's name as men in red coats rushed the gypsy camp—more hordes of killer locusts. Gunshots went off followed by a round of explosions that rocked and broke her world.

Heart pounding and the last echoes of a scream on her lips, Velvet woke up. She opened her eyes, panting heavily, the starched sheet beneath her hands crumpled under her punishing grip. She felt a waft of air brush her heated skin, followed by a cool hand falling on her forehead, the soothing touch of an angel.

"Hush," murmured Nora, and she made small, sympathetic sounds. Velvet looked at where Nora's face should be and blinked her eyes in disorientation. Three fiery-red heads and six pairs of eyes drenched in concern floated above her.

"Please…water," Velvet croaked. Was she still burning? Where was the fire? She looked at Nora's multiplied, pinched features looming over her and struggled to compare memory with reality. Velvet tried to clear the burning dryness from her throat by coughing, then cringed at the unexpected pain. "Where am I? Where is my grandmother?" The words came out before her feverish mind could stop them. She tossed her head then clapped her hand over her mouth. There was a roaring furnace in her chest…perhaps she died, and this was hell.

She felt tears of pure misery trace scalding trails down her flushed cheeks. Tense muscles in her legs and arms jerked, spasming from tiny cramps that seemed to target her most sensitive nerves. She had never, in all her life, imagined such uncomfortable pain existed.

Nora, who was already pale, went a few shades whiter. "Don't thrash, Velvet, or it will force me to tie you to the bed again." Nora's three floating heads shook in tandem; her lips pulled in a tight, pained line. "Where a small girl like you got such strength is beyond me. It took two redcoats to hold you down while I tied the knots...still, you managed to strike me...twice."

"Sorry," Velvet groaned.

Nora's skirts rustled, her lips softened, but the trouble stayed present in her eyes. "Think nothing of it, dear, you've had a touch of delirium—been quite out of your mind for days."

Velvet swallowed a dry lump of nothing. Nora helped Velvet lift her head and pressed a cup to her lips. There was a high-pitched twang when her front tooth struck the metal rim. Nora muttered something, then repositioned herself, using both hands to steady the cup. Sweet, cool water touched her tongue and Velvet gulped at it in unabashed greed. The crisp, wonderful liquid cleansed her dry mouth, blissfully soothing the parched contours of her tongue.

"How long?" Velvet rasped when Nora took the cup away.

"Three days now."

Nora placed the cup on a small bedside table where sat a plump gas lamp. Velvet saw a golden flame spinning in the confines of its sheltering glass tube. Nora touched a curved knob at the base of the lamp; instantly the flame grew causing a luminous saffron light to spread through the room. The light touched Nora's face adding peachy highlights to her pointed chin and shadowing her pursed lips. More sparkling lights danced through her hair, which, Velvet noticed, was clean and redone. Half of the glimmering mass was twisted atop her head in a neat bun, and a small diamond pin held it in place. A charm dangled from the tip of the pin. Velvet saw it was a ruby, carefully cut into the shape of a heart, deftly pierced by a tiny silver arrow. The rest of her hair tumbled over her bare shoulders in sets of perfect ringlets that smelled like rosewater and strawberries.

"Believe it or not," said Nora, gently touching Velvet's clammy cheek, "your fever has actually gone down. Last night I thought your skin would set the bed alight." Nora turned back to the table and reached behind the gas lamp. There was a splash of water, then she pressed a cool, wet cloth to Velvet's head. Velvet shivered as a chill wracked her bones. Nora's fingers twitched slightly, her words continuing to tumble out with irrepressible speed. "Katie went to the nearby village yesterday, she found an apothecary, located more yarrow and white willow crushed in chamomile, we mixed them in tea tree and garlic oil. Nasty-smelling stuff! Katie slathered it all over your wounds. I also have a tea I swore to make you drink. Katie made me promise to use force if you refused."

"Why would I refuse?" Velvet asked, too disoriented to care much about the answer.

"Because," said Nora primly, "it tastes like Satan's toilet water." The door to their small room opened noiselessly and a thin shaft of light spilled in, hallowing Katie in a smoky-grey glow.

Katie moved to stand beside Nora. "The fever is still burning," said Katie, touching Velvet's cheek. "It's lost a good portion of that deadly heat, though." Katie made a clicking sound with her tongue, brushing Velvet's hair, her touch feathery and pleasant. "Awake too, that's good. You had us properly scared, my lady, you've spent the last three nights in purgatory, make no mistake." Katie stopped talking on a tired sigh and picking up her skirts she made her way to the other side of the room.

A stout wooden tabletop squatted on stubby legs next to an overstuffed, yet comfortable-looking chair. A clean gown of peach silk lay draped over the armrests, a pair of scuffed, but freshly polished boots sat by its clawed feet. Katie lifted a small, round pot and a teacup from the cluttered contents of the tabletop. A bundle of herbs plummeted to the ground. Katie's free hand flashed out to catch a falling bottle, saving it from certain destruction at the last second. She set it carefully on the table and retraced her steps, then sat near Velvet's feet at the edge of the bed.

Velvet saw that Katie had also bathed and changed. Her hair wrapped her crown in a thick braid. Newly washed, it shone like a polished acorn under the shifting lamp light. A cap of white lace topped off the hairdo with a sensible flourish. More lace framed the collar of her high-necked black dress, clean and freshly pressed. A spotless cream apron belted her waist. Her skin was slightly pink, and her features held a drawn determination that belied her slender, youthful frame.

"Are we...?" Velvet cleared her voice and tried again. "Are we at the tavern? The Blind Boar?"

"Pig," corrected Nora. "The Blind Pig." Velvet made a face, and Nora let out a long put-upon sigh. "Yes, it is the worst name in all of Christendom. But it's clean and the beds are quite comfortable. Katie and I are staying in the next room, it has a pretty view of the surrounding properties. If you look out that window there"—she pointed to the one near the washstand —"you can see bits of the village from here. Katie and I have been taking turns watching over you, sleeping in shifts, that sort of thing. This room has the only *salle d'eau* with running water." Her pointing finger shifted to a curtained alcove on the left side of Velvet's bed. "So we've been in and out of here often. Henry said he must speak to the King. The blasted man promised he would return before nightfall; that was three days ago. He took Devon and left us here with a contingent of redcoats who—I am told—have sworn to protect us with their lives." Nora tossed her hand in the air as if all that was of no consequence. "They are a polite group of gentlemen—for the most part—two of them run in my social circle, Lord Byron and Sir Jeffers."

Velvet listened to Nora, a million questions running through her boiling mind. She asked none, there was one thing far more important than all the rest. "Please," she wheezed, sitting up as far as the pain in her side would allow, and she took Nora's hand, effectively cutting off her incessant flow of words. "Can I have a bath?" The utterance of this short sentence was all it took to make Velvet's strength give out, and she flopped bonelessly back on the pillows. "I'm filthy," she moaned. "Disgustingly so."

"Humm, what do you think, Katie?" asked Nora, pulling a face and winking at Velvet. "She could use one."

Katie did not smile at Nora's jib; her wide doe eyes watched Velvet. "I think it would be alright. The priest at our parish says it is evil to bathe a wound—I do not believe them—on the premise it makes no sense, of course. How can water let the Devil in when air cannot?"

"Is that a yes?" Velvet croaked.

"Very well. I will speak to Miss Jenny," said Katie. Standing up with a hand pressed to her lower back, she did not bother to hide her exhausted groan. "I'll have water brought up and a fresh fire lit, after which I leave you in the capable hands of Lady Nora. There is a pot of tea here. I want to see every drop drunk when I wake up."

"Yes, ma'am," Velvet said obediently. There was no response from the departing Katie. The door swung firmly shut.

"She's so tired," Velvet said, feeling misery and nerves band together to make a knot in her gut. "I hope she isn't... I mean, I hope I haven't been too much of an inconvenience." She stared at the wooden slats, crisscrossing the ceiling in harmonious lines, and felt sizzling tears gather in the corners of her eyes. Who knew humans cried so much?

"You are not an inconvenience," said Nora firmly. She placed a sharp fingernail beneath Velvet's chin and turned her head to meet her eyes. "If the roles in our little play reversed, would you have just left me in the street to die? Or after the carriage accident? Maybe abandon me right after my house blew up?"

Velvet shook her head then felt a tear slip free of the cluster bordering her lower lashes and roll down her cheek. Sniffing painfully, she wiped it away. "No. Of course not."

"Well, then," said Nora in a *that's enough of that* tone. "We will hear no more of it...don't worry about Katie, she is tired, but hell"—Nora sat back, stifling a yawn—"we all are. She's strong though, stronger than I, she always has been. We grew up together on Newcastle land—did you know that? No, of course you didn't. She was the only other girl besides myself, after Henry's mother and sister died. She was the miller's daughter. He's dead too, heart attack, very sudden." Nora rearranged the pillows bracing Velvet's neck and fussed with the hair clinging to her sweaty cheeks. "He was kind to me when I first arrived on Newcastle estate, him and Katie both. A grand misfortune blessed Katie with five older brothers who constantly tormented her. I met Katie about a day after my mother discarded me. I was playing in the pond near the stables, under the shade of a big Elm. I remember my shift, soaked to the knees, transparent as water.

"Katie came shrieking out of the stables; she was so tiny, almost completely obscured by her hair. She had a snotty nose and a ripped dress. Apparently, her eldest brother had made it the mission of his day to set her dress on fire. That girl has always been lithe as a squirrel. She scrambled up the Elm and crawled out onto the furthest branch before I had time to blink. I looked up, and there she was. Her little stick figure clinging to the leafy branch and blowing in the wind. She dangled precariously for a few tense moments above the rather deep pond. Then, her younger brother, desperate to join the ruckus fun, shot an arrow at her.

"She dodged it successfully but lost her hold in the process and plummeted headlong into the pond. I shooed the boys away. They were terribly afraid of me, a princess *and* a cursed bastard. I dove in after her. It was freezing. She didn't know how to swim; she was very brave, holding her breath, kicking her feet like a drunk mermaid. The chit thinks I saved her life, hung onto my shadow ever since." Nora sighed. "Perhaps I did, but she saved mine too. I was alone in the world before Katie and Henry took pity on me. Eventually, Henry's father made Katie my lady's maid, seeing she had already assumed all the duties. I honestly don't know what my life would be without her." Nora started to yawn again but broke off when she saw Velvet's struggling movement.

"Oh, here," she said and gasped. "Let me help you sit. Just go slow, okay, I don't want to open your wounds. I had a devil of a time sewing you up."

"You sewed me up?" Velvet asked, startled by the notion.

"Yes," said Nora proudly. "It appears I am made of sturdy stuff."

"I owe *you* my life so many times over," Velvet said.

"True." Nora smiled. "It's nothing. I think you would do the same for anyone. Besides, it's all quite exciting. I never thought I would apply a needle to a task larger than stitching frillery. I've always demonstrated talent with a needle and thread. One of my forced accomplishments, don't you know? I also speak four languages, paint beautifully of course—watercolors only—

anything else is too scandalous for a lady, and I play piano like the masters..."

"You put me in a nightgown?" Velvet said, cutting off Nora's tirade. She stared down at the starched white material, already stained bloody around her wounds.

"I did. Miss Jenny's girls had a few gowns going spare; that nightgown belongs to one of the maids downstairs." Nora looked at the garment like it had caused her a great offense. "A kind girl had the courtesy to wash it first...alas, that was three days ago." Nora wrinkled her nose. "Here, drink this while we wait for the bath." Nora handed her a cup of tea. Velvet took it, and her nose also twitched at the vile odor it released.

Nora grimaced. "I warned you," she said solemnly.

Finger hooked around the curved handle, Velvet raised the delicate cup in salute. She drank it in one horrendous gulp, gagging helplessly when it slid down her throat like a glob of old snot. Nora took the cup from her and helped her settle back against the pillows.

Velvet must have dozed because the next time she opened her eyes a cozy fire roared in the hearth. In front of the fire sat a wooden hip tub, resting its bulk on four legs carved to resemble dragon feet. Thick swirls of steam rose up from the surface of the tub and bubbled over the uneven, slatted sides. A lush cut of fur was spread beneath the bath, and on it lay a bar of sweet-smelling soap atop a pile of fluffed towels.

"Can you stand?" asked Nora.

Velvet nodded, determined to try. She would crawl over broken glass to get to that bath. *Why were humans so filthy?* She swung her feet over the side of the bed; her limbs trembled but held her. Nora took her elbow as if they meant to take a morning stroll in the park. Slowly, they made their way to the steaming water. Velvet undid the small tie at her neck and let the ruined nightgown fall to her feet. Nora held her hand for support and Velvet stepped in the scalding, wonderful water. Beyond bliss she sunk down into its soothing depths.

"Sweet saints." Velvet ducked her head beneath the sparkling, firelit surface; she came up seconds later gasping, the sheer wonder of the water muted the pain of her wounds. "Nothing has ever felt so good!" Velvet scrubbed her hands over her scalp, and her locks of golden hair rippled.

Nora smiled and handed Velvet the soap. "I think I said the exact same thing three days ago. I stayed in for over an hour, just scrubbing. Here, lean your head back, I'll help you with your hair. You know," she babbled, "you really are the most beautiful girl I have ever seen in my life. You are perfect actually. Strange, but I bet something like that doesn't matter to you at all, does it?"

"I only saw my face for the first time three days ago, and to be honest I didn't much care for it—very soft. I don't think it matches me. I don't remember how it looked when I lived in Paris. I don't really remember much."

Nora smiled and said nothing more on the topic of beauty. "Did you always know you were a princess?" she asked instead.

Velvet took a few seconds to answer. "No," she finally said, deciding to tell the truth. "My grandmother told me the day she turned me back into one." Velvet shrugged and water rolled off her shoulders in sparkling, pearlescent strands. "I suppose when I was a little girl I might have known it. I was born in a palace, after all, but the spell my grandmother cast on me wiped away most of my childhood memories. It left me nothing but storied shades hiding in questionable shadows."

Nora paused in the process of sudsing up her hands and gave Velvet a piercing look. "What did she change you into?" she asked bluntly. "You can tell me the truth, even if it's crazy. I promise to believe you. Was it like my fairy tales?"

Velvet held Nora's gaze studying the way blushed freckles swirled over her cheeks and stood out on her pale skin turned pink by the fire's heat. Velvet knew honesty was all she had; who even knew if she could make up the right lie? Besides, were her truths really *that* unbelievable? Surely, stranger things had happened.

"Yes," she said when she could think of no real reason not to. "It was exactly like your fairy tales—my grandmother used Gypsy magic to transform me into an owl." Velvet braced herself; letting out a nervous breath in a puff that made ripples dance over the surface water.

Nora's mouth dropped open.

"And she changed my brother into a…" Velvet swallowed a tear-spiked lump in her throat as visions of Louis exploded in front of her closed eyes. "She changed him…"

"Into a golden stag," breathed Nora, every ounce of flushed color drained from her face. She sat down rather abruptly and braced her hands on her knees. "Oh my God, Velvet!"

"I know," Velvet could not help her fearful flinch; she did not even wonder how Nora had guessed such a thing. *At least she wasn't screaming or laughing*, Velvet thought. Out loud she said, "I told you it was unbelievable."

"No," said Nora. "It's not that. I mean, it is of course completely crazy. There would be no way I could ever believe this, except…except…oh God! I've seen your brother!" Nora's blue eyes were now the only points of color in her face. "Twice, actually. Christ and bastards on a biscuit! I thought I was hallucinating!"

"What?" Velvet screamed and jumped up. A large slice of water sloshed on the ground. "Where? When? Why didn't you tell me?"

"Tell you?" Nora looked aghast. "I didn't tell you because you were bleeding, and I was too busy telling *myself* it wasn't real. I fainted the second time he showed up. Right outside of my house he was, all regal and glowing—naturally, I assumed I was losing my mind."

Velvet found herself at a loss for words so—it seemed—did her flummoxed friend. She kept quiet while Nora scrubbed her hair.

"Take a breath," said Nora. Velvet did not ask why, only obeyed, having already developed a healthy fear of Nora's erratic actions. True to form, Nora placed her hands on the top of Velvet's sudsy head and shoved her under the water. Velvet did not care about the dunking, she was grateful to hide under the cleansing liquid, refreshing as any lake she had ever swam in.

"I can't believe you actually saw him!" Velvet said when she emerged for air. "He's invisible to most people." She wiped her face. Fluffy suds chased down her cheeks and onto her lips.

Nora declined comment, only wrinkled her nose and sat back on the fur, crossing her legs beneath her, her fingers twining through a long curl dangling over her bare shoulder. She twirled it around her slender fingers, blinking solemnly. "Everyone thinks he's dead, you know? Louis, I mean."

"I know," Velvet said. "I remember the day my grandmother told us. We had just arrived in England and were staying with a band of gypsies near Dover. My brother was smaller, his antlers only little stubs I liked to make fun of."

"Were you an owl then?" asked Nora, not breaking eye contact.

"Yes," Velvet replied.

"And you remember things? As an owl I mean. Process thoughts, you know? Like a person."

Velvet smiled. "Much better than a person. Humans have a very limited view. They forget things very easily. Human sight is tainted by emotion, which can cloud their perspective."

"Well!" Nora sat back and pressed her fingers to her temples, touching her head gingerly as if afraid it might blow apart in her hands. "That is a rather deep thought, I shall investigate it later. Could you talk to your brother? The way I can talk to you?"

Velvet considered that, using the time to wring out her hair and twist it into a loose knot. "All animals can speak to each other, they just have to learn the language."

"This is quite incredible!" said Nora.

"Do you believe me?" Velvet asked.

Nora dragged herself to her feet using a wobbly stool for support. "I think I need a drink." Walking over to the fat table she lifted a decanter and poured herself a glass of crimson wine. Like she was receiving holy sacrament, Nora brought the cup to her lips and drank in reverence. She left the crystal rim resting against her lower lip while she swallowed, then she took another long gulp that closed her eyes.

"I have to believe you, don't I?" said Nora finally. "I mean, I saw him. Twice."

The irregular clomp of stomping feet sounded behind the closed door, fracturing Nora's reverie. Velvet slung her arms across her naked chest and lowered her body further under the water until only her chin brushed the delicate bubbles floating along the surface. Nora set the glass of wine on the table, straightened her shoulders, and folded her hands in front of her, clasping them together in prim perfection.

A loud series of knocks rapped against the door. Not a single muscle twitched in Nora's limbs or stubborn, ramrod spine.

"You may enter," called Nora in a voice Velvet assumed might be used to summon kings. The wooden door swung inward without preamble; it crashed against the little table shaking it unmercifully, a teacup broke free of the tabletop mess and shattered. A burly man sporting a neck thick enough to hold two heads stepped into the room. He wore the hated red coat, a pistol, and a sheathed sword. Velvet saw the lantern light play over the engraved silver buttons dotting the front of his red coat and had to gulp back a growl of rage.

The man removed his hat and when his eyes settled on Nora he bowed politely. "My lady," he muttered, miraculously holding his ungainly pose. Considering the paunch under his coat, Velvet wondered how he did not fall flat on his face.

Nora cleared her throat in haughty impatience and tilted her small chin higher, perfectly affecting the look Velvet had previously thought to cast on Henry. Nora held out her hand—Velvet saw a slight tremble in her noble bones—and the balancing man snatched it up. His jowls swung ponderously as he bent even further to place a smacking kiss on her wrist.

"What can I do for you, Lord Bryon?" said Nora in tones that could have chilled an ice cap. "We are bathing, sir."

Lord Bryon blushed to the roots of his starched, linen wig. Sweat popped on his mottled, pale brow and dripped down his fat nose, fast turning the color of a ripe tomato. His eyes—a flat silver color—were abnormally tiny, squished together like peas in a pod. His eyebrows, however, were in their proper place, and the overall effect gave him the look of a confused ferret.

Silently, Velvet lowered herself further beneath the water, wondering why the awful man did not just leave instead of loitering in their doorway, staring at Nora.

"I'm...I'm...so sorry," he finally stammered. "I mean, I do beg your pardon, my lady...ladies."

"It is difficult to give it, sir," returned Nora. She waved her hand sending impatient little strokes through the charged air. "What is so urgent you must burst in on two ladies in such a state of *déshabillé?*"

Lord Bryon coughed wetly and wiped his mouth on the back of his hand. His eyes flashed to Velvet, then rushed back to Nora. "Lord Melton asked me to inform you that we're sending out a small contingent of men in search of His Grace Newcastle."

"What? No!" cried Nora. Lord Bryon's statement snapped her carefully cultured composure. "Henry said you must stay here and guard us; what if someone comes?"

"You are perfectly safe, my lady," said Lord Bryon, casting another furtive glance over Nora's shoulder at the hidden creature in the bath. His height was such that Velvet wondered if he could see past Nora's head. She flowed further down in her soapy water, shuddering in horror, hugging her bare chest until her arms ached.

"We will station twelve dragoons here to guard you and your guests. Miss Jenny asked the rest of the patrons to leave."

Nora snorted. "What did that cost?"

Lord Bryon smiled ruefully, and the action squeezed his tiny eyes even closer together—now the confused ferret appeared mildly intoxicated. "Your safety is priceless, my dear."

One of Nora's feet tapped out a rhythmic pattern on the wooden floorboards. "Is there anything else? If not, then I must bid you good night; I fear you have found us indisposed." Lord Bryon was in the middle of stuttering out a reply when Nora slammed the door in his face.

"What an idiot!" said Nora rolling her eyes while simultaneously giving the door a sidelong glare. She looked pale, and fear made a fine tremble touch her fingers when she finished the wine in a single gulp. There was no conversation beyond the necessary as Velvet stepped from the tub and patted the water from her body.

"What a great...prized...idiot!" sputtered Nora. She refilled the glass and handed it to Velvet.

"I think he meant well," Velvet said. She took a sip of wine; her eyes went wide in shock. It slid down her throat and left a streak of fire in its wake. Velvet's next cough pushed a little of the wine out of her nose.

"Not Lord Bryon." Nora threw her hands in the air. "I wouldn't know enough to comment on the state of that one's intelligence—I was talking about Henry."

Velvet sat on the bed and tried the wine again. It burned worse than the first time; she held the glass up to the light regarding the bloody liquid and scowled. "So, everything tastes bad to humans, then?" she observed.

Nora removed a clean nightgown from a magic drawer somewhere and tossed it at Velvet. Velvet slid the fresh-smelling shift over her head. Silk settled on her naked body like a thousand butterfly wings, making gooseflesh trace her tingling spine. "Do you think he's alright?" Velvet whispered, speaking through the airy confines of the cloth.

"What?" Nora looked up. "Oh." She waved her hand and drank more wine. "The officers all have chambers, the rest are sleeping in the common room. I imagine they'll be comfortable."

"I meant Henry," Velvet said, yawning hugely. "Do you have a hairbrush by any chance?"

"Yes, here." Nora went to a cabinet near the curtained portion of the room. There were several unusual sounds as she rummaged through the mystery drawer. When she found the desired item, she walked to Velvet and made a swirling motion with her index finger. "Turn around, I'll brush it for you."

"Thank you," Velvet whispered, feeling incredibly shy, not able to remember the last time someone had performed such a service for her. Nora hummed a pleasant song as she attacked the tangled ends of the blonde mass of Velvet's hair with a purposeful vengeance in each stroke.

"So," said Nora, after a silent moment filled by a host of unasked questions. "How long have you been human? I mean since *she* changed you back. I'm sorry." Nora sighed. "I just can't call her your grandmother because she wasn't, you know? Maria Theresa Walburga Amalia Christina—who, incidentally, is your namesake—and Maria Josepha of Saxony are your grandmothers."

"Oh," Velvet whispered. "I didn't know that. I mean, I knew she wasn't my actual grandmother, but…"

Nora shrugged one slender bare shoulder. "There is probably a lot she didn't tell you. What was her name?"

"I don't know her real name actually," Velvet said in dawning surprise; she had never thought to ask. "Everyone called her Queenie."

"Hmm…" Nora made a soft thrumming noise in her throat. She nodded her head but seemed unsatisfied by the shoddy information. "Why are you a human and your brother still an animal?"

"There is a spell," Velvet explained. "It consists of an amethyst, blood of the caster, and some ancient words. Queenie only had one amethyst left; she told me the other was stolen from her by her own blood—her brother, Antonio. She tried to break the amethyst down to dust and make a potion; there simply wasn't enough. Queenie said she waited too long to make the change. So, I am as you see me, and Louis is still under the spell." Velvet's words dropped off abruptly. Queenie's face flashed in her mind, every detail clear as if she stood right in front of her. Little wrinkles bracketing soulful eyes, hair black as a raven wing flowing effortlessly in a summer wind.

Nora brushed in silence while Velvet stared out the small circular window bordering the wash closet. Outside the confines of the hand-blown glass the storm howled, banging against the dripping pane like a hungry ghoul. Nora dropped the brush, then scrubbed her hands over her arms. "Where are you supposed to find this other spell?"

"In a place called the *Bahamas*? I don't know where that is…" Velvet said honestly. "But I have a map. I hid it in the Heath, the night the redcoats came."

"Can you find it again?" asked Nora.

"Of course," Velvet replied wistfully.

Nora pressed Velvet back against the pillows. "Well, yours is the craziest story I have ever heard in my life." She hiccuped a snort, patting Velvet atop her cool, damp scalp. "Sleep now, when you're feeling better and Henry gets his derriere back here…"

Velvet smiled at Nora's reference to that part of Henry's anatomy, but she was far too warm and content to say anything, so she kept her sleepy lips closed. Nora yawned carrying on. "Henry will return soon. He promised, and he never breaks his promises. Oh!" Nora started. A pastel blush painted her freckles while she reached in her pocket. "I didn't want to take it from you, but I didn't want you to lose it." She opened her hand. The silver necklace coiled in the center of her palm, its small links pouring over the emerald pendant.

"It feels so strange," said Nora, a low reverence in her voice. "I thought I heard it singing the other night, while you battled fever dreams. It seemed crazy. Now, I don't know if crazy is even a thing anymore, perhaps it's all just something we don't understand."

The pillow *smushed*, cradling her head in softness. Crisp, white sheets warmed by the firelight shrouded her in a cocoon of comfortable dreamy bliss, and Velvet felt herself already falling asleep. "Just something we don't understand," she agreed, speaking through a noisy yawn that threatened to dislocate her jaw. She was wondering how a human could feel so wretched, yet blissful, then decided—not for the first time today—that humans were strange things, very strange things indeed.

Nora leaned in and linked the chain around Velvet's throat, carefully settling the pulsing emerald to sit pretty in the small dip between her collarbones.

Air whistled through the little gap in Nora's front teeth when she inspected her work. "There you go," she said proudly. Her eyelids lowered and the shadow of her lashes dusted her freckles, gone pale again under the glow of the blaze flickering in the hearth.

"Go to sleep now, love, I'm watching over you," said Nora, pitching her voice to be low and soothing as possible. "Just sleep, I'll try to keep away the dreams."

8

PEACE IN THE STORM

One fine day, a witch cast a spell…and rang that soldier's head just like a noisy bell…

The next five days passed in blessed uneventfulness. Velvet spent a vast majority of the time sleeping. She healed quickly, thanks to the snotty tea and Katie's constant ministrations. Nora loitered in and out of the room babbling, tidying, and bouncing off the walls. As though by magic she wore a new gown every day, and Velvet noticed each one of them appeared more beautiful than the last. Each morning she would open her eyes to find a smiling Nora at her bedside, laughing and telling some grand new tale. Having lived most of her life in silence, Velvet found she relished the high-pitched babble; often pinching her own thighs to keep herself awake while Nora took her time getting to the exciting part in some new drama.

Tea parties and masked balls full of scandalous gossip. Hushed stories told at night, the intrigue of dashing lords in collusion with soldiers of fortune and fate. Many of her stories included terrifying creatures named *dowagers,* or something to that effect; they ruled a place called the "drawing room." Velvet imagined them as potbellied monsters looking out of beady eyes situated over long noses specked in warts. It was confusing and wonderful as Velvet tried to learn an unknown world through the brilliant eyes and thoughts of another. Just like learning to talk to a deer or a fox, first see the world from their perspective, then from your own.

Soldiers in red coats would often wander in the room spitting some lame excuse or a bit of nonsense they had concocted as a discussion point for Nora. Velvet would scowl at their uniforms and hiss when they asked her a question. Nora informed her once, in clipped cultured tones, that it was a distinctly unladylike greeting, and suggested she stop it immediately. It was difficult to obey as the sight of those hated coats struck Velvet in the gut and always brought on a bout of acute nausea; she trembled until they left, sometimes, for a while after.

Katie, the very soul of kindness, was ever amiable. Yet, her answers were clipped and monosyllabic. Velvet often struggled to carry the conversation. Still, over the last few days an easy repertoire had grown between Velvet and the strange doe-like girl who granted their wishes—always graceful and polite, always offering her endless strength, in a quiet, unassuming manner. Velvet, who had mentally plotted her escape from this room for the last three days, concluded her first herculean task would be to get past the quiet, watchful girl.

Today, the storm had raged its fury for six days and five long nights. There was not much for them to do but talk; it was that or go mad staring at the walls. Velvet had spent every piece of her life —which she could remember—outdoors. Staying confined to this small chamber, listening to the song of the blue jay through a pane of glass, hearing the wind and not feeling it on her face made her feel like a mermaid in a bubble dangling over an endless expanse of water. The wind howled briskly over the hills, there was an icy chill in the air, and the rain had finally stopped. Through the window Velvet could see brave slivers of evening sun playing over the dewy grass. Nora and Katie had left her alone for most of the day, and she was going stir-crazy because of it. The final dregs of her fever had burned away the night before last, and she was feeling good for a girl recently stabbed. Twice.

Velvet stood up and wrapped a dressing gown of blue silk over her chemise-clad body. The material flared out, and the firelight captured the shimmering threads in the weave, making them sparkle. Shivering slightly, Velvet walked to the fireplace to throw another log on the dying flames. The fragrant wood contacted the roasting coals and spat out flickers of orange and green.

Velvet held her hands out to the weak blaze, then watched the sparks turn to ashes and flutter down to the sooty grate. When the fresh log caught fire Velvet went to the washstand, filled a porcelain bowl full of clear crystal water—which she poured from a large pewter jug—then splashed the sparkling liquid over her face.

A dusky, speckled mirror rested against the washbowl. Velvet regarded her reflection in critical speculation. She appeared mostly recovered from her ordeal of the last eight days, though a few traces of the trauma left shadowed aftershocks on her pale skin. She touched a bruise in its final, yellow stage, that decorated her right cheekbone, and saw another, still blue on her neck. The image of the fleshy face of the strangler in the conservatory flashed through her mind. She could almost smell the sweat and feel the meaty hands on her throat, squeezing and squeezing!

She did not see beauty in her face. Not the way others did. To her eyes, she looked weak, her features too soft. *I look like my mother,* Velvet thought. *That's why they see beauty. If I was an ordinary girl living peacefully somewhere, they would see me through different eyes. If I was not a princess, if, if...*

A princess with no castle, ruler of a dead court, current heir to a burnt throne. Velvet splashed water on her face.

The door banged open and she jolted up. Her hands hit the water bowl and knocked it to the floor. It shattered loudly, and Velvet screamed, consequently sniffing a great deal of water up her nose.

Nora flounced in, her dress the yellow of noonday sunshine. "Good evening, Velvet," she said, and threw herself down on the bed; lace skirts and pillows flew up around her stocking feet. "The skin you just jumped out of landed somewhere in Scotland," she said, then giggled at her sarcasm. Her laugh died quickly though, and the smile went out of her eyes. Brilliant cream lace wrapped her pale shoulders, it crinkled when they slumped in frustration and fatigue.

"No news yet?" Velvet asked, reading the answer in the pinched expression on Nora's face.

"Nothing!" wailed Nora. "It is certain now that my father has arrested them. Henry is his closest friend, and if he's put him in irons there is no telling what he will do! If I go to him in this state, he may well kill me. I feel it is only a matter of time 'till our own redcoats turn on us before the assassins and whoever else find us." Nora stopped talking and threw up her hands, her face a picture of pure despair.

Velvet caught Nora's hands midair and held them in her steady grip. "Go to the King. Tell him you didn't know he wanted me dead, tell him you found a wounded girl, did what any well-bred lady would do. Tell him everything you know, let him help you, Nora. You have done more than enough, the fates will not judge you if you walk away now."

Nora vaulted from the bed and fluttered to the oversized chair by the door; it was yellowing in certain places, showing pieces of stuffing through a thick layer of dust. Nora lifted the peach gown resting delicately over the armrest and shook it firmly; the satin material snapped to attention. A giant cloud of infinitesimal grey particles exploded around her. Nora coughed prissily, then sneezed a great, wracking heave that made her stomp her feet.

"Go to my father?" She gasped, lifting a dainty handkerchief from the front pocket of her gown and dabbed at her reddening nose. "Leave all this scintillating intrigue? My dear, I am caught up in the scandal of the century alongside Marie Antoinette's daughter. Galloping horses couldn't drag me away from you. Besides…" She shook out the gown once more; this time she held her breath and turned away. "From all I have read, the fates were tempestuous creatures who did as they pleased. Now, enough of that. Get up, get dressed. I am releasing you from this cage," she announced casting her eyes disdainfully around the small room. "I think an evening stroll would be just the thing." Nora flung open the door and stuck her head out. "Katie!" she bawled.

Velvet jumped to her feet shushing her. "Please, don't call

Katie!" Velvet insisted when Nora hollered the girl's name again. "I am more than capable of getting dressed on my own."

"Oh?" Nora's brow arched suspiciously as she eyed Velvet in considerable curiosity. "Have you ever done so before?"

"Well…no," Velvet stammered out. "But how hard can it be?"

"Ah! The question asked by a thousand ladies the world over."

Katie chose that moment to arrive at the door, panting from her exertions. Her heart-shaped face was flushed and wind-burned, her lips were parted and moving, but no sound emerged. She wore a plain black cloak and the hood was thrown back showing her mussed hair. Strands of it hung limply in her rapidly blinking eyes. She held a letter in her steady hands.

"Katie!" Nora swayed on her feet, hand to heart. "*Mon Dieu*! What do you mean bursting in here?" she said, forgetting she had done much the same thing to Velvet only moments ago. "Do you want me to die in front of you, or worse, faint again and fall victim to your awful smelling salts?"

"I have a message from Lord Eden," wheezed Katie.

"Christ!" screamed Nora, and all but grabbed the missive from Katie's hand. She snapped the wax seal.

"Lord Newcastle has, to this day, been imprisoned in the Tower of London," said Katie. Her words fell like pristine glass ornaments, and they shattered loudly in the silent room.

Nora's eyes scanned the missive, each word she read further dropped her jaw. When she had read it twice over, Nora finally read aloud in a low, tragic voice.

Dearest N & Katie — I cannot speak to the rest:

I write to tell you the worst is true. Old George was furious, called Henry's deed an act of treason against himself and the Crown. He screamed at us for hours, enough to make me long for the days of here-here and what-what. At the end of what proved to be a rather punishing ordeal, his own men clapped Henry in irons and hauled him to the Tower. There was much resistance on Henry's part, I assure you, it took four men to subdue him. Finally, they dragged him away, many wept. It was all desperately emotional if I do say. In the struggle, Henry wounded Lord Hardgrave; we wait to hear if he will live. Understandably, the events of the last few days have sunk the court into deep mourning. You know there is none so well loved as His Grace, my Lord Newcastle. I, having only followed the orders of my captain, am confined to a small room at court. I sit alone by day, at night I am under constant guard. I do not bemoan my fate for Henry's is far worse. They allowed me the small favor of a paper and pen, so I may inform you of our imminent release. It seems Henry has re-sworn his allegiance to the Crown. Pledged on pain of death to kill Velvet and her lost brother, or as the English court call them, diables français—the French devils. I am sorry for these tidings; I leave it to you to decide what must be done.

Yours respectfully, Devon E.

"Christ, and bastards on a biscuit!" Nora's forceful exhale landed her in the wing chair, crushing the dress she had so painstakingly shaken out. "Perhaps we could go to the Americas? I have money saved, we run, make a life for ourselves. There is nothing here for me in England, there never has been."

Katie fervently crossed herself. "That seems drastic, my lady," she said.

Nora shook the missive then laid the paper over her face. It fluffed up at the edges riding on the wind of her breath when she spoke. "Please give me your suggestions. I am all ears."

Velvet watched the whole scene unfold in that strange detachment which had been present in her since the changing. There was only one solution to this unsolvable problem, and that was to remove the problem, which just so happened was her.

She kept her silence, knowing full well what the girls would say. Velvet would not put it past them to tie her back to that bed if she refused their gentle cajoling. Marie Antoinette's daughter was the problem. If the daughter died, or disappeared…well, it was not difficult to decode the rest. She had to leave, that was that. Tonight…when the girls slept, and the hired soldiers gambled.

"Well," Velvet said and clapped her hands. The palms smacked together making a fantastic bang; the paper resting on Nora's face flew off as she exhaled a giant draft of repressed air. Eyes rolling, her hand went to cradle her galloping heart. "Good God, Velvet! Both of you! Why all the drama?"

"Sorry," Velvet muttered, shocked. She stared down at her hands wondering why she had felt the need to clap at all. She had never done it before and was unsure if she would do it again. A hot rouge soaked her palms, and they smarted miserably. "I wanted," Velvet cleared her throat and tried again. "I wanted to say if we plan to run for our lives—again—we will need a good night's sleep. You two should sleep in here tonight. The bed is much larger than the one in your room." The room that was closer to the front door of the tavern, the one she thought might come in handy during her grand escape. "I've been hogging all the comfort," she finished lamely.

"How can you talk about sleep right now?" asked Nora. "I couldn't think of such a thing."

"I could," muttered Katie. "I could find a bed and sleep for a week."

There was a cursory knock at the door. Katie and Nora exchanged a look, at the end of which Nora gave Katie a tiny nod. Katie straightened her apron before brushing the wandering strands of hair off her sweat-dappled forehead. The knock sounded again, hesitant this time. Katie opened the door, her movements quick and careful.

A young lady garbed in a clean white cap and smart maid uniform entered, pushing a small trolley. Velvet's stomach roared audibly. The maid smiled at her in a good-natured way. Her round cheeks were plump, and her homely face hosted a pair of sympathetic eyes. "I have just the thing for that. There's a lovely braised lamb in a mint sauce, some baby carrots fried in butter and parsley, chicken soup, and some hot biscuits."

"I couldn't even look at food right now!" Nora avowed, rising in a rustle of sounds to shoo the lady from the room. To Velvet's relief, Katie intervened.

"That all sounds wonderful, thank you," said Katie. Quickly, she gave the startled maid a consoling pat on her hand. The maid, grey eyes dramatically magnified through a pair of delicate spectacles, blinked owlishly; she pulled a pouting face and stammered out a reply.

Nora was already on her feet rifling through the dinner cart, lifting the polished silver lids and sticking her finger in various sauces. To Velvet's surprise, Nora placed a kiss on the maid's cheek and apologized for being a shrew. Hot color flushed the maid's cottage cheese complexion. Another curtsy, a whispered word to Katie, and the maid backed out of the room. She took a while to leave, pausing every third step to make an additional curtsy. Eventually, she reached the door and closed it quietly behind her.

"What would you like?" asked Nora, facing Velvet and holding out a curved bone, dangling a piece of fragrant meat.

Velvet's stomach growled again, but she shuddered in revulsion. Nora read the look on her face and drew the meat back, treating it to the full heat of her quizzical regard. "What is it?" asked Nora.

"I don't think I can eat that," Velvet said, fairly appalled by the thought of skipping dinner. "I don't think I can eat a lamb. I mean, they are babies, really the sweetest things, besides, they're some of the few creatures in the world who can speak to flowers. To take a bite of its flesh would just be…" Another shiver of revulsion wracked her body, and she covered her mouth to stifle her gag.

"Speak to flowers? Really?" Distress washed Nora's face. "But it's already dead and just sooo… delicious and…"

"So are you," Velvet said crossing her arms over her chest. "But I don't think you would want me to eat you with a mint sauce."

A musical peal of laughter burst from Katie, startling Velvet. Nora made a sour face at Katie. "I am glad the idea gives you such joy."

"Oh, my Lord!" said Katie, recovering herself slightly. "It was the mint sauce that got me."

Nora made a disbelieving sound, picked up a biscuit, and gave it a look chock-full of disdain. "Speak to flowers, really! Banquets will never be the same," she said, and Katie laughed again.

After a dinner of biscuits, carrots, mint sauce, and cranberry wine, they sat together on the cut of fur before the fire. Nora lay on her side resting her weight on her hip and elbow. Her right hand cradled her head, her other caressed the crystal stem of her wineglass, swirling the crimson liquid. "I can't believe old George imprisoned Henry, they share blood for Chrissakes! I swear I don't know what this world is coming to." She took a sip of the wine; the tart berry left a light pink stain on her bottom lip. "What if you were Queen of France, Velvet? I mean, you are the current heir to the throne. I could help you, we could raise an army. I know you have supporters, here and in Austria. We could take revenge on the parties who put your families to death. Do you want to be Queen?"

"No. I have never wanted that," Velvet said without a second of hesitation. She had never given it much thought, yet once asked she knew her heart. "Louis is heir to the throne, and I don't know why, but I feel in my heart that's the way it has to be. I don't want to rule, I am not sure someone like me would be a good custodian of all that power."

"I think you would be, Lady Velvet," said Katie. "You are brave, your heart is good, a little naive—if it's not too bold of me to say—but I think it somehow adds to the mystique of you.

"It is too bold, Katie," said Nora, mouth stern, eyes smiling.

"What on earth is our Queen, Lady Charlotte doing in all of this?" asked Katie, taking Nora's jibe for what it was—an open invitation to speak her mind.

Nora shrugged. "Who can say? Running down the palace halls, screaming and breathing in a bowl of smelling salts—I imagine—while trying to calm her love, it's what she always does."

"They are in love, aren't they?" asked Katie, unusually wistful.

"I've never seen such a love," agreed Nora. "What I wouldn't give to have a man look at me the way my father looks at his queen."

"One can only dream, my lady," said Katie. She leaned forward to quickly squeeze Nora's hand. She sat above them in the overstuffed chair carefully mending a gown Nora had torn during a hasty escape from the privy earlier this morning, after a harrowing encounter with a hairy-legged spider. Velvet saw Katie nod and knew they both understood something she did not. She loved Louis, but she did not think that was the kind of *love* that had them both sighing and staring dreamily off into the unknown like victims of a sleeping draft.

"Have you ever been in love?" Velvet heard Nora ask. Katie said nothing, the silence stretched until the drop of a feather would have created a catastrophic din. Despite the fire, the room was chilly—still, color bloomed in Velvet's cheeks when she realized that Nora had directed this question at her. She took another sip of wine, choked on it, and wheezed.

"N…no," Velvet stammered. "A couple of gypsy warlords wanted to marry me when they heard of the change. I loved none of them, they brought me many gifts, fine dresses of silk, skirts dyed pink with pomegranate juice…"

"Were they handsome?" asked Nora.

"They are in *your* mind," muttered Katie.

"Always," said Nora, an exaggerated sigh lifting her breast. She laid her head on the fur and rubbed her cheek against its springy softness.

"Don't you love Charles?" Velvet asked. "Or, do you not need love to conceive a child?"

"Oh, you certainly do not need love. More's the pity!" moaned Nora rolling onto her back, holding the cup aloft so it would not spill. Her glossy lips twisted in a bitter line. "Charles embodies everything wrong with the British aristocracy. He is ill-mannered to those less fortunate than himself. He cares only for the latest fashion and keeping with the current trends. His words are vapid as his empty mind."

"I see," Velvet said. As was often the case, she was completely in the dark. "Then why did you…you know?"

"Take him to my bed?" supplied Nora. A flash of real pain washed over her face, and Velvet thought she saw a glimpse of the girl beneath the lady. "Because he has the face of a fallen angel. He can be warm and romantic, he danced with me in the moonlight…" She sighed. "His smile is so sexy it curls my toes. He looks like Henry, only a little shorter…and blonde." Nora rolled back onto her stomach, buried her face in the fur, then pounded her fist beside her head. "I should never have done it! My life's greatest regret will be the final nail in my coffin of ruin. A bastard bearing a bastard. Perfect."

Katie sat up, apparently deciding the drama had gone too far. She slid off the chair, kneeling beside her lady, and lifted Nora's head into her lap. Her slender fingers weaved through Nora's hair, while she whispered words of comfort, then wiped at a tear which escaped Nora's closed eyes and spilled down her cheek. "I am a living cliché," sobbed Nora. Velvet, not knowing what else to do, took Nora's hand, held it tightly between both of her own.

"A ruined woman crying over a lost man."

"He's not lost," crooned Katie. "Charles would take you back if you asked."

"I will never ask!" cried Nora. She sniffled loudly and used her trembling fingers to dab at her eyes, then fanned her face. "He has broken every promise he ever made, he is a scandalous cad. I will forget him if I must take a knife and carve him from my mind. Men break promises, fast as they break hearts."

Velvet thought the knife and the carving were extreme but said nothing. Images of Henry flashed in front of her, the room full of a million crimson-flecked emerald eyes seen through sheets of whirling rain. Her hand twitched when she remembered holding his and recalled the safety of his arms around her body. In the silence, she heard his whisper, promising he would never harm her. Then, she thought of the message from Devon telling them he had sworn to kill her—again—and felt compelled to agree with Nora. Promise breakers the lot.

Velvet excused herself, quietly letting go of Nora's damp hand, and stood up to use the water closet. After a brief struggle with the complicated architecture of the toilet's flush, Velvet emerged from the floral curtain to find Katie helping a half-dreaming Nora to her feet. Velvet muttered out a few polite words of good night to them both, and Katie closed the door behind them echoing more of the same.

Alone, Velvet flopped back down on the fur, feeling ruffled by the day's events; she knew the night would bring her no reprieve. She did not want to run away, could muster no desire to be alone and scared again. The only comfort would be relief from sickening guilt. Guilt for dragging them throughout this, guilt for not being strong enough to leave sooner. That guilt would fade with the distance she put between herself and the two girls she had come to love.

The parameters for her escape were not ideal. Velvet did not have a clue where she was; the timing felt wrong, she had done no planning and collected no supplies. Against her will, her eyes fell closed, her mind wandered freely into the realm of imagination. She dozed fitfully, dreaming of emerald eyes and a hand held out to her in the rain.

9

LOST AND FOUND

You didn't leave me and now I've found..
so many dead bodies lying around.

$\mathcal{V}$elvet woke with a start, her heart racing in her chest, shallow breaths tangled in her throat. She wondered, hand to dazed head—if it was normal for humans to wake this way —their consciousness struggling so hard against reality, reluctant to shake off the oblivion of dreams.

Banked firelight glowed through the room and a melting warmth fused the fur to her body. Velvet's gaze flew to the window; she blinked her eyes firmly determined to dislodge the last clinging remnants of sleep. Through the misshapen bubbles in the glass window, she instantly judged the indigo quality of the night. The sky swirled like the contents of an inkpot, the moon full, pulsing hotly in the blackness as it threw beams of silver light on the rolling hills.

Disembodied voices rose from downstairs, and anticipation knotted Velvet's stomach. She could feel her nerves jumping in her throat, persistent ticks that made cold sweat mist her palms. Velvet lifted the apricot dress and held it up to the fire. It was a delicate satin weave, rose leaves embroidered along the corset and silk inserts threaded through the puffed sleeves. A sweet, slightly cloying smell rose from the garment, it was the last thing in the world she wanted to wear, but Velvet told herself that beggars were simply souls who had relinquished the option of choice.

She took off her nightgown and stood shivering in her clean shift. The silver chain slid over the soft skin on her neck and she felt the emerald settle in the hollow of her throat. The heat of it was a sharp reminder, furthering her resolve in what she meant to do. Velvet stepped inside the wide skirts of the dress, sighing. It felt smooth as silk and moved around her legs like a fluffy cloud. She thrust her arms through the belled sleeves…and ten minutes of frustrated insanity ensued.

Shrieking in miserable rage, Velvet conceded defeat—Nora was right. If the fates kept her alive 'till ninety, she would never, could never hitch up a gown on her own. The laces of the blasted thing ran down the back? Humans could only see what was right in front of them; more's the pity, so how was she meant to accomplish this task? She was not a moth caterpillar with eyes in the back of her head!

Velvet dropped the useless gown groaning vengefully. There was a brief flurry of noise from the common room downstairs, a shout followed by a crash that boomed low in the distance. She froze, but all went silent again. She was stalling now; it was time for action.

Velvet did not even know if she could do what she planned to do, but she meant to try. Her hands found the borrowed cloak Nora had given her in the conservatory moments before it all went to hell, or had it gone to hell before that? The timeline was hazy, just a lot of running, bleeding, laughing, and trying not to die. The cloak smelled of rosewater. A good washing had removed the mud and dark blood streaks previously gracing the material from hem to hood. A swish of her arms settled the cloak around her, and she shoved her feet in a pair of boots some wonderful soul had left at the edge of her bed. They were a little too big for her, but fur lined and toasty warm.

Velvet tied her hair back in a knot, then inspected her reflection. There was nothing to be done about the tendrils which escaped the knot to flutter in her face. She sucked in her cheeks and lifted her brows, trying to make them touch her hairline, then pursed her lips. The pose gave Velvet the impression of a dizzy fish, her lips reddened, and her eyes stuck out like blue stars. A strange face indeed. She had disliked it the moment she saw the pale features looking blindly back at her from the shifting surface of the lake near their camp. Too pale, lips too full and childish for her liking. In the days before the attack, she had trained in swords and daggers with the Romani warriors. Velvet learned quickly that many of her animal instincts had remained; she was fast and uncommonly strong. She found herself wishing her body reflected some of the strength felt in her soul. Maybe add a couple of muscles to the slender, white arms, some height of any kind, a little heft to her bones? Wide blue eyes stared back at her from the dusky glass, Velvet let her face relax. She looked nothing like a warrior, she noted in accepted resignation—only a lost waif made of moonbeams and shadows.

She lifted the cloak, covering her bright hair, listening to the wind whistle across the open fields of Stanwell Moor, the hallowed sound muted by the glass pane of the small, round window she hoped never to see again. Measuring her steps, Velvet counted each steady beat of her heart as she gave one last longing look at the dying fire then walked silently to the door.

Twelve redcoats lounged restlessly in the dark belly of the Blind Pig. Velvet saw the layout of the common room had them sectioned off into three groups of four. The first group played a game of cards around a rectangular table covered in strange green stuff resembling well-trimmed grass. The table was situated near a grand piano, fat as a pumpkin and pressed flush against a couple of dying fichus plants. A tall, dark-haired woman wearing a peacock feather stuck in her high coiffure, played the piano with gloves of black lace. She wore a sad expression on her face and bit her lower lip when encountering a difficult chord. The haunting strains of Mozart flowed through the room. The song was one of her grandmother's—Queenie, she corrected herself—one of Queenie's favorites. Whoever that woman truly was, the sweet music made Velvet miss home.

More clusters of wigged redcoats draped themselves over the numerous, plush cushions and one long chaise lounge which decorated the back wall of the Blind Pig's lush salon. The room was much larger than Velvet had expected, having only previously acquainted herself with the four walls of her recovery room. Velvet saw satiny paper—its design a braided ribbon pattern— covered the walls. She had a strange memory of such paper coating the walls of a different room a long time ago, a huge room strung by golden chandeliers and chairs that looked like thrones.

The hazy images flitted away. Velvet hoped they would return from whence they came and lie in peace beside the rest of her repressed memories. Drawing in a silent breath she moved like a shadow along the hall, stopping momentarily at the top of the staircase. The floors and doors of the room were stout and well-constructed, but finery of the items filling it spoke of deeper fortune. Women strutted through the smoky space swathed in risqué gowns and low-cut necklines, and whispered to the soldiers in low, sensual tones from lips rouged the color of blood.

Velvet felt a throbbing sensation in her hands and feet. A few drops of sweat misted her brow. She must have looked truly alarming—a ghost escaped from the haunted moors or the spirit of the girl who might have died in the upper room.

The first man who saw her jumped up knocking over his chair, a mug of ale dropped from his hands, the thick liquid surged out in a smelly puddle.

Velvet's own hands went to the emerald hanging around her neck. Only a slight disturbance in the air marked her passage down the stairs. When her booted toes touched the last step, every redcoat in the room gained their feet. The woman at the piano cut off mid-note, a discordant tone that twanged unpleasantly and died harshly.

Silence fell over the room. A man, whose bearded face was unfamiliar to Velvet, walked in front of the stunned assembly, removed his hat, and offered Velvet a stiff, formal bow. Lamplight caught the red threads in his coat, illuminating them until Velvet saw nothing but that hated color. Her hand went to the latch at the back of her necklace and the hook gave way. Velvet sighed when she heard the small click and release.

"Good evening, my lady, I am Lord Melton, how can I be of service?" His red-rimmed eyes sagged badly, but the gleam in them was sharp and focused. His voice caressed the last word, his lips parted in what she supposed he meant to be a smile. Behind the leering man, a wavering outline resolved itself by the door, Lord Bryon stepped from the shadows. He had a dagger in his right hand, and its naked blade looked thirsty. There was no kindness for her in his swollen visage, he looked at her like a rat he found wandering the privy floor. It seemed he had heard the stories of who she could be, listened to the whispers of the hideous danger she represented—whatever that was. From the hostile looks on the faces that cluttered her vision, they all had.

"I am in search of food, sir," Velvet said, surprised by the haughty command she heard in her voice. "If you would point me in the direction of the kitchen, I will bid you good evening." An old woman elbowed her way to the front of the gawkers. She had a small, tight figure and a leathered face. Miss Jenny, Velvet assumed. She opened her mouth to speak but the leading man held up his hand. She fell silent, her throat working hard when she swallowed her nerve.

"There is no reason for you to leave the comfort of your room, my lady. I'll have a tray sent up to you." Lord Melton's purplish tongue came out and swiped at his lower lip. His eyes, colorless in the dimmed interior, held hers in a steel vise. He reached out a gloved hand. Velvet skittered back, and the sleeve of his coat brushed her arm. A silver buckle stitched on the seam of his cuff caught Velvet's eyes. She studied the familiar engraving while a bitter shot of fear filled her mouth.

"That is unnecessary," Velvet said. "I was hoping to take a small breath of air afterward."

Lord Melton shook his dark head, slowly mouthing the word *no* before he took another determined step in her direction, prepared to take her back to her room, lock her in if need be.

Velvet had one last try; she was afraid to do it, afraid she did not have enough magic, terrified the gem would malfunction, leaving her a prize fool, a child witch who ran out of borrowed tricks. Searching her soul for the steel she knew lay buried somewhere, Velvet took a deep, bracing breath. It was her only choice. Did magic come from the stone? Or was it only a tool for what was inside her? One of the many questions she would have asked Queenie if they had not so cruelly run out of time. Velvet's fist closed around the heated emerald, and she held it out in front of her defensively.

Here goes nothing, she thought. Her eyes fixed stoically on a slender hat rack stationed near the front door. The burning started instantly, in a place just beneath her heart. Queenie did not tell her the spell caster also felt pain. It was not surprising though—since becoming human she learned that being in pain was just another part of being alive.

For a moment nothing happened. Velvet almost rolled her eyes, feeling the worst of her fears come true. Fears that stood at the edge of her escape, jewel in her hand, waiting for magic that would never come.

Yet, finally it did come. Slow at first, just a green glow that enveloped her fist in a smoking glove. She heard her own shattered gasp, but it came from far away, the sound tangled in the racing thuds of her surging heart. Velvet had no spell committed to memory in preparation for this encounter, and she had only seen a stonework once before. She could not remember the spell Queenie recited during either changing, but Velvet remembered her words afterward. *"Hold the stone in your hand and your desire in your mind. Say what you want and believe it."*

Velvet tore her eyes from the expanding glow and settled them on the man who stood poleaxed in shock. At close range, she could see each bristle of dark stubble on his chin, smell the sweat collecting in a little puddle below his long nose. Her mind went blank as a clear blue sky. Velvet waited, then said the first word which appeared in that empty space. "Dance."

Something cracked in her palm. A shower of sparks burst out of the emerald; golden lights tinged in aqua green spewed from her hand. The lights spun in dizzy concentric circles, securely wrapping her in a glowing orb. Velvet made a sound of undiluted wonder, and Lord Melton did the same. Bolstered by the heat, the pain, and the growing glow, Velvet straightened her spine. She felt chilled when her hood fell to her shoulders. An invisible wind whipped her hair around her face.

"Dance," she said again, this time her voice was low, enchanting. She took another step. "Dance, sir."

Another soft series of explosions went off in her palm. Velvet was covered in cold sweat, vibrating in every limb. The emerald released its hidden magic and lit the room in a silvery green light like the harvest moon had fallen on the earth. The light darkened in the places where the colorful swirls of endless sparkles twisted into themselves, flashing and sizzling before shooting off into volleys of hot sparks. Spears of light burst from between her fingers, and Velvet wondered, with detached curiosity, if the light would split her hand apart.

White light slithered through the room layering the ground in a moving, milky fog. The redcoat standing in front of her shook his head, and his eyes rolled around in their soggy, bagging sockets. The sad-faced girl, the peacock feather poking from her brunette head, played again, a Mozart waltz in F major. The redcoat stumbled, Lord Bryon was there to take his elbow. The latter's long fingers curled almost delicately over the other's coat; they turned until their mouths were only inches apart. Wearing twin looks of stunned consternation, the two men held out their arms. In the first second of touching there was some confusion on who would lead. Velvet saw that a few of the other soldiers had encountered this same problem, though some fell to the dance as naturally as breathing. The sweet strains of the waltz harmonized through the echoing room, swaying the smoke that swathed her legs, while the emerald in her fist continued to beat like a heart. The men stared into each other's eyes, blank, directionless—almost shy glances. Then they clasped hands, wrapped their arms, each around the other's waist—and obeyed her—vigorously. A little click of Lord Bryon's polished heels, a bow from Lord Melton, and the big soldiers started to dance. Every other body in the room did the same.

Each dragoon had a partner, but none of them spoke—the

confusion of the moment too real and current. They spun in swirling circles like dancing specters in a ghost house, locked eternally to the endless, repetitive rhythm, unable to do anything else. Velvet shook her head, sure she would never see such a sight again, then pocketed the emerald, weaved through the waltzing dragoons, and escaped into the night.

10

ALL WE COULD DO WAS FOLLOW

Nora, Nora, what do you see?
A little owl sleeping in a tree…

"*D*o you feel like dancing, Katie?"

Katie groaned and rolled onto her side. "How can I feel anything at all? I'm sleeping."

"Are you?" Nora asked in a soft, leading voice. "You sure you don't feel like dancing?"

Katie flipped onto her back and opened her eyes. "Yes," she said miserably. "But I don't know why."

"Me neither," Nora declared, throwing her hands in the air, elated as a child at her first ball. "Isn't it magical?"

"Not particularly," muttered Katie. "It's the middle of the night, and I'm so exhausted! Hours of tossing and turning in this tiny bed. I finally fell asleep, only to wake up five minutes later possessed by an incredible urge to dance a gig. Magical is not the word I would use."

"Wonderful, then! Let's dance, shall we? I hear a waltz, it's been sooo long since I waltzed."

"My lady, please," whined Katie, shutting her eyes definitely.

"You, please!" Nora retorted. "Don't you want to?"

"Yes, I do," admitted Katie. "I am struggling to resist the urge and go back to sleep." Katie turned on her side giving her back to Nora. "I suggest you do the same."

"Oh, I can't. I can't remember the last time I heard a good waltz, I almost forgot how it sounds!"

"You attended the Northumberland ball less than a fortnight ago," said Katie, shooting Nora a confused look from over her shoulder.

"I know," replied Nora. "An eternity." She let out another sigh that turned into a tired moan.

"And this is not a good waltz, by anyone's standards," muttered Katie.

Nora made small, mewling noises, kicking her leg in the perfect imitation of a frustrated kitten, but otherwise held silent. The silence remained until Katie's breaths deepened into a gentle cadence of soft, sleepy sounds. Nora finally heard a snore. Katie muttered something unintelligible, her small features gathered into a relaxed frown.

Nora vaulted from the bed, springing up like a fired cannonball. Katie screamed, instinctively diving for her knife, then rolled lithely to her toes, coming up in a low crouch, naked blade held at an angle in front of her face, teeth bared in a snarl.

"You know," said Nora conversationally, eyeing Katie's warrior pose in critical assessment. "For someone who has such pleasant features you can look ridiculously ferocious."

"You scared me," returned Katie. "I am fairly certain you did it on purpose." Katie did the unthinkable—and stuck out her tongue. Nora laughed and returned the elegant gesture, then giggled as her hips swung from side to side. It was all very confusing because while her mind may object to her craving for song and dance, her heart wanted to spin, twirl, and kick her heels. Nora rubbed her eyes and shook her sleepy, bobbing head. What in Dante's hell was wrong with her? She glared out their double set of wide glass windows, framed by long, dark curtains which were tied back by little ropes tipped in golden tassels. Through the misty glass, the outside world was silent, haunted as a grave. Tall grass swayed in a soundless wind, and the moon

140

illuminated the lively green blades in the brilliant shadows of violet light.

"I'm not dreaming, am I, Katie?"

"I wish I was," muttered Katie in exhausted frustration. She relaxed her hands, set the knife at her feet, then rubbed her eyes. Katie's frilly nightcap had shifted in her mad dive for the knife, so a square of delicate lace covered the right side of her face.

"I'm sorry, Katie! But I have to dance," Nora pleaded, the need so strong she feared it would pull her physically out the door. "Come downstairs for a moment. I have to see what all the commotion is. Come on, I can't just lie down and pretend it isn't happening!" Nora stomped her foot until her toe ached. "Fine, if you won't come with me I will see if Velvet is feeling adventurous. Ah!" Nora screeched. "Katie! You're dancing right now!"

Katie did not reply, only froze mid-spinning jump. She landed and tripped, and her hand flew out to break her fall. "What is going on?" she whispered, half frightened, half dazed.

"This has been the strangest fortnight ever! First Marie Antoinette's daughter is alive, yet different than the one we thought already lived...? I run for my life...not once, but twice, then... learn that magic is real..." Nora's words broke off abruptly. "Oooh!" she moaned. "It feels like a dream or a spell, I have heard far too much about such nonsense lately. Velvet told me some stories which were quite beyond my imagination!"

Nora ran her hands down her front, dimly realizing Katie had let her fall asleep in her dress—it was strange, but it suited her fine. There was no time for such a mundane thing like dressing. Her hands trembled when she pulled on her boots, and she could count the clacks of her teeth while she fastened the silver clasp of her cloak under her chin. Briefly, she caught her reflection in the night-darkened glass—her face was terribly pale, but her smile and eyes were bright and shining.

"What is happening?" howled Katie desperately, throwing herself to the floor, trying to stop her incessant, involuntary twitching. "What in God's name is wrong with me?" Katie crossed herself. Her movements jerky and awkward, when she reached "Holy Spirit," her finger rested lightly over her right shoulder.

Nora watched the lifelong symbol comfort Katie, as it always did. The girl's terror-stricken features relaxed; Katie lifted her hands to kiss her fingers and say Amen, just before they touched her praying lips, the hand twirled in front of her face. Katie's slender body twirled with it.

Nora rolled her eyes and laughed. "Velvet! This is her doing, I'm not sure how, but I swear it is. Quickly, Katie, dance into your clothes," she said, unable to resist then spun toward the door. All she wanted to do was dance. Nora felt like she would forgo silks, lush red wine, winter carriage rides, masked balls, and good books beside warm hearths. She would give it all up to do...all she wanted to do. The sentence rhymed in Nora's mind making her smile. Her dancing thoughts added a beat to the words and turned them to a little song, which got stuck in her head. *Would give it all up to do, all she wants to do. Would give it all up to do, all she wants to do...*

Katie returned Nora's smile with her best dignified glare. "I see nothing funny about this," said Katie, though her hands tapped out the first five beats of the *quadrille*. "Why would you think Velvet has anything to do with this?"

"Oh, I don't know, but I would bet my life on it! You wouldn't believe the things she told me." Nora reached for the handle and threw open the door. "I am not using that as a figure of speech, I mean, you really would not believe it."

Nora flew out of the room, rushed down the hall, and opened Velvet's door. Her mind registered Velvet's absence long before her eyes adjusted to the emptiness of the darkened room. She stood there staring stupidly at the crumpled gown left discarded on the floor until Katie tapped her on the shoulder.

"Did you see the smoke everywhere?" asked Katie. "It is very strange, it moves like vapor or steam." Katie kicked at the white stuff swirling between her feet, and it fluffed up around her legs. "Mayhap the Devil is here, my lady."

Nora snorted. "Unlikely, though if he is, I do have several questions for him regarding the Garden of Eden and his role in painting us women in such an unfortunate light." Her body spun in another circle before she clenched her fist and gritted her teeth, her foot tapping lithely all the while.

"She probably did the right thing leaving us here, my lady," said Katie, keen eyes reading Nora's crestfallen expression.

"I don't care what the right thing is. I wanted to help her, without us she will die. The things she told me, Katie! My mind is still spinning. A real adventure is all I have ever wanted in my life, and here is the real thing fair tumbled in my lap. I have to see how it all comes out in the end."

"Even if it means your life, my lady?"

"Oh, heavens! I don't think it will come to that. If it does, well then...it does. I would rather die doing something right than live feeling I have forever missed out...what do I have to live for anyway?"

"The baby, my lady!" said Katie scandalized.

Nora growled to the rhythm of her stomping foot. "Come on! We have to go after her."

"Do we though?" asked Katie. "My lady, you helped her. She is alive because of you." Katie shook her hand, struggling to dislodge Nora's death grip. "She wants to go. You need to make peace with your father, get some rest, maybe not in that order. Can we not leave well enough alone?" Katie kicked her feet, did another little jump, then buried her face in her hands. "This is ridiculous!" she howled.

"It's certainly powerful, huh? My first spell," Nora whispered and closed her eyes at the wonder. Dead children were alive, animals could change to people, and spells could make you dance. It was like bloody Christmas. "It's magic, Katie, real magic. People go their whole lives without it."

Katie nodded. "Yes, they do, my lady, it is probably for the best. Nothing good will come of this, mark my words."

"Consider them marked," Nora said, recapturing Katie's hand.

Half walking, half dancing, they spun to the top of the stairs, where the strangest sight of all met her eyes. Nora grasped the polished wooden railing in both hands and looked down into the common room. In a swirling cloud of mist, twelve dragoons regaled in military finery, danced. Twelve men, four women, and Miss Jenny weaved between the tables, kicking lazily at the sparse items, which had the audacity to remain in their path—a felled chair, an overturned table, a misplaced jug of wine. Nora watched them move, showing all the grace of stumbling youth, their enchanted bodies struggling to keep time with the sad strains of Mozart ringing off the stout timbers and doors.

Nora felt herself blanch, and her mouth went dry as sand. It was haunting as any sight she had ever seen. The men held each other, their limbs wooden from exhaustion. A few wigs were askew and pinched, disillusioned expressions painted their faces like Halloween masks.

Katie crossed herself again, this time pulling it off without the dance move. It seemed to Nora the shock of the moment had snapped them into stillness.

Katie's hand covered her mouth. "It's the Devil, my lady." She breathed, shoulders vibrating, voice shaking in terror. She crossed herself again.

"Snap out of it this instant, Katie! Now is not the time to abandon your nerve."

"But my lady," moaned Katie, her eyes swishing from the dancing men to Nora's face.

"It's a gypsy enchantment, Katie."

Katie looked startled. "How do you know that?"

"It's a long story, about spells, princesses, and princes."

"A story you know?"

"Yes. One I know."

"Tell me, then!" Katie rounded on Nora, her small face fiercely flushed, mottled grey by the light of dying fires.

"Now is not the time," Nora said.

"Dancing dead men," said Katie and crossed herself again.

"Frozen, dancing dead men," Nora replied.

Around her feet, the mists swirled faster; before she knew what to make of it, Nora held Katie and they spun to the music, twirling in a small circle. Their feet kicked at the mists, and it rose up enfolding them like angel wings.

Nora smiled at Katie. "Well," she said over a laugh. "At least this isn't boring."

Katie returned the smile, which lit up the dark places in the spinning backdrop of the room. "I concede," she dipped in a small curtsy, and rose beaming. "This is terribly fun."

"You really are the most wonderful person in the world, Katie," pronounced Nora, and kissed her maid's flushed cheek.

Katie giggled when Nora stepped on her toe. "Come on," Nora urged after another long, flowing twirl. "Let waltz our way out of here."

Katie raised a thin, brown brow. Her eyes glistened in the lamplight and she looked at the soldiers, a hesitant frown playing over her lips. "What about them?"

"What about them?" Nora repeated. "Look at us, dancing like fools—and we, only feeling the aftershocks of whatever transpired here. I don't think the targets of such a spell are going anywhere for a while."

"They look so ghostly," whispered Katie and moved to cross herself again.

Nora caught her hand. "If you do that one more time, I will go mad."

"Well," Katie said and shrugged, reclaiming her hand. "It won't be a far journey from where we are now."

Nora squinted, trying to see through the swirling mists collecting at the base of the stairs like steam in a boiling pot. "We need weapons, food if we can find any," whispered Nora not knowing why she felt the need to keep her voice down. One last look at the mists and Nora found her nerve. She ran down the stairs listening all the while to the patter of Katie's following feet. There was a sort of whistling noise above her head, which made Nora duck and throw up her hands instinctively. A candlestick holder crashed against the wall behind her. Katie grabbed her arm and dragged her away just in time to avoid being hit by the rebound.

"Someone kicked that at us!" said Katie, her mouth falling open in horrified astonishment. She shut her eyes, breathing heavily. "You go for the door, my lady, I will get the weapons and food."

"No." said Nora firmly. "You grab food, I will get the weapons.

Thirty seconds, no more, then we run." Katie nodded, gnawing at her lower lip. Nora swallowed hard. "Go!" Their words clashed in simultaneous commands before they spun off in the dancing crowd.

Were they really under a spell? Nora's mind struggled to comprehend the enormity of the situation and keep breathing at the same time as she passed in front of two soldiers. Deep exhaustion slumped their eyelids. Nora had to resist the urge to wave her hand wildly in front of their faces. It had to be a spell, it just had to be. That meant Velvet was not lying. That meant it had to be true—all of it! Nora felt like fainting again.

Careful, measured movements disarmed one of the men—a sword, a dagger, and a pistol. She planned to search his boot, but his dancing feet made it impossible. The soldier opened his mouth to speak, but only a strangled squeak emerged. His throat worked up and down as he swallowed a gulp of air, dazed, eyes returning to the task at hand.

"One, two, three, one, two, thee, one, two, three…now step together!" Nora hummed, briskly leaving the man and shaking her head. She ran past Miss Jenny. The woman's unseeing eyes traveled over Nora's face; not a single spark of recognition flickered in the lost gaze. Strange, Nora thought in passing, she was not dancing like the rest of them. Just watching, here but gone. Very strange, indeed.

Nora stumbled to the door, grabbed the knob, and flung it open. Night wind hit her in the face and blew the clinging white mists off her body. She had the odd feeling that the rest of her life —the parties, gossip, Charles and his cruelty, were falling away, disintegrating in the vapors behind her—and she, a scandalous bastard, more a story than a person—now ran headlong to her future.

Nora's boots touched the wet floor of the outside world; she sighed, her toe beating a silent tattoo on the grass. It was a few moments before realizing she was looking for him. Searching the moonlit night for the sight of his golden skin, and towering antlers glowing from that strange, interior light. Nothing greeted her eyes, save hills and fields rolling to darkness. Katie came up beside her, a small bundle of cloth in her hands.

"How on earth are we meant to know which way she went?" Nora asked, not taking her eyes off the dark woods bordering her vision.

When Katie brushed past her and began to sniff at the air, Nora threw up her hands. "Do you also have powers I am not aware of?"

"Maybe," said Katie lightly then dropped to her knees. She stood up after a moment not taking her eyes off the ground. Nora saw what the girl was looking at. Small imprints of a boot marked the mud in a clipped pattern leading west. To the dark forest and all the creatures waiting inside.

Nora swallowed a sudden burst of fear. She wondered if she was being stupid. Stupid and stubborn. *Was Katie right? Was it time to leave well enough alone?* Nora turned to the strange interior of the Blind Pig, looked at the swirling vapors wreathing through the legs of the dancing men, then at the warm rooms resting just at the top of the stairs. Longing made her spin back to the open night, one hand touched her midriff and she watched a small, shining ring of green circle the moon.

Katie took her hand, and fine droplets of sweat glittered on her face as she watched Nora's indecision through hopeful eyes. "My lady?"

"Oh, I just don't know," Nora moaned. "I really am so tired. The last thing in the world I want to do is go traipsing through these hills and forests in the middle of the night, freezing cold and scared."

"But?" There was open pleading in Katie's voice. "You're going to go anyway, aren't you?"

Nora searched the night, looking for him. "It's like I must! I feel something out there, it's calling to me."

"There's nothing out there, my lady, save animals, bandits, and highwaymen," said Katie.

"I know," Nora said.

Katie released an exhausted, foreboding sigh. "Very well, my lady, if you must, you must—though from my perspective you've done your part."

If she knew that for sure, Nora thought, *her voice would not be shaking...she feels it too.* Nora's eyes continued to scan the night. Four horses stood hobbled to a straight post near the back entrance of the tavern. They nipped lazily on the grass at their feet, licked the last of the rain from the air. One mare, taller than the rest, had a snowy-white mane and wore a pair of matching boots. A white star decorated her silver nose and giant almond eyes blinked at Nora through the darkness. Her silver coat was shiny, reflecting the soft moonlight, fresh from a recent brushing and new shoes.

"What a beautiful girl you are," Nora crooned. A grey, leather saddle, gold stitching and pocketed sides graced the mare. "Finders keepers," Nora whispered. The horse stuck her cold nose in Nora's palm then licked it.

Katie's shoulders slumped in defeat, muttering beneath her breath. She made her way to a brown gelding, a few hands smaller than Nora's silver mare. She put the few things she had gathered from the men in one of the empty packs swinging from the rough leather saddle, and mounted with a swinging grace, the horse nickered, seeming to barely register the weight of his new companion.

"He likes you, Katie," Nora said. "Perhaps he was Lord Bryon's horse, and currently thanking his horse gods for a rider who won't bow his knees."

"I hope you know what you are doing, my lady?" said Katie.

"I rarely do," Nora admitted. "At least your years of running through these woods and doing battle with your monstrous brothers will not have gone to waste—now is your moment to shine."

"It's too early in the morning, and I am far too tired for shining," said Katie.

"Enough of your doom and gloom, Katie. My house exploded, I don't know what happened to Spencer, Miss Croy, Laura, Philip, and the rest of the household." Nora ticked off the names of the missing persons on her right hand, her voice rising in passion. "My mother abandoned me in childhood, my father has never openly acknowledged me, Henry's brother—who consequently is also my lover—and all of London think I'm a whore. This baby will prove them right!" Nora paused her rant to gather the red silk train of her cloak; it bunched up like roses in her hands. She mounted gracefully and took the reins. "I am the daughter of kings, I have old, royal blood—I am young and strong. I can do anything. I am more than just the latest topic of the gossip rags, I can be anything I want. And I want magic!" Nora clicked her tongue. The horse understood her desires. A toss of her snowy mane and she started off at an easy canter. Katie said nothing and silence rode alongside them and stayed until the Blind Pig was the size of an apple on the horizon. They entered a dark, familiar forest—Nora had always thought it a terrible place, ever seeming stuffed full of murky, crawling things. The naked, winter branches of the trees stood tall and gangly like the ghosts of dead, old men.

Katie lifted her hand, yet it was she who first completed the symbol of the cross and kissed her fingers. *Amen. Bless us, oh Lord, in the hour of our death.*

The full moon floated in its glittering green ring like a swollen soap bubble, looking ready to pop at any moment. Nora thought that when it did, its glow would sink to the ground and the spongy earth would consume the light thrusting them all in darkness. Nora shuddered. The dark and all the hidden things would always be her biggest fear.

"What is it, my lady?" asked Katie looking over her shoulder apprehensively. Nora saw her hidden shudder when she reached for her dagger.

A horse and rider blasted from the distant tree line. The cape of the man rode the racing wind, flaring out behind him like batwings. Seconds later another rider shot from the same spot. Nora watched the two men gallop flat out toward the Blind Pig.

"It's the Devil, my lady. He is here to punish us for trespassing in his house." It appeared Katie meant to slide out of her saddle and fall to her knees.

Nora shot her a quelling look. "For heaven's sake, Katie! It's only Henry, though I do see the similarities—point of fact, I always have."

"Oh, thank God!" said Katie, relief flushing her pale cheeks a deep rose. "We are saved!" Katie clapped her hands together dropping the reins in her excitement.

Nora shook her head and breathed through her nose, as her mouth was otherwise occupied by gritting her teeth. "No! We have to get to Velvet. Henry swore to kill her. I won't let that happen, I just won't! Who's to say what that beast will do if he gets to her before us!"

Hot blood drained from Katie's cheeks, and she looked on the verge of tears. "You can't be serious, my lady. You really don't think the Duke would hurt her, do you?"

"I certainly hope not," Nora said derisively. "No way to know for sure. Come, let's away before they see us."

For a brief second Nora imagined Katie would abandon her, and the thought made her ill. The girl stared at the riders, naked longing in her eyes, leaning so far forward in her saddle Nora thought she would pitch herself over her gelding's chestnut head.

"You don't have to come, Katie," Nora said, cringing at the words. "Go back to them, tell them you woke to find me gone. Your search turned up nothing. Tell them whatever you want, then go see if Spencer and the rest of our people are still alive."

"Uh!" exclaimed Katie; she looked appalled. "I will not leave you, my lady. I have told you so," she scolded. Recollecting the reins and straightening in her seat—a pose that lifted her stubborn, pointed chin. "I promised you fifteen years ago I would not leave you until death, and if the blessed saints allow, not even after that. I don't care if she is a princess! You are the royalty I serve. You are all I have, my lady, and if you die I will follow close after."

Nora felt her eyes prickle at the impassioned speech. "Oh, Katie," she said and sighed.

Katie *humped* again, and her small feet dug in her horse's sides. She leaned over his neck and whispered something in his twitching ear. The horse neighed riotously kicking his restless feet. He had stayed tied for too long and was in the mood for a decent run.

Nora followed suit; she dug tense feet into the leather stirrups and begged her own beauty to gallop. The horse shot forward, and Nora felt the wind reach its long fingers beneath her hood to fling it back. It rushed through her hair, pulling tears from her eyes, painting a smile on her lips. No one had asked Nora what she wanted, not in many years—maybe not ever.

Tonight, no judging eyes trailed her movements, waiting for her to slip, hoping she would be herself so they could later whisper amongst themselves of all the ways she did not measure up. Here, in this untouched wilderness, only the moon witnessed her flight, and none but the wild wind would hear of it. For the first time, Nora felt free, and what was freedom if not the ambition of life? Succeed or fail, at that moment she was truly alive, and securely wrapped in the wonder of it.

A PROMISE TO A KING

Henry, Henry, why do you cry?
Is that a lie I see in your eye?

enry walked through the common room of the Blind Pig, his steps magnified by frequent contact with random debris littering the ground. Devon slumped on the leg of an overturned chair; the look on his face was one of such dumbstruck confusion that Henry felt the incredible need to belt out a hysterical laugh. He did not.

"If only we had a caricaturist to capture the grandness of this tableau," said Devon. "Most incredible thing I've ever seen." Though his tone was light, his voice sounded uneasy.

Henry felt the mood as he surveyed the room. A couple men lay on each other beneath a toppled whist table. Their faces were puffy, discolored by drunkenness perhaps, yet Henry had seen many a drunken soldier, and these men did not carry the telltale signs. Their cheeks were deathly pale instead of rouged by an elevated blood alcohol content, no loud snores rocked their slumbering frames, they were silent, motionless as dead men.

To his left, a woman lay face down on the keys of a grand piano. Still locked in their last note, her fingers twisted in strange, opposing angles. A peacock feather rested beside her mouth and moved up and down on the waves of her shallow breaths. Yet, it was the center of the room where the real attraction took place. Four couples held each other, revolving in waltzing circles, moving to music only they could hear. One man rested his heavy head on his partner's shoulder. Bent at the waist he swayed back and forth, teetering on the verge of a bad fall; still another lay asleep on the chest of his waltzing companion, a long stream of clear drool hanging from his slack mouth. Henry rubbed his tired, stinging eyes hoping the vision would alter when he reopened them. It did not.

Devon stood and moved languidly to the nearest couple. He tapped the leading dragoon on his quivering shoulder, and the man twitched like a spooked fawn. His partner, Sir Bryon, crumpled. His knees buckled and his face hit the floor with a splat.

"So sorry, old chap," said Devon tossing a bemused glance at the felled man. "May I cut in?" He did not wait for a reply, only stepped up, took the smaller Sir Bronn in his arms, and spun him full circle around the room. "What do you suppose is wrong with them?" Devon called out. Bloodless as a dead man, his dancing partner swayed dangerously. His head rolled back, open eyes showing only their whites. Henry had no answer, but the corner of his mouth twitched as Devon let go of the weary Sir Bronn. The dazed man spun one last time on his own, then folded bonelessly, landing on a pile of waiting cushions.

"Enough," said Henry when Devon went in search of a fresh partner. His voice came out harsher than intended, the sound it made shocked and unsettled him. He was not at all himself, hunger and a bone-weariness gnawed at his achy limbs, and he surmised if given the chance he could sleep until the new moon. There had been no sleep for him in the Tower. Henry thought it possible the cold chill of those old stone walls would never leave the marrow of his bones. The food was an abomination, he had eaten nothing but bare scraps for days. The nights moved in suspended animation, rolling out dreams from which he had no reprieve. It was of no matter. Henry knew any food he tried to eat would curdle or turn to sawdust in his mouth. The pervading chill of the Tower was nothing compared to ice coating his soul. He had spent every moment of his captivity in hideous worry for the small waif of a girl, whose golden features refused to leave his mind.

Devon strolled casually to a table which had remained standing during the impromptu ball. On it sat a crystal goblet of half-drunk wine, wearing a smear of lipstick on the rim of the glass. Beside it, a plate holding a loaf of bread, a few cakes, a wedge of cheese, and a small pot of strawberry jam. Devon reached for the clump of bread, tossed the sweaty block of cheese in his mouth then spoke over it. "Should we knock the rest over? Seems a bit cruel to leave them in this state."

Henry looked up at the two rooms atop the stairs. "No time," he called over his shoulder. "George didn't trust my word, he's known me for too long. He's a wily old fellow regardless of his mental state. There will be others, many others hunting her tonight. They'll kill anything in their path."

"Good gods! What did you tell him?" Devon asked over another bite then tossed Henry a large cut of bread. Henry looked up in time to catch it absently and sunk his teeth into the fluffy loaf. He chewed it before he answered and went to search out a mug of ale or a bottle of wine. Really, anything alcoholic at this point would suit him like ambrosia. He rubbed his knuckles hard over his forehead and absently brushed the dark curls to the side. He found a jug of warm ale and drank straight from the wide mouth, not bothering with a mug. His throat clenched tight; the *thunk* of ale and bread hitting his empty stomach sickened him. "I told him I would do exactly as he would wish," said Henry finally and wiped his mouth on the back of his hand. "I did not lie. He would never put this girl to death, were he in full command of his faculties. During my audience, he took a piss in a potted plant and spat on his prime minister." Henry paused to firmly squeeze the bridge of his nose. "It was a humbling sight. If the power of the mind thus turned on its user, can reduce even a king to such… what hope is there for us mortal men?"

Devon shrugged. "I piss in potted plants all the time."

Henry ignored this, swallowed another mouthful of ale, grimaced, and drank again. "Said he dreamed of the children coming through his window at night, they kill him in his sleep, he says, then eat his eyes and take his throne."

"I like to do it in ballrooms," continued Devon undaunted. "Those stuffy places always bring on the urge to relieve oneself."

"I can't understand it!" Henry continued, speaking over Devon's voice. "They have no claim to his throne. Unless Velvet and her brother amass a huge amount of finance and raise a large army, they don't have a prayer of reclaiming what France stole from them."

"His fear is born of his sickness," said Devon seriously. "Nothing else."

"You may be right at that," Henry agreed, then turned away from the macabre scene of the common room and took the stairs two at a time. In Velvet's room he found the gutted candle, then lifted her discarded gown. "It's cold." He heard the hitch in his voice and wondered when he had begun to care, when exactly it was that the thought of her pushed out all else.

Past the cloying smell of the gown, the faint scent of Velvet lingered. He brought the cloth to his face, and each inhale added further sustenance to his imagination, feeding the vision he had of her lying in a ditch somewhere, her golden hair bloody, her fighting spirit gone.

"Is she taken?" asked Devon. "Nora, Katie?"

Henry nodded his head, sickening fear congealing in his gut like lard. "Gone."

Devon groaned and gave the room a needy look. "Good-bye, sweet bed." He brought his hand to his mouth, kissed it, then tossed the kiss aloft. "Farewell, warm bath, sweet *adieu*, roaring fire. None of you will be my companions tonight. Hello, cold, hunger, and pain...only a few moments more, my loves, and I will be in your arms again."

"You are a true poet," Henry said sardonically.

Devon gave a self-satisfied snort. "Don't I know it. Alas, I have squandered my endless talents in battle and blood."

"You are one of the best swordsmen I have ever met."

"Yes," said Devon and scratched his smooth chin in thought. "One of my few talents not going to waste." He faced the cold ashes, kicking morosely at a shard of coal. "Henry, I need you to know—if it is in my power, I do not mean to let her die."

"Nor I," said Henry. He scrubbed his hands through his hair, shifting to the small table near the window. A hairbrush lay discarded beside a gas lamp. Deep chips marred the wooden handle and twined through its few remaining bristles were a few strands of honey-blonde hair. Someone turned the covers of the bed down, but the pillows and sheets were indent free. Protocol told Henry to search the property for signs, any evidence of force or struggle. His gut told him she left of her own accord. After the troops he had seen marshaling at Buckingham Palace, he knew her quest could only conclude in violent death.

"I wrote to them the day before we left the place," said Devon.

Henry set the brush back down beside the lamp and turned in time to see a wash of guilt drench his friend's classical features. "I meant no harm, Henry, please understand." Devon took a few steps back, telling Henry more than he needed to know.

"You told them I swore to kill Velvet," said Henry. It was not a question.

Devon retreated to the doorway, holding out his hands before him in surrender. "It had been days with no word. If you did indeed swear to kill her, I wanted to give them a running start."

"You thought they broke me." Another statement. Henry felt unreasonable anger surge. Devon's milky skin went a few shades lighter. Suddenly, Henry felt the anger flow out of him quickly as it had come, the sudden loss of its strength slumped his shoulders. "I understand," he said. He heard his voice again, this time low and shaken. He did. Truly, the thought of seeing fear in Velvet's starry blue eyes sickened him. He had promised to protect her, promised to find her brother, and had thus far failed on all accounts. There was a pull in his soul, dragging him toward her— he felt bewitched —like every shadow in the night called his name, as if instinct alone would take him to the place where she was. Gritting his teeth, he tampered down the surge of hope in his heart—chances were, she was already dead.

12

VOLUNTARY CAPTURE

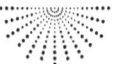

...but of course, the robin knows best, for he built the...oops—I shan't tell the rest. Put the three little somethings in it—I'm afraid I shall tell it any minute!

*H*umans were the worst creatures in existence! Velvet came to this unshakeable conclusion while falling and screaming. She had taken one blind step—and that was that—she had tumbled right off the edge of a rocky embankment. Her body hung weightless in the air for a split second before it crashed to the earth. A small patch of rocks near an outcropping of mossy ivy broke her fall. Her left leg landed in a puddle, and her backside followed, and she felt wet mud slowly crawl into her boot and work its cold, slimy self between her toes. A flock of chattering birds fluttered above her head, flapping little black wings capped by crimson and scarlet. Velvet lay unmoving, her spine screamed, and her backside smarted something awful. Sticky sap clogged her nostrils and she could taste gritty earth on her tongue.

Whispers of air ghosted over her cheeks, chapped by the ice-tipped wind, and coated in fresh, stinging scratches. Another bruise on her forehead, which Velvet suspected grew by the moment, throbbed like a heartbeat in her right eye.

Velvet mused that she had spent her life devoted to the acceptance of the things she could not change. She had no control over her parents' death, no ability whatsoever to alter the course of the dreadful, magical years following it. She did not remember the first changing, due perchance to her youth, but more likely to the overwhelming fear of the moment in which it had transpired. From one day to the next she saw the world through a different set of eyes, so foreign to everything she knew. The first time she spread her silky wings and flew in an open blue sky, all traces of fear disappeared from her mind, the rippling memories of childhood had gone. There was only breath, life, and flying, always flying. All of that had come to an abrupt, screeching halt when the second changing took place. The moment her tiny, bird bones snapped, and some punishing force ripped her beautiful feathers from her skin, Velvet knew nothing would ever be the same. And why should it? She had lost everything she was, not once but twice. Two families, two lives.

Velvet felt an unwelcome surge of self-pity rise in her throat. *Why me?* was the question she wanted to scream at the sky—would have if she had the strength. The wind rose to an eerie whine and black chunks of night sky showed through the swishing leaves of the closely linked trees. The pale light of the moon covered the blackness in a transparent veil, tinting it a deep, lucent green. Busy, familiar scents tickled her nose and something furry skittered across her bare ankle. She twitched but felt no real alarm. It was entirely her fault for being in the poor animal's way, lying here in the muck—just where she did not belong.

Velvet well knew the notion of finding her brother and actually doing it were two separate things. She anticipated obstacles, hell, expected them, but she had not prepared for being human. Did not know how bad her legs would hurt after a five-mile hike, or how blue and wooden your limbs and digits were when frozen solid. Her cloak and the soft dressing gown may as well be pure air, for all the warmth they offered. Wracking shivers evolved into fierce cramps about three miles ago; now, Velvet felt numb. Empty.

Finished. It was futile to expect she could find Louis in her condition. She had no idea how to hunt with her two clumsy hands or run on the obnoxiously tiny feet she found herself fated to walk on.

Standing up took every ounce of determination she had left in her worn-out soul. London was her goal; if she had any notion where on earth she was, she might determine where to go. As it was, Velvet looked around her and saw nothing more than dark shapes. Rippling shadows cut out and stuck to the sinister sky swaying in concentric circles. Velvet sat up and wiped the mud from her cheeks as best she could. Little rocks in the mud grated over the scratches, stinging them miserably.

Just when she collected enough composure to scramble to her feet she heard the crisp clip-clop of hooves and deep, low voices of men too close for comfort. The reek of tobacco smoke interlaced with gunpowder infused the air. Velvet dropped to her knees, quickly ducking behind the outcropping of rock, which had been her downfall. She put a hand over her mouth to stifle her erratic breaths, mentally commanding her nerves not to quiver.

The muffled voices grew louder. Closer. Velvet could see white threads of tobacco smoke weaving through the night air. A small squeak shoved her body against the rocks, and she tried desperately to sink into a patch of soggy moss hidden behind a waterfall of vines. Cold drops of water dripped off the tips of the heart-shaped ivy leaves and rolled down her stinging cheeks.

"The skies fillin' and looking to belch," a deep voice called out, a strong accent adding a layered timber to the words. "We'll make camp here. Just before the bridge. It's the only open area in this godforsaken forest. We have a view of the crossroads. Give us plenty of time to see a threat riding in."

"Or a sweet country lass out for a stroll."

Velvet closed her eyes and prayed to all the goddesses she knew for invisibility. She did not know what happened to girls who wandered into the darkest places of the forest in the middle of the night, but knew she had no desire to find out.

"A lass out on a night like this, desires only sin," the accented voice replied. "Makes it less fun when they want it."

Velvet realized the jerky spurts of conversation were taking place just above her head now; she thought she would go mad from the suspense. From her vantage point, all she could see were a few pairs of mud-caked boots and shoeless hooves. A jagged crack decorated one of the restless hooves, and it stamped a half moon of blood on the sodden road. Yellow pus oozed from a huge abscess at the base of the heel and Velvet fingered the hilt of her dagger. For a brief, happy moment she imagined giving its owner's foot a good stab, see how he liked it when the poisonous fire of infection attacked his blood.

"I gotta go splash my boots," the first voice said. Something thumped when he dismounted, and the rocky wall shivered at her back. A few bits of dust sprinkled her face. Velvet inhaled the tiny motes up her nose. The itch was instant and incredible. It sent a sharp spark of distress to her brain. There was no help for it. Velvet knew she was going to sneeze. She held it in until her eyes rolled in their throbbing sockets, and her chest expanded.

The man with the full bladder walked down the south edge of the small embankment, stopping a few feet from her hiding place. Sizzling tears trickled from her wide eyes, and her nose burned like she had snorted hot ash. One hand pinched her nostrils until the tips of her thumb and forefinger turned white. Lips miming a silent prayer, Velvet pressed her other hand against her mouth hard enough to leave a bruise. It was going to happen now...

The man fiddled with his belt for a second, then his black-and-red striped trousers fell in a puddle at his feet. He was the largest man Velvet had ever seen. If she was not about to sneeze, she might have screamed.

The violet light of the moon cast his dark skin in harsh relief, showing each scar and bulge. Thick black hair ran from beneath the tail of his linen shirt to his swollen vein-streaked ankles like a fur pelt. His knees bulged under the weight of his derriere and sagging paunch. They bowed badly and stuck out in all directions, swollen and fat as cannonballs. A great heaving cough erupted before the man spat on the ground. Grunting loudly, he bent forward at the waist, violating each deep place in Velvet's imagination—then broke wind with a force that rippled his thighs;

it rustled the hairy surface of his skin and howled like a dirty tornado. The event ended in a wet splat that bubbled between his clenched cheeks. Huffing a relieved sigh, the man relaxed his seat, leaned his head back, and groaned at the moon. A stream of liquid splashed the dirt.

Velvet knew she could not fight it anymore. Her small body heaved, and her cold toes curled. She gritted her teeth violently and used all her strength to plug her nose. Alas, it was to no avail. The sneeze shot out of her. The sound was monstrous—the dying squawk of a crow mixed with the mating call of a rooster. Ivy parted around her and she pitched forward, another strangled squeak breaking free of her sealed lips.

The stream of liquid flowing from the man in rapid spurts cut off like a squelched faucet. Velvet shut out the voices overhead and tried to focus her eyes. It was a useless enterprise. After being nocturnal for nearly eight years, her human sight amounted to little more than glorified blindness. Silently she drew the dancing dragoon's dagger from her boot and stepped into a pale shaft of moonlight.

She held the naked blade at a right angle, crisscrossing her heart. *More butterfly than assassin,* she mused, shoving away a tinge of fear. The man rose to his full height, considerable enough to make Velvet wonder if she had finally encountered a mythical British giant after all this time. Pebbles shifted soundlessly under her leather soles, wind-washed her shadow—it blew away her scent.

Velvet saw a muscle in his wrist twitch a second before he unsheathed his sword. She sprang up behind him and straddled his massive waist while her arms wrapped around his neck. The smell of tobacco laced by sulfur and urine assaulted her senses, but she pressed her lips to the tepid air near his jaw, and the knife to his throat.

"Make a sound and I will kill you," Velvet whispered. Her voice sounded strangely flat to her own ears, heavy, breathless.

The man's massive shoulders slumped. He relinquished his cutlass, hands going up in the age-old sign of surrender. Velvet saw he wore a red cloth stitched in gold; it covered his weave of black braids, golden beads, bells, and long, tasseled cords that streamed haphazardly down his broad back. Bells sang when the wind swished through the mass and tossed each strand that sprouted from his head, thick and wiry as horsehair.

"Midnight Madonna," he rumbled. A wet smile jiggled his bottom lip. "You have me at a disadvantage." He gestured toward the puddle of his pants, using the divot in his chin to point the way. "I stand unable to defend myself. 'Tis a great comfort to know my death is not tonight— otherwise I would be sore afraid."

"Why are you so sure?" she hissed.

"I am the great Alfonso. The great Alfonso is not fated to die with his nether parts swinging in the wind. Come now…" His chilling smile slithered away, his voice turned husky, cajoling. "I have many bargaining chips, you must want something."

"I want nothing from you. Only to be left alone," Velvet whispered.

"Young lady. You attacked me," returned Alfonso in a condescending tone, like attacking him had been the height of stupidity. He tipped his head slightly, glancing over his shoulder, trying to get a decent look at her face. Velvet drew her head back into shadow. Silence deepened into a pulsing ring, not a flicker of movement disturbed their surroundings, save a faint glow lacing the edges of her vision in crystal moonlight.

Velvet gripped the handle of the knife, unconsciously digging the blade deeper. She hated death, yet she had taken many lives since the changing—each was felt like a dark stain on her soul, a stain she feared would never wash out. "I attacked you," Velvet said, lowering her voice to its deepest reach. "Because I don't like being the one at a disadvantage."

"It was unfortunate timing for such a tremendous sneeze," agreed Alfonso. His mouth twisted in a wry smile and he glanced at his raised hand. "Good hiding place though, I would have walked right past you."

"You did," she said.

A deep chuckle issued from Alfonso's chest. "Remove your knife, kindly allow me to lift my trousers, and I give you my word, I will leave you unmolested."

"The word of the scoundrel is meaningless," Velvet said. "Everyone knows that."

"What makes you think I'm a scoundrel? Ah, you heard us on the road. Well…" He coughed, a deep racking sound then spat something dark on the ground. "I *am* a scoundrel."

Velvet saw pride further swell his chest, as if the *nom du plomb* was his life's goal. It was unlikely he would let her go without a fight. Based on his size and her body's current state of exhausted affairs, it was a fight she would lose. Cold made her clumsy—her trip off the embankment had proved that—she was hungry and wanted nothing more than a warm, safe ride to London.

"I am going to move my knife," Velvet whispered, forcing her unsteady nerves to remain calm. "I want you to keep your hands where they are."

Velvet saw a twinkle flash in the creased corner of Alfonso's eye, but he acquiesced. A light dew of sweat broke out at the base of her spine, and she twitched her head but did not wipe it away. Instead, she carefully removed the knife from between the rolls of Alfonso's neck and stepped back. Quickly, she lowered the blue hood to cover her face.

"Alright," she said.

Alfonso let his hands fall in a dramatic gesture, then he put them on his broad hips and turned around. Velvet had never seen a naked man before, the shock of her first time was her downfall. Her mouth fell open, her eyes locked on his face while her mind scrambled to collect her scattered thoughts. Alfonso just stood there for a second, naked from the waist down, brow furrowed, regarding her curiously from a pair of thickly lashed kohl-lined eyes, dilated pupils black as tar.

Diamond studded rings pierced both his chunky nostrils; the big rocks winked cheekily in the night light. More giant hoops threaded through his earlobes, and a fat, gold chain straddled his neck tight as a slave collar. Velvet could feel the dumbstruck expression freezing her face. The man was obviously a gypsy, his white linen shirt, leather jerkin, and flashy jewelry spoke to his bloodlines. She was not sure how to feel about this; she had a strange urge to run into his arms and beg him to take her home, then realized she had no home. No people; she may long for the sight of his people, but to him, she was just another pale girl in a country full of them.

Bending to retrieve his pants, he grunted slightly and with slow, practiced movements buckled his belt. He moved his gut and settled the leather band around his waist, then took his time in adjusting his jerkin and fluffing the ruffled trim falling from the cuffs of his shirt. All the while Velvet felt his eyes boring deep into her own. It was disconcerting, to say the least. She was glad when his pants finally covered what she had not cared to see.

Recovering some sense, she opened her mouth to speak. Alfonso's sharp whistle cut her off as it pierced the air like the cry of a lark. Every muscle in Velvet's body tensed, her hand clenching on the dagger's hilt.

The wind blew across her face carrying scents of wet earth and sap-soaked pine. Beneath the forest's fragrant perfume, an underlying taint of sweat and horseflesh permeated the air. The smells told her the men were close, mere seconds before she saw murky shapes pour from the shadows. Velvet swallowed a lump in her throat, one of frustrated resignations. More than a dozen men in white or red fringed shirts—covered by dark leather jerkins— dotted the empty spaces between the closely knit trees. Moonlight bounced off their bare blades and stroked their faces in shades of blue-black, illuminating dozens of laughing eyes.

Alfonso brought his hands in front of his paunch, folded the fingers together, and swiftly cracked his knuckles. More men stepped through the curtain of trees. Velvet heard the snapping of twigs, running alongside the splat of boots meeting the waterlogged ground. She thought about going for her emerald but decided to wait until a more opportune time; it took serious energy to cast it last time and she was not sure how much more she had left to give. It would not do to reach some and not others, or saints forbid, miss altogether. Velvet promised the moon which looked down at her from its vantage of safety that she would not go down without a fight.

"You gave me your word, you would let me go," Velvet said trying to add a touch of command to her tone.

Alfonso rocked back on his heels and laughed, showing every sign of enjoying himself immensely. "And you told me that the word of a scoundrel was meaningless."

"Ah!" Velvet said, trying not to show her nerves. "And you mean to prove me right…" She gave a small curtsy. "How kind of you, sir."

Alfonso clapped his hands and laughed, a deep belly laugh that rocked his gigantic frame. "You have made my day, my Midnight Madonna." He swept into a low bow, graceful somehow, not despite his size, but due to it. The bells in his hair sang when he moved, whipping braided ropes—studded by colorful beads—across his face.

Men advanced on all sides, their accelerated breaths ragged and close. Very close. Velvet drew the cloak tighter around her body; she could not step back—there was nowhere to go. The reality of the situation in which she found herself held limited options and even fewer outcomes. She squared her shoulders, determined to be prepared for whichever one should come.

Alfonso walked a slow circle around her and stopped behind her back; she felt the sting of his black gaze raise the hairs on her neck and commanded her body to stay still. The rainy air clung to her skin. In it, she could smell her own fear, hear the thump of her heart, doom-filled as a war drum.

"What is such a beauty doing alone this blustery night?" asked Alfonso. Velvet felt his breath rustle a curl dangling against her ear, and the pinnacle of his rotund belly brushed the base of her spine.

"I'm lost," Velvet said, telling herself to stick to the truth as best she could. The truth was always simple—she had no experience of such things yet feared for her it would be dangerously easy to lose the plot of a lie. "I need to find my brother."

"A quest!" cried Alfonso. "I do love a good quest."

"Do you?" Velvet whispered and spun to face him. Alfonso raised his brows in surprise, retreating a step. His lips were so red, Velvet thought they looked rouged. They moved widely when he spoke showing her a grill of gold.

"Love it like a hot fire or a warm woman," he confirmed. A nod of his dark head set bells in the braids singing again. "Quests usually end in a pot of gold. The great Alfonso loves nothing more than gold."

"I have gold," Velvet said, keeping her eyes buried in his. Peripheral vision trained on his feet and hands, she watched for the slightest movement—watched and listened—listened to the sounds of the men surrounding her; a cough, a snapping twig, a loud exhalation of breath. Velvet sensed their restlessness, it told her she was running out of time. She lifted her chin and nearly bit her tongue to keep the tremble from her voice. "Escort me to London and I will give it to you. All of it. Every single piece of gold I have."

Alfonso's brow wrinkled, and Velvet thought she saw a flash of interest in his eyes. "Do you think I'm lying?" she asked when the silence had gone on too long.

Alfonso tossed his dark head. "Shockingly, I do not." A huge blast of wind whizzed past, its freezing fingers tossing back Velvet's hood. Her golden hair flew free of its cloth binding. Acting on instinct only, Velvet dropped the dagger as her hands darted to retrieve the hood. It was too late.

She saw recognition spark in Alfonso's keen eyes as he sucked in a breath then laughed again. This time it was a hearty guffaw which shook his belly, forcing him to hold it in place. "Well, well…" he murmured. "What do we have here?" He whistled through his teeth, rocking back on his heels. "You are the missing daughter of Marie Antoinette!" he proclaimed, fairly licking his lips in pleasure. "Redcoats plastered that pretty face of yours all over London. Offering five thousand pounds sterling for you, they are. Dead or alive."

Velvet stood completely still. She could feel each of her senses, pulsing and vibrating in a high alert as she waited for his next words to fall.

"You, my Midnight Madonna, are worth a fortune." A look of pure animal instinct touched his face. He buried it in another lewd chuckle uttered through a wet-lipped smile. "Strange to be worth something after death…makes you special."

Special was not the word Velvet would use, at least not in that context. She thought of telling him so then decided against it. She needed to escape, not engage.

"What princess?" a new voice hollered. "What are you talking about? Get off me! Let me see!"

Velvet instantly recognized the high, ringing voice. Her heart plummeted to the depths of her gut. She would have known those cool, cultured tones anywhere.

"Take your bloody hands off me! *Let me go!*" A thump proceeded a low growl, then Nora screamed.

Velvet drew in her breath. "Don't touch her!"

Alfonso shrugged and wiggled his fingers. "My hands are over here, princess."

"If you hurt her, I will kill you," Velvet hissed, meaning it. She heard stories of what gypsies did to Gadje maidens. Katie would never leave her lady—that much she knew as fact, which meant this monster had them both. Velvet's mind raced through a short list of impossible options. Each scenario played out before her in hyper-color and in acute disaster.

"Providence smiles on the great Alfonso today," he said, ripping her from her reverie.

"Why, sir?" she asked, fearing she had no desire to know the answer.

"Why? What a question! Many reasons, Midnight Madonna. First, you did not slit my throat," he said and gave a mock bow. "For which I am most grateful. Second, fate has allowed me to keep my word and retain my honor this night, however jaded it may be."

Two long braids slid free of his bandanna, the wind tugged them here and there. Chunky gold and silver rings sat on each of his fingers. His flesh bulged on either side of the beveled bands, giving Velvet the distinct impression of sweaty sausages. "You see," he continued. "I can leave you unmolested." He paused his speech, tugging on the wandering braid, which set bells to ringing. "I will give you over to our glorious King." Alfonso spat on the ground after he said the last word. "If I leave you in his loving care, two birds, one stone. I have done a great service for my country. The King will place a generous reward in my worthy hands…and you? Well, that is your own fate, is it not?"

Velvet rallied, and fists clenched she took a punishing step forward. "You are a gypsy, you know the story of the stolen princess. It was Queenie who raised me." Velvet spoke the word hoping he would know the name, praying the invocation of it would carry its own warning. "She gave me her magic. Beware I do not use it on you."

Alfonso fingered the braid in his hand and searched her face with a penetrating glare. Thick brows drew together over his hooded eyes as he rocked back and forth on his heels for a long time. *Keep talking,* she thought. *Press your advantage. What advantage?* her mind argued. Queenie was dead, her friends captured, her brother lost, her dark rescuer intent on her destruction once again. Velvet felt like surrendering…wanted nothing more than to throw herself on the ground and howl her frustrated mystery at the smoky moon.

She did neither of those things. She would not risk the lives of the two girls who saved hers. Alfonso placed a hand on her shoulder. She wanted to cringe and cower away; she wanted to scream, bite, and put up a gigantic fight. Again, she did not. In a show of steely determination she did not feel, Velvet gritted her teeth and held her ground.

"Queenie, you say? Hmmm?" A bar of moonlight cut across the gypsy's face. It swept over his smile, highlighting the flecks of gold in his front teeth, glinting off his nose rings. "Powerful woman, but a dead one," continued Alfonso. "If the stories are true, and I have learned that in these times they usually are." He resumed walking. "We do not speak of the dead as it hinders their travel into the next world."

"I can speak of her," Velvet breathed, positive she spoke the truth. "She is not dead to me. A little thing like death would never prevent Queenie from protecting me." A deep emotion resounded in her voice as Velvet felt thoughts of Queenie give her strength. "I am not lying," she told him. "In fact, I do not think I know how to lie. Let me on my way and no harm will come to you and your men."

The forest hooted out its normal evening songs, but the shifting sounds made by the surrounding men died. Abruptly his warm fingers closed around her chin and snapped her head to her left. A shock of pain lanced down her neck; she hissed through her teeth and glared at him.

"You have the look of a murderous fairy," said Alfonso. She had never in her life felt more like the prey than she did at that moment. She may have lives on her conscience, but her tally was nothing in comparison to this man's. Each of her thrumming senses told her she stood in the presence of a real killer.

Velvet slapped his hand away, then scrubbed the wet left from his touch off her chin. "I am many things, but I am not a fairy. If you will not release me, I beg you...take me to London, I swear I will give you every ounce of Queenie's gold." She straightened her shoulders, taking a single step away from the hot wash of his breath. "You know the stories? Gold from Marie Antoinette, my mother," Velvet finished. This was the first time she said the word aloud in many years— *mother*— the sound of it made her want to cry and howl at the moon again, so she pushed it away. Another time, another day, she would sit, think, and cry until her waterworks took the edge off the pain. But not now. Now she had to survive.

"I swear to the moon goddess, offer my pledge to the riders of death, I will give you three times the King's ransom. One for myself and twice again for the two English women you hold captive."

Alfonso's smile never wavered. "Friends of yours I assume?"

Velvet gave a small, nearly imperceptible nod of her chin. "They are innocent in all of this. Please let them go."

He pretended to consider this for a moment, more to mock her, Velvet assumed, than to engage in any real thought. "If I take this gold, and your devil's deal, you will still die. The promise of your blood sweetens the air, many men thirst for it tonight." He wiggled his eyebrows sardonically, bells jangled out a toxic song. "I fear the others you encounter will not be so kind and fair as I."

This gypsy had no animal. Velvet fancied if he did it was one long ago driven to extinction. A minotaur perchance, or an old woolly mammoth. "My fate will be my own," she said. "I trust leaving me to it will not lose you any sleep." Velvet shuffled her feet restlessly, waiting to grab the lapels of his jerkin and shake a promise from him. "Do we have a deal, sir?"

Alfonso dropped his eyes to inspect her small frame, hidden in the thick folds of the sky-blue cloak, dusty grey in the night light. "We shall see. I do not wish to stand here for the rest of the night bantering with an angel, no matter how alluring. Come with me." He held out a hand. "As it is, you have no choice. Come with me, ward of Queenie, French devil, and bringer of blood. Walk with me now, I will take you to our camp, then we will see what is to be done."

Velvet closed her eyes and slowly exhaled. She had no choice. This was the path, it was foggy and twisted off in strange places, but it was the one her feet were on. Another breath is what it took to gather her resolve and nod an affirmative. "Thank you, sir," she said firmly. "I will owe you."

"According to your promise, Midnight Madonna, you owe me quite a lot."

"Then it is to your fortune that I never break my promises," Velvet replied. "It creates a terrible *qi* that follows one, provoking great harm." She pushed her wet hair out of her face as a particularly dark cloud burst overhead, and freezing rain crashed down in renewed vigor.

Sheets washed over Alfonso's face. He let out a garbled curse. "Come now," he barked, holding out his giant hand. "If you force me to ask a third time, I will not be so kind."

Velvet gave his proffered hand a disdainful look but nodded mutely. Together, they made their way with sloshing steps up the soggy embankment while she studied his profile. His cheeks round, rouged, and shiny as ripe apples obscured nearly all other features, save the lips. Alfonso licked them giving her a sidelong inspection of his own. "Do you really have Queenie's legendary gold?" he queried in blunt curiosity.

Velvet raised her chin in a show of bravery she did not feel. "Yes. I really do. I hid it, in a fantastic spot mind," she said. "Don't think you can kill me and find it yourself because you can't. It is under an enchantment," she said, and realized much to her chagrin that she could lie, albeit badly. Velvet took a panting breath and met his amused eyes. "I am telling the truth, it will shrink your manhood." Velvet held up a pinky finger to show him exactly what size it would shrink to. She fingered the emerald at the base of her throat wondering if the old stone even had such a curse in it. The threat was classic Queenie, but Velvet felt Queenie would not mind if she borrowed it once or twice.

Her hand fell away from the emerald, a wash of heat spread through her skin, pulsing over her collarbone before climbing up her face, and Velvet wondered if she had it in her to do such a dastardly thing. She listened to the erratic beats of her heart and decided she probably did. Her teeth sunk into her lower lip while she concentrated on each footfall. It would do none of them any good if she took an additional face-plant in the mud.

After an endless moment of stumbling, they reached the base of the ridge. Velvet saw two caravans set against the backdrop of a moonlit night. Bright splashes of color decorated the wheels and walls, groups of hobbled horses wore bells on their saddles and chains in their hair. The familiar blues and yellows made nostalgia twist in her chest; absently she lifted a hand to rub it away. Two small campsites hosted baby fires that sent ribbons of smoke in the air. Above the camp a pocket opened in the sky and swallowed the moon, the night fell to blackness absent its goddess.

"Take your hand off me, you blasted brute!" Velvet heard Nora shout and spun around in time to see her deliver a swift kick to her attacker's booted shins. The man lifted his hand aloft intending to return her attack with a casual backhand.

Alfonso whistled a single piercing note, and the man froze. Nora took the opportunity as a godsend. She slammed her hands into the gypsy's chest and gave him a push for all she was worth. The man's mouth went wide, and he stumbled. His heel caught a loose stone; it skillfully tripped him, and he landed on his backside. The sound of tearing cloth rent the air as the seam in his pants split. Nora barked out an unhappy laugh, determinedly shaking muck from the hem of her gown.

"It serves you right for being so awful." She spared the fallen man a withering look then rushed at Velvet. Velvet let go of Alfonso's arm just in time to catch the fragrant bundle that nearly bowled her over. Katie struggled out of her own captor's hold—who let her go with little fight—and she fell to her knees beside them.

Grasping Katie's hand and clinging to her remaining air, Velvet held Nora tightly while the girl continued to scream in an octave only dogs and gods could hear. Velvet did not mind, point of fact —it was wonderful. Tears scalded her lashes and her nose burned from the pressure of not crying them. "Nora, what are you doing here? I left you safe! Why would you follow me?"

"Oh, don't be absurd. I am not going to just let you run off on your own, don't you know anything by now?" Nora's hair tumbled into her eyes and stuck to her teary cheeks; Velvet brushed it away and looked into her friend's glittering gaze. Giant teardrops magnified her pupils and her lips were deathly pale, the thin line quivering under the force of her emotions.

"You are the bravest soul in the world," Velvet whispered.

"Said the pot to the kettle," murmured Katie. Impulsively, Velvet kissed her cheek.

"An exceedingly touching reunion, if you all are quite finished...?" Alfonso coughed up a wad of mucus and spat it out violently.

It hit the ground near Nora's feet; she hissed and shrank away from the snot. "We wouldn't expect you to understand," she said through clenched teeth. "I'm sure there isn't a soul in the world who would greet you in happiness."

Alfonso made a ticking sound, tongue in cheek, before he took Velvet's elbow in his big grip. "The great Alfonso has many who love him. Many who call his name and stare at the sunrise awaiting his arrival."

"I don't see how that is possible since you are the most horrid man I have ever had the misfortune to meet," snapped Nora. "You practically stole the horses out from under me! You have brutalized me...and..." Nora's words fell away, and her eyes went wide as realization's strike cut her off mid-sentence. She clapped a hand over her mouth. "He recognized you."

Velvet nodded an affirmative.

"It would be hard not to," acknowledged Alfonso. "If it was not

I, it would have been another man. The bounty on the head of the princess states 'alive or',"—he let his voice hang for effect—"'dead.' Many others would have killed first and consulted the spirits later."

"I am only breathing because I held a knife to your neck, then offered you a king's ransom in gold," Velvet said.

"Do not belittle your charms, Midnight Madonna," replied Alfonso. "It was your beauty which stayed my sword. I dislike destroying beauty." He nodded his head as if he agreed with the voices in it. "Then it was the gold." Velvet saw a quick flash of golden teeth. The grip on her elbow tightened until she could feel her small bones grind together.

"Please unhand me, sir, I am more than capable of walking on my own." That was not why he was holding her and they both knew it; still, she felt it needed saying, if not for him then for her quaking knees.

"What do you plan on doing with us?" demanded Nora, angry strokes of her hand pushing hair and rain out of her face. Velvet flexed the fingers of her right hand, slowly going numb as Alfonso's monster hand cut off the blood flow from her heart to pulse. "I too am a princess," continued Nora. "There is no bounty on my head. My father will kill you if you harm me."

"So you have informed my men, repeatedly I am told," said Alfonso. "Earlier I felt inclined not to believe you, now...? Now, I am not so sure."

"I do not lie," said Nora, more miffed than defensive. "My father will—"

"Kill me," Alfonso released a fake yawn and made a great show of covering his mouth. "I know, I know. I have received many death threats tonight, it has not put me in the best humor. I need a long drink in a warm bed. We'll make camp here, try to sleep out what remains of this night." Alfonso gave Nora a meaningful look.

Nora's eyes sprang open so wide that a rim of white showed around the sharp blue irises. "Don't even think to touch me, you beast!" Nora stuck her forefinger in her mouth, then mimicked vomiting.

Alfonso stared at her for a long, tense moment. Then he burst out laughing and shrugged. "'Tis your loss," he heaved. When his bout of rumbling chuckles subsided, his fingertips tightened on Velvet's elbow, and she gasped at the small burst of pain. Nora scrambled to her feet, grabbed Velvet's unmolested hand, and held it between her two freezing ones. She squeezed it, clinging to Velvet like a vortex would suck her into its eternal, dark void if she did not. Velvet returned the squeeze, their fingers linked, the grip feeble in their exhaustion. The fresh falling rain made their palms slide against each other so Velvet had to struggle to keep hold. It was not much, but she refused to let go—the small touch gave her strength. Katie wrapped her arm around Nora's waist and rested her head against her lady's shoulder.

On the other side of the small clearing Velvet saw a few men had set about the business of fire and food. They laughed and ripped the skin off small rabbits before they shoved sharp sticks through the dead, twisted bodies. Twirling threads of tobacco smoke rose around them like a malevolent spirit. Memories stole over her making grief rip through her soul. Feeling as if she would never make it, Velvet straightened her spine and motioned for Alfonso to lead the way. Her hands were drenched in sweat, and slippery as an eel they held onto Nora like a lifeline. *Don't let go,* Velvet thought, struggling to keep up with Alfonso's wide steps. *Just for a little while longer, Nora, don't let go.*

13

THE OATH OF A SCOUNDREL...

The world was fraying at the seams. Five endless days of riding and four nights of terror had set Velvet on edge. Alfonso took his time, stopping often to rob, pillage, sleep, and feast along the way. Last night, on first sight of the new moon, he had ridden out with a group of men, leaving them in the loving care of three remaining warriors. He had not returned since. Nora, Katie, and Velvet spent their torturous days and nights either tied to a galloping horse or a slumbering tree. For her part Velvet had enough. All the muscles in her body—even the ones she had not known she owned—screamed, and her joints yelped in protest at her every move. The only time she or her companions were free to walk and stretch their legs was to use a bush or tree as a privy. They spent those embarrassing interludes trying to shield their nether parts from the watchful eyes of the guards and curious forest creatures.

Velvet let her lashes flutter to her cheeks in useless frustration. She rested her head against the bumpy body of her current tree and used the corner of her cloak to wipe the evening dew off her clammy face. A thick hemp rope wrapped her waist and ankles, and linked her to Nora and Katie, both similarly bound. The rope ended in a chunky knot at the rooty base of the tree, thus, their position was such that none of them could fully lie down without violently yanking on the other. Beside her, Nora sat completely

175

still, but Velvet knew she was not asleep. Real sleep was impossible in their position. Just a dodgy slumber that was more exhausting than anything else.

Velvet put up with these numerous injustices for one reason only. *Louis.* She would bear it until they reached her destination, then she would use the emerald. The thought did not bring the same comfort it once did. By now all magic was sure to have left her. Velvet felt almost certain of this. The stone had gone cold a few days ago. On their stilted rations of food and water, Velvet could hardly think past the gnawing strain of hunger; even lifting her head was an impossible struggle. She tried to imagine the strength it would take to cast a spell—the size of the one needed—and drew a blank. It did not matter, it would finish her regardless…then what? She would leave Nora, Katie, Louis defenseless innocents marked as traitors. No. Unthinkable. There had to be another way, Velvet decided that she was just too tired to think of it right now.

"Nora?" Velvet breathed. "Are you awake?"

"Unfortunately," moaned Nora.

"I recognize this area," Velvet said, staring at the open expanse of green fields and rolling hills. "I've been here. At least I think I have. If I'm correct, we're less than an hour's ride from Hampstead Heath."

"Pity," muttered Katie. "I shall be dead long before that."

"None of us will die," Velvet said. She reached blindly for Nora; her shaking hands encountered cheek, jaw, she felt a wet trail left by tears and wiped it away. "I will not let either of you die. Not if it kills me."

Nora sat up a little straighter, and the motion made Katie wince. "Kills you?" huffed Nora. "Really, Velvet? What good would that do anyone? I'm sorry, Katie, it's just that…oh!" She shifted her arms, releasing a trembling groan when something popped audibly in her shoulder. "Ah, God! How's that? Is it still pulling?"

"A bit," whimpered Katie. "But it's better." Splotches of red dotted Katie's pale cheeks; her lips, stained blue by cold, were littered in numerous red, angry cracks. A smart bruise bloomed on her right cheek just below the bone, and a series of small, jagged scratches decorated her neck. From the feathered look of them, Velvet knew their ever-present friend—the rope—was the culprit.

Katie's lacy cap was a thing of the past; its absence left her hair hanging in clumpy tatters around her small shoulders. Pain collected her pinched features in the center of her round face, her eyes were wide in their bloodshot frames, and the sharp tip of her nose looked dipped in rouge. Every line of her body was tensed in eloquent distress.

All three of them had turned a deep brown color from the muddy roads, the lack of a bath, or a decent change of clothes. Velvet touched the emerald at her throat. It was a cold, dead weight in her palm. The vibration in its core was so faint Velvet feared she imagined it. "I can get us out of here," she said, praying her words were true. "We need a distraction. I have a spell, but I don't have the strength to cast a large net for it. One or two men, maybe, not a crowd."

"So, no dance party?" asked Nora. "What a shame, I've always wanted to hear a tambourine song."

Velvet threw her a look and Nora returned it with one of innocent confusion. "What?" She shrugged then rolled her eyes. "You think we walked downstairs, saw a bunch of dancing redcoats, and naturally assumed everything was copacetic? It's not a secret, is it?" Nora took a deep breath. "I can keep it if that is your wish, but I would so love to tell all of snobby London that I know a real, live witch. In America, they burn women like you." Nora's eyes sparked, making a spray of color return to her freckled cheeks. "What are you going to do?"

"I don't know yet." Velvet twirled the emerald between her fingers silently, regarding it in pained confusion. "I don't really even know how it works."

"But you must!" declared Nora.

"No, not really. Before Queenie died, she told me to hold my desire in my mind, speak it, and believe it. My desire was to run away from my own life, dance in the forest until sunrise. I held the emerald in my hand, the thought in my mind, then…I commanded them to do it—dance! The emerald seemed to act as a conduit for my thoughts, or something to that effect, before I knew it…" Velvet shrugged and mimicked the moves of a waltz to the best of her mobility.

"That's incredible," breathed Nora. "Why now? Why not days ago before all this mud permanently became one with my skin?"

Velvet smiled despite herself. "They're bringing us to London—eventually, that is where I need to go. Even if we don't find Louis, I have gold and more precious stones. If they get us there, I can take us to safety."

The quick flash in Nora's crisp blue eyes told Velvet she thought this possibility dubious. "Well, we have to come up with a solid plan." She cast a disdainful look at their tree, then the bumpy roots beneath them. "We don't have anything better to do. Alfonso and his merry band of miscreants haven't returned yet, so we will have peace for a few hours if nothing else."

Katie used her red nose to gesture to the man who sat on his haunches, his chin resting on his chest, less than ten feet away. "What about *that* charmer?" she asked. The tone of her voice dubbed him anything but. He had a thin, wiry frame and long braids that draped his slumped shoulders like a cluster of dark vines. He cast an uneven shadow against the ground, its smoky-grey body ran into a shaft of pale, dying sunlight and dissolved.

"He doesn't see us," Velvet said, waving her hand past her blank gaze in demonstration. "We are dirty white women, captives, slaves. Nothing. He will pay our conversation no mind."

"Underestimation," said Nora. "A woman's true, secret weapon." Nora held out her hand. "Let me see it."

Velvet hesitated for a moment. Unsure what would transpire, she was bone-tired of putting everyone near her in mortal danger.

"Nothing will happen," said Nora firmly, reading Velvet's mind. "I need to look at it. Before I die of filthy cold, I choose to hold real magic in my hand at least once more—besides, I've already held it, nothing happened then, so nothing will happen now. Give it over!"

Velvet surrendered the emerald. The green stone winked once, a big sparkle that sprayed verdant light in all directions, then fell into Nora's waiting hand. Nora's eyes widened in awe, and the bright blue orbs reflected flecks of emerald green. "It's so heavy," she said, stroking the spiked ridges of the stone, her touch reverent. Velvet made a soft sound of agreement and shifted her weight to the small portion of her backside still unmolested by sharp pins and needles. Against the horizon, the sun was settling into a vivacious bundle of colorful clouds painting the sky in crimson and purple light. Velvet could hear the rise and fall of voices coming from the remaining men loitering around the camp. The sweet scent of tobacco lingered in the cold air.

"I only saw Queenie use it once," Velvet said. "Actually, it must have been twice. I only remember the second time. I sat on her lap, still a bird, and watched her through slitted eyes. I didn't know exactly what she was about, yet I could see she feared or at least deeply respected the stone. It was clear in the way she held it over my head, reciting a sonnet of chanting prayers, right before she dumped a bottle of stinking liquid over my feathers." Velvet shuddered under the weight of memory that crashed down on her, and the lump in her throat caused her eyes to smart suspiciously. "It hissed and stunk terribly. While I burned she kept the emerald in her fist, hovering above the pinnacle between my eyes. The words she spoke ran over me like the spell. I don't know what language she said them in, but it was guttural-sounding, ugly, and powerful. I must have passed out from the pain."

Velvet pushed the hair out of her face and tried to focus on her surroundings rather than the images conjured by such painful memories. "When I opened my eyes, the potion had taken my feathers, burned to ashes all that I was. I wasn't a princess or a spirit animal flying through endless clouds; I was just a girl lying flat on her back watching a blue sky thrash overhead."

"Amazing!" breathed Nora, her eyes still locked to the emerald in her palm. "I wonder where on earth it's from?"

"Queenie told me a story once, I haven't thought of in many years."

Nora tore her eyes from the jewel and met Velvet's gaze, a look of encouragement in her own. Velvet hesitated, as the hungry beast in her stomach growled. She rubbed her hand absently over her waist, then turned her attention to the filthy hem of her gown. Velvet wondered in which century it turned awkward to talk about magic, what year was it that the fear really kicked in, what final, crushing event made people skirt the topic with twitching noses and eyes like hunted rabbits.

"My God, Velvet! Getting a story out of you is one of the world's seven wonders, to be sure!" Nora locked her hands around Velvet's upper arms and gave her a small shake. Velvet's teeth rattled but she could not help a weary smile.

"Oh, fine, I'll tell you." The uneven bark of the tree stabbed into the base of her spine. She bit her bottom lip in sharp discomfort and shifted. "I warn you now, it is just a silly story."

"One I fear we will never hear," said Nora.

"Honestly, Velvet," Katie cut in. "The suspense is ghastly."

Velvet hesitated for only a second, took a deep breath, and began to weave her tale. "The story goes, a long time ago, an old woman stopped to ask a gypsy girl for a drink of water. The old woman wore a hideous face, warts all over her nose. Her skin was wrinkled like a sour raisin, and deep grooves cut harsh paths through her cracked bloody lips. Clumps of hair jutted out of her bald head; scabs and open sores covered her neck and encircled her withered arms. Streams of puss ran down her fingers when she raised them in greeting.

Fear paralyzed the gypsy child, but she did not scream. She remembered what it meant to be brave, knew from the teachings of her mother she must help all those in need. She recovered her wits, then gave the old lady a drink from her own jug. The spring water was fresh and sweet. The old woman lapped at it in ravenous greed. Cool streams dashed over the jarring slope of her chin to tangle in the wiry hairs sprouting from the deep cleft. The woman drank every drop in the girl's jug and sank to her knees demanding more. The child ran to do as bidden, returning moments later, her jug filled to the brim. The old woman drank until the jug was empty once again. When the woman hastily disposed of a third jug, she lay down on the bank of the spring and fell asleep in a sea of mist.

The child took off her own cloak, covered the twisted limbs of the old woman, then said a prayer for the sad soul who had begged her help. She plucked a daisy from a bundle of them and set it in the center of the old woman's palm. The sun sunk deep into the mountains, while approaching twilight forced the child to hurry back to her camp. Through the veil of a dancing fire, the girl told her parents what she had seen and done. That night she dreamed a thousand crystal pools surrounded her, yet she was dying of thirst. She put her hands in the water—it was wet and cool—and when she brought it to her mouth, nothing. The skin of her palms was dry as bare bones stranded in the desert.

The next morning a beautiful woman walked into their camp, and an eagle perched proudly on her shoulder. She held a bag of precious stones in one hand, in the other a single daisy. She gave the stones and the simple white flower to the little girl. Told her the jewels came from an ancient family of stones, hailing from Avalon. Stones enchanted by an old, lost magic; whatever the child wanted she had only to hold them in her hands and ask for it."

Velvet stopped talking. Nora and Katie stared at her, their bodies so tense and still Velvet was sure she could have felled them with a feather. "It's a strange story I know, but it's the only information I have. Obviously, Queenie believed this is one of the stones from the legend. After all I have seen, I am inclined to believe it myself. Magic was in her blood, there is no doubt of that, and I don't know if it is in mine. Part of me says the first time was just a fluke, maybe bits of Queenie still clung to the emerald, fueling the stone in a way. Perhaps I used up the last of her in the dancing spell." That thought was so miserable it hardly bore considering.

"Well," said Nora, "if it's one of those stones, it's clear what we have to do."

"It is?" asked Katie, her face blanched even whiter, if such a thing was possible, her chapped lips twisted in deep concern.

"Are you sure?" Velvet blurted simultaneously.

"Yes. Yes to both of you. Velvet is not strong enough to cast a spell on her own? Fine, then we will help. The three of us should be able to conjure the strength. I read a novel once about the power of three witches...I think they were sisters."

Katie closed her eyes. "My lady, you read too many novels. We are not witches or sisters."

Nora flung her hand in the air dismissing this as nonsense.

181

"Mere details," she said. "We can't fight, there are too many of them. We can't escape this cursed rope—heaven knows we have tried. This stone is our only chance."

"It's not a chance, it's insanity," said Katie. "It's suicide." She threw up her hands. "Which means of course, we'll do it! Fine, I'm all for it. Better than this rope."

"True," said Nora. "I can't take one more day or night spent in this fashion. Prisoners condemned to the gallows are less filthy than I am."

"It is all rather revolting," said Katie.

"This is not how all gypsies live," Velvet muttered, feeling the need to defend.

"Of course not!" said Katie. "Every race on the planet has their fair share of imbeciles. You should've seen where I grew up, before my father became miller for the great lord—"

"Velvet spent some time in Cheapside," said Nora.

"Not that I remember," she whispered. "But I'm glad you understand. My people, well, those I grew up with, they were clean, well-mannered, hard-working, and kind. They tended helpless animals carefully as their children. Sang songs that told incredible stories…" Velvet's voice trailed away as she heard the echo of those very songs in her mind.

They stayed in a cocoon of cold silence until another faint tang of roasting meat floated through the air. Nora sniffed, then growled in surprising menace. "I say we eat and kill the first man we enchant. I mean, it isn't normally the thing one does, but these are trying circumstances."

"I would rather starve!" gasped Katie.

Nora raised an arched, auburn brow. Her cherry lips twisted in derisive consternation. "Would you though?" she asked in her pitched, leading tone.

"I fervently hope so!" Katie snapped back.

"Well, I would not turn down my nose at a good flank of roast guard. Despite my status, my life wasn't always roses. The first two years I spent on the Newcastle estate, I slept in stables on a bale of hay and often retired hungry. Never once did I contemplate eating one of the stable boys. I am considering it now. What does that tell you?"

"You're a starving pregnant lady," Velvet supplied helpfully.

Nora's hands went to her stomach and shock flushed her pert features. The emerald fell into her lap; it caught a beam of sunlight spraying a pretty pattern of green sparkles on her knee.

"Oh, my lady," said Katie, her voice remorseful. "Forgetfulness can often be bliss."

"I…" Nora's mouth turned down at the corners. "I just…didn't remember for a moment." Nora sighed and collapsed back against the tree, groaning. "It was a nice moment," she whispered. Katie patted her shoulder with soft, consolatory taps.

"We'll figure it out," said Katie. "Together."

"Yes, together," whispered Nora. "A family."

"Yes…" Katie nodded. "Always family, always."

Velvet picked up the fallen emerald and pressed it against her heart. She closed her eyes whispering a prayer to all the goddesses, of earth, seasons, water, and the four pillars of the wind; Velvet drew a draft of cold air in between her teeth and sent up a final prayer to the goddess of the hunt. *Make my steps sure, sharpen my aim so the kill is quick and clean. Help me save life, my lady. Give me the strength to take it.*

The emerald remained cool to the touch and Velvet made a funnel with her hand. Slowly, she breathed on the stone. Her breath heated the interior of her palm.

"Anything?" asked Katie. She sounded both interested and wary.

"No." Velvet hissed. "There must be some spell, words maybe, to activate the object." She turned the stone over in her palm, her eyes fixed on a single hairline chip in the otherwise perfect jewel. Like the touch of a butterfly landing on her skin, Velvet felt Nora's right hand cover her own, the left went atop the other. Nora linked her fingers, engulfing Velvet's hand and the emerald.

Katie's hands joined the fray until there were thirty cold fingers laced together. "I'll help you," said Nora. She glanced at Katie smiling sweetly. "We both will. You did it before. I know you can do it again. Who says you don't have magic in you? You were an animal once, for Heaven's sake." Nora's eyes flared in her flushed face. "That has to leave a remnant of lingering magic, no?"

"I hope so," Velvet said.

Using her bottom lip as a directional tool, Nora blew a gust of air through the auburn curls obnoxiously swinging in her eyes. The hair fluffed up for a second, then settled back in exactly the same spot. Rolling her eyes, Nora tried to use her shoulder to push the hair away, and her quick movement tugged on the rope around her waist. It pulled taut—a hissing flash, cutting a groove in the soft skin of Katie's waist. Katie hissed in pain, unconsciously throwing her body away from the source. This action tightened the rope dramatically. Velvet jerked forward, then crashed against Katie so forcefully it toppled them all.

"Stupid rope," Velvet groaned. She shifted her weight back into place. Wet, knobby roots arched beneath the tender skin of her knees. A small cry of shocked pain escaped her dry lips as she settled hard on her derriere.

The small sounds of the scuffle made the guard lift his head, and he fixed his hazy gaze on them. One hand went to the hilt of his dagger then he stood up.

Nora's eyes bulged until the blue of the irises seemed to seep into the white. "He's coming over here!" she said in a whispered yell.

The man coughed, did a swipe at his nose, and mumbled something in Romani. Nora's fingers tightened on Velvet's, her nails left half-moons in her cold skin. "What did he say?" asked Nora.

"He wants to know what we are doing," Velvet replied, then turned to the advancing man and cleared her throat before calling out to him in French. "*On essaie de trouver une position comfortable*," she told him, not wanting him to know she spoke their language. "*Nous avons échoué.*"

"We're trying to find a comfortable position," said Nora, laughing and smoothly translating Velvet's French. "If only," she finished under her breath.

The man took another step in their direction. His chest and arms were bare—a light sweat misted him, leaving his skin glowing beneath the hard lines of his leather jerkin. A thick purple scar ran down the left side of his chiseled face, from the outside corner of his eye to the base of his chin. It gathered in ugly clumps around the edge of his bottom lip, twisting the soft skin into a large knot, giving him a drunken, perpetual scowl. Their tower of hands slowly retreated, taking cover in the folds of their overlapping legs.

The man's gaze never faltered. Velvet felt like she was being eyed by a hungry hawk. Braids swinging in the restless wind, he took another step. Velvet's waist expanded under the rope and it squeezed her, tight as a boa constrictor. *Minotaur, panthers, hawks, and snakes,* Velvet thought. She wished they would all go away. *Slither away,* then…*yes. That was it!* Exactly what she wanted. Her eyes fell to the rope. *Slither away, strange, sleeping snake. Come alive, slither away.*

Katie's breath rushed out in a gasping squeak. Velvet realized she was saying the words out loud, repeating them rapidly.

"Yes!" said Nora. "Slither away, awful rope. Slither away." Her eyes looked dizzy; a rose flush infused her muttering lips.

The man took a deep breath then let it out in a pale, misty cloud. Slowly, he shook his head. The braids swung around his waist in wild abandon, tangled through the iron hilt of a sword dangling from his leather belt. His once white pants were brown in all the wrong places, and Velvet could smell him on the wind.

She believed these men were nothing like the ones who had sung songs around roaring campfires on the starry nights of her childhood—but perhaps she was wrong. Perhaps her memories were flawed, seen through a glowing pair of spectacles that had the magical ability to change a dank reality into a plausible fantasy. Perhaps they were all giant brutes who looked at women the way this man now glared at her.

Nestling in their tower of hands the emerald was silent, no threads of heat emanating from its hard surface. Velvet rolled her eyes, silently realizing she was trying to feel the pulse of a stone.

At long last, cursing under his rancid breath, their scarred guard returned to his makeshift bed nestled in the crook of a skinny oak. He settled cross-legged on the ground, a vile expression twisting the good side of his mouth.

A faint shadow crossed Nora's face. "I don't even know why that was so scary. We're not doing anything, not that he would notice."

Velvet heard her words but did not respond. She had a sinking feeling that this situation would get a lot scarier before it got better...no, she corrected herself—*if* it got better. She opened her mouth to tell Nora this exact thing, and that was when she felt it. It was not much, but it was something. A faint ticking against her hand, a small pinprick of heat that flooded her soul with the first rays of hope. The sudden wash of relief made her feel sick and dizzy. Velvet breathed a breath of thanks to whatever goddess answered.

"Do you feel that?" asked Nora, her voice tacked in wonder.

Katie lowered her head toward their stack of shaking hands listening to the jewel. Velvet did not fault the girl, she had once conducted the same experiment herself.

"You can't hear it," Velvet said. "At least I don't think so, but it felt this way the last time, and it was a few seconds before it worked."

"Slither away, rope!" commanded Nora in a tone that had controlled the working class for centuries. The stone trembled; shafts of smoky sparkles spread out from the place where their hands joined. Coral green light poured around them like someone had overturned a bucket of luminous paint.

Three things happened simultaneously: the rope spasmed, Katie screamed, and their guard bolted to his feet.

"Slither!" cried Katie. "Slither off, you awful thing!"

"Slither away," Velvet repeated. The light from their joined hands expanded into a giant sphere encapsulating them in a ward of radiant dawn.

"It's so beautiful," breathed Nora. Her lips moved in a soft pattern as she mouthed the word *slither* once more. The light pulsing convulsively in the center of their hands snapped into itself before it exploded like a stick of dynamite. A shuddering took hold of the rope. The tiny, twisted fibers vibrated so fast they blurred, and in the center of the blur an evolution occurred. Rough hemp smoothed to silk. Velvet held deathly still while the bumpy lines of the rope morphed and changed, the sinewy body of a snake began to take shape, rippling scales that glowed under the banked light of the emerald.

Even as an owl Velvet had an extreme aversion to snakes. She felt awful about it, as she believed on the whole snakes had cultured a bad reputation over the years, through little fault of their own. This one, however, made of pure magic, was uninterested in her baser fears. He lifted his diamond head, tilted it, and peered at Velvet out of slitted, yellow eyes. Velvet held the word in her head. *Slither!* Velvet found the word floating in the aether; she took a firm hold of it then threw it at him with all the power of her mind. The snake reared up, hissing, a forked tongue speared the air, and the thin lips drew back to expose a set of deadly fangs.

Katie's shriek ended in a grunt of amazement. "Saints! It's worked."

"I believe a man named Moses used a spell like this once," said Nora. "It terrified and converted an entire race of people for centuries."

Velvet felt gooseflesh ripple down the skin of her torso as the snake shifted, sliding against her, slippery as a gutted fish. Then, with a definite thump, they were free. The hissing snake landed in a flat coil on a loitering, hollow stick, shattering it to smithereens. Their approaching guard stopped dead in his tracks; briefly Velvet watched his eyes struggle to assimilate the scene before she jumped to her feet.

The snake recoiled, swinging its head dangerously, hissing at the two-footed strangers. The man looked at the snake in blank confusion, and his blush turned his scar a bloody color. Velvet saw an understanding in his eyes that had not presented itself in her previous victims. He was a gypsy—stories of magical, bloody arts filled his childhood the way sonnets and nursery rhymes did for others. He knew a curse when he saw one. Every muscle in his body appeared frozen in shock, his jaw hung askew letting the wind whip hair into his open mouth. Velvet stuffed the emerald into the bodice of her shift and grabbed Nora's hand.

"*Run!*" she screamed.

Katie hesitated, her wild eyes jumping between the writhing

snake and the scarred man. Velvet's free hand flashed out, her fingers locked fiercely on Katie's arm, and delivered a solid shake. "*Run!*" she yelled again. Katie obeyed.

They ran with the wind, stumbling, panting, holding onto each other for support. Katie glanced over her shoulder in a timed series of jerky, repetitive movements, checking to see if the man had recovered his senses sufficiently enough to give chase, or at the least send up an alarm.

Nightingales cried out in the rising wind. It finally stopped raining—the phenomenon seemed a glimmer of hope, and Velvet took it as a gift from fortune; the grass swishing under their running feet was damp but not overly slippery. They raced across the clearing and broke through the first line of forest in record time. Velvet could still smell the skinned rabbits roasting over pine-charred campfires, but it was fast fading.

"We have to go east," panted Katie. "Toward the Heath."

"No," gasped Nora. "Don't think, not yet! Run!"

They obeyed. No direction, just freedom. Barren trees stretched out their long, gnarled branches reaching for her, fiercely raking sharp talons through her matted hair. Velvet scarcely felt the wet bark lay open the skin on her cheeks in fresh slices. The earth, wind, and sky cartwheeled around her. Exhausted breaths sawing out of her lungs, she ran as fast as her slender legs would take her. She jumped over a patch of wet leaves blanketing a bundle of mangy roots and landed on her toes never breaking pace. Her boots were waterlogged, their soles caked in mud, they were little weights on her ankles, slowing her down. Wishing she could throw them off, yet not daring, Velvet let go of Katie's hand to collect the ends of her cloak, one less thing to trip on.

A leaf, the color of her hair, dangled down onto Nora's forehead clinging stubbornly to a bouncy curl. Nora slapped it away, her hands shaking. Velvet released her other hand, letting Nora gather her own flailing garments. Void of support, Velvet vaulted over another clump of roots and landed wrong. Something pinged in her ankle, and a shock of bright red ribbons twined painfully up her leg.

"Stupid feet!" Velvet gasped. Pure fury at life in general heated her blood to an unbearable degree. "What a horrible design!" Velvet felt Katie's cold fingers wrap around her upper arm, helping her stand. The second she put weight on it, Velvet's ankle twisted in a sickening crunch. The joints in her knees liquefied and she buckled, one hand held in front of her to take the fall. Nora caught her around the waist seconds before she hit the ground. Using their combined strength, the girls kept her standing.

"It doesn't matter," Velvet panted. "Just go on without me. Give me a second to catch my breath, I'll be right behind you."

Nora gave her a tired look. "If you say anything of the kind ever again I am going to bop you on the head."

Velvet smiled. "Bop?"

"Of course, bop!" huffed Nora. "You probably twisted your ankle; my father says walking on it improves the condition."

Katie snorted but kept silent.

A few choice words for Nora's father sprung to Velvet's mind, which she assiduously kept to herself. "I can't see how that would be true," she said instead, but leaned into place weight on it. It was bad, so bad she thought the pain may take her consciousness as its toll. "Okay, I can keep going."

"I don't think it is so much a matter of *can* as *have to*," wheezed Nora. Velvet did not have the strength to disagree. She was right anyway so what was the use? Velvet knew she had to keep going, she could not stop. Not now, not when she was so close, to Louis, the map, the jewels, Cerberus—all the things she had lost—each individual element required to put the shattered bits of her life back together. She was so close she could smell it—the flowers, trees, sap, and soils of home.

Katie gently lifted the hem of Velvet's cloak to prod her smarting ankle between a cold thumb and forefinger. Velvet saw, rather to her dismay, that her ankle had already doubled in size. It was also turning a strange color—tomato red, and purple as a ripe eggplant.

"It's not broken," announced Katie, when she had concluded her poking. "You twisted it something good, my lady."

"Perfect," Velvet whispered. "I guess I am still remembering how to run." The statement depressed her. It was a bad joke. The universe had sent her on an impossible mission and just for extra kicks, handicapped her in almost every way. Near blindness, ridiculously small feet…

Katie stood, and tossing her lank mane, she lifted her head sniffing at the air, then turned full circle hands at her sides, pert nose pointed at the mesh of leaves obscuring the sky. To Velvet she was once again the deer, standing proud in the sunlit center of a silent meadow. Her ears perked for danger, nose sniffing out the horrid odor it wore.

"Yes," said Nora, throwing Katie a forbearing look. "Apparently she has magical powers as well. I am only learning of them just now. I believe she may be a different species." She sighed then leaned in, brought up a hand to shield her mouth, and whispered in a conspiratorial fashion. "Once, I saw her walk barefoot over a bed of hot coals. Not one flinch or a single sound." Nora closed her eyes over a visible shudder. "Just watching it made me cry."

The thought horrified Velvet; she scrunched her nose and tickled the soles of her feet. "Why on earth would she do that?"

Nora threw her hands Heavenward. "Who knows the mind of Katie?" she said wistfully. "I believe it was an ill-placed bet with her eldest brother." Nora waved her hand through the air. "I prefer not to dabble in the politics of Katie's escapades, only pick up the pieces."

"I'm impressed, amazed…also, a little scared," Velvet said and smiled. "How much time do you think that snake bought us?"

Nora looked behind them biting her lower lip in a fresh wash of nerves. "I honestly don't know. Katie, what are you doing?"

"East is this way," said Katie, not turning around. She pointed to the only portion of the forest which carried any light of the rising moon. "There is a small patch of stars breaking through just here. You can see the constellation of the Seven Sisters, which means…east is that way." Katie sounded triumphant, and Velvet felt inordinately pleased for the girl. Unexpectedly, it also made her quite sad. She should be the one doing these things, helping them, giving them directions to safety. Unaccustomed to being so helpless and not liking it one bit, Velvet grit her teeth and stood up. Her foot felt like it was seconds from exploding, but she stood on it anyway.

"You are a magical creature, Katie," Velvet said, meaning it.

Katie laughed. "Never say so, my lady."

Velvet's eyes passed between her two companions, and she could not help but smile at the picture they made. "We look like the wives of some ancient dirt god, mud and travel grime streaking our faces in the war paint of our adventures," she said. "Torn clothes and all manner of forestry twisted in hair gone too long without a wash."

"Far too long." Nora sighed. A patch of leaves fell in a triangular pattern down the right side of her brow like a solstice crown—or a queen of the woodland fairies. Velvet had spent the first ten years of her life in a great household full of people, though she remembered not one. She had been in the company of these two girls for a very short time but knew she would remember them for the rest of her life. Adrenaline sparked in both sets of vivid eyes so vibrantly, Velvet felt sure that two more brave and beautiful women did not exist in this world or any other. Velvet started to tell them so before a huge, resounding crash interrupted her. As one they dropped to the wet earth.

"What the devil was that?" cried Nora in a whispered wail.

"What now?" moaned Katie in time.

The anger was back, thrumming in Velvet's heart. She wanted to kill that entire band of mangy fools, she wanted to spread her wings, soar into the twilight sky, then she wanted to shoot at them like a snowy comet...use her razor-sharp claws to scratch out their eyes. The very real, present knowledge that she could do none of these things made her want to clench her fists until her nails cut little bloody half-moons in her skin while screaming her rage at the sky.

She found the wide eyes of her companions and pressed her finger to her lips, telling them to be silent. Nora made a gesture with a different finger that Velvet did not entirely understand, mouthing the word, "*Obviously!*"

Velvet rolled onto her stomach behind a felled tree, its center hollowed out by the elements and time. She tucked her knees up to her chest, and her feet disappeared from sight. The bark of her pine protector was old, fat, and interspersed by patches of wet moss. Vines twined its frame like leafy bracelets, the fragrance of rosemary recalled her hunger. Velvet buried her face in the aromatic leaves. She lifted her head the barest of an inch, looked through the foliage and over the rippling body of the wood. Swaths of brambles cluttered her view; she could see nothing past the first line of trees, save a soft violet fog carrying colors of twilight.

The loitering forest creatures, having recovered from the shock of the boom, dispassionately carried on with their various evening activities. A squirrel—red-tipped ears and a bushy tail, and too adorable for words—gave her a quizzical look. Judging her as no threat, he chewed on the soggy shell of a walnut. Velvet offered the squirrel a polite nod, the squirrel saw it but felt no need to return such a gesture. She was no threat to be sure…yet, the squirrel had not deemed her interesting enough to command his full attention. One wary eye trained on Velvet, in case she thought to offer such acknowledgment again, the squirrel continued eating.

"I think everything's fine," Velvet whispered.

"Did the squirrel tell you that?" Velvet visibly saw the effort it took Nora to keep her tone calm.

"What? No, why?" Velvet asked.

"What do you mean why?" responded Nora, forgetting even the concept of a whisper. "You were an animal, so how do I know you can't still speak to them?"

"You know, at some point, someone really must tell me what on earth is going on?" said Katie. "Does it have something to do with the witch's stone?" Katie's tone was conversational, if overly bright, and she lifted her hand.

"Don't do it!" Nora commanded, pointing a punishing finger at the first signs of Katie's cross. Katie inspected Nora's shaking finger for a moment then her hand dropped, leaving the symbol of the cross unfinished.

Nora cast a bleary eye over Katie's despondent hand. "I swear you curse us every time you do that."

Katie huffed in true offense. "I certainly do nothing of the kind, my lady." The humor faded from Katie's face, thinning the curved arch of her lips. "If we are speaking of curses tonight, there are very few fingers pointing at me."

A flash of movement caught the corner of Velvet's eye. She snatched her head back and ducked behind the log, scraping her chin in the process. "Hush!" she hissed. "Someone is coming."

Nora pressed her body tight to the ground, her cheek lay flush against the earth. Slowly, Katie rolled onto her back and drew her cloak over her body. The filth of it blended with the dirt. Thus shrouded, Katie held still until she all but vanished into the ancient belly of the mythical British forest.

"Jesus, I see them!" squeaked Nora.

"There's two," said Katie.

Velvet said nothing. From her vantage point, she could clearly see the dark riders break through the mists, and the breath of the horses fogged the air. Through it, the menacing forms of the advancing men swirled in and out of focus. Velvet's hand went to the emerald nestled near her heart. Cold sweat broke out across her palms and she held her breath. She could try, saints knew she could always try...

Seconds ticked by like hours yet were over in less than a blink. Nora placed a hand across her mouth to muffle her involuntary sounds and Velvet did the same. A minute, maybe less, and the wobbly path of the King's road would bring the riders in spitting distance. Velvet placed her finger over her lips again, and this time there was no return gesture from Nora. That one's eyes stood out above her hand, white-rimmed and liquid in terror.

Velvet's hands combed the forest floor for a silent, desperate moment before her right hand hit something rather slimy, yet sturdy. Velvet wrapped her fingers around it; some obscure yet alert part of her mind identified it as a tree branch, and she prayed it was not hollow.

A horse brayed in sudden alarm and kicked up its front hooves in boisterous strokes. The rider meticulously maintained his seat, muttering words too low for Velvet to hear. The hooves returned to earth crunching wetly; the rider pulled in on the reins and lifted his hand. A lingering snort, and the other horse came to a skidding halt.

These men were shifting shadows, nothing more, Velvet told herself. She was faster, smarter. A branch snapped less than a foot from her head and Velvet's eyes flew open. Oh, she tried, but there was no way to hold back her scream.

Only one lone rider remained on the mist-drenched path.

14

ALL I SEE IS HIM...

*V*elvet scrambled backward, the stick held firm in her shaking hand. Nora's muffled gasp echoed through the woods. She suspected she did not have the strength right now to take on two gypsy warriors with what was possibly a hollow, rotten stick and knew for a fact she did not have the strength to cast another spell.

Now or never, Velvet thought, then determined, not for the first time in the last fortnight, that she would not go down without a solid fight. Velvet leapt to her feet, flinging leafy twigs in all directions. Her ankle screamed when bones grated over nerves. She tensed her legs and pulled the stick to her chest, yelling her battle cry, then struck out blindly, swinging the stick in a wide arch, using all her strength.

Velvet thought she heard someone yell a warning, but she had already committed to the attack. Her stick struck something solid, and the jarring impact sent blue lightning shooting through her bones. The stick fell from her numb fingers.

Somewhere, a horse screamed in outrage; Velvet screamed with it and opened her eyes just in time to see a black stallion bearing down. Two hooves kicked wildly over her head, so close Velvet felt the wind they disturbed. The nostrils of the screaming horse flared, Velvet had a moment to feel quite terrible—it was the man she meant to hit, not the horse. Then, her thoughts vanished as another wrenching scream was shoved out of her chest when nearly a thousand pounds of horseflesh hammered into her gut with the force of a rupturing supernova, knocking her to the ground. It felt like the universe itself punched her, smacked the wind from her lungs in a hollow *thunk* that spun her eyes in their sockets. Her head hit the ground and bounced, her neck flopped from side to side.

A dark apparition fell from the sky, landed on her making a low, blunt sound, and taking what remained of her air.

The apparition possessed a heartbeat which pounded rapidly against her breast. Abruptly, a massive pair of hands sprang up out of the darkness and pinned her shoulders firmly to the sodden ground. Alarm bells went off in Velvet's stumbling mind. Yet, the fall seemed to have shattered her thoughts; they floated around her like dandelion seeds riding a spherical wind.

Beside her, the stallion thrashed, uttering a stream of repetitive screams. Velvet felt immense relief that the horse was not doing all that from on top of her body; she was not sure she would have survived it.

The apparition rose above her, using his hands as leverage, and pressed her shoulders deeper into the earth.

"Don't move," a deep voice whispered. Velvet objected strongly to this command. Her hands thrashed at her sides. She struck something solid, a grunt of discomfort issued from the apparition.

"Velvet, it's Henry! Hold still!" The harsh words had the desired effect. Velvet fell deathly still. Her breath came back in a painful screech as her eyes flew to his. She focused on the face looming over her, further materializing with each erratic pulse in her throat.

Henry's body covered her from bare neck to throbbing ankle like a warm blanket. The hardness of his lean, corded frame fused to her hips and breasts, until she could not take a breath that was not full of him.

"*Oh, merde de alors!*" Velvet tried to kick her legs. It was good for nothing. Henry held them between his own in a vise of iron. "Get off me," Velvet whispered, but there was no conviction in her breathless voice. She was well and truly caught. "If you are here to fulfill your promise to the King, I forgive you. Just do it, get it over with. In the name of all that's holy, do be quick about it."

"I am not here to kill you," panted Henry. His deep, rasping breaths triggered a mesmerizing flutter in her breast. "I've been going out of my mind, goddamn it—" He pressed his forehead against hers, hissing in relief. "I'd begun to suspect I was looking for a body."

The legs clamping hers flexed strongly. Unconsciously, Velvet bucked her hips. Henry sucked his breath in through the white line of his clenched teeth. "Hold still," he ground out; his eyes jumped like the tip of a candle flame. The green irises expanded, shedding burning light on his face. To Velvet, he looked like the archangel Gabriel come to claim his virgin prize.

"If that is true, and you are not here to kill me, please get off before your crushing weight yields the same result! You're suffocating me," Velvet moaned, afraid of the light in his eyes, the effect of his body pressed against her own.

"I'm sorry, Angel, but it appears I am equally trapped. Peter landed on my leg and seems disinclined to remove himself. Peter is quite tired, you see," continued Henry in a reasonable tone. "He's been searching for you these past five days, with hardly a thought for himself, barely thinking of food or water. Upon finding you— at long last, you launch a firm attack and strike him in the leg with a branch, is it little wonder he cannot find the strength or will to rise?"

"I was aiming for you," Velvet muttered under her breath, wondering why she felt the need to be so honest all the time. She twisted her head to the side trying to see past Henry's huge frame. She saw only a leg clad in mud-stained white breeches. The top of a leather boot was encircled by a silver line of buttons that ran down the length of his calf, then disappeared into darkness—presumably, the felled body of the much-ballyhooed Peter.

"Oh!" Velvet whispered. "Is it painful?"

"Quite," said Henry. His voice sounded entranced, and Velvet wondered if perhaps she was not the only one lost in the invocation of the moment. She felt a warm thumb trace her bottom lip, and that traitorous body part quivered under his touch.

Her breaths puffed out like fluffy clouds, shading his face in dusky swirls.

"It does me good to see you breathing," he whispered. His thumb moved to her cheek, then ghosted along the tip of her chin. Her skin tingled to life in the wake of his touch. She felt his breath like fire on the tip of her freezing nose, then his tense muscles relaxed, and his weight settled. No longer posed for defense or restraint, his body smoothed out on top of hers, not crushing but caressing. He pressed down with his hips, and Velvet arched up into him. She gasped, surprised and confused by her reaction.

Somewhere in his throat, Henry made a deep sound like tearing cloth and both his hands slid into her hair. In that second, his expression was entirely defenseless. He cradled her head gently. "God, Velvet," he rasped. Shocked breaths sawed through his lungs. His hands touched her neck and shoulders, his fingers reverent on her skin like he merely meant to assure himself of her reality. "Haven't slept...or eaten in days..." she heard him say. "You've played the very devil on my constitution. I left you safe," his voice trailed off. "Safe."

"I thought you meant to kill me," Velvet said, and she felt him tense at her words, saw a portion of light in his eyes going dim.

His mouth lowered until not even a breath would dare the space between their lips. "Did I not tell you I would die for you?"

Velvet struggled to make sense of his passionate words. Her eyes focused on his face, feeling the cold night wind washing over her skin, stark and shocking in contrast to his burning heat.

"I'm sorry," she returned in a subdued voice, like running for her life had somehow been her fault. What on Gaia's earth was wrong with her? Her eyes met his; she knew in them he could read all the questions written on her soul.

"Hush. You have nothing to be sorry for. It is we who are the villains." A flush of red glowed on the high arches of his cheekbones. For a wild moment, Velvet felt sure he would kiss her. She should be horrified; it would be her first kiss...this was not how she had imagined it, lying in the mud, sick from fearful confusion, in a fever of hot desire. She should be fighting for her virtue instead of wrapping her arms around his neck to bring him even closer. She should be kicking and screaming, not melting under him like heating ice.

"I've never seen anything like you," said Henry, his voice so husky it was nearly inaudible. "So magical, like I'm holding handfuls of starlight."

The contents of her stomach collected in a tight knot…it was going to happen now. This was her last thought before all senses deserted her. Heavy lashes brushed her cheeks, as her eyelids tumbled closed, she lifted her head…his lips moved closer…closer.

"If you kiss her, Henry, I will brain you over the head with this branch until I have knocked sense into your thick skull," hissed Nora.

Velvet jumped in Henry's arms, and her eyes flew toward the sound of the irate voice. Nora stood poised like the statue of some mythical war goddess. Displeasure flushed her cheeks, the gentle slopes of her peach lips pulled back in a menacing snarl. She held Velvet's branch above her head like a battle club.

"Indeed," Devon called from somewhere to their right. "Unhand her, I say."

"I'm stuck," Henry grated out. He looked down at Velvet, a quizzical glare in his eyes. "If someone might help Peter to his feet, I could release my attacker."

"I didn't know it was you," Velvet said. Shivering and breathless, she gasped like she had just fallen from a very high place.

"Ah," breathed Henry against the shell of her ear. "Would *knowing* have stopped your assault?"

"Probably not," Velvet said. Then, she mentally rolled her eyes. *Seriously? A little lie every now and then,* she told herself. *Throw it in to shake things up.* "You promised King George to kill me. Alfonso told me there is a bounty on my head. It appears I am safe nowhere, with no one." Her eyes found Nora then drifted to Katie. She corrected herself. "Almost no one."

"Well," said Henry in a husky undertone. "I have no clue who Alfonso is, but I never made such a promise. Devon was a fool to tell you so. I gave my vow to George, to do what he wishes. I will. The King is a good man, he would wish you safe."

Velvet raised a dubious brow. "Do you mean it?" she asked, wanting to know the truth, shying away from his answer.

"I would never hurt you, Velvet," said Henry, returning her glare, his heart in his eyes. A real depth of sincerity rang out in his tone, then he cleared his throat and glanced up at Nora's confused features. "A little help please?" he asked.

Nora made a noncommittal sound and moved to stand beside his invisible foot. From the vantage of flat on her back, Velvet watched Nora lightly stroke the arching tendons in Peter's stressed neck. She gave the horse a few pats, whispering soft nothings in his flicking ear. Peter nudged her cheek and rose in a sleepy, unhurried fashion. Velvet saw Henry grit his teeth then Peter rolled over. Henry's back went ramrod straight. He locked his jaw but could not hold back a hiss of pain.

"Are you alright?" Velvet asked.

"I will be," grunted Henry. "Little thanks to your well-timed attack. You really are terribly quick for a tiny wisp of a girl."

Velvet had spent years swooping through the skies at speeds that would dizzy a two-leg but decided not to mention this to him. "It had nothing to do with speed or talent, I swung blindly, hoping for the best."

Peter sneezed in exhausted frustration, then began the laborious struggle of getting to his feet, assisted by a cursing Nora. Henry let out his breath in a low whoosh that drained the golden color from his swarthy skin. Velvet felt an invisible shudder running down the length of his taut body. "Well," said Henry. "Your best knocked me quite solidly on my ass."

"Not your ass, per se," Velvet said, hoping she had the correct meaning of the word, "I think you fell more on mine."

Henry looked at her in surprise then laughed. His shoulders shook, his chest rumbling like a storm. Velvet was not sure what she had said to bring on such a bout of hilarity, yet in the middle of pondering it, she laughed too.

"Oh Jesus," said Henry, sitting up to wipe at his eyes. Velvet noticed his hair was slightly longer everywhere, and a smattering of dark stubble shadowed his jaw, dusted his upper lip. He looked tired and desperately road-worn, as if the events of the last few days had aged him in some indefinable way. Feeling a touch of envy, she noticed the dirt and travel grime did not seem to harm his appearance in the slightest. If anything it added to the dark power writhing inside him, the power she knew he held on a shaky, cultured leash. Despite the grass stains smearing his shirt collar and the wet mud streaking down his cheeks, Henry, Duke of Newcastle, remained the most beautiful creature she had ever seen, in this kingdom of animals or any other. Her distraction was such, she feared she would say some nonsensical thing to this effect.

Gratefully, Nora's scream blasted her thoughts away.

Something invisible, yet somehow bright as a sunspot hurtled out of the sky and smashed into Henry's side forceful as a flaming comet. Warm wind coasted over Velvet's torso. Then, Henry was lifted off her and flung through the air. His body spun a full 360 degrees and hit the ground a few feet away—he did not move.

"Oh my God! He's here! He's here!" hollered Nora, rounding on Velvet, her eyes so wide they seemed to fill her face. "Velvet?" A thread of confusion crept into her voice. "Katie? Devon? Aren't you seeing this?"

"Seeing what?" asked Devon. "I don't see a thing, who's here?" His hand went to the hilt of his sword. "Henry?" he called. "Henry, are you well?"

Nora spun full circle, flinging up her hands. "Is no one else seeing this?"

Katie shook her head, barely sparing a glance at her distressed mistress, her eyes strictly trained on Henry's unmoving body. "I see something," she intoned. "It's like glowing rain, do you see that, Devon? Right there by Henry's feet?"

"I see nothing of the kind. Ladies, I believe exposure to the elements may have messed with your sanity."

Nora made a strange squeak in her throat while her head shook out an adamant negative. Unblinking, she walked to Henry, stopping a few feet from his unconscious form. Lifting her hands, reverent movements constrained by wonder, she ran them down the surface of the thing only she could see.

Suddenly, Velvet knew what it was. Knew exactly who Nora saw, who she touched. With a cry she left floating behind her,

Velvet scrambled to her feet and dove for the shimmering piece of air.

"Louis, Louis, Louis!" Velvet crashed down on her knees beside Nora, shaking arms folded across her stomach to stay the force of her tremulous breaths. "Louis." She felt herself rock back and forth. "It's him, isn't it?"

Nora said nothing, her coruscating eyes fixated on her vision. Velvet knew humans could not see through an enchantment of spirit and bone; only the one who cast the spell had the sight.

"Yes," said Nora. "Yes, it's him."

What was happening? Why was he invisible to her? Her! She had seen him before, had run with him through the open Heath. "Where is he?" she whispered. "I can't see him…" Velvet gulped at a sob she could not hold back, and both her hands searched the air. It was no use, she was fully human now, he was lost to her. It appeared all lingering remnants of her own magic had truly faded away.

Devon moved to them, Katie at his heels. "What on earth? Will someone please explain?"

Velvet ignored his command. Harsh despair sucked the last strength from her limbs, her shoulders dropped in defeat. Tears traced down her cheeks. She let them fall to her lap, no heart to wipe them away. She would never see her beautiful brother again, at least not as a magical stag…maybe not even as a bright-eyed boy.

Devon threw Katie a defeated glance, wide-eyed Katie only shrugged.

"Here. Let me help you see him," said Nora.

Velvet looked up and through her tears she saw Nora's face glowing from a borrowed light. Velvet acknowledged that while the universe may have handicapped her, it left a few gifts, like this girl, along the way.

"His nose is right here," said Nora. Velvet watched her pale fingers ghost though husky twilight air. The forest held its breath; the wind ceased swishing, and all the many leaves hushed their incessant gossip with the blue-tinged moon.

"Here is his neck and…oh, now you're touching his ear. His eyes are so beautiful. He loves you very much, I can't hear him, but you were right. It's not a sound, not really. It's more of a feeling. There are words lighting up in my mind, I see them when I look in his eyes."

Velvet felt a fresh wash of tears rush down her cheeks to splash on her trembling lips. "Louis?" She moved her fingers, and Nora said, "That's his heart," in a soft, wondrous tone. "He's knocking his nose into your forehead. Can't you feel it? I'm surprised he didn't gouge Henry with those incredible antlers." Nora turned her gaze to Velvet, her cheeks the color of sunrise. "I love him, Velvet! He is the most magical thing I've ever seen, ever even imagined seeing!"

"He really is." Velvet's hands fell dejectedly into her lap.

"All the remnants are gone?" asked Nora.

"Yes," Velvet said. "All gone. I can see the glow, but,"—she shrugged in resignation—"anyone could do that."

"Anyone but me," said Devon.

"I saw him on the run through the Heath. When the soldiers stuffed me kicking and screaming into their coach, I saw him one last time. Now that I think about it, he seemed…diminished, faded in a way. I was quite *à côté de moi* from being hit in the face and stabbed; at the time I believed my eyes were playing cruel tricks. The murder of Queenie, everyone…it all happened so quickly after the change. I was barely getting used to my own two feet when suddenly my world was burning. I never thought he would disappear from me…never." Velvet's eyes returned to the space where Louis's aura shivered like the reflection of a ghost.

"Why do I see him?" asked Nora.

Velvet shook her head and let go of Nora's hands. She lifted the grimy hem of her cloak, attempted to find a spot not carrying chunks of mud, then used it to wipe her running nose. "I really don't know. The only thing I can think of is…because you're pregnant. Magic manifests itself differently to women who carry life. Queenie always said, *une sorcière enceinte, est une sorcière riche.*"

"A pregnant witch is a rich witch?" asked Nora, then smiled. Velvet looked at her smile and felt sure that Nora's spirit animal was a monarch butterfly. In her mind's eye she could see Nora's aura as a pair of glittering wings, burnished bronze, lit by all the colors of a sun-drenched autumn day.

"Louis's resting his forehead against yours now," said Nora. "I think he is smiling at you."

Velvet felt the shimmering glow touch the skin of her brow and fall down her face. Vividly she remembered what it felt like to fly with him running alongside. Saw him sleeping in front of her oak tree, guarding her from the safety of its mottled shadows. Her mind stumbled onto a childhood memory. It was filled by the dark face of a gypsy man, looking down at her, the hard feeling of his hands as he dragged her from her cell, the pale blue eyes of the little girl who took her place and her life.

"I love you so much, Louis," Velvet whispered as the old memory left her. I'm going to make this right. I swear I will. I'll get the spell. Let's go back to the Heath, okay? Promise me you'll stay there until I return. Don't shake your head, promise me."

"How do you know he's shaking his head?" asked Nora, leaning over Velvet's shoulder, running her hands through the air. Velvet suspected she was touching his antlers.

"I can feel him," Velvet said. "A little, it's something."

"Feel who? See who?" howled Devon. "I say, what the devil are you two doing?"

Velvet shot a quick glance at Devon. His face expressed comical befuddlement, but she had no answer for him. Katie stood behind him like a spectral shadow, hand clasped over her open mouth. Somewhere to her left, she heard Henry stir. Velvet turned away, instantly forgetting them all. She wrapped her arms around Louis's neck and spread kisses on the shimmering air near his face. "Come with me." She sniffed through a single, wracking sob. Then she pushed it away, determined to show him only strength. "Let me take you home."

"He's nodding his head," said Nora. Bejeweled tears spiked her lashes like brilliant crystals. "This baby is quite the best thing that has ever happened to me," she declared. She cast her eyes toward the evening sky and the numerous gods sitting proudly in their starry constellations.

Velvet turned away from Louis, and gently she touched Henry's hair, let it slide through her fingers. *Black silk,* she thought. Abruptly he coughed, sputtered, blinked rapidly, then his eyes were wide open, regarding her in crystal clarity.

"That was…" Henry broke off and prodded his ribs, wincing once, soundlessly. "Quite the hit."

"I'm so sorry," Velvet said, no idea what else to say.

"What the devil happened?"

Devon made a sound of disgust and threw up his hands. "Couldn't tell you even if I wanted to, old boy."

"It was my brother," Velvet said.

Henry gave her a befuddled look, before doing a quick scan of their immediate surroundings.

"He's right here," said Nora. Holding out her hand, she was touching the shimmering air. "I know it's going to sound quite insane, but a gypsy spell is nothing to be trifled with, after all, and none of us really knows what magic can do, do we?"

"Nora, what are you saying?" asked Katie.

"I'm saying, eight years ago a gypsy woman named Queenie turned Velvet into an owl and her brother, Louis the Seventeenth, into a golden stag. She saved their lives, and the night before her death, she changed Velvet back into a princess."

"Oh, of course," said Devon, rolling his eyes Heavenward. "That entire scenario was going to be my next guess."

Nora sighed. "Since none of you are the spell-casters, none of you can see him."

"You can't be serious," gasped Katie.

"I truly am," said Nora. "If I wasn't staring right at him. I don't think I would believe it either."

"I'm glad he's alive," said Henry.

Velvet smiled at him. "Thank you."

"How are we standing here even discussing something like this?" demanded Devon. "Henry? Katie? Anyone want to take a closer look at the insanity option?"

"Really, Devon," said Nora, hands on hips. "Can we all freak out about it later? We have to keep moving. Katie, you ride with Devon; Henry, you will take Velvet."

Henry sat up and Velvet helped him to brush the clinging

leaves off his red coat and trousers. When her hand ghosted over his upper thigh, he caught her eye and winked. Velvet felt the roots of her hair flush deep scarlet.

"I don't like that coat," Velvet blurted, her tone full of far more anger than she intended.

Henry's shoulders hunched as if he meant to absorb a blow. "I can only imagine. Would you like to burn it?" he asked reasonably.

Velvet rolled her eyes. "Yes. I would."

Henry smiled pleasantly. "Now?"

"Well." Velvet threw up her hands. "Well, no…"

"To the Heath, then?" he asked, offering her his arm. She noticed a slight limp to his step, and there was a dark smear of blood over his right eye. Without thinking, she reached up her hand and wiped it away. Henry shifted his head, and his lips burned a kiss in the center of her palm.

"I'm sorry," Velvet said helplessly, shivers tracing a relentless path through her arm, down her spine.

"For not liking my coat?"

Velvet's giggle turned into a hiccup; she feared she snorted. Her blush called reinforcements. "No. I am not sorry about that. I'm so sorry for everything else."

"Hush." Henry's arm came around her waist as he pulled her to him.

"Sometimes I truly wish I had not been born," she whispered.

"No. Never say that. Listen to me, Velvet, look at me, hear me. There is a word for a woman like you in Gaelic, *Seann Anam*."

"What does that mean?" she asked, lost in his gaze. She was thinking one would need a detailed map to get out of his eyes.

"Old soul…" His thumb touched her bottom lip. "Magical soul. They fill up the legends of my childhood, their lives always fraught with conflict." His voice dropped. "But always worth preserving."

"I have no magic, I can't even see my own brother anymore." Misery threatened to overwhelm her. His big arms pulled her closer. Velvet made a busy show of wiping more blood off his cheek, dropping her head, shying away from the blaze of his glare.

Nora stared at Louis, wearing a beatific expression of rapt awe.

Her mane of frizzy hair hallowed her in a soft rouge light, blending flawlessly in Louis's shimmering glow. Nora raised her hand and wrapped her finger purposefully around Louis's right antler. Her fist hovered for a moment, while knuckles whitened by pressure gripped the sizzling air. Suddenly, her legs cleared the ground, her body swung to the side, arching like a sunset fountain; she kicked her leg, locked it to something unseen, and hoisted herself onto Louis's back.

Katie screamed, Devon went a sickly shade of grey, and Velvet saw a rush of moisture dampen Henry's brow. Beneath her hand, his arm trembled. He swayed slightly like he meant to faint, tried to say something, but choked on the words. He coughed and tried again. "Nora, do you realize you're riding thin air?"

Nora purred like a cat with her bowl of proverbial cream, patting her invisible mount, and wrapped in a crescendo of smiles. "Actually, I'm riding a giant golden stag," she said in dreamy tones. "Oh, you should see him, Henry, he's glorious."

TO SAVE A LIFE

But if the tree and the robin don't peep, I'll try my best the secret to keep; though I know when the little birds fly about—the whole secret will be out.

arrions circled the moon-drenched light of early dawn, flapping their sparse wings or picking flesh off the numerous bodies strewn across the ground. The massacre had taken place nearly a fortnight ago, but the acrid smell of charred flesh still lingered like muggy smoke in the air. The fire had eaten down to the bones of the caravans; the remaining pieces jutted up from the earth like strange, morbid headstones.

Velvet knelt dry-eyed in the middle of her broken family. Little Keziah died clutching her rag doll, someone had shoved a knife in her chest before she burned. Hester and Mercy had both caught fire, their arms extended toward the burnt child. Velvet could remember watching them dance by the riverbank, shaking tambourines that caught the campfire light and reflected it in prisms of gold.

She closed her eyes and buried her head in her hands. She had no idea how long her body had remained trapped in this shocked repose, but she knew time was ticking. Alfonso and his men would not be far behind, she had stupidly told him of her destination… the gold. It did not matter if he showed himself; she would keep her promise, she would give up every single golden coin without a flinch. All that mattered was the bag of jewels she retrieved from the body of her old oak, which—because of her—also lay in ruins. Burned to a crisp.

The four of them had ridden until the first violet light of dawn touched the horizon, Nora and Louis leading the way like twin comets fused together in a darkened sky. Velvet traveled curled up on Peter's back, wrapped in Henry's arms. She could feel Henry's chin resting on the top of her head, his heat burning through the fibers of her thin shift and cloak. Feeling warm, secure…dare she think it…safe? The notion of safety had a strange, tongue-loosening effect on her. Consequently, she had told him everything, each painful detail of her story from the first moment she could remember, right up until the moment she first saw him.

Henry listened to the entirety of her tale, asking few questions, making small, encouraging noises in his chest while he took it in silent contemplation. It came spilling out of her with the force of a tsunami. Velvet talked for hours in long babbling spurts. When the wave passed, she felt at peace, and that beautiful peace had stayed all the way until the dead bodies.

They had passed her oak first, the place where a white owl with red-tipped feathers had once called home—to see charred pieces of its ancient body strewn on the blackened ground. Fearing the worst, Velvet launched herself from Peter's back, landing on her knees in the rubble. By instinct more than sight, she shoved her shaking hand in a hollow knot, piercing the center of the tree's ringed middle. Miraculously she found the only place fire had not reached. When she touched the bag, holding the precious gems and her map, relief made her dizzy.

The burnt, broken body of her long-time home screamed a shout of warning—a warning Velvet had ignored. On that fateful night, before she and Louis ran for their lives, she had seen real disaster and watched Queenie burn. Yet nothing in her imagining could have prepared her for the carnage that met them in the clearing. The death.

A touch fell on Velvet's shoulder, returning her to the present. She looked up, lifting her hand to shade her eyes against the piercing rays of the rising sun. Henry stood silhouetted in front of her, his fists clenched at his sides. Bloody dirt smeared his fingers and breeches. Slowly, he removed his coat. She could see the golden color of his skin rising from the loosened collar of his white shirt.

"The graves are dug," he said. Velvet noticed a husky quality to his voice, like it had been a while since he used it. He took a step backward, wiped his hands on his pants, then hunkered down beside her, arms resting on his knees. "Devon and I will gather up the bodies and lay them to rest." He reached out a hand and with tenderness in his touch he brushed a lock of hair away from her dry eyes. "Do you want to say good-bye?"

Velvet nodded her head, yet she could not seem to force the words past the lump churning in her throat, dry tears that would not fall. Was she ever to have peace? Or had the very substance of her blood cursed her before birth?

Body limp and lifeless as a corpse, she let Henry help her to her feet; his big shoulders blocked her view of the bodies. The new morning light burned her eyes making them cry like her heart, and lungs heaving, she buried her face in his chest. Henry stroked her hair, whispering hidden words against her temple.

It was the shock, Velvet told herself. That was why she could not think, breathe, or even cry. It was the way little Keziah's face looked, the soft whites of her eyes melted on her cheeks, her crispy lips stretched in their final scream. That was what had done it, Velvet decided. Sent her over the edge into this world of buzzing darkness.

"I know there is nothing to say at a time like this," said Henry, his voice almost too low for Velvet to hear. "I won't say I understand exactly how you feel, though I have some idea. I buried the only blood relations I ever loved. I remember watching men lower my sister's coffin into the hole they gouged in the ground. I heard her little body bounce against the sides of the wooden box, which sounded just like a broken toy. I felt a piece of me go into the earth with her."

Velvet's eyes went to his face, yet he was not looking at her, instead he searched a distant spot behind her shoulder. There was a distinct vacancy to his gaze, a look which told her he too grappled with nightmares of his past.

"England was a haven for me," Velvet heard herself whisper. "I forgot Paris, stopped dreaming of its bloody ways. I forgot my mother, father, my brothers, sisters, and country that wished me nothing but death. I got lost in this sky." She motioned weakly to lush, green curves of the clearing. "This beautiful land—the old magic here—captivated me. I think it healed or at least replaced some pieces I lost." Velvet wiped her nose again, keeping her eyes locked to his. "I don't think I can heal a second time."

"Aye, you can," Henry assured her. "It won't appear that way, not for a long while. But you will find yourself again." He ran his hands through her hair, then gripped her face between them. "You come from a long line of queens, women of real strength and flawless bravery. Great ladies who snarled in the eyes of death." He held her head in a grip of iron, and for Velvet there was nothing in the world but him. "You are not alone," Henry said and kissed her cheek, and Velvet finally felt the welcome pressure of tears sting her eyes; her shoulders shook as she tried to blink them away.

"I'm so sorry! God, Velvet, I'm so very sorry," he breathed. "Just cry or scream if you need to."

Velvet knew she was about to do both. His hand lightly stroked her back, the other cradled her neck, and he whispered more nonsensical words against her temple. And they stayed that way, locked in the moment while she cried out her broken bits of soul.

When Velvet had wept her senses into oblivion, Henry lifted her in his arms. He carried her to the edge of the clearing and a patch of lumpy shadows clustered at the base of a squat sessile oak, then set her down, tucking her filthy cloak around her trembling shoulders.

Nora took her hand, Katie stroked her hair. Velvet wanted to thank them for their support, but she felt blank, like her body was here while her soul floated uselessly up in the sky. She could only stare silently as the men piled bodies on top of each other, then covered them in the mound of freshly dug-up dirt.

When it was done, Henry fashioned a headstone out of branches and laid it at the base of the mass grave. Devon knelt down beside Henry, cleared his throat, and placed his hand on the other man's shoulder. "Someone should say words over the bodies," he said.

Henry grunted. He had rolled his sleeves to the elbows, and grime streaked his forearms wet from the sweat of his exertions. He looked at one arm dubiously, shrugged, and used it to wipe his brow. "Velvet? Would you like to do the honors?" he asked. The fragrance of the Heath filled her scenes—fresh grass, wet sap saturating the cool wind that carried lingering hits of rain. His tense features softened. "Only if you want to," he said.

Velvet nodded, swallowing hard, still unable to find words. Nora helped her to her feet. White pain exploded in her ankle, and she swayed slightly but felt glad for the pain. It told her she was standing, walking, and most of all...breathing. She limped to the grave, keeping her eyes trained on the distant horizon, and rested her hand atop the knotted wood pinnacle of Henry's makeshift cross.

The men had picked a lovely spot to host the morbid gravesite, a small sunlit hollow nestled in a place betwixt the clearing and the settled ash of her lifeless oak. The new morning carried on unaware of the turmoil in her soul; it was, after all, another day. Velvet took a fresh breath filled by pain, but also a possibility; she cleared her throat and spoke.

"Queenie was both parts good and bad, like life and death, two sides of the same whole. No one would have called Queenie a good woman, yet she loved Louis and I like we were her own. Queenie cared for her own. Because of her I spent the invisible years of my life among a tribe of people who didn't need sight to see me. Louis and I were alone in the world, but she never let us feel that way, she made sure we grew up loved. She taught us of the wind and sky, of laughter and truth. Right and wrong, magic and curses. I want to think that what she did for my brother and I, helped to erase the slate of her past. Many say she was a dark witch or an evil spirit walking in human skin." Velvet sniffed, blinking tears from her eyes. "To me…she was my grandmother. For the rest of my life I will remember her in only love."

Nora placed a small bundle of wildflowers on the grave. Devon said a simple prayer finishing it with a symbol of the cross over the flowers. Katie's soft voice rose sweetly on the notes of "Amazing Grace."

Velvet closed her eyes in bliss, listening to the song. It was one she remembered from long, long ago. Remember. She did remember, her lips formed the words. *"I once was lost, but now am found, was blind but now I see."* She had not heard the melody since childhood—suddenly, smells, sounds, and strange pictures rushed through the darkened corridors of her mind. All at once, she recalled the face of her mother with a vivid clarity that had not touched her memories in years. When the final strains of Katie's ballad concluded, Velvet drew her cloak tighter, then lay down beside the grave, slowly placing one hand on the bundle of flowers. She pillowed the other beneath her cheek, shuffling slightly to find a comfortable position.

Let Alfonso come, she thought. The gold was his for the taking. At any rate, it was out of her hands. If the Four Horsemen of Death were bearing down on her, and the Grim Reaper himself held a pistol to her head, Velvet knew she could not have taken another step. Henry's silhouette loomed over her, the ground beneath her shifted as he knelt. Velvet's thoughts scattered in the morning breeze. It felt like little weights linked to the tips of her lashes forced them to droop. Limp and submissive, she slid through the glittering barrier of consciousness into the vale of dreams.

16

DON'T LEAVE ME

In the name of the Father, the Son and the Holy Ghost…Amen

Something was drastically wrong. Velvet sat up. "Wh…
what?" Her voice was dusty, and a piece of scalp just above
her right ear stung horribly. Through her dim, sleepy thoughts, she
slowly realized Henry was kneeling on the ends of her hair. Wind
knotted her wayward locks; she grabbed them in both hands and
tugged. The trapped hair did not budge an inch. Scalp smarting,
eyes leaking liquid like primed pumps, she tugged again. Henry
swiveled in her direction, his eyes hot as firecrackers, beautiful—
deadly if you got too close.

"You promised this bastard a bag of gold?" he roared.

Velvet sputtered in confusion. "E…excuse me?" She felt her
tired eyes blink rapidly, the rhythm of her pounding heart more
baffled than afraid. "I did what?" she asked. If he answered, she did
not hear. Her head was on fire, her hair ready to rip out a piece of
her scalp. "If you don't mind," she said and tugged again. "You're
kneeling on my hair."

"What? Oh. I do beg your pardon." Henry lifted his knee,
looking at her from hooded eyes, his expression harsh. The sun
beamed down from its perch, high in the crystal blue sky. Velvet

felt the sun do its level best to sear her retinas. She lifted her hand to cast a shadow against the blue blaze. How long had she slept? Had it passed noon? Why couldn't she properly wake? She wondered for a dizzy moment if perhaps something broke while she slept, left her stuck in a fog-drenched world, lodged somewhere between life and dreams. She shook her head. Scurrying footsteps dominated the forest sounds—loud twangs of steel bumping steel, the scratch of rustling leather chaps.

"Henry, what is it? Why do you look so...?" Velvet's words broke off as the ripping fog obscuring her vision cleared, and she finally saw what the rest of her companions already knew. Men surrounded them on all sides. Swords were unsheathed, daggers glinting daylight, thirty or more, each armed and feral.

"Alfonso's here," said Nora helpfully. Her hollow tone implied the sky was currently falling.

Henry spat on the ground, body rigid, eyes fixed on Alfonso's face. "Let him go," he rasped in a low, deadly voice that made a chill of dread sweep up Velvet's spine. "Let him go. I may let you leave this place with your life."

Velvet's eyes flew to the shadowy figures bordering Alfonso's bulk. What she saw had the power to stop her heart. A sharp scream rang out and she understood that it was hers. Devon knelt in the grass, the scarred gypsy—victim of her snake attack—pressed a knife to his throat. He held a fistful of Devon's golden hair and tilted his neck backward, stopping just before the breaking point. The white skin of Devon's throat stretched dangerously beneath the blade. The scarred man's other hand was empty, save the blood covering it like a red banner. More blood smeared his bare chest, and there was a delicate splatter of it across his twisted face.

"I don't know what's going on..." Devon called out, his voice strained badly by the kink in his neck. "But don't do anything you don't want to, Velvet, dear. Not for my life."

"Shut up, you!" the scarred man roared, jerking hard on Devon's hair. His scar bulged, and mangled tissues distorted until his eye winked in slow-rolling motions.

"Let him go!" shouted Henry. He unsheathed his sword.

"My wounds are great," the scarred gypsy said. What it cost him to use the hated *Gadgo* language further distorted his face. "I will only take the golden one's life in payment." He pointed one long, bloody finger directly at Velvet, then wiped the arm over his face. Blood from his wounds sloshed on his forehead and streaked down his face like war paint. "Your snake! He bit me. It hurt very terrible."

"A phenomenon common to all snake bites, I fear," said Nora thoughtfully, looking at the man's mangled arm, seeming deeply impressed at the damage done.

Velvet moved into the narrow space between Alfonso and Henry. "Let him go, Alfonso. I'll give you all the gold. You don't need to hurt anyone. Please. Let Lord Eden go. I don't break my promises."

"No?" asked Alfonso. His baritone voice was irritated. His dark, huge eyes left Henry for a moment to focus on her. His lips pulled into a smile so wide and red they shamed a carnival clown. "You only weave dark spells, make pacts with the *le Diable*, and set snakes on my men."

"Snake," said Katie. "There was only one snake." She cocked the pistol in her hands, keeping it where it was, squarely pointed at the scarred gypsy's head. *Make a move,* her eyes said, *make any move. I swear my bullet is faster than your knife.* Alfonso saw her look, made a tsking sound in his mouth, then let loose the hated whistle. Instantly, the net of surrounding men tightened.

"A curse touches this place. I can smell Queenie's magic. It lies low, like a plague in the air." Alfonso tugged at a braid hanging over his left brow; it twitched in the wind flicking him in the eye. He tucked it firmly behind his ear. "I have no need for cursed gold," he continued. "The great Alfonso realizes there is one thing he loves more than gold, and that is his life."

"What do you want, then?" Velvet asked though the question was unnecessary. She read the answer in the bloodshot eyes.

"You," he said.

Henry growled again, a low dangerous sound. Alfonso raised his brows. "I see you have acquired a protector. It seems the accommodations I provided were not on par with your standards, for that I apologize, we do not live well when we raid."

"You live just fine," said Nora tartly.

"*This* is Henry," Velvet said, trying to soften her voice in an attempt to defuse the tension. "Captain of his majesty's dragoons, His Grace, Duke of Newcastle."

"A Duke!" cried Alfonso, clapping his hands in unbridled joy. His laugh was humorless and coarse. "A Duke must bow before a King. You, my lord, stand in the presence of the great Alfonso, King of these lands."

Henry grunted by lieu of response to Alfonso's grand statement. Nora made a great show of clasping her hand to her heart and gasping in blushing chagrin. "*Mon Pere?*" she breathed.

Alfonso ignored her, his expression blank. Black seemed to seep into the whites of his eyes turning them the color of a winter storm. His hand went to the hilt of his dirk, and he shook his head regretfully. "Kill the men," he said simply. "Take the women."

"Not likely!" said Katie and squeezed the trigger. The sound of the shot cracked the day.

The scarred man—still holding the knife to Devon's throat—dropped like hammered lead. Devon was prepared, his wide eyes locked on Katie's weapon, his body braced for the shot. He moved the moment the bullet left the chamber and came lithely to his feet, retrieving his sword, and unsheathing it in the same smooth movement. He spun to face three men racing at him, knives and teeth flashing, trailed by the discordant battle cries rippling from their screaming mouths. Alfonso's smile widened to an impossible degree. Velvet's throat closed tight. She could see it all happening at once—Devon lifting his blade, Katie reloading, and Nora...Nora stepping into a patch of sunlight and placing a hand on Louis's glimmering neck, a look of indecision narrowing her eyes.

Velvet gave a wild nod. *Yes, go!* she thought and mouthed the words, waving her hands. "Get Louis out of here!"

Nora opened her mouth to speak, wide eyes studying Velvet's face, then flashing back to the melee in the meadow.

Cerberus broke through the trees, a low howl rumbling his swaying jowls. A squat man brandishing a cutlass swung to face the giant dog and died before he raised his sword. Cerberus ripped off the man's head in one, clean bite. The bones of the skull crunched when he noisily swallowed them down.

Alfonso spared a single glance at the shaggy beast and drew his own sword. Henry brought himself up to his full height; he was a tall man standing several inches above six feet, his body broad and brawn, Alfonso dwarfed him by nearly two feet. Velvet knew, were the men to stand face to face, the top of Henry's head would not have cleared the base of Alfonso's monstrous jaw.

In that earth-shattering moment, Henry, her god of golden bronze, seemed reduced to a mere mortal daring to challenge a giant. Each moved in time with the other, like a panther and a minotaur circling a fresh carcass. Alfonso's braids whipped around him, his hooded eyes drew tight over the bridge of his long, bulbous nose. She could hear Henry's breath catch in his chest, like he too was inspecting his own mortality.

"Enough of this!" Velvet yelled. She jumped to the right, deftly dodging Henry's leg despite her yelping ankle. Her hand flashed out, and she ripped the freshly loaded pistol from Katie, who gave a shrill squeak of alarm. Velvet put her finger on the trigger, pulled back the hammer, and pointed it at Alfonso's head.

The muzzle hung between them for a long moment. Alfonso halted his advance, dark braids swung, bells shivered, and sang his terrible song. "You must kill me in one shot, Midnight Madonna," he said, eyes running up and down her body. "Do you think you can? Many brave men have tried."

"Doesn't say much for those men," Velvet said.

"Doesn't say much for you either," said Katie, her small quick hands already pouring powder into another pistol. "That many people have sought to kill you, I mean..." She bit her lip thoughtfully. "Perhaps it's your manners," she suggested sweetly.

"I can give you more than gold," said Henry. "Land, ships," he flung his words like knives. Alfonso declined a response. "Take your choice," demanded Henry. "You're not leaving with the princess."

Alfonso turned back to face Henry, the chunky heels of his

mud-caked boots cut grooves into the soft earth. "You are not in a position to bargain. We surround you five to one."

Henry tossed his head in Devon's direction. "Your numbers dwindle."

Velvet's eyes scanned the clearing, and she saw that he was right. Three men lay at Devon's feet. Two of the bodies emitted low, mournful sounds, one—most likely the scarred recipient of Katie's bullet—did not move at all. As she watched, a short man sporting a missing front tooth and wearing a misshapen eye patch charged Devon, bellowing a full-throated roar. The guttural shout wrinkled the leathery skin bracketing the corners of his dark eyes. Devon deftly dodged the blade directed at his middle and returned the slash in a practiced uppercut, giving the man's broadsword hell with his own slender cutlass. The swords kissed, and hot white sparks flew.

Devon shuffled his feet, flipping one in front of the other like a ballerina in the throes of the finale— spinning with graceful flourish, causing the man to miss his next swing. Devon pivoted to the right and smacked the man on the back of the knees with his blade. The gypsy pitched forward, holding out both hands to break his fall. In the middle of his rapid, downward trajectory, Devon punched him in the face. The man's nose broke and made the distinct sound of a dry, snapping twig, it spewed a geyser of dark blood. A silly groan whistled through the gap in his teeth, his rolling eyes closed. To Velvet, it seemed he lost consciousness in slow-motion.

"That's quite a man you have there," said Alfonso, real appreciation in his fierce glare. His grin widened. "Does he sell his sword for gold?"

"He is a King's guard and a lord of the realm," responded Henry. His deep voice balanced on the precipice of a shout.

Alfonso laughed. "So, yes then?"

"Enough of this!" bellowed Henry. "You just lost another," he said as the next man fell under Devon's relentless attack. Lord Eden is the finest swordsman I've ever met. Once, in the Americas, I watched him take on five men in a bar without spilling a drop of his scotch."

Alfonso laughed, hitching up his pants with his free hand as the other swished his cutlass through the bright air. The sharp blade pointed at the end like a needle, the tip flashed and winked under the high sun. A throaty growl had Velvet swirling to her right, in time to see Cerberus lay waste to a shouting man, using deadly skill and very little guilt. His long tongue lolled out of his grinning mouth. He looked up at her like she called him, licking his bloody lips in loud, happy smacks. He lopped over to her with wide, uneven steps, leaving huge imprints in the earth.

"A gypsy familiar?" said Alfonso. "Midnight Madonna, you are full of surprises." The high sun wrung sweat from his pores, and he let it run in unchecked rivulets down his face.

Velvet met his eyes, her own desperate. "Please," she begged. "Just take the gold. Go. Get out of here. Death already haunts this place—the ground has tasted blood— it craves it. Do not give it more."

"You do not have the gold it would take to buy my departure. You have cost me time, resources, and many men," roared Alfonso, visibly losing composure. "I will get the price of your golden head or die in the trying."

Velvet raised the gun. "I will shoot."

Alfonso spun with incredible speed, shocking for his size. His sword raced at Henry's ankles, and Velvet screamed his name.

Henry met her eyes before the scream cleared her lips. One look at her horrified expression, he jumped, booted feet clearing the ground in the last possible second. Henry closed the space between them, slashing his sword in a wide arch aimed at Alfonso's head. Alfonso threw his body into a roll, and Henry's sword cut the earth sending up small volcanoes of mud. He retrieved the blade, grunting, swiping at the hair stuck to his wet brow.

Velvet drew a deep breath full of sweaty, fresh blood, and reached her hand out to Cerberus. The big creature nuzzled her palm, all the while keeping a wary eye trained on the unfolding drama. Velvet clutched handfuls of his fur, not able to tear her eyes from the two men now circling, death in their darkened glares.

Velvet knelt and placed her hands on either side of Cerberus's bloody jaw. "Go now, boy. Take Louis, keep him safe." Her forehead fell against the dog's wet, blood-streaked nose. "I will come back for him…for both of you. Please, don't let him die."

A shout made her whip her head around, her eyes searching frantically for Henry. She found him on his knees, jaw clenched, sword extended to take Alfonso's next punishing blow. Velvet looked down at the gun in her hand. She eyed it speculatively, loosely fingering the trigger. She had no clue how to use it. *Just like learning to fly*, she told herself. *Don't look down. Just jump.*

Finding Alfonso's head down the shoehorn site was easily done. She raised the gun to eye level and released the hammer. A man sprung from the brush behind her, caught her around the waist, and tried to stuff a fist down her bodice. The thin shift gave way like smoke under his punishing fingers. Velvet heard the sick shriek of tearing cloth as a rush of air washed over her chest. Inwardly she resolved not to scream, as any distraction may mean Henry's life.

She tensed her shoulders, set her teeth, and thrust an elbow deep in her attacker's midsection. The man let out a shocked grunt; spit struck her in the eye and ran down her face. The hand on her breast loosened just a fraction, but it was enough.

Velvet whirled and fired the gun without thinking.

The report was a deafening thud. Black smoke billowed. In the ringing confusion she heard Henry call her name. Two eyes filled her vision, glowing like hot coals for a split second before they blinked, then a fist flashed out. It connected to her cheek—a smack that put stars in her eyes and sent her to her knees.

Velvet gasped, hand flying to her stinging jaw, and already staggering to her feet, she brought the butt of the gun down. The ivory handle of the borrowed weapon struck the man on his upper lip and busted apart with a wet smoosh. Velvet drew back her arm and struck again. This time the man fell. She closed her eyes, bit her lip until she tasted warm blood, then hit him once more. The crunch of his bones made her gag. She swallowed it, threw the empty gun to the ground, and went about the process of disarming the fallen man. With a fleeting prayer for strength and nerve, Velvet rushed to join the fray.

17

THE WORST POSSIBLE CHOICE

*H*enry faced many opponents in life: strong, fast, skilled, tall, red, white, black, and all the colors in between. He had never encountered an opponent who was all those things at the same time. He heard Velvet cry out, and the sound made rage shoot spurts of acid in his mouth. Alfonso hurled at him like an enraged berserker; Henry braced his legs and lifted his blade in the last second, narrowly avoiding a killing blow. If he looked at her a second longer, this giant would split his skull in half like a spongy coconut, yet he feared some terrible danger would befall her if he did not. The girl attracted tragedy like bees to a rose.

Alfonso swung his blade in a quick uppercut. Henry jumped, sucking in his stomach to avoid being gouged by the razor-sharp tip. His next weak parry was badly timed, it glanced off the gypsy's golden bracelets. The jolt of Alfonso's brutal response resonated through his bones.

Henry would not say he had a death wish—not entirely; however, he had no fear of it. Some part of him believed the absence of it kept him alive during his dark days in the Americas. A man with nothing to lose is harder to kill; he takes dares, chances others may not. Sometimes, luck is on his side…sometimes it is not. He did not dread death in this glen; it seemed as good a place as any to meet his end. He only feared what would happen to the princess if he fell. Fury backed his next riposte, his flashing sword caught a bolt of sunlight and flung it in Alfonso's eyes. The blinding beam caused Alfonso to stumble, and Henry pressed his advantage.

A man came at Henry from the left, his filthy face obscured by sweaty hair. Henry dodged the well-aimed blow, drew back his sword, then shoved it upward into the man's heart. Growling he withdrew his sword, and the man dropped like an upended sack of flour. He had time to wipe a streak of blood off his lips before two more were on him. Time and fear faded to nothing—there was only the fight.

One man—delicate ink designs decorating his scarred cheeks—stuck a dagger in Henry's shoulder. Henry glared down at the smaller man, then at the knife protruding from his deltoid, still vibrating from the blow. A dark, wet patch expanded through the grit-smeared fibers of his shirt. Henry gripped the hilt, sealed his jaw, then tore the knife loose. The severed muscles and tendons screamed while hot sparks shot down his arm and sprayed his tense spine. Queer patterns of blue spots exploded in his vision. He winced, shaking his head to clear it. *Focus, man!* he told himself, *You do not die today.*

That thought resounding in his skull, Henry let the bleeding knife fly. It cartwheeled for a breathless moment then found its mark precisely between its previous owner's eyes. The man died instantly, fell boneless, legs and arms splayed out like Leonardo da Vinci's *Vitruvian Man*.

Henry shuddered, resisting the urge to be sick. He hated the sight of blood; it made him dizzy, it always had, a truly unfortunate affliction for a warrior. He stood where he was a moment longer, focusing on getting his breath, his attention locked on the giant hell-bent on taking Velvet from him. Henry knew she was not his. He had no claim to her, other than he had once sought her life. He had not taken it, perhaps that meant he had saved it. Some would say the act of salvation commissioned him to protect. It was of no matter, not worth speculation, the forgotten laws of ancient cultures could have no effect on his course…she was his now and he would not let her go.

A brief survey of his chaotic surroundings told him Devon grappled with three men. Katie stood beside him, reloading her gun, her familiar movements swift and efficient. Strange, Henry thought. He did not recall hearing a third shot. Alfonso's bells clanged and chimed.

Henry moved to the sound, his sword clutched before his heart in a defensive stance. It was too late. Alfonso's wide, sun-blackened face loomed inches from his own, scarcely visible amidst the mass of dreaded hair. He held his arms aloft and the broad blade of his massive sword blocked out the sun.

Henry lifted his own sword, closed his eyes, and commended his soul to God.

The death blow never came. Henry's eyes flew open.

Alfonso's sword lay forgotten on the ground less than a foot from where he stood—poleaxed in shock. The man looked to be in the throes of demonic possession. He tossed back and forth, jumping and hollering for all he was worth, like a host of wasps found their way into his striped trousers. None of the surrounding men moved. Weapons held at the ready, they waited; it seemed to Henry *everything* waited. The wind stopped mid-flight, fluttering out white puffs that disappeared into the blue sky.

Alfonso shouted the cry of the damned, screaming, cussing, and hopping on one foot, gracefully as a broken top. There was a sharp noise, like an ice cap meeting rock, and Alfonso's threw his head back, making bells chant. That is when Henry saw what everyone else had already seen. Ice congealed in his stomach as the urge to breathe abandoned him.

Feline eyes flashing though long hair that whipped about her like a golden cloud, Velvet straddled Alfonso's shoulders, giving the impression of a butterfly attacking a mountain. She squeezed the giant's ears between her knees, and her slender arms braced his head. The red silk of Alfonso's bandana poured over her bare arms like blood.

Henry called out her name and started to run. Nothing…he called again, but not one head turned in his direction. He felt like one of the ghosts haunting this place, as if he *had* died moments ago and now watched the world go on without him through the pale eyes of a fading specter, frozen in death, unable to do anything to help the living.

Henry wiped his forehead, his muscles stiff, gone cold from shock. He understood the reason for his shock; he did not know fear, not really, not the way most people did. Not even on those dark days when his father beat him within an inch of his life. Pain, yes...dread, sorrow, deep, soul-wrenching anger...not fear. He used to think something was broken inside of him. Somewhere, somehow, a fundamental part had gone missing. Or perhaps the terror of his early years had simply inoculated him against it, like a smallpox vaccine. He felt it now, proudly raising its demon head in his heart.

Breathing fast, he rushed at the spinning pair. Velvet delivered a hard blow to a soft spot just above Alfonso's ear, using the base of a little dagger she held. He had no time to wonder how the girl had armed herself, or how she had managed to vault on the giant's back. All that mattered was she had saved his life; if he did not recover his senses, it would cost hers.

Velvet gritted her teeth, the small muscles in her arms bulged, and she hit Alfonso again, her endless blue eyes spraying flames of rage. Alfonso went to his knees. Henry did not hesitate; using both feet to brace himself, he drew back his arm, then stabbed his blade into Alfonso's chest. The sword he used had once belonged to his father, fashioned by Scottish silver, the old blade was strong and battle-tested. Henry believed a sword's soul thirsted for blood, consequently, rarely missed. This was one of those rare times. Alfonso jerked his body to the left in the last possible second. Henry's sword went in less than an inch, slipped, and pinged off Alfonso's sternum.

Alfonso threw Henry a look of absolute disdain, one of his hands left off defending himself against Velvet's assault and went to the blade. Sharp metal cut his palm, splitting the meat like a cleaver, and Alfonso barely flinched. He ripped the sword out of his flesh and dropped it. Henry dove for the hilt, but Alfonso was faster. The freshly bloodied hand gripped the front of his shirt. Henry found himself lifted off the ground and hurled through the air for the second time that day. He heard his breath punched from his lungs as he hit the earth thumping, his flailing limbs, limp and floppy. One of his ribs snapped loudly, and he cringed to hear it, with a grunt he rolled to his feet, staggering like a drunkard. Through slitted eyes he surveyed his worst nightmare.

The scene that met his eyes had undergone a drastic change. Velvet was now the one on her knees, a handful of her gold-spun hair wrapped around Alfonso's bloody hand, a knife to her throat. A tall gypsy stood over Devon, who lay flat on his stomach, his hands held out on either side of his head. The gypsy's bottom lip still spurted fresh blood and his left hand cradled his lower gut, where another torrent of blood gushed from what looked to be a fatal wound. The right held the cold muzzle of Katie's gun to the base of Devon's head.

Katie struggled in the arms of a man who sniffed her hair and ran a long tongue along the edge of her jaw. From the cover of the leafy underbrush, two men burst free, dragging a furious Nora from her hiding place. She was a wild thing, biting and shrieking in painful rage. Cerberus and the sparkling reflections of Velvet's brother had vanished into the smoky, moaning wind.

Something solid hurtled past the corner of Henry's eye. It hit his face, a firework of blinding stars, and knocked him to the ground. His teeth bit the dirt, his left incisor pierced his bottom lip, and a warm, metallic taste filled his mouth. He heard his own grunt of pain and cursed himself for a fool. His attention had wavered, just for an instant, but that was all they needed. A scarred fist struck him in the mouth. Henry felt his lip bust and his head snapped back. A booted foot kicked him in the gut, steel-toed and hard as a rock. Another bashed his ribs, air shot from his mouth in a visible spray of blood. Henry fell on his side; the boot struck his face. There was a sickening crunch that tingled over his back molars, and he felt blood burst in his nose. The pain of his snapping nose had the effect of a slap, clearing his head, bringing back his focus.

Fine, Henry thought. *Have it your way.* He stuck the pain, dizziness, and overall disorientation in a corner of his mind. Bloody fists surrounded him, another struck him in the back of his skull. They were fighting to kill. Henry stood up. A dark, toothless face and bloodshot eyes wavered in front of him. Henry drove his fist into the man's left eye and listened to his own enraged shout. He could see sunlit drops of blood fly off his face, and he had to swallow back a gulp threatening to pour from his busted mouth. He gagged, shuddered, and hit the face again. The bones of the man's nose crumbled like dry chalk under his bleeding knuckles. Then, he was yelling and hitting with both fists, again and again.

"Enough!" shouted Alfonso, his voice clearly ringing through the buzzing in Henry's head. "I will kill her, I swear it, cut her throat like hot butter. End the curse she brings."

Henry said nothing. He found Velvet's eyes, wide but clear, fury brimming over their frame of dark lashes. The small tears clinging to the tips of those lashes acted like drops of acid on his open heart.

"Just go, Henry," whispered Velvet, looking at him like it was her last time. "Just live." A tear slipped from her eye and he listened to her broken gasp. His own throat felt so tight it was a struggle to draw breath.

"I can't take it." Velvet's shoulders drooped. "I won't cause one more death."

Alfonso's punishing grip on her hair intensified; she made a small shuddering sound that screamed across his nerves. "No more," said Velvet. "I want to go with him. Let it be over."

"No!" Henry was not sure he said the word out loud, so he screamed it again for good measure. "*No!*"

"She is mine," said Alfonso.

Henry thought if he could do just one thing before he died, he might cut off Alfonso's swollen lips so the man could never cast that deadly, learning smile at anyone again. "Take her from me," Henry spat, and thick blood hit the earth like a curse. "I vow mine will be the last face you see before you die."

The steel-toe boot kicked him hard in the kneecap, and Henry stumbled. Strong hands caught at his right forearm, and he sharply twisted it up behind his back. He kept his eyes on Velvet until the increasing pressure on his spine drove him to his knees. Blood trickled like a scarlet ribbon down the left side of her beatific face, muddying her golden curls. Long lashes fluttered, and her eyes met his, enraged, resigned.

"I'll come for you," he told her. "Wherever you are, I swear I will find you."

Alfonso flashed a mouthful of gold. "No, Your Grace. You die today!" He lifted Velvet by the hair, raising his arm so she hung from his hand like a rag doll. The cold wind caught her cloak and flung it out behind her. It flared up around her shoulders like sky-blue wings. In his battered eyes, she was Persephone in the grip of Hades.

Horses galloped past him, kicking up huge clouds of dirt, partially blinding him. Henry's vision strained through his one good eye. It was useless. Hands shoved his face to the rumbling ground. When the settling dust blew away, Henry peeled open his swollen eye and watched Velvet go with it.

He took another beating then; his forearms braced in front of his face, his fingers gripping handfuls of hair to shield his skull from the worst. He could hear deep grunts, punctuated by shouts of pain, and knew Devon received similar treatment.

In the distance, a clutter of noises clung to the last shreds of his consciousness. Wind stuffed by birdsong, water lapping at rocks, and the furious clomp of cantering hooves. For a split-second Henry imagined it was Alfonso returning Velvet—he had changed his mind, decided to take his offer of lands and gold. Even as his breath hitched in hope, he knew it was a fantasy. Every expiring moment took her further away from him, and each footfall, each bracing blow on his head and spine took him closer to the grave.

A volley of shots silenced the birds. The familiar, acrid scent of gunpowder rose up in the air. More shots erupted. Abruptly the beating stopped. Two bodies hit the dirt on either side of him. Gaping in shock, Henry lowered his arms then opened his one good eye and looked into the vacant gaze of a dead man. The bullet that took his life had blown a hole in the nose and gouged out a portion of the mouth. Henry fought off a wave of fresh dizziness. God, he hated the sight of blood! Halting breaths cut painful grooves in his nostrils; he swallowed, and his stomach heaved powerfully. He bent forward, bracing his weight on his hands, and vomited forcefully enough to arch his beaten spine.

When his body finished its purge, Henry sat up and placed the butt of his hands on either side of his nose. He closed his eyes, locked his teeth then snapped it back into place. The joints popped as the broken bones scraped, and hot liquid flooded his mouth. He spat it out and looked up, squinting against the rare sun, and tried to make out the wavering silhouette of a horse and man.

Spencer! Good gods! The shock of seeing the stooped manservant wiped Henry's spinning mind blank. "Bloody hell!" His words were overly raspy, harsh even to his own ears. "What are you? How…?"

Spencer's stoic features paled, but he gave no other outward sign that anything was amiss. He knelt down in front of Henry and withdrew a handkerchief from his inner breast pocket. He handed it to Henry then went to retrieve a metal flask. Henry took it and barely muttered out a haphazard thanks before he poured the contents over his burning face. "How?" he asked again, rubbing gingerly at the bloody water tracing his cheeks, trying not to knock his throbbing nose.

"Well, sir, we, the household I mean, knew something was amiss after the shooting began. I was waiting by the cellars since it's the best exit from the house, you see? When Katie and my lady never showed, I hustled the rest of the household to safety. We watched the house go up in smoke from the comfort of the Strand. We've searched every day since. I was greatly distressed when I heard of your imprisonment in the Tower." Spencer's eyes twinkled, but his expression remained placid. "I'm right pleased to find you alive and well, Your Grace."

"Thank you, Spencer," Henry croaked. "I don't know if *well* is the correct sentiment."

"Of course, my lord. I apologize for my timing. When our search finally led us to the Blind Pig, a fairly upset regiment of dragoons waylaid me. After much cajoling I convinced a few to join my quest, hoping they would be of help, were it to come to that, my lord."

"It has come to that," said Devon, stepping out from a clumpy grey shadow cast by a tall, unbridled mare. He held his arm at an awkward angle, his nose was a bloody, broken faucet, and a deep cut furrowed his brow. Otherwise he looked to be unharmed. "Bastards," spat Devon then offered Spencer a clipped bow. "Came just in time, you did. Good man! My ribs are screaming like pigs." Devon rotated his right shoulder and groaned. "I haven't taken a beating like that since I was a boy at Eaton and dared to kiss the girl you like, eh, Henry?" His voice held a trace of amusement.

Henry barked out an unexpected laugh, which made him wince and groan. "That happened the other way around, you bloody well know it."

Devon tried to shrug in his usual nonchalant flare, but his face twisted in sharp pain and his hand flew to his ribs. "Ah! Man, don't make me laugh. My ribs are quite shattered beyond repair."

Clouds danced on the face of the sun, and a thread of ice crept in the air. Devon held out his hand. Henry took it, and Spencer caught his elbow. Henry felt his feet beneath him, and the world careened out of control. Devon patted him on the back. Henry choked then spat out another mouthful of blood swaying drunkenly.

"Ugh!" Devon shivered. "Sorry, old man, are you going to make it? Or must Spencer and I leave you here and race off after our damsels in distress?"

Hands shaking like a debutant, Henry wiped the cold perspiration off his face. "I will do more than *make it*. I will kill *the great* Alfonso with my bare hands."

MAGIC IN THE SOUL

Pirates, virgins and gold...oh my.

*D*im candlelight painted the cabin room in soft flushes of crimson and butterscotch. Drops of water carrying flames in their spherical centers, rolled like liquid gold down Velvet's naked calf. More water sloshed over her shoulders, coasted in warm streams down her spine. It splashed over the wooden slats on the floor, making a pool of pure amber around her feet. Velvet opened her eyes and wiped a hand over her face. She felt sure she was moving, swaying in a sickening motion from side to side. Hands the color of caramel-chocolate ran a soapy sponge down her arm, a thread of frothy water dripped off her fingernails. Abruptly Velvet stiffened, gaining full consciousness with a clap that echoed in her head. The hand passed the sponge along the edge of her shoulder and a gentle voice hushed her.

"There, there," the voice whispered. "You hold still now and let Abigail tend you. That's it...hush." Suds spilled onto Velvet's lap, puddled laboriously under her bare hips. The bench was smoothly polished and so tall her feet scarcely touched the ground. Her toes ghosted through the glassy water and she watched more suds fill it. The woman with the beautiful mocha skin had nearly finished bathing her; Velvet felt clean as one of the soap bubbles bursting under her heels.

Velvet understood these things with that same distant sense of attachment, like part of her was still in the clearing, struggling in Alfonso's arms begging, crying…watching the men beat Henry, listening to him break and bleed. Velvet knew she would never forget the sound of his bones snapping—it had felt like each one of hers broke in time.

"You've been sleeping for some time now, missus, I was thinking you might be dead, then you call out some man's name, I was right relieved. Knew then you would come out of it. You're just tired. Never seen no one so tired."

"Where am I?" Velvet croaked. She had the distant memory of riding till nightfall, Alfonso's hands on her body, his breaths pummeling her cheeks, while visions of Henry's bloody, battered face assaulted her mind. "How long have I been…?"

"Just a few hours," said Abigail, raising a hand to flick a lock of hair off her cheek. She had an oval face, high, sloping cheekbones, and a strong, yet well-rounded nose. Her lips were full and painted bright red, the color stunning against the burnished hew of the skin beneath. Deep lines of coal tipped her eyes in satiny black diamonds. Teardrop jewels hung from her earlobes and she wore a turban of cranberry silk looped around her riotous mass of curly dark hair. "Now, settle child," said Abigail, her soft voice passing like her fingertips over the top of Velvet's head, as if she performed some ancient protection rite. "Don't start questions you don't mean to know the answer to."

Velvet caught the woman's hands midair in the act of throwing more water on her head. "Please, Abigail." Velvet met her eyes. "Please," she said again, her pale voice threadbare in desperation.

Abigail's eyes darted to the ground, and she shuffled her feet nervously. Velvet repeated her plea, putting every ounce of soul into her own teary eyes. Abigail capitulated with a shaky sigh. "You are on the Bacchus child. It be belongin' to the dreaded Captain Chance and…"

Velvet squeezed the calloused hands in her own. "The two women with me, where are they?"

"We're right here," said Nora, her voice calm and strangely muffled. "Where we have been for the past two days, locked in this room—watching you sleep. It was very strange, like you were hibernating."

Velvet turned, startled to find Nora laying in the cabin's corner, her feet kicked up, her head resting on her tilted arm, body limply sprawled over a plush heap of satin pillows. Picking lazily at a piece of salmon with a silver fork, she popped a grape in her mouth and closed her eyes in bliss. "I've been eating for hours," she said, wholeheartedly stabbing at the salmon. "Everyone should get a last meal." She patted her stomach and let out another gurgling groan, her arms stretched above her head. She spoke loudly through her yawn, "Mine was fabulous! *Très délicieux!*"

"Last meal?" Velvet echoed, feeling a little like a drunk parrot.

"Oh." Nora sighed and ate another grape. "They're definitely going to kill us, I believe they are fattening us, much like the proverbial cow!" Her tone was wistful before her teeth clenched; the fresh grape popped audibly, purple juice sloshed over her bottom lip.

Katie's head shot up from the mound of pillows and a few strands of hair jutted out like tiny electric bolts. "I don't think that's true," she said. Her forehead lined in concentration, her lips pouting like a rosebud. "Abigail? Are they going to kill us?"

"Oh, no, my lady!" Abigail shook her curly head, her hands fluttering anxiously with the bow of the apron perched saucily on her rounded hip. "Not kill you. Not yet, anyway."

"Well," huffed Nora. "That's a great relief."

"Do you know what they mean to do with us?" asked Katie.

Abigail said nothing, only poured more water over Velvet's head. Humming in her slender throat, she set about the process of wringing out Velvet's hair. The water rushing down her naked body was cool and…pink? Velvet stared at it in stunned confusion.

"You're not hurt," said Nora, watching Velvet intently, an unreadable expression flitting through her sleepy eyes. "Alfonso deemed you too recognizable with all that golden hair of yours so,"—she shrugged and gestured helplessly at the swirling rosy water circling a small grated drain—"he made Abigail change it."

Abigail shuffled her feet again wringing her hands. To Velvet, she looked like a woman in need of a good cry. "I didn't want to, my lady. Your own hair was so…" The lovely girl sighed and threw her hands in the air moaning fitfully. "I used henna, it will wash out. I never wanted to touch it…honest, my lady." Abigail stopped talking and flexed her hands as if she could somehow undo the action by the power of wish alone.

Velvet ran her hands through her damp hair, then flipped it over her shoulder. It poured along the slender line of her arm then tumbled over her hip, thick, luxurious, and red as a ripe cherry.

Abigail's hands fell away from her and Velvet stood up. She walked to a small, smoggy mirror hanging on the wall near a series of dusty bookshelves and pressed her finger against the glass then studied her reflection. Abigail offered her a rough towel. Velvet muttered a soft thanks and wrapped it absently around her body.

She did not recognize herself at all and that was a strange feeling indeed. Bruises decorated her face in bluish yellow-rimmed splotches, and her eyes seemed older in the muted candlelight. The skin beneath the bruising cuts was white as fresh milk. Velvet drew in a sharp breath; that face of hers—the one she had barely grown accustomed to—stared dizzily back. Capped by a crown of hair waving down her back in kinked streams, fully cloaking her naked shoulders in soft, vibrant, red velvet.

"Oh, goddess," Velvet breathed in wonder. She spun helplessly, reverently in a full, sweeping circle. She could not help it, she looked like a mythical, whimsical creature. Red curls flared up like the frilled skirts of a ball gown. The hot color lit the close spaces between the stubby cabin walls, a rosy glow that extended to the face of her observers. Velvet laced her fingers through the locks then let them slide down her arm and settle around her hips.

"I like it," said Nora, peering at Velvet over a loaf of bread. "Makes you look dangerous. Sinful."

"I like it too," Velvet said, bashfully studying the hypnotic movement of her mouth in the glass. It was an understatement. She loved everything about it—the way the hot color sparked against the blue of her eyes—it stirred the cream in her skin, enhancing the rosy glow constantly heating her cheeks.

"Are you sure, my lady?" moaned Abigail.

Velvet patted the worried woman's shoulder. "You did beautifully, I like the change, really I do. More than anything, I love the idea of being someone else. Seems like I have a reason to be grateful to Alfonso after all. Not sure how I feel about that." Velvet cast a furtive glance at her dripping, towel-clad form. "Do you have any clothes I could wear?"

Nora snorted, the sound of it more painful than irate. "Gah! If you can call this clothing?" Clumsily she jumped to her feet gesturing dramatically to her own garment. Two strips of peach gauze crisscrossed over Nora's breast, clearly showing their shape through the transparent cloth. The ties disappeared behind her back leaving her midriff bare, a yellow diamond sparkled in her navel like a fallen star. Chains dangling fat coins and chunky jewels encircled her slender hips. More of the same gossamer material fell around her legs like a dozen tiny waterfalls, skillfully eluding to what was beneath. "Nora!" Velvet heard her own gasp from far away.

Nora darted a sideways glance at Velvet. "I know, I know," she said, falling into a deep curtsy for no one in particular. "I look like a prostitute. I consoled myself in the fact that I at least look to possess some class, and…" Her eyes shot up and she fixed Velvet with a strange look. "It's not a bad outfit to die in."

"We will not die," Velvet said and meant it. "Not today anyway. Abigail, tell us everything, please."

"He'll kill me," breathed Abigail. She scrubbed her damp hands over her pretty face. She did not sound afraid, just very sure she spoke the truth. Palms pressed to burning cheeks, Abigail walked to the corner of the dark cabin and knelt before a barren bookshelf. She ran her hand along the base of the shelf. Velvet took a step closer, going up on her tiptoes to see what the girl was about. There was a small click, followed by a whirring sound, like grinding gears or an old clock unwinding. A stout drawer popped out as if by sheer magic. It was empty save a small satin bag. Abigail's fingers closed over the bag, then she stood, her movements slow and hypnotic, like the contents of the bag had suddenly bewitched her.

Velvet's eyes flew around the room. Her heart stopped. The jewels!

Abigail stood up, a small groan escaping her lips. The hand not holding the black satin bag went to the small of her back. She came back to stand beside Velvet and held out the bag in a shaking hand.

"My jewels," Velvet breathed. She did not need to open the bag to know its contents, the collection of ancient, precious stones pulsed against her palm. Velvet felt her eyes tear in relief. "Thank you!"

"I don't know what they are, my lady, but they feel mighty powerful. Like I'm holding all the energy of the world in my hand."

Velvet shivered. A strange way to put it—yet stunningly true.

"There be a map in there too…" continued Abigail.

"I know, somewhere in the Bahamas, I need…"

"Not the Bahamas, my lady," Abigail cut in, her voice soft and firm. "That is a map for St. Mary's Island. Don't be going there! You hear me? It's a pirate isle. The Bacchus docks there in the winter months. A wicked godless place, full of evil men." Abigail shook her head, real fear flickered under her sooty lashes. "My master, the dreaded Captain Chance, is lord of that island." Hands balled into fists, she moved back to the small cabinet and retrieved a wad of sheer crimson cloth. Candlelight danced over her taut features then rippled through the cloth. It unwound of its own accord and a flick of Abigail's wrist sent it sailing. She shook it out once, twice, and dust motes filled the air. Finally, the luminescent material settled. Abigail met Velvet's eyes. "That giant monster who brought you here…"

"The great Alfonso," said Katie.

"Well," huffed Abigail. "He is great. I've never seen a man that size. And since the day cruel men took me from the white shores of my home, and sold my body to the dreaded Captain Chance, I have seen many men."

"What about him?" Velvet said, desperate to return to the topic at hand, the map leading to the spell she would give her life for.

"He means to sell you to my master. There's an auction tonight, you—" Abigail broke off. "Oh, my lady, I am so sorry."

"Sorry?" Velvet said. She felt a smile of epic proportions light her face. She wondered if she should throw caution to the tempestuous wind, give in to her impulses, windmill her arms, jump up and down. Instead, she pulled the larger girl into a backbreaking hug. "How wonderful!" she gasped, hardly able to contain her glee.

Abigail's expression was horror-struck. Her glare said she feared Velvet had suddenly taken leave of her senses. "What do you mean, my lady? Surely I do not have to tell you what kind of man my master is?"

Velvet placed a kiss on Abigail's hot cheek. "You do not. I am sure he is a cad of the worst form. However, I would set sail beside the Devil himself to reach that island. If necessary, take on the Kraken and his cronies along the way."

"There's a spell on that island. She needs it to change her brother back into a human," said Nora, floating over to give Velvet a heel of bread topped by thinly sliced cheese. Velvet took the bread, it was still warm, the smell of it richly divine, and her mouth watered until it felt like her tongue floated adrift in a sea of weeping taste buds. She swallowed, thanked Nora, but eyed the cheese dubiously.

"No one died making it. You will literally fade into smoke if you don't eat."

"He...he is not a human right now?" asked Abigail. Not in disbelief, Velvet thought, or even mockery—just genuine interest shining in her exotic eyes.

Katie cradled her head in her hands. She wore a clean black dress, a row of pearl buttons running down the bodice. Her hair was pulled back in a severe knot. The knot bobbed up and down as she moaned in her palms. "It is a very long story. What do you mean he will sell us? We are British citizens! He can't just sell us, I mean...can he?"

"You are traitors to the crown. Wanted women..." said Abigail. "You have bounties on your heads. Your Alfonso means to claim them by selling you to my lord as concubines."

Nora coughed. "He's not *our* Alfonso!" She coughed again and the grape in her mouth shot out and soared across the room. It hit the wall with a splat.

"Well, we have to make sure he buys us," Velvet said.

Nora's pale brows arched high as she threw Velvet a daggered look of real concern. "That is *sooo* not what I thought you would say."

"You don't want such a thing, my lady! I swear you do not, you mustn't even speak those words. If you can escape tonight, that is all you should do. A rough man like my master would decimate a delicate thing like you." Abigail's nervous chatter broke off, and she fell in a hurried curtsy. "Meaning no offense, my lady."

"None of this *lady* nonsense, my name is Velvet and there is no offense taken. I am much stronger than I look."

Abigail's eyes darted to the smooth bag clutched in Velvet's hand. She sighed, the tense set of her shoulders sagged in defeat. "I believe you are." Her small chin tilted in thought. "My master...he is a monster wearing human skin. Tall as Lucifer, beautiful in his own way, but my lad—Velvet." Abigail let the wad of satin cloth she held shimmer to her feet and folded her hands in prayer. "He is evil, Velvet. Pure evil."

"It doesn't matter," Velvet whispered. "It's fate. More than that even, it's a gift." She squeezed the satin bag. She could feel it—the power of the old ones tingling in the tips of her fingers, rushing everywhere, flooding her veins in magic. "There is one thing I have learned since exchanging wings for legs, human love is something different. Something strange. I thought at first it was weakness. Now I realize it's the only real power. Love is its own dream—for good or bad, it's a purpose."

"Love?" scoffed Nora. "Oh, Velvet, please, you're talking nonsense. What are you going to make him do? Make them all fall in love with you? Then what? They'll just drop to their knees and do whatever you wa—" Nora's final word died on her lips as the light of understanding dawned.

Velvet opened her mouth to reply. The door to their small room flew open. Two men, one fat, one tall, strode in.

"Which one of you wenches answers to the name of Katie?" the tall one asked.

Nora jumped to her feet. "I do," she said instantly.

Katie put her hands on her hips. "That is Lady Nora Harrington, I am Katie."

"Very good," the fat one said. "Come with us then. It seems our good Captain has found employment for you."

"Get out!" roared Nora.

"You can't just take her!" Velvet insisted.

"But she is not yet ready," begged Abigail.

Both men unsheathed their swords. "We can, and we will." The fat one laughed. "We're pirates, dearie, we take what we want. Do what we please with pretty little maidens like you."

Katie walked to the men, her small chin held high. "I will go with you," she said. "For now."

"There's no coming back from where you're going." The tall one wiped a filthy hand over his scoffing mouth. "It's not a bad life, just ask sweet Abigail here." He smacked his free hand across her derriere, the noise of the hit cracked like a whip in the small room. Abigail bit her lip but made no sound.

Nora grabbed Katie's hand. "Wait!" she cried. "You can't have her, I am the daughter of the King, and she is my lady."

"King?" the fat one crowed, tugging languidly at the thick golden chain hanging around his neck. "What king?" He looked up at his tall friend. "Do you see a king?"

The tall one shrugged his massive shoulders and shook his head. "I don't see no one."

Katie put her hand over Nora's. "It's okay. You'll be okay, they won't separate us, and if they do, I trust you will come and save me."

"I love you, Katie," said Nora miserably. "More than I've ever loved anyone, more than any sister or brother. I'm going to find our way out of this, I swear it."

"I know. I love you too," said Katie. "You're the family I chose." Katie lifted her eyes and met Velvet's gaze. "You are a princess of France, Velvet. You're not an owl anymore, take what's yours."

Velvet nodded. "I will," she promised, and prayed it was true.

∼

Lanterns cast their light over the tall shrouds and the moon spilled its glow on the foremast. It filtered through the sails and touched the crow's nest. A group of men waited on the main deck, watching the spectacle taking place atop the stern. The scream of a crow sounded overhead, and Velvet looked up to see it land on the bowsprit, its wings glistening blue-black in the dark night. Nora squeezed her hand and Velvet squeezed back.

"At least you look pretty," said Nora sotto voce. Velvet glanced dubiously at her body. Crimson cloth swathed her hips, a thin, sheer strip of it wrapped her breasts like an alluring bandage and left the rest of her skin bare to the ice-studded wind. In the last, after Abigail rouged Velvet's cheeks and lips to her satisfaction and applied charcoal lines to her eyes, she placed a string of pearls around Velvet's neck, then stabbed a butterfly comb—its delicate wings made of ruby—deep in the swirls of her upswept hair.

Alfonso shouldered his way to the front of the crowd. His dark eyes roved over her scantily clad form, and a wicked thing sparked his hooded glare. He climbed the stairs two at a time, and they squealed wretchedly under his punishing weight.

He wore a well-cut coat, purple with threaded gold piping. It had large ivory buttons and a wealth of golden tassels hanging from the shoulders. His hair was washed and brushed, he had polished his golden teeth, and they winked like rogues behind the cover of his smiling lips. "My Moonlight Madonna, I fear this is where we part ways."

"Pity," Velvet said sweetly. Keeping her eyes well trained on a distant spot hovering just beyond his head, she closed her lips.

"I do not wish you harm," he said, tossing up his big hands—the bangles on his wrists clashed, harmonizing badly with the bells in his hair. "Alas, I cannot give you freedom. Perhaps your new owner will offer kindness."

"Perhaps," Velvet said, in what she hoped was a note of finality. More than anything she wanted to see the back of this man's head as he walked out of her life.

"I will leave you a gift," he said, his smile firmly fixed, vapid eyes devoid of humor. He leaned in until Velvet smelled whiskey and raw meat. He paid her shudder of revulsion no mind, only took another step until his moist, lower lip brushed the soft shell of her ear. "A secret I leave with you, one fixed and true," he whispered. "It was a gypsy who betrayed you. A gypsy who went to the King with rumors of your life. Told him you had English sympathizers with deep pockets who pledged to support you in taking back the French throne. Swore you and your forgotten brother would come for England the day after you left your own homeland soaked in bloody ashes."

Velvet felt like she swallowed a cold stone, heard it hit her gut, and the hollow *thunk* was sickening. It made no sense. None at all. "Why? Why would he do that? Who could hate me that much? I know no one."

"Why?" Alfonso drew back and scratched at his close beard. "Why? Ah! Now she looks at me, speaks to me."

"Just tell me you...you..." Velvet found herself at a loss for words, her mind stuttering under the fresh information as her train of thought flew off its shoddy rails and crashed into a wall.

"Bastard," supplied Nora.

Velvet nodded. "Just tell me."

"An old blood debt," said Alfonso bluntly. "Queenie had many enemies, fought many battles which were no concern of mine. Gratefully, my little enchantress, no longer are you." His eyes swept her from head to toe and a rumble started up in his chest. "'Tis a true shame." He reached out a thick forefinger and stroked it down her cheek. "You are a Botticelli angel come to life, a sensual masterpiece and...good enough to eat. If the great Alfonso did not need the gold he likes to think he would keep you."

"What did you do to Henry?" she snapped, wishing to bite off his wandering hand.

"Your knight in broken armor? He is crow food," he said, and his leer overtook his face.

Leaving that wrenching pronouncement hanging in the air, he turned and held up both hands. A deathly silence settled over the crowd.

"Brigands," he roared in a clear baritone sure to carry across the Thames. "I have for you tonight, two virgins of immeasurable beauty."

Nora darted a look at Velvet's hands tightly clasped behind her back. Wrapped in the gauzy mesh of her fluttering skirts, she held the bag of jewels like a loaded gun. "Are you ready?"

Velvet nodded but said nothing. She had no words. The power of the jewels wreathed her in electric strength; like each of their colors—ruby, amber, emerald, and topaz—were alive and shooting bolts of lightning, wreathing up her arms, sharp and biting as thorn-studded vines.

"I think the sleep really helped," Velvet said struggling to keep her voice subdued. In the center of her chest bubbled something old and powerful, it was a battle to contain it. She took a long breath through her nose. The wild thing wanted out. "I feel…" She did not know what she felt. "Rested."

Nora's freckled face flushed, and she rolled her eyes. "That's the understatement of the century. You look like you could spread your wings and fly."

"I have no wings," Velvet whispered.

Nora pursed her lips, considering Velvet in thoughtful affection. "I wouldn't be so sure about that."

Alfonso raised his voice then, saying something that made the crowd roar in gleeful anticipation. Nora threw his satin-clad back a withering glare. "If he is alive, I hope Henry kills that man. Cuts his stupid nose off his swollen face."

If, if he is alive. If… Velvet could not force out a reply, her mind was a whirl with the overwhelming force of the stones and Alfonso's *gift* ringing in her ears. It was not enough, his words only shot more holes into her confused story. *What had Queenie known, or dear gods…what had she done? What had she not told her?* There were no answers for her in the night wind coasting over the body of the ship.

Nora shivered, then growled under her breath. "We could make a run for it. Grab Katie and Abigail too? I mean if she wants to come for a freezing midnight swim, that is."

Red hair tangled in Velvet's lashes when she shook her head. "No. I won't run. I will take this ship and its crew." She closed her eyes and felt for the power of the ruby. Velvet listened to its music, drew it into her soul, and the rest—Alfonso calling out the starting bid; the guards silently dangerous at her back; and Nora's frightened, expressive eyes—just faded away.

Nora's sharp voice cut through the singing fog. "There is a bid for you. Five hundred pounds."

"Is that good?" Velvet asked.

Nora winked, and her shoulder moved in a shrug. "It's passable."

Velvet felt herself smile. She would do her best to get Nora and Katie back to whatever passed as safety, then she meant to take this ship and retrieve the spell for her brother, even if the cost was her life.

From the corner of her eye, Velvet glanced at Nora, head held high, chin strong, the regal posture of a queen. Wild auburn hair fell in a thick mass around her body—beautiful hair, matching a personality so vivid, and bright, it spilled out of her unawares—Nora knew who she was. Even Katie with her steely determination and quiet faith had no delusions of self.

Not her. Since the moment her feathers burned, her bones cracked and reformed, Velvet knew nothing except the need to survive. She had no idea who she was, or her capabilities. All she knew was that she loved her brother. If she did not take this ship and somehow win her freedom, she would literally never see him again. That was simply unacceptable. *Love—love in this human body*, she told herself, *was truly the strangest of things.*

Alfonso's voice blew away on the night wind. The ship lumbered under their feet, bobbing up and down like a beached cork. Velvet felt the small, now familiar heat of the gems pulsing against her palm...she waited. The moment had to be perfect. All eyes on her.

Alfonso moved, his hand shot out, fast as a striking snake. His fingers closed on the back of her neck, yanking painfully on her hair. He hauled her in front of him. Her toe clipped a loose board on the ship's deck, and she stumbled. Alfonso kept her standing by his hold on her hair. A few pieces ripped free of her soft scalp, making her eyes water fiercely.

"Have a look at her, Captain. She is truly a prize fit for kings." Alfonso's hot breath coasted over Velvet's flushed cheek, and she jerked her head away. He ignored her struggles and raised his voice. "Do I hear a thousand?"

Footfalls sounded to her right, Velvet's head automatically snapped in their direction. Her eyes started on a pair of black boots and moved slowly up. He wore dark canvas breeches tucked into the top of his boots, a thick red belt held them up, and a metal skull buckled it tight. The white shirt covering his chest billowed like the sails. Slung back over his shoulders was a long leather coat hemmed in inky rabbit fur. It shrouded his tall frame like a blackening rain cloud. The head sitting atop the muscled neck was handsome for its irregularities; jagged patches of absent pigmentation splattered his face like zebra spots. White as snow, his hair fell across his forehead in flowing sweeps. He wore a wide-brimmed cap, there was a violet feather sticking from the deeply curved brim, and his gloved hand rested on the diamond hilt of a golden sword. Moonlight glanced off the stone hallowing him in a ghostly light, cold and grey as a grave. His head dropped.

Velvet gulped a hitching breath and stepped back. His gaze pierced her from beneath white lashes, eyes red and shifty as a rat's peering out of a darkened cellar. The dreaded Captain Chance, she assumed.

The broad grin splitting his face like a gash showed her a straight line of white teeth. He grabbed her hand then bowed over it. His warm moist lips pressed hard against her bare wrist. Velvet had the urge to scrub that spot with a metal sponge until it bled.

"I will offer a thousand," he said. "*Tres belle. Maginque.*"

Magical? Velvet thought and wanted to scoff in his face. You have no idea, she would tell him, then she would slap him, just because she felt he deserved it. That made her smile. Nora saw the smile and looked at her suspiciously but said nothing, only returned her mission of sending daggered glares into Alfonso's heaving chest.

The humming body of the crowd moved restlessly and spat out the dark figure of a man who held up his hand, one finger raised. "Fifteen hundred pounds," the voice, deeply muffled, was unrecognizable.

Thick fog poured off the tattered shore of the Thames; it settled on the main deck covering the bodies of the muttering men, shrouding their deeds from prying eyes. Velvet could see nothing, just shifting shapes dancing in smoky shadows. It did not matter. All that mattered was that they saw her. Velvet knew somewhere in her heart she felt fear—her mind had no time for it, all thoughts were centered on the ruby. "Alfonso," she breathed sadly, hoping this time no one would die. "I would've given you more."

Alfonso's head whipped around, his eyes locked hotly to hers. "I don't want your cursed gold," he said. Fury pinched his mouth and fat drops of sweat popped out on his brow.

"More fool you. Now, the deal has changed…" Velvet's fingers clenched the stones so tightly that she could feel their small edges cutting into her cold skin. The heat of them was everywhere, breathing in her chest, singing in her mind.

Velvet moved and his body went very still as she pressed her cold lips to the perspiring skin of his cheek.

"Love me," she breathed, and the heat from the ruby permeated her bones. Velvet knew she was beginning to glow from its endless light "Look at me," she said again, then demanded, "Love me."

Alfonso's eyes went wide; he started to scoff in astonishment but broke off mid-leer. Sweaty hands fell away from her neck, an abrupt motion that took more of her hair. Velvet barely felt the small, stinging pain. She took a determined step forward. Fear broke out like a rash across Alfonso's exaggerated features. He stumbled back, his mottled complexion going grey as the fog that sheltered them. His hand made weird grabbing motions at a pendant, hanging from a gold chain low on his chest.

Velvet ran her fingers up her neck, then threaded them through her hair. A flick of her wrist and she sent the red locks cascading off her shoulders. For years she had flown the skies, watching the light of campfires, dreaming of the day when she could dance with the women spinning through the flames, flashing wings of shimmering scarves. She could hear the music rushing out of the gems, rising in an echoing crescendo. The heat of the jewel's combined power engulfed her. Velvet saw only red. One thought pounded in her mind as she started to move, sway…be. *Love me…*

love me... love me, she thought, and the thought became everything.

She could not fight the music any longer—it was part of the spell, she was enchantress and enchanted. Hands lifted above her head and fingers twirling in the fog, she swayed her arms, rocked her hips, spun in a flurry of silken mist, and slowly began to dance.

Alfonso's brown eyes were pools of liquid confusion, his stubbled jaw fell wide, his free hand fumbling desperately for the stair rail. Somewhere amidst the music Velvet heard Nora gasp. She thrust her hips to the left, then slowly swirled them to the right. A low *hum* rippled through the crowd. Velvet saw Captain Chance turn and fix his eyes on her, the crimson finish of his unfocused gaze irradiated his pale face.

Suddenly, Nora scrambled backward, yelping incoherent commands before crashing to the ground. Katie landed half on top of her. A discolored lump crouched against the floor emitted a low moan.

"Good God, ladies!" a confused voice heaved. "I am half dead already! What do you mean by this?" Somewhere in the music Velvet recognized it was Devon's voice. On the ground near Nora's feet kicked a pair of regiment standard boots.

"Don't look!" Nora howled. "It's a love spell, she...she..."

"It's a what?" Even in the grip of her dizzying magic, Velvet heard the clear shock in Devon's voice.

"An enchantment," said Nora. "For whatever insane reason, Velvet wants this ship. She is enchanting the men, so they will... oh, *mon Dieu*...give it to her I guess." Nora rolled her eyes. "A ship and an island."

"A ship and a what?" Devon struggled to sit up.

"An island, she—" Nora's voice cut off. She moved abruptly, kneeing Devon in the back. He yelped, muttering a foul word under his breath.

"Where is Henry? How are you even here? Oh, this is just all too much..." Velvet lost the rest of Nora's words.

Captain Chance recaptured her attention. Wind tousled his halo of white hair; his body was taut as a bowstring, red lips and eyes the only slash of color on his face. A moment of clarity flickered in his glare. Velvet watched him visibly struggle to break the spell gushing from her very pores, weaving around them all like fog in a dream.

Another flicker...and he was lost. His body swayed in her rhythm, and he made small circles with his shoulders. Moonlight winked off the skull head on his belt buckle when his hips moved in tandem to her own. Velvet threw back her head, her spine arched, her locks of hair swept the deck. Ruby light erupted between her fingers, her body arched further, until her forehead nearly brushed the polished, cherry wood floor. Gauzy material stretched tight across her breasts; she watched it ripple over her arms, run like silky starlight down the length of her legs. The ends of the glimmering cloth floated around her—a million fairies dancing in the light of a crimson star.

Velvet closed her eyes. The feeling was indescribable, because by exquisite happenstance or vibrant magic, she was that star. She was the twirling light that in the end, drove every standing man to his knees.

19

BLOODY DEATH

The heat slowly diminished, the jewels drew the light back into the center of their beating hearts—the brilliant ruby shimmering longer than the others. Surreal reality seemed to suspend time; blood tingled in the tips of Velvet's fingers as sounds returned to normal and her breathing calmed. She heard the water lapping against the hull, listened to the whisperers…the halting, broken whispers—whispers she had heard before—whispers of men in a trance.

She was so dizzy, shocked, and stumbling—the ship swayed, and she reached out a hand hoping to catch onto something—anything—for salvation. Her hand touched the cold metal spoke of the ship's wheel, it was wet, slippery as an eel, and she gripped it hard. Wind whipped hair across her eyes, taking what little sight remained to her; it stuck to the wetness on her cheeks and burned.

Fever rolled across her skin, and her stomach lurched dangerously. Velvet fell to her knees, shaking from the intensity of emotion roiling through her, terribly afraid she was going to be sick in front of all these men.

It's not right! her mind screamed. *I've done the spell wrong,* she told herself. *That's all. I only need rest.*

Hands touched her shoulder. Gasping, Velvet pulled back and opened her eyes. Nora's face hovered in front of her, white as cotton, blue eyes soaked in concern.

"That was..." Nora sucked in her breath and cast her gaze to the surrounding scene. "Well," her voice shook badly. "I think it worked...the guards." She motioned to the men who had carried them bodily to this craven place. They stood still as stone statues, unremarkable faces blank, their eyes—showing her reflection—were unblinking.

"Captain Chance, Alfonso...all the men. You were brilliant, Velvet...so beautiful, the most exquisite thing I have ever seen." Nora's voice turned breathless, and a strange, limpid light swayed in her eyes. "And it's possible I watched you for too long..." She put a hand to her head. "We tried to cover Devon's eyes, but I saw some of your dance...I am—" she broke off and touched Velvet's cheek, a butterfly stroke that was over almost before Velvet felt it. "I'm so in love with you."

"Oh *merde!*" Velvet gasped, torn between laughter and dismay. "You are not in love with me. It's a spell, that's all. I did a spell to save my brother, but I think I've done something terribly wrong. I feel so weak...there's *sooo* many of them. It was too much magic." Velvet felt her nose burst blood, saw a big drop of it splatter the deck. Nora screamed.

"What's done is done," said Katie, ever the voice of reason. "No sense crying over it. What are we going to do now?"

Nora ripped a strip of gossamer cloth from the hem of her skirt. "Look at me, Velvet, your nose is a horror show."

"It doesn't matter," Velvet heard herself gasp. She looked past Nora's shoulder to the carnage she had caused. Devon stood beside Alfonso, a hand resting on his dirk. Wind tousled his blonde hair, brushing a face that was bloody and bruised. He had a wild feel about him, like a predator kept too long in a cage—Velvet thought he looked as shocked as she felt.

Katie sat at his feet, one arm wrapped around his calf, her forehead resting against his knee. Devon took a deep breath, then looked up with the hesitation of one fearing to meet a cyclops. He opened his mouth, trembling lips moved, but no words made it out. Instead, he ripped the dirk free of its sheath and pressed the blade to Alfonso's unprotected throat.

Alfonso moaned and reached for Velvet. A stream of drool

hung from his slack mouth and dripped between the front gap in his shiny, gold teeth.

"No!" Velvet shouted. Devon froze. She shouldered Nora out of the way, accidentally putting her in the path of the stunned Captain Chance. "Don't kill him!"

"Are you serious?" growled Devon. "The dream of this moment is all that's kept me alive." He looked at Alfonso. The bigger man ignored Devon's glower, only stared into Velvet's eyes whispering words of love.

"He knows something. It's no coincidence he meant to sell me to the king of the island where the spell I need is hidden…ugh!" Velvet buried her head in her hands. "I think he knows everything."

"What do you mean everything?" asked Nora, coming up behind her, placing a cold, solicitous hand on her bare shoulder.

"I don't know," Velvet whispered, not turning around. "But if you use your knife, all my hope dies with him."

"Your hope?" squawked Nora. "I thought this ship was your hope."

"He knows about Queenie, he knows who betrayed me to the King!" Velvet said. "Just tie him up, please? We need him."

She felt the diminished heat of the stones and tightened her fingers around the satin bag. Something was definitely wrong—it was a nameless thing in the night haunting the air she breathed. Pricking shivers accosted her skin lifting the soft hairs on her neck. Sucking in a breath for her nerves, Velvet faced Captain Chance. She squeezed the jewels until their sharp edges again pierced her skin and held out her hand to the pirate king.

"Give me your sword," she commanded.

The captain nodded his albino head. He handed her the jeweled piece. Velvet clasped the hilt, then pressed the shining, razor tip to his heart. "This ship is mine," she said, hoping her voice sounded more authoritative out loud than it did in her head. "I am the captain now. I command this crew."

"Only the man who kills me will be captain, and you are not a man…" Captain Chance made a fist and beat it twice against his heart, one pale brow tilted in a dramatic arch. He took a step and the point of the blade pierced the fibers of his coat. Eyes dazed but lucid, he licked his lower lip and one long forefinger coasted down the edge of the blade. "I am alive, and you are mine," he stated.

Oh Jesus! Velvet's throat closed. "Get on your knees," she said. She bit her lower lip, struggling to collect her power and steady her senses. The jewels were rapidly cooling, the soft buzzing in her ears nearly gone. Wrong—it was all so very wrong. Pounding, screaming, tearing, breaking, dying. It was happening all around her—her shield was shattered, this was done for personal gain—and soon the terrifying darkness would pierce through.

Captain Chance lifted his hands in surrender. Moonlight poured down his features, and he bent a knee. Velvet relaxed the grip she held on the blade, letting out a gulping sigh of relief. Seconds before the pirate's knees hit the deck he moved, his hand shot out, his fingers burrowed into Nora's hair. He hauled her to him and pulled a knife from his boot, then placed the tip against the underside of Nora's left rib cage, inches from her heart.

"You are mine," repeated Captain Chance. "Come with me or I kill her now."

"But...?" Velvet's voice cracked. "You have to obey me." Her eyes darted to the other men, frozen in Madonna poses, looking at her as if she was the very soul of the universe—as if they would gladly fall on their swords if it was her wish.

"Umm..." said Nora, her voice calm, almost thoughtful. "I don't think the spell works the same for everyone. It's possible we overlooked a few pitfalls in our plan."

"Oh God," Velvet said. She threw the captain's golden sword to the deck; it skittered across the uneven planks and came to rest near Nora's small, pink-slippered feet. "You can have me," Velvet said. "Just let her go. I will be yours forever." She meant it. If he let Nora live, she would leave with him and never look back.

The shadows on the main deck moved. The ship rocked violently, and there was nothing to hold onto, so Velvet fell.

"She is mine," a new voice said. Somewhere through the screaming, breaking, tearing sounds in her mind, she recognized it.

Captain Chance showed his teeth. "Mine," he said again. He lifted the knife and Nora flinched. Velvet felt her insides turn over.

"Yes. I am yours!" she cried. "Let her go, I will be yours forever."

"*No!*" roared the voice she knew. "*No, no, no! She is mine!*"

Now she was sure... "Henry?" Velvet did not realize she whispered the word aloud until it echoed around her. She said it again, a catch in her throat and a hot pressure building in her eyes. "Henry!" He was alive, he was here. Velvet lifted herself on her arms and searched the dark body of the crowd for his face. She saw nothing but murky shadows, stuffed by waving hands. Crows screamed overhead, circling their company like starving vultures. One of them landed beside her right hand. It opened its cracked beak and squawked in her face.

Captain Chance rotated Nora's head, tilting it in the direction of Henry's voice. "Take another step, I'll bleed her. I swear I will!" he promised.

Velvet felt for the stones, and squeezing them in her hand, she listened for buzzing. There was nothing, only the racing thuds of her heart. All the magic had gone. Abandoning her when she needed it most. A hot wash of hatred for the stones made her groan. Anger made her teeth clash—she wanted to hurl them over the side of the ship, pray they plummet, lose themselves in the endless murk of the Thames.

"Henry." Nora's voice broke the silence. "Don't do anything stupid! Do you hear me, Henry? I don't think I could lose you."

"Just take me," Velvet said. She struggled to her feet. Captain Chance made a squelching sound in his throat. He jerked, his legs striking the metal base of the swing gun. Nora screamed—then the world went mad.

A small shape, dove-grey and pale, rushed in front of Velvet, knocking her back. It crashed into Nora, the base of it struck her slender ankles, and she buckled. Captain Chance pitched forward —together they hit the deck with a crack that made the cherry wood planks groan and scream. Limbs and cloth swirled, and Velvet saw Captain Chance forced to relinquish his hold on Nora. That one drew her arms across her stomach, rolled over, and threw herself down the short flight of stairs that fed onto the main deck.

Velvet dove at the pirate with a snarling scream of rage,

slamming thoughtlessly into the fluffy shape tussling with him. Something blunt and sharp struck her chin. She flew backward, landing on the solid deck. Sharp pain lanced through her rattled skull, murky red smoke blooming like winter roses in her shattered vision. She rolled over, hands going up to shield her head—the ship's swaying deck wavered in and out of focus.

Just in front of her, only inches out of her reach, she could see strands of white hair spilling over the deck's well-worn slabs. Velvet blinked her eyes and tried to see through the fog. It was impossible, the shadow of the foremast thrust them in utter darkness. So she closed them, and everything went very dark. Closed them and listened to all the little sounds, listened to the wind in mast, listened to the panting breaths of the red-eyed captain. *Hish, hish* —through the sails, *hish, hish* through his hair.

Velvet went for the hair. Grabbed two handfuls of the silky stuff and yanked on it—then the unexpected happened. The hair —all of it—let go of his scalp with a small *shucking* sound. White locks dangled from her fingers, blowing in the night breeze, obstructing her view.

Velvet screamed, gagged, screamed again, then threw the wad of hair. The breeze caught the strands and lifted the gauzy mass. It flew for a moment, then hit the helm, and the rushing wind tangled the long strands around the spokes. To Velvet they looked pale and tentacle-like.

The pirate arched his neck; moonlight bounced off his skull, bald and speckled as the head of a poisonous mushroom. Velvet saw his fist flash, the shape grappling with him, cried out.

Suddenly, strong hands closed around her upper arms and lifted Velvet bodily out of harm's way.

Captain Chance gained his feet, holding the shape in front of him like a shield. Velvet whirled to dive at the Captain once more, but Henry linked his hands around her waist and pulled her to him. He breathed a groan that sounded like a prayer and crushed her cheek to his heart.

He smelled like blood, rain, horses—and most of all, he smelled like safety, warmth, and…just him. "Henry," Velvet said, unable to believe her eyes or her words. "You're alive."

He said nothing. Just locked a set of blank, glazed eyes to hers, and lifted her chin—before she could say his name or think to utter protest—his lips crashed against hers with the force of a falling star. She tasted blood and closed her eyes as her bones turned to water. She had never been kissed, not once, not even close—even in the heady daze of her spell, Henry knew what he was about. His mouth was relentless, desperate—insatiable, breathless kisses that stole the mind. His lips were firm and gentle, blistering and cool.

She heard herself moan when he let her go—and it was so many shades of darkness and insanity. Her hand flew to her mouth, and she studied his face in shock—just another layer of horror. Bloody streaks crisscrossed it, a bad split marred his full bottom lip, and his dark hair lashed at his swollen eyes. To Velvet he looked like an ancient god of war, fresh from battle, ready for the next kill.

"Henry!" hollered Devon. Velvet snapped her head in his direction to see him lowering his blade. Alfonso blinked his eyes— unhurried, almost alert.

"Don't move, Devon! Don't let him go!" she begged, raising her voice till it was hoarse. His lips thinned but he gave her a tight nod.

A crash drew her attention back to the pirate still struggling with the shape in his arms, yet the dust of the tussled had settled. Velvet saw the shape clearly, ice congealed in her veins, snowed in her heart—suddenly, she knew the horror she felt was merely a premonition. She knew the worst was yet to come.

The fighting shape was Katie. Her teeth locked in struggle, her hands clawed, she raged like a berserker wearing the face of an angel. Velvet struggled out of Henry's hold, he tried to clutch her arm and she kicked him in the shin, then dove for Katie. She made a fist, lifted it, meaning to strike the Captain in his smiling mouth. He was much faster. The backhand took her across the face. Pain blazed in her jaw, and her eyes saw only blue stars. It did not matter, this was her fault, she would not let him hurt Katie because of her own stupidity. Yet, when Velvet lifted herself on shaking arms, it was to see the scene had altered in the worst possible way.

Captain Chance now held his blade to Katie's throat, a thin line of her blood laced the edge of the knife. Her eyes were calm, her mouth forming the prayers to her goddess, her soft words reciting the Hail Mary.

Nora screamed, a long horrible sound. Velvet could see her trying to drag her body up the stairs, trembling hands made her arms give way. Velvet's muscles twitched to help her, but she stayed frozen, her eyes locked to the pirate's face.

"If you kill her," she said cautiously, her voice shaking over every word, "I will throw myself over this rail, and you will never have me. Please," Velvet sobbed and held out her hand. "I'll do anything you want, I swear it...please don't hurt her!"

The pirate king smiled a white toothy grin. He was a sea snake wearing human skin, and Velvet knew what he meant to do. She rushed at him, fingers tensed to claw out his eyes. He lifted a booted foot and kicked her in the gut. The force was incredible and crushing—she heard a rib crack as she fell. Her breath screamed when it left her lungs and refused to return.

Katie's eyes went wide, and her grey gaze found Nora. She pursed her lips and blew her lady a kiss. A soft serenity painted her face, and her smile was sad. "It's okay," she said. A crystal tear rolled down her cheek. "You're worth my life a thousand times over."

"*No!*" Nora kicked her legs, digging her fingers into the boards of the deck until her nails cracked and bled. She made it up one more step—two—three.

Too late, Velvet thought. *She will never make it, too late—my fault—too late.*

"Don't worry, my lady—I won't go far—I'll haunt you always," said Katie, then lifted her hand to mime her last tribute to the cross. Nora screamed again. Velvet threw her body at the feet of Captain Chance, wrapped her arms around his thick shins, and tugged. His foot struck the side of her head—she did not care. She pulled harder, trying to break his balance, all the while reaching for Katie—yelling—begging.

Through sharpened teeth, the captain yelled out a maniacal laugh. Velvet saw it all happen in a speed too slow for real movement—her aching muscles begged for mercy, but she did not stop. She punched and screamed—but the pirate was unmoved—his red eyes stayed pinned on her face while his smile broadened, and with a kiss blown in her direction, Velvet's heart stopped as he sliced the blade across Katie's throat.

Blood fanned out like a fountain of rubies; it splattered Velvet's cheek, ran down her neck—the feel of it was hot and final. Behind them, Nora screamed and screamed—it was a sound Velvet had never heard before—a sound past pain, past the darkness; it was a sound to break the soul.

Katie's body crumpled, limp as a marionette who lost its strings. Her head hit the deck. Everything fell still save the blood expanding between her lips as her frozen eyes filled with the images of their last sight.

20

MISTAKENLY LOVED

And then we fell to dreaming, like all good poets do, lost ourselves to fantasy—long lovers overdue…

*N*ora crested the ridge of the top stair—the hair whipping around her flashing eyes was unbridled and wild as a forest fire. Tears rained down her cheeks as she crawled to the body of her friend—screaming, then locking her jaw when her hands slipped in the ever-expanding pool of Katie's blood.

Captain Chance howled out another stream of chilling laughter.

Crying in rage and pain, Nora grabbed his discarded sword and threw herself at the cackling pirate. Her bloody fingernails raked furrows in his cheek.

He squealed and tried to bat her away. The dagger he held fell from his shocked fingers and clattered to the deck. Nora closed her eyes, then butted his chin with her forehead. "You bastard!" she raged. "Katie was the most precious soul on earth, you had no right to take her life."

Captain Chance made a wailing sound, eyes rolling around in their red-rimmed sockets. He balled a fist to hit her, Nora tucked her chin to her chest, and slammed the top of her head into his cold heart. His eyes went wide as he lost his balance, his arms jutted back, and his feet slipped. In a flurry of peach silk, leather boots, and bare skin, Nora and the pirate flipped over the short, wooden rail. A lingering scream, a heavy splash, and they vanished into the Thames.

Dark, crimson bubbles rose to the top of the river. The bubbles exploded, rising and sizzling like boiling oil. After a time the final bubble popped, returning the water to its calm surface of fool's glass.

Velvet ran for the railing screaming Nora's name. *It's too steep,* she thought, the price of this magic far too high. *Don't take her, not her, please not her! Not her!* Velvet did not know what deity she prayed to, yet the words fell from her mouth just the same.

"Bloody hell!" cursed Devon. He kept his eyes closed. Whether in acknowledgment or denial, Velvet did not know. He removed his coat and shoes, paused for a moment to throw Henry a disturbed look, then shook his head, vaulted over the ship's rail, and plummeted into darkness.

Henry did not move. His muscles were tensed to the point of quiver, while a small ticking counted down in the corner of his jaw. Astonishment parted his full lips. His dazed eyes remained locked on Velvet.

"Henry!" she shouted, reaching up to shake him.

"You are mine," said Henry in a blank tone reserved for the walking dead.

"Henry! Nora, she's fallen...and...Katie." Velvet's voice dissolved in a sob, she grabbed the soft linen of his sleeve and shook hard. "Look at me, Henry! Can you see me?"

"I see you," he said. "You are mine."

"*Ah zoot alors!*" Velvet wailed. Her front teeth worried at her lower lip for a second before she drew back her hand and slapped his cheek. The hit was a thunderclap in the silence. Henry's head snapped back. His big, booted feet remained firmly planted, Katie's blood lapping at his heels. She saw the red imprint of her hand forming on his wounded cheek and felt sick.

"You are beautiful," said he, seeming to register the hit—not at all.

Wind snapped the sails and somewhere another crow screamed. Velvet looked around quickly, her eyes struggling to see through the dark fog. On the main deck the group of men remained on their knees. Night light played havoc with their garish clothing, rendering princes, lords, pirates, sailors, and slaves in black-and-white rippling light. Under it they were all one and the same, shapes of forgotten men held captive to her spell. A few of the men roamed the edges of the crowd. An arched tricorne here caught the pale moonlight, another buckle sparkled there, and jaunty feathers bobbed atop the forecastle deck. The sails snapped again, and Velvet looked up, seeing them for the first time. The top sail was done in black silk, a white skull decorated its swishing face —two dark bones made a severe X over the hollowed-out nose. To Velvet it seemed each gust of wind opened the toothless mouth in a soundless scream.

Henry whispered her name; she turned suddenly—and froze. He stood less than a foot in front of her, and his beautiful smile dazzled like a star in his swarthy face. Calloused hands cupped her chin; even in the throes of the spell, his eyes glowed exquisite tenderness. With a sigh of the victorious, he leaned in until they were so close Velvet could taste his warm breath—it was whiskey, storm, and fire.

"I look at you and I can't breathe," he said. "You are beauty and fairy tales. The shadows of mystical queens dance in your eyes, lost histories—memories. I think...I need you..." His voice whispered chills over the shell of her ear, down her cheek, and again to her mouth. Velvet felt her resistance waver, her hazy thoughts scattered like ashes in the wind. *This was madness! Madness!* The flames of insanity incinerated the world and she was burning in them.

He linked his fingers through hers, then lifted her hand and pressed it to the quarterdeck railing, cold against her back. Engulfed in the heat of his grip, a wash of pins and needles rushed up and down her arm. His body was hard as steel, his legs moved against hers in tandem with the rocking ship, he squeezed her hips and pulled her closer.

Suddenly, it seemed like he had sprouted an abnormal amount of hands. They touched her everywhere, leaving her skin in sparkling cinders before she had time to make sense of it. His fingers sunk into her hair. "I want to touch you, have you," he said, and Velvet knew the worst *was* true—she was lost in the intoxication of her own spell.

"No!" she said, shifting her face away, and his scalding lips coasted over her cheek. She shoved at his chest with all her strength. "*No*! Stop—Henry—It's just a spell. I cast a spell on you. Oh, gods of earth and sky, I didn't mean to, Henry…now everything has gone so horribly wrong. It's the price, Queenie always warned me about the price. I…I just didn't think about it. Saints!" She was gasping, rumbling, she was so weak, so tired. *I can't think, I can't breathe—breaking—breaking.*

"Maybe I just didn't care," she whispered, her eyes watering mercilessly. "But you don't love me, Henry. Katie is dead! Do you hear me? Dead! It's just a spell, a stupid goddamn spell! I don't know how long it will last. So you have to snap out of this, alright? I need you too. I need you to help me! I need this ship, this can't all be for nothing…" Even as the words were coming out of her mouth, Velvet knew how selfish they were, yet nothing mattered, not anymore. Only Louis.

She tensed her hands on his chest, meaning to give him another shove. Katie's blood streaked her fingers; she smelled it, tangy and metallic, the crimson currency of any good spell. "I'm a monster," she whispered. Not Queenie's blood, but her spawn."

Night wind undid the three top buttons of Henry's shirt, and as she pushed him, her fingers touched flesh. He was like sun-warmed steel and she wanted nothing more than to rub her cheek against him and lose herself in this madness. "It's not real," she whispered again, not sure to whom she spoke. It was the most real moment she had ever experienced; death, spells, pirates, and gods drifted away. "I don't want this…not if it isn't real." Lies. There was only him.

"I don't care," he rasped. "Gods and monsters be damned, all I see is you."

The dark clouds shifted, and the moon grew bright in the midnight sky. Then, he was kissing her, and the fire was everywhere. Velvet could not breathe, did not want to breathe. His tongue touched her lips—she listened to them part with an audible gasp. The indescribable sensations curled her toes, arched her spine, put stars in her eyes. She felt the cool touch of the wooden deck on her back and thighs.

Henry rose above; his dark hair falling down in waves tented their kiss, and they were alone in their breathless, burning world—and she no longer cared—gods and monsters, enchantments and lost princesses be damned. Her hands twined through his thick curls as she held onto consciousness like a lifeline praying the ticking seconds would loop in on themselves, and this moment would never end. Reality was evil; bloody and cold…this—oh *this* —his hand cupped her breast, his kiss turned rough, achingly desperate—this was golden, glorious, and hot as the sun.

21

A WATERY GRAVE

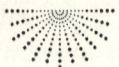

*F*ilthy. That was the main thing. It was so freaking filthy! The splash when she hit the dark surface had shattered her eardrums, and the water rushing up her nose was probably killing her, but it was the filth that would haunt her memories until she was old and grey. *A watery grave.* Nora found this strangely fitting—her and her baby, drowning together. Poetic justice for having not wanted it. Well, she wanted it now. More than that, she did not want to die, not here, not swimming with chunks of what she deeply suspected was human excrement floating past her face, and Captain Chance's hands around her throat.

Captain Chance, Bacchus, the fall…Katie…oh, gods! Katie! Grief, sudden and bright, tore a black hole in her soul. She kicked her feet badly, the inky water fought back. The strangling vise tightened on her neck, and she sensed more than felt her eyes bulge. Nora screamed. A hollow, empty, bubbling sound, like screaming in a dream, or into a very fluffy pillow. Strange, being strangled underwater, having your breath cut off in a world where there was no need to breathe. Nora told herself it was not the time to wax philosophical, she would soon be very dead if she did not kick her feet. So she did—with incredible gusto. The vise constricting her larynx loosened. She struck out again—blindly, desperately. Her slippered toe hit a shin. Streams of muddy bubbles burst from Captain Chance's mouth, he made choked popping sounds that echoed in her ringing ears. Her right leg kicked again, slippery silk tangled around her ankles; she ignored it and put every ounce of her misery and rage into her next kick.

Suddenly, Nora was free. Blessedly, wonderfully free. Good work too, she thought. Sure, her lips were bright blue and her face a dastardly shade of purple. One of her hands stroked at the inky black waters drowning her—suffocating, murderous waters—and the other moved to cradle the flutter in the pit of her stomach. The tiny speck, she imagined, struggled for life just like her. She kicked again. Her lungs were burning now, she could feel them expanding against the confines of her silken harem dress. *Ridiculous thing to be wearing when one attacks a pirate captain,* Nora thought.

"Note to self," she muttered, and fresh bubbles raced from her mouth. "Go back in time and don't get on the ship,"—more bubbles—"don't lose Katie, don't lose her…don't let her die…" Nora knew she was crying, but the filthy Thames washed away the evidence.

The distance to the surface seemed endless, at times she was not sure she could make it. Some annoying muscle in her thigh cramped horribly, her arms were lagging, and her heart…each beat just that much more exhausted. She was not swimming—she was falling, the light at the end of her path dimming.

Hard fingers closed around her ankle. Cold and slimy as sea snakes. Nora reared up and screamed, a giant flare of bubbles enfolded her like a shroud. Her lungs were at the breaking point; screaming behind her arched ribs, it was nearly impossible not to take a huge breath. Only the sure knowledge that it would be her last kept Nora from throwing back her head and gulping in a massive killing gasp. Feet kicking furiously and arms battling the rank blackness, Nora fought for her life. She was lost in it, caught between the hand and the drowning waves.

Enough! her mind shouted. She adamantly refused to die down here. If it was all the same to Davy Jones, she meant to keep her grave site on land. Water slapped her in the face, knocking her skull back, allowing cool wind to wash her cheeks. Wind? Nora's mind drew a sudden blank. A froth-capped wave hit her chest.

Nora sucked in a swill of air. A tornado of filth rushed down her throat—excrement, rotting food, and thick, sticky smog. She heaved and gasped, hiccupping back the urge to retch. The need was so strong it brought a surge of acid to the back of her mouth. She heard the smack of water breaking against a hull; it sluiced over her head and thrust her back under. Ghostly hands burst from the darkness, and clawed fingers made a grab for her face. Nora batted them away. The swallow of air she took was filthy and clogged with all manner of evil, but it had given her new life. Her strength came back in force. She arched her body and dove for the pirate. Her left hand grabbed a fistful of his linen shirt, while the right gouged at his eyes. A cold pupil squished under her fingertip, his face wavered in her focus as fat purple lips opened to release a soundless, grating screech.

To watch him die screaming. *That* was all Nora wanted. She swallowed the acid-soaked bile flooding her mouth and dug her fingers deeper into his eyes until she felt her fingernails scrape bone. Rocks, sharp as razor blades, cut her bare shins. Nora held in a scream of pain by sheer force of will, her head broke the surface, and a wave crashed into her rear. Nora flipped through the air, had a good view of her flying feet, then the retreating wave sucked her back. She was momentarily weightless, soaring through space and time. The wave surged again and threw her boneless limbs into the craggy bank. Groaning and coughing for air, Nora rolled over and looked up at the moon, glowing like a flame behind a veil of rain. Clean, cold air poured down her lungs—sweet, precious air!

She lay still, simply marveling that she was alive. Was he alive? That was the pertinent question. If he was, she needed to take his sword and rid his bones of his rotten soul. The golden sword dropped from her hand during the fall, or perhaps when she hit the water? It was all a big, terrifying blur. Swaying in unsteady circles, she lifted her head, resting the weight of her drenched body on shaking hands, and hauled herself forward over the rocky shore.

Sounds from the docks reached her, muted noises ringing hollow in her waterlogged ears. Sitting up, she wiped the hair from her eyes and looked at the waters breaking against the black skeleton of the Bacchus. Katie was up there, hidden somewhere in the thick blanket of fog cloaking the ship. Dead and lying in a pool of her own blood. Henry, Devon, and Velvet too—she had to get back to them. But first, she needed to see Capitan Bastard to the underworld.

Find the sword, her mind commanded. Nora jumped to her feet, ignoring the rivulets of blood rushing down her legs from places where the stone's sharp bodies had done their work. Her waterlogged eyes scanned the dark, clumpy shore. Rocks and shrubs were black cutouts against the grey mists, the fog painting the ground so thick, that her feet and hands disappeared in its shifting body.

She tried to listen for the sounds of a grunting survivor finding their way to solid ground, but there was nothing save the whistling wind and the screaming crows who left their shadows on the moon. One of her slippers was missing, and a couple of scattered shells stabbed the arch of her foot. Something snapped behind her, and the soft hairs on the back of her neck stood up straight. She froze in her bloody tracks.

The pirate's fingers were a coiled fist. It was him, oh God! Too late. A hand sunk into her hair and yanked her head. Nora cried out, swinging her arms and wildly kicking her legs. Another hand soaked in slime crawled up her waist to her breast, then slowly encircled her throat.

"Killing is a passion for me," he hissed in her ear. "I love the way the body tenses up when the brain knows its host is about to die. I love the sound of the heart racing, the feel of fear heating the veins. Most of all, I love to see the blood flow. I adore the pattern it makes, like a Baroque painting by one of the greats, Rubens or Caravaggio.

"You wax rather poetic for a dead man," she said. The stench of him was sickening, but if her body wanted to vomit she would aim downwind and serve him right.

"I'm going to make you beg for death," he promised. He spun her to face him, still keeping a firm hold on her neck and hair. "You cost me a good eye."

Nora bit her lower lip until she tasted blood. She did it so she would not scream. His bleeding black socket gaped inches from her face. In it, she could see remnants of the eye she had crushed, bits of white goo clinging to exposed bone. Trails of black blood marred his cheek, more poured from his nostrils and ears.

"It is well deserved. Now I know why pirates all have missing eyes," she said, trying to distract, ignoring all, save the flash of gold in his hand. "Everything costs something. Even killing."

"Admit it, you love death too. Tell me it wouldn't give you great pleasure to see me dancing at the end of this blade and you'll be a liar."

"You killed my friend for no reason. She had more goodness in her tiny pinky finger than you have had in any of your lives combined. She was brave and stronger than ten men. You had no right!"

He pulled her close so his whole wet length was pressed tight against her, then scoffed in her ear. "I had every right—she was nothing—a woman and a servant who got in my way, as did you. Neither the prize I desired." A red tongue dripping blood shot from the thin slash of his white lips. He licked her from earlobe to chin in one long wet stroke. Nora shuddered in revulsion and fear. She was scared—badly! Only an idiot would not be. Yet she knew fear was not her friend in this moment, it would scatter her thoughts and shake her fingers. Nora combed through her plethora of emotions, grabbed firmly onto rage, balled her hands into fists, and lashed out. The reckless movement surprised him; he jerked his head back a second too late, and her right knuckle glanced his jaw.

"Little bitch!" he growled. Nora's knee found his groin, nicking more than striking what she meant to. Captain Chance roared, drew back his hand, and slapped her face. Blue light pounced on her vision and sent her reeling to the side, her heel caught a stone and she fell with a broken scream. Captain Chance advanced on her like a hyena, his lips contorted in a sneer, his one good eye glowed red in the dimmed light. He made a low, gobbling noise, one hand grabbing at his crotch, and he lunged for her. The blade of his sword swished through the air. Instinctively, Nora threw her arms up to shield her eyes and watched moonlight dance over the blade rushing to take her life.

Then, everything went incredibly still. His jaw seemed to come apart at the hinges, swinging off to the right like a broken window knocked loose by a storm. His one good eye widened in shock. Nora struggled into a sitting position, then crab-crawled backward, putting a few feet of distance between her and the frozen pirate. Lost in the sight of his strange face, it took Nora a moment to notice the golden antlers jutting out of the pirate's chest. He began to shake, his arms and legs jolted up and down as if gripped by a powerful seizure.

Nora grinned from ear to ear. She felt terrible, wicked even, but it did not stop the grin. Her shoulders relaxed and she let out a long breath that turned into a laugh. She scrambled to her feet, not caring that more broken shells cut her grasping hands and bare, bleeding foot.

"What...? I do not die...? I am Captain Chance of the nine lives...how?"

Louis muttered a series of soft, consistent grunts and Nora wondered if the captain could hear him? If he had any idea what was killing him? His one good eye rattled in its bruised socket, glancing to the invisible wounds in his chest, then up to her smiling face. Louis arched his spine; the pirate's twitching feet cleared the ground, his mouth widening in a startled snort. The golden sword clattered to the ground.

"You will not be free of me," he rasped, his words muffled by a mouthful of blood.

"Maybe?" she said softly as though to herself. "But if you come back, I'll kill you again. There is no place in this world for the likes of you."

The pirate made a mottled sound, his trembling arms splayed out like the crucified Christ. With a final howl of denial, he threw back his head and died.

Louis snorted and shook the limp body off his horns, stomping his hooves in what Nora figured was a combination of relief and disgust. He nudged once at the white corpse, then stepped aside.

"Cut off his head."

The words echoed in Nora's mind. They came from everywhere and nowhere, flashed through her heart imprinted on the lids of her eyes. She felt her right hand clap over her mouth, her knees gave way, but she barely felt the fall. "Did you just…?" Her mind spun in a circle—did he what? What was the word?

"Telæsthesia," replied Louis in that mind voice hell-bent on making her faint.

"What does that mean?"

Louis made a sound that could have passed for a laugh. He was so…Nora rolled her mental eyes, sighing long and loudly. There were no words for all that exquisite golden beauty. *Magical,* yes, that would have to do. He was so incredibly magical.

"Telekinesis," he said.

"Is that really a word?"

Louis lent her a long searching look. *"It will be."*

"Why can I hear you?"

"I don't know. It's never been this easy with anyone."

"But you've done it before?"

"Yes."

"Oh my God!"

"No, I don't think your god has anything to do with this." Louis squinted at the moon. *"Some of mine, perhaps."*

Nora laughed and felt real pleasure flush her cold cheeks—a pang of acid pain told her Katie was dead and took it away. She stood up again, shaking out the strips of cloth that stuck wetly to her legs. "You saved me! You wonderful creature! How are you here?"

Louis snorted, kicked at a sharp stone, and sent it flying. It landed in the dusky surf, thudding a distant thud. *"My sister used the ruby. I felt it singe my soul. Those stones carry dangerous powers, the ruby more than the others. It always demands a life."*

"Yes," Nora breathed, feeling a fresh agonizing surge roast her heart. "It took one."

Louis's eyes fell to the body on the ground. *"Two…I pray it is finished."*

"She did it for you," she said, not sure why she felt the need.

"I know," he said and made another rough sound that clenched the muscles of his chest. He nudged dispassionately at the bloodless body. *"Take his head."*

"What? No." Nora shook her head adamantly. "I couldn't."

"You must. His men will only follow if they know you made the kill."

Nora shuddered and dropped the sword. "I…I can't. This is foolishness. Really, I can't even make a proper cut of tea, what makes you think I could decapitate a man?"

"Necessity is an incredible motivator."

Nora felt her arched brows reach for her hairline. "You are very witty for a deer."

"Stag," he corrected.

Nora eyed the sword, giving it the same venomous glare she might have afforded a giant spider or a poisonous snake.

"Pick it up!" The words flashed brightly in her mind, illuminating the darkness in brilliant blue lights.

Her heart said no, yet her hand reached for the hilt. The metal was cold in her grasp, foreign in the extreme. Nineteen was just too young! Nora decided. Far too young to have a baby, too young to fight a pirate, and certainly too young to chop off a man's head. "I can't do it…I won't," she whispered.

"You must. Do it now. I can feel my sister slipping, succumbing to the magic of that cursed stone." Louis grunted and sniffed at the air, his hooves kicking a restless pattern against the earth. *"She is with that man again, I can smell him."*

"Who? Henry? Oh, heavens! He must have seen her dance."

"She danced?"

"It was beautiful, you should have seen her glow."

Louis snorted and she felt his relief that he had not.

"Yes, it probably wouldn't be the best if you fell madly in love with your sister. It's frowned upon in our times, you know, the world is turning quite modern." More kicking shifted the restless mists.

"Stop stalling." A burning force shoved the command in her mind.

"Hey!" She lifted a hand to shield her head—a useless action if ever there was one. "That hurt," she breathed, still shocked she could feel him at all.

"Do it, Nora! You're running out of time."

"You can't be serious," she moaned, though she knew he was.

Cringing, she lifted the sword—slick metal, cold as ice, and surprisingly heavy.

Less than two weeks ago she had ridden beside Charles in Hyde Park down to the corner of Serpentine Road. The sun was cheerful as a fresh-faced daisy, and the skirt of her pink riding habit fluttered like cherry blossoms in a summer wind. She was witty, appropriately so, and laughed at a silly joke she had not understood. They had taken the afternoon tea in the drawing room, then strolled through her rose garden and watched the purple sunset. She had worried desperately about the latest gossip, wondered what new stories they told of her. Obsessed over how she would face the crowds at their next soirée. What foolery to think the girl she had been then knew anything about fear or choices. In this moment, thoughts of her bastardy and tenuous social standing were tremendously far away.

Nora lifted the sword above her head. Her heart mourned the girl who had died the second her body hit the Thames. The naive girl who never thought to ask more from life than what had been offered. She grit her teeth until her jaw squawked and brought the sword down with all her strength. The blade struck flesh. A geyser of blood drenched the waiting mists.

She would never be that girl again.

22

LIGHT, PASSION, MADNESS

*H*enry was out of control. Heat arched his back and his hands tightened reflexively on the flesh they tenderly held. His mind was a whirl with inky ghouls, his reality a shifty thing, hazy and disturbed. He struggled to lift his head and open his eyes. Scattered memories rushed at him, riding the four corners of the wind. They carried pictures of the endless, cold ride to the ship and the long walk to the rocking haul. He remembered seeing Velvet standing so proud beside Nora, holding her hand while the wind buffeted and braided their hair. He remembered a moment of shocking horror when he realized Alfonso meant to sell her.

The pirate's bid was easy to beat. Henry would have given title, land, and name to wrap Velvet up in his arms and spirit her away. He had taken one step, then two, intently watching her eyes widen as they searched the dark crowd—imagining she looked for a savior in its depths. Praying she looked for him. Then, she let go of Nora's hand and walked in his direction. He sensed approaching chaos as she thrust a long, shapely leg through an angular slit in her silky dress. She arched her delicate foot, took a deep breath, and started to dance. When she moved, his world funneled to a single, luminous focal point—her. Only her. Like a siren sprung from the sea, like Helen disrobing for Paris, like Venus herself—beauty incarnate.

He remembered a ruby-red light pouring from her fist, then her slender arms twined above her head, the action lifted her breast and they swayed hypnotically through the near-transparent silk of her strange gown. Red hair instead of blonde coasted over her swirling hips, and her feet tapped out a sensual rhythm Henry knew only she could hear. She was a living vision, a goddess made flesh, the very spirit of allure come to steal his soul.

Then, the memories changed—flushed bloody—full of need and pain; they raged before his closed eyes. He shook his head to drive them away. His cheek touched something warm and familiar which shared the darkness with him. Cold hands clutched his hair and scalding lips tugged at his own. *He was drunk,* he told himself, that was the cause of his spinning world and disintegrating will. But he did not believe his mind, the taste of the drink was absent from his mouth, and his brain was not foggy so much as lost. He looked down at what he touched. A deep red light bordered his vision hallowing the wild thing in his arms.

Velvet.

The name lit up the night like a racing comet. He leaned back and shook his head. "Velvet?" he croaked.

"Henry," she breathed, and her rose petal lips parted. The hands in his hair pulled him down, while her soft, bare legs linked around his own. Blood rushed hard in his ears, reverberating through his head. He kissed her. He could not help it. Her mouth was hot as the tip of a flame, the moan he summoned from it low and intoxicating. She tasted faintly sweet, like honey or plum wine. Tearing away from her was nearly impossible, yet he did so with a groan and buried his face in her neck, breathing deep. A single fingertip traced the line of his jaw and touched the throbbing tendon in his neck.

How had he come to be here on this deck, surrounded by blood? This burning woman his only anchor in a reeling swell.

"What's happening?" he said stupidly, his words muffled by her thick, silky curls. Velvet did not respond. Her eyes were closed, her flushed mouth bruised from his kiss. Henry could see the marks on her cheeks where his spiked stubble had rubbed her soft skin raw. He leaned away until all his weight rested on one shaking arm. Her body bucked again as she fought to drag him back. He resisted, his will bent so far, it nearly snapped in the last second. Wordlessly he began to lift his weight from her silhouetted form—her eyes opened, their azure light dreamy and golden.

He looked away from her hypnotic gaze blinking rapidly. *What in God's name was wrong with him? He had almost taken her here, on the dirty planks of a ship's deck, as if she were a common strumpet.* He tried to remember what had happened, yet it was like a bonfire had taken place in his mind, now, only soot and ashes remained.

"Velvet!" he said again. His voice was acidic, and far harsher than he intended, but he could not help it. He wanted to shout and shake her until at least one of them regained some sense.

Awareness returned to her fevered gaze, and her angelic features crumbled in sadness. "Aw, *merde!*" she breathed. "I'm sorry."

Henry had to strain to hear her halting whisper, and that infuriated him too. "What in hell and damnation is going on?" he nearly shouted.

"It's a spell, I cast a spell on you." Her lips had gone bloodless, her eyes were open and staring deeply in his—right to the heart of his soul. "I didn't know you were in the crowd. I wouldn't have…I couldn't…I did it for my brother." She put her trembling hands against his chest and pushed him lightly away. He moved swiftly, caught her hands, and locked them above her head bracing her wrists to the cold deck, then closed his eyes, hoping that would make the sight of tears fade away. It did not. He wanted to forget his question and kiss her again, God and monsters, pirates and death be damned.

"A spell?" he rasped. "What the hell are you talking about? I told you, I don't believe in spells."

"Of course you don't," she said.

He made a deep sound in his throat—one he had never heard himself make before—something betwixt a snarl and a sob, then let go of her hands and wiped his knuckles over his mouth wishing for water.

There was a confusion of screaming and shouting coming from below deck, and his eyes flicked momentarily toward the restless crowd, wondering if like him, they too were waking in foggy agony.

Velvet rolled her body toward the noise, then struggled to sit up. Henry let her go. His limbs were heavy and clumsy, gravity was at war with his desires, insisting he lie down and die. He wanted to obey the urge, having never felt so horrible in his life. She sat back on her knees and tried to draw the pale slips of silk over her shivering body, struggling with the fluttering cloth for a moment before her lips pulled into a pout and she threw her hands in the air, making a furious gesture of frustrated despair. Her eyes flicked across the deck to a pool of blood. Henry had a brief flash of Katie's wide grey eyes; he heard her soundless scream and remembered a blade slashing her throat. He swallowed hard. His eyes followed Velvet's and came to rest on Katie's lifeless body. Beads of cold sweat broke out across his brow, and shock kept him from wiping it away.

"I killed her," she said, her voice flat and empty as a desert. "It's my fault."

"I don't remember," he said.

Her gaze returned to the bloody deck. "That's my fault too."

"You're serious, aren't you?"

She nodded miserably. "I didn't know you were onboard, I wanted the ship and the crew. It was a good plan." She hiccupped over the last word and swiped the back of her hand over her streaming eyes. "It almost worked."

A beam of silver moonlight struck her face and took his breath, he had to look away or reach for her again. His mind was full of bits and pieces; the last thing he truly remembered was the moonlight stroking her body, highlighting the strips of silk clinging to her pale limbs as she danced. After that, the memories came to him in picture shards and boisterous sound bites that rattled his ears. Confusion sparked abruptly into anger.

"You had no right!" he said, the words rushing out before he could hold them back.

Her eyes stayed on Katie. "No," she said. "I suppose I didn't, but we were captured, and I felt we had no other choice, no better choice. I have to save my brother!" Her hands curled in tight fists and she rocked on her knees. "I have to! He's all I have! I just have to!"

"He's not!"

"Not what?"

Henry almost growled at her. "He's not *all you have*, at least he wasn't."

"Oh, gods, I know," she whispered. Crystal tears cut tracks through the blood and dirt on her face—Henry thought it possible they would rip out his heart. "I think I made a promise once, I don't remember it really, but he is what matters, not me. I am afraid, if the chance presented itself, I could do far worse," she confessed miserably, then bit her lip to keep from saying more.

That thought unnerved him, helping to shake off the last of his daze. "Worse?" he said. "Worse than taking a man's memory and commandeering his will? Worse than murder?" Henry realized he was shouting.

Velvet's eyes flashed. "I only meant to take this ship and gain a freedom I richly deserve." Tears blurred her blue eyes, and he could feel her struggling for words, then she relaxed her hands and reached for him. Henry flinched away. She saw it—her lips thinned into a harsh, white line and she dropped her eyes. "I have been hunted, chased, and abused since I can remember," she said, and the broken tone of her voice was just another vise ripping into his heart. "Surely I have a right to try and retrieve some of what I have lost? Surely I have a right to love and freedom."

"By stealing the will of those sworn to help you? At the cost of their lives?"

Velvet rolled her eyes and threw up her hands. Henry knew her argument had sense but felt no desire to hear it. She bit down on the nail of her forefinger, and there was a distinct click as the nail snapped between her teeth. At the sound, she jerked and dropped her hand. "Is it possible to hate me later?" She gasped. "We have to take care of Katie…and Nora…" Her voice broke and more tears escaped her shattered gaze.

"What about Nora?" he roared, realizing he was towering over her.

"Nora went over the side with Captain Chance. Devon jumped

in after her…" She fell to her knees. "I'm sorry. I tried. I tried to save them both."

Henry thought his mind might explode. He had an immediate impulse to get up, take her in his arms, kiss her again until they both ignited, and he forgot all this madness. He did nothing, only stood still and listened to their racing hearts.

"Four lives for one?" he said finally, and watched a hot blush infuse her cheeks. "It seems the King *is* right. You bring only death."

Velvet's hand went to her heart, like his barbed words had struck her there and she swayed on her knees.

"Maybe," she finally said. "Yet, I mean to save Louis! You, the King…the people, they have no right to hunt his life. He is good, innocent, and pure. Too good for this bloody world. I will save him."

"No matter the cost?"

Velvet lifted her chin in a brief flash of defiance and nodded faintly. Henry felt gooseflesh ripple across his chest and shoulders. He was breathing like a winded stallion, but had possession of himself again, that was something at least. He looked in her eyes wanting to read her truths. The glint of stubbornness darkening the blue irises told him all he needed to know. It would kill her to do it, but she was not lying. She would do whatever it took and worry about putting together the pieces of her humanity later.

Velvet made a small, dreary noise that could have been a laugh, though Henry suspected it was not. Her hand restlessly smoothed the silk over her taut stomach. He felt his breath catch; her beauty seemed to have the power to suspend time.

His. The word was a powerful boom in his brain, she looked up at him like she heard it, her gaze forever piercing.

Mine! his mind roared. His feet moved to her, his fingers twitched, wanting to crush all that soft silk under his hands, take her down to the deck and have her, over and over before a host of watching eyes until she was locked to him, body and soul, forever.

Velvet threw him a wary look and shot to her feet, retreating a step, then another. "Do you still want me?" she whispered. "Has the spell not faded yet?"

The plethora of possible responses nearly overloaded his brain. He felt venom rise in his gut. "As a boy I treasured the memory of you, and I've wanted you since the first second you attacked me—wounded and feral as a wildcat," he heard himself snap—answering her first question and ignoring the other. "But that man kissing you just now...that was not me." He threw her a dark look and watched her shudder under the weight of it. "I would never let Nora and Katie die for common lust, I would've never..."

"I loved them both!" she shouted.

Dear, holy God! He was seconds away from grabbing her—to blazes with hurt pride, curses, and the Devil. "You should've woken me, cast another spell, for God's sake!"

"I..." her voice faded to a squeak. "I don't think that's how it works." Her front teeth gripped the lush swell of her lower lip. "I tried to stop it, Henry, I swear, I would've died in their place."

He knew that was true and the useless knowledge further enraged him. He could hear men milling about a few feet away, some muttering curses while others strained to see the shadowed bodies. A commotion broke out near the stern and the remaining crowd of sailors scurried away from the redcoats. The precision of their retreat seemed rehearsed.

Hardly aware of his actions, he turned his back to Velvet and faced the advancing men. Even behind the cover of a dark mask he quickly recognized Lord Bryon. His face was pale and his pinched features gaunt. His baleful gaze launched daggers at Velvet, and Henry realized he too had been a victim of her spells. Henry felt sickened by himself and the world at large. *How had he let a pretty face cloud his judgement?* He was not a traitor, loyalty to King and country was all he had. How had he not seen it? Sensed the evil in her, glowing right in front of his eyes. Had it been nothing but dark magic all the while—every feeling, every thought he had of her? It seemed plausible, probable even—he had been reeling since the moment they first met.

Velvet held out her hand, her pale fingers trembling in the space between them. "Henry, they'll kill me...please," she said, her heart in her eyes. "Please, no! Henry, you promised."

Henry sucked in a long breath that trembled down his throat.

No, he could not do this thing. She was his, her tears his to wipe away, her body to hold, her soul to own.

"Take her," he said.

Lord Bryon gave a stiff nod and moved toward Velvet—a dark purpose hastening his stride.

Velvet retreated. "You swore, Henry! You gave me your word."

Henry turned away, the sound of her bewitching voice, the vision of her heartbroken face forever branded in his mind.